WHEN I FOUND YOU

WHEN I FOUND YOU

BRENDA NOVAK

THORNDIKE PRESS
A part of Gale, a Cengage Company

When I Found You
Copyright © 2021 by Brenda Novak, Inc.
Home for the Holidays
Copyright © 2021 by Brenda Novak, Inc.
Thorndike Press, a part of Gale, a Cengage Company.

Thorndike Press® Large Print Romance.
The text of this Large Print edition is unabridged.
Other aspects of the book may vary from the original edition.
Set in 16 pt. Plantin.

LIBRARY OF CONGRESS CIP DATA ON FILE.
CATALOGUING IN PUBLICATION FOR THIS BOOK
IS AVAILABLE FROM THE LIBRARY OF CONGRESS.

ISBN-13: 978-1-4328-9133-6 (hardcover alk. paper)

Published in 2021 by arrangement with Harlequin Books S.A.

Printed in Mexico
Print Number: 01   Print Year: 2022

CONTENTS

WHEN I FOUND YOU 7

HOME FOR THE HOLIDAYS 509

■ ■ ■ ■

WHEN I FOUND YOU

■ ■ ■ ■

To Ginger Lyman, one of the most generous people I've ever met. Thank you for all you do to support and uplift others. You are a true inspiration!

ONE

The old Victorian looked nothing like the pictures she'd viewed online.

Dr. Natasha Gray sighed as she stood in the entryway, peering at the place she'd rented, sight unseen. No wonder her landlord had been willing to leave the key in the mailbox. She'd assumed it was because the town was so safe he wasn't worried about someone else finding it. Now she understood that a key wasn't necessary — a large window on the side had been broken out. Although the hole had been taped off with black plastic, the barrier would do little to stop anyone who really wanted to get inside.

"*This* is where we're going to live?" Her six-year-old son, Lucas, had slipped past her and was turning in a circle, surveying the dilapidated interior.

She could understand his disappointment. Living here would be different, in every way, than what they'd known in Los Angeles.

11

There, they'd had a nice upper-middle-cl
home in the suburbs. This was an old, one-
of-a-kind house located in a small town
ninety minutes to the northwest of the
sprawling metropolis they'd called home,
with the town's main drag in front and a
small patch of worn grass in back. But it
was all she could currently afford. And they
were far enough from where they'd lived
before that she'd no longer have to face the
stigma of everything that'd happened this
past year.

"This won't be so bad once we get it fixed
up," she heard herself say, but she'd expected much more after seeing the darling
pictures online. They must have been taken
a while ago, because it was obvious the
house had been vacant for some time.
Whoever had cleaned up the glass from the
broken window had left footprints in the
dust on the hardwood floor.

"Who will I play with?" Lucas asked.

Since there were only commercial businesses in the immediate vicinity, they'd have
no neighbors — none with children, anyway.
"Silver Springs might be small, but there
will be other kids," she told him. "You'll
make friends once school starts."

"When school starts! It just got summer,"
he said in a sulky voice.

She tamped down her own disappointment. "It'll be fall before you know it. You'll see."

The way he shoved his hands in his pockets and bowed his head let her know he wasn't even slightly mollified. But she hadn't asked for what'd happened; she and her family had been victims of it. The nightmare that had destroyed her practice had also wiped her out financially and proved to be the death knell for her marriage.

But there were others who'd been hurt — and some of them had suffered much worse. She couldn't think of them without wanting to cry.

If only she could've figured out what was going on sooner . . .

"Why can't I live with Daddy until school starts?" Lucas asked.

Natasha wished she could let him. As much as she'd miss him, she had no doubt spending the summer with his father would be easier on him — less lonely — than spending the summer with her in this strange new place. His father didn't give him a great deal of attention. Ace never had. But Lucas would have been able to associate with his grandparents, who were more hands-on, and some of his friends had he stayed in LA. Natasha might've considered leaving him with his father for a month, just so that the summer wouldn't seem so long and lonely for him. Except she and Ace had lost the house when her practice failed, and he'd made it clear that there wasn't room for Lucas to stay with him in the condo he was now sharing with two roommates — not permanently. Visits would be crowded enough.

"I'd rather you stick with me and we both get settled here," she said. What else could she tell him? Not only had Ace agreed to let her move to Silver Springs, he'd only requested two weekends a month and every other holiday for visitation. Natasha suspected her ex preferred to be free to play the field, so he could find another woman.

"But I don't like it here." Lucas pinched his nose. "It stinks."

He was right. The scent wasn't strong, but it was distinctive. "Smells like a skunk to me." Had one died under the house? She couldn't say until she looked, but she wasn't ready to brave what she might find under there, not when the part of the house that was supposed to look good didn't. "A thorough cleaning will make a big difference," she insisted.

The dust and dirt she could contend with.

14

Natasha was more worried about the integrity of the roof and the rat droppings she spied in one corner. Did they have a rodent problem?

This was hardly the sanctuary she'd envisioned. But since when had anything ever been easy for her? With a mother who'd dragged her all over hell when she was a child and consistently put her own needs first, Natasha had always had to fend for herself.

She'd get through this, too.

"Maybe you should play on the porch while I sweep," she said.

He peered out the door. "When will Uncle Mack be here?"

"Any minute."

"Uncle Mack" was driving the rental truck that carried all of their belongings, other than what she'd been able to squeeze into her car. He wasn't really her son's uncle. As far as she was concerned, a long-ago marriage that had, for a fleeting time, joined her family with his didn't qualify. It wasn't as if they'd grown up together. He'd been twenty-five when they first met, and she sixteen. Neither did they get together for the holidays or anything like that. His father was just another man in the long line of men who'd been in her mother's life, except that

15

he'd had five sons who'd stepped in to help her at a critical point when she was a teenager.

But she and Mack had always struggled to figure out exactly what role they should play in each other's life. Ever since she'd lived with him and his brothers before she went to college, she hadn't had a lot of contact with him, especially since her son was born. So she'd been surprised when he'd called, out of the blue, and insisted on coming to help her move.

No doubt he'd heard about what'd happened to her practice and her marriage and felt sorry for her. She hated being the object of his pity, once again, especially after all she'd done to make something of herself. Not only had she put herself through medical school, she'd survived the insanely long shifts required during residency — while raising a young child, no less — and, after eleven years of pushing for all she was worth, had *finally* achieved her dream. She'd become a pediatrician and started her own practice — only to be leveled just when she'd thought she was home free.

"He left when we did," Lucas said.

"He can't travel as fast in that big truck," she explained. Her son had taken to Mack instantly. Maybe it was because he'd lost his

16

father and his friends all at once, but the relationship worried her.

"Maybe he doesn't know how to get here," Lucas said.

"He has his phone, and GPS will lead him right to us."

She went out and got the cleaning supplies from her Jetta, which she'd parked in the unattached garage. She was eager to get started on the house.

After setting the supplies inside the door, she gingerly picked her way up the stairs. Because she was afraid they wouldn't hold her weight, she made Lucas stay in the living room until she'd scaled them first. But they seemed sturdy, so she let him come up.

Fortunately, the bedrooms weren't as bad as the living room. There were no broken windows, no water damage, no rat droppings. She tried to tell Lucas that his room would soon look as good as the one back home, but he wasn't buying it. He trailed slowly after her, so dejected he could hardly put one foot in front of the other, but he didn't want to be left in a different room, either.

The rumble of a large engine sounded as they were checking out the laundry facilities, which were — along with a plethora of

spiderwebs and Lord knew what else — in the musty, unfinished basement.

"There he is!" Lucas exclaimed and ran up to greet him.

Natasha took a few seconds to compose herself. She didn't want Mack to know how disappointed she was in the condition of the house, just as she didn't want him to know that she wasn't bouncing back as readily as she'd hoped from everything that'd happened in LA. She didn't have a lot left, but she had her pride.

"This is it?" Mack said, as she met him in the living room.

"It won't look so bad once I get it fixed up," she replied.

He removed his sunglasses. About six-two, he had powerful shoulders, dark hair and large brown eyes that were currently filled with doubt. "Really? Because it looks like a bulldozer would be the best way to fix it."

"It's structurally sound." She wasn't sure she fully believed that, but she preferred to pretend that she'd known what she was getting into when she rented this place — that it hadn't been the act of a woman so desperate to escape her current situation that she'd jumped from the frying pan into the fire. She had to convince him that she was going to be fine so that he'd leave. The sooner,

the better. Then she could get on with the business of rebuilding her life, wouldn't have to deal with the conflicting emotions he evoked.

He'd been with her for three days, and she still wasn't entirely sure why he'd come. To help, certainly. He'd done plenty of that. But why did he want to help her? That was the question. Since when did what happened to her matter to him?

Actually, that wasn't fair. Mack, like his brothers, had tried to look out for her during those few years when her mother was married to his father. He was the baby of the family, so although she was nine years younger, she was closest to him in age. After she graduated from high school and confessed her love for him, however, he'd pulled back a great deal. Although he'd continued to check in and let her know he cared about her, and she would visit him and his brothers whenever she returned to Whiskey Creek, he wouldn't allow their relationship to go any deeper, especially after that one night during Victorian Days. And after she got married, she'd actually heard from his brothers — Dylan, Aaron, Rod and Grady — more than she heard from Mack. She wasn't even aware of how he'd learned that her life had imploded. The news hadn't come from her own lips. If she could've hidden it from him, she would have.

It was possible he'd read about it, though. It'd been such a shocking and horrible situation; the media had been all over it.

Or her mother could've told him. Although Anya had divorced Mack's father years ago, she was still in Whiskey Creek. Mack and some of his brothers still lived there, too, where they ran the original location of their family business, Amos Auto Body. Knowing her mother, Anya stayed because she considered them the only family she had, and even though Natasha doubted they felt the same way, they continued to help Anya whenever she got down on her luck.

Natasha refused to lean on them the way her mother did. She preferred to stand on her own two feet, had decided long ago that if she couldn't have Mack's love, she'd at least have his respect. That was why it was so difficult to let him see her now. This should've been a moment of triumph, when she faced him as a practicing pediatrician who no longer needed him.

Instead, because she'd hired the wrong nurse, she was standing amid the rubble of everything she'd established so far.

"Well, *structurally* sound or not, I can't

bring in the furniture," he said, hooking his thumbs into the waistband of his faded jeans, which had a hole in one knee, as he surveyed his surroundings. "Not until we get a few things done in here, anyway. And —" he wrinkled his nose "— it stinks."

"That's a skunk," Lucas piped up. "Oh, look! A potato bug!" He dropped down on his stomach so he could examine the insect crawling on the floor.

At least he wasn't by the rat droppings.

"I'll be okay," she said. "I'll check under the house to see if we have a dead animal there. It's probably nothing, just residual spray —"

"Which means we can't do anything about it," he broke in.

"It'll fade with time," she said. "And I'll work around the furniture, once we bring it in, so that you can take the truck back to LA." After all, she didn't have that much; her ex had taken their bedroom and living room furniture and their washer and dryer. "I can get this place fixed up on my own, a little at a time."

He gave her a look that said she must be crazy. "You want me to leave you alone with this mess?"

"Why not?"

"Have you ever put in a window?"

21

She had no idea what she was going to do about the window. She'd poured everything she had into becoming a doctor. When would she have had the time or the opportunity to learn anything about home improvement? "I can probably get the landlord to handle that much."

"You told me the lease you signed was 'as is.' That the landlord had no money for repairs, which is why he gave you such a sweet deal."

"That's true, but . . . he can't leave me without a window." The landlord had mentioned that the house needed work, but this was ridiculous.

"Why fight with him when I can fix it?" Mack asked.

"Because it's not your job to fix it. I can hire someone."

He cocked an eyebrow at her. "With what money?"

He'd been there when she'd tried to rent the truck and her debit card had been rejected. She still cringed when she remembered him stepping forward to front the money.

"I have a job," she said defiantly. She'd been lucky enough to land employment nearby, which was why she'd moved here. She'd be the medical professional at New

Horizons Boys & Girls Ranch, a year-round school for troubled teens located not far outside of town, until she could save up enough money to once again open her own practice. She was overqualified for the position. Aiyana Turner, the woman who ran the school, had stated as much in her interview. Mrs. Turner had been looking for a nurse, not a doctor. But at least the school would have someone on hand who could provide expert medical care, and Natasha would soon have a steady income. She was grateful for the stopgap. And she'd pay Mack back as soon as she received her first paycheck.

"Your job doesn't start for another week," he pointed out. "And then it'll take at least two weeks to get paid. You're staring down the barrel of three weeks without income. You realize that."

"I've got a few bucks in my purse." She hoped he'd let it go at that, but he challenged her instead.

"Oh yeah? How much?"

"Enough to get by," she retorted. No way was she going to reveal the specific figure; then he'd know just how poor she really was.

"Probably three bucks exactly," he said with a roll of his eyes. "I don't know who you hired to do your divorce, but your ex must've paid him a lot more than you did."

"Her. It was a woman," she said. "And that's not funny. After what happened, there wasn't much to divide between us."

"I heard you on the phone yesterday when you were talking to your mother. You admitted you agreed to pay alimony, for heaven's sake, even though you have primary custody of Lucas. Why would you ever agree to spousal support?"

Although she'd seen the scowl on Mack's face when she'd made that revelation, he hadn't said anything about it until now. "Once he told me he wanted out, I decided not to prolong the split by fighting over possessions."

"Why would *he* fight over them? That's my question. Especially after everything you've provided already — and everything you've been through?"

"Because they mean more to him, I guess." And because he wasn't working. He hadn't worked for a number of years, which made it much less likely that he'd be able to replace those items — unless he found a job or another wife to take care of him. Ace wasn't the most motivated person. He'd sold her on his dreams, droned on and on about all he was going to accomplish in the future. But once it became apparent that

24

was all talk, that he'd probably never accomplish anything, she'd consoled herself with the fact that it would be nice to have him home with Lucas, and it didn't really matter if he contributed financially as long as she could earn enough to support them.

It wasn't until Lucas started preschool that it began to bug her that Ace was spending most of his time gaming. At that point, she'd asked him to come in and run her front office so that she wouldn't have to hire someone else, but he did such a lackadaisical job she would've let him quit even if everything hadn't gone to hell right about then for an entirely different reason.

"Is he unable to work?" Mack asked.

"No." She lowered her voice so that Lucas wouldn't be able to hear her. "He comes from a wealthy family and has never had to work for anything."

"So he's lazy."

She checked Lucas again, who was, thankfully, still absorbed in examining that bug. "Stop. I don't want to talk about Ace." She'd just had a baby when she married him. Because she'd been frightened to be a single parent, especially one who was juggling so much, she'd made a bad decision. But she'd been willing to compromise as much as possible to make the marriage

25

work. So it was pretty ironic that *he* ended up finding fault with *her* and felt he'd be better off on his own. "I can get by. And if I have to, I can sell what he did let me have to bring in some quick cash. It's not as though I have any kind of sentimental attachment to these things. There's no need to hold you up any longer."

"God, you're stubborn," he said with a scowl. "I can see that hasn't changed."

"You're just as stubborn as I am," she retorted, pretending to be irritated, but really she was just trying not to admire the handsome face that'd fueled so many of her dreams over the years.

"Damn right," he said with an unrepentant grin. "Did you bring any tools?"

She dragged her mind back to the focus of the conversation. She couldn't allow herself to admire Mack, couldn't fall into that trap again, especially after the Christmas before she got married. But it was difficult not to at least acknowledge that he'd only gotten better with time. Although he'd recently turned forty-one, he didn't look that much older than when she'd first met him. "What do you think?"

"If I had to guess, I'd say Ace got those, too, which means I'll have to buy some, because I'm not going to leave you like this."

She wanted to tell him to just walk away. He was good at that. But she didn't feel the barb was warranted — at least not right now, when he was trying to help. Maybe this was about penance for the pain he'd caused before. Maybe he was looking for forgiveness or something. But she didn't dare let him into her life now — not in any big way. She couldn't pile more hurt on top of what she'd endured so recently. "The truck has to be back by the end of the day, or they'll charge me — er, *you,* until I can pay you back," she said. "You don't have time."

"So I'll pay the extra thirty bucks." He shrugged as if it was nothing. "Give me the keys to your car. Lucas and I will go find a home improvement store."

"What?" She blinked at him. Surely he wasn't planning to stay any longer. She'd already let him off the hook. "Seriously," she said. "You've spent three days getting me out of the house in LA. I appreciate your help — truly — but there's no need to hold you up any longer." She started for the door. "Come on. Let's unload so that you can be on your way."

He caught her by the wrist. "You need the help, Tash, and I'm standing here, offering it. Why won't you let me? Are you really

27

that angry with me? After seven *years*?"

Yes, she was. So angry that she couldn't believe he'd even bring it up. She might forgive him. Since when had she ever been able to hold a grudge against Mack? But she would certainly never forget. "I just don't want to inconvenience you any longer," she said.

"It's not an inconvenience. I've been planning to visit LA for a while now to scout a good location for another shop."

He and his brothers had been talking about expanding into LA for years. Aaron, the second oldest, had opened an Amos Auto Body in Reno, Nevada, but he was the only one who'd broken away so far. "LA's ninety minutes from here."

"That's not very far. I can take a week to get you set up before I go back."

He still hadn't let go of her wrist. Her whole arm tingled at his touch, and a memory danced around the edges of her mind — a memory she'd banished long ago. "Who would run the new shop?"

"I would."

"You'd live in LA."

"Yep."

Which meant he'd be much closer to her. Whiskey Creek, where he and his brothers had grown up, and she'd once lived with them, since they'd taken her and her mother in while their father was in prison, was six hours away, not far from Sacramento.

"Are you going to stay with us, Uncle Mack?" Lucas cried, finally abandoning the poor bug so he could hurry over.

As soon as Mack let go of her, Natasha stepped out of reach.

"For a few more days," he said.

"Yay!" Lucas yelled and launched himself into Mack's legs.

Mack laughed as he tossed him up and over his shoulder like a sack of flour and her son squealed in delight. "You got those keys?" he asked her.

She almost refused. But on what grounds? That she wasn't sure she could deal with their history?

She'd die before she'd ever admit that — to him or anyone else — so she retrieved her purse and handed him the keys.

Two

Mack glanced at Natasha's little boy in the rearview mirror, but he was driving, so he couldn't let his gaze linger as he was tempted to do. This was the first time he'd ever been alone with Lucas, the first time he'd been able to study the child without having to worry that Natasha might figure out what he suspected.

Did the boy look like him?

It was hard to tell. He'd watched Natasha's son carefully ever since he first met him three days ago, but it was hard to say. He'd never seen Natasha's ex, hadn't run across a single picture of the man while they were packing. Maybe the boy resembled Ace so much the answer would be apparent, but from what he'd seen so far, the boy was the spitting image of Natasha.

He pulled into HD Home Supply, parked and walked around to let Lucas out of the car.

The kid had already unfastened his booster seat.

"Good job," Mack said. "Let's go."

Lucas insisted on taking a plastic sword into the store, and Mack couldn't help smiling when he brandished it at everyone they encountered. Maybe the boy didn't look a great deal like him, but he couldn't hold still for two seconds, which was exactly how Dylan described Mack as a child.

Mack let his gaze run over the boy again. Was this his son?

"On guard!" Lucas yelled, frightening an old lady who was trying to purchase some paint.

"Let's take it down a notch, okay, buddy?" Mack said with a chuckle, ignoring the dirty look the woman gave him.

"Why are we here?" Lucas asked, sword fighting with phantom opponents once they reached the main aisle, which was momentarily clear.

"We're getting supplies, remember?" Mack told him.

"What kind of supplies?"

"A window, if we can find one that's the right size. But as old as that house is, we'll probably have to order a custom one. I'm also going to need a hammer and some nails. A socket wrench. A drill. A saw. A

Shop-Vac. Those sorts of things."

"My dad has a hammer," he announced.

Mack wished he could borrow it and any other tools Ace had. It seemed silly to purchase everything again when it was unlikely Ace would need them in the near future. But he wasn't going to ask, even if he was willing to make the drive to get them. Any guy who could leave his wife in the situation Natasha was — heartbroken over what'd happened to her practice, barely able to eat or sleep because of the pressure and worry of everything that was going on in her life, and alone with a child to care for and no money — was a total douchebag. That Natasha didn't expect any more from her ex spoke volumes. Maybe that was why Mack felt completely justified when he took advantage of this opportunity to speak to her unsuspecting little boy and, hopefully, satisfy some of his curiosity. "What's your dad like?"

"I dunno."

"He nice?"

"Yeah."

"What types of things does he do?"

"Plays video games on TV."

Lucas would've knocked a stack of batteries off the shelf if Mack hadn't reached out to redirect his sword. "Anything else?"

32

"No."

"Where does he work?"

"I don't know. On the TV, I guess."

Ace should be set, then. Mack didn't remember loading a TV into the truck, which meant any that Natasha and Ace had owned together had stayed with him.

The aisle where he could find the windows came up on their right. Mack took hold of Lucas's free hand to guide him down it. "Can you tell me when your birthday is, buddy?"

"Yeah."

"So? When is it?"

The boy screwed up his face as though he was thinking hard but ultimately shook his head. "I can't remember."

It was in the fall. Mack knew that much. The instant he'd learned that Natasha had had a baby, he'd counted back the months, and would never forget how hard his heart had started to pound when he realized he'd been with her about the time she'd gotten pregnant. She'd returned to Whiskey Creek to see her mother for Christmas, they'd bumped into each other at the annual Victorian Christmas Days Celebration, and things had moved quickly from there — years of pent-up desire had exploded all at once.

"Look at all these windows," Lucas said, obviously impressed.

"Pretty cool, right? Now we just need to see if we can find one that will fit."

Before he could check the various sizes, Mack's cell phone vibrated in his pocket.

He pulled it out to see that his oldest brother was trying to get hold of him.

He punched the talk button. "Hey, Dyl."

"What's up, man?"

"Not much. We made it to Silver Springs. But you should see the house."

"Is it nice?"

"No, it's a piece of shit."

Lucas's eyes widened. "Oh . . . I'm going to tell Mom!" he said, covering his mouth. "You're not supposed to say that word."

Mack gave the boy a sheepish look. "Don't tell on me," he whispered.

"Okay." He grinned as though he liked having a secret, but then he started saying, "Shit. Shit, shit, shit," to himself, as though he was practicing it.

"Who's with you?" Dylan asked.

Hoping Lucas would forget what he'd learned before they got back to the house, Mack returned to his conversation. "Natasha's boy."

"What's he like?"

"He's a cool little dude." He didn't add

that Lucas might be *his* cool little dude. He wasn't going to tell anyone that, not until he knew for sure.

"I'd like to meet him," Dylan said. "I'm surprised that Natasha has never brought him back to Whiskey Creek."

So was Mack. That she'd stayed away felt intentional, and he thought he knew why. "She was busy with her residency, then starting her practice."

"It's amazing what she's achieved, especially considering what she started with. I thought she was in the clear, you know? I can't believe what's happened. How's she handling everything?"

"She's lost weight, isn't sleeping well." He'd heard her walking around the house late at night, could see the weariness in her movements and the dark circles under her eyes as they packed up the van. "What happened would be a nightmare for anyone. But she's tough. She'll pull through." He planned to see to it. That was another reason he'd packed up and headed to LA almost as soon as he learned about her divorce.

"I wish there was something more we could do."

"I'm doing what I can."

"Whatever happened to the woman who

destroyed her practice?"

"She's in prison and she won't be getting out." He dodged a sword thrust that would've hit him in the nuts and couldn't help laughing as he once again guided Lucas's sword in a safer direction.

"What's so funny?"

"Nothing. This kid — Never mind. Has Natasha ever mentioned to you what went wrong in her marriage?"

"No. I called her when the news about her nurse first broke, and we discussed the stress it was putting on the relationship. She admitted things were getting rocky, but that's it."

"She didn't say why they were rocky?"

"Even if she did, I couldn't go into it, Mack. She wouldn't like me discussing the details with you, and you know it."

"With me specifically? Why not?"

"Come on. Things have always been . . . complicated between you two."

That statement bothered Mack, but he didn't want to examine why, so he let it go as Dylan followed up with, "When are you coming back?"

"Do they have the window?" Lucas asked at the same time.

Mack smoothed the hair off the boy's face. "We'll check in a sec," he told him. Into the

36

phone, he said, "I'm not sure that I am coming back."

"What? You live here, remember?" Dylan sounded shocked.

"I'll get my stuff, of course, but I think it's time we go ahead and expand into LA."

"Now?"

"Why not?"

"No reason, I guess. Just seems sort of sudden. It isn't because Natasha would be close by and you could help her get back on her feet, is it?"

Mack heard the wry tone of his brother's voice, but he wasn't going to apologize for wanting to take care of Natasha. "That's part of it. She needs me," he said simply. "Her bastard ex took almost everything."

"That makes me defensive, too, but I don't know that you'll be doing her any favors if you stay."

"What are you talking about? I've always done my best to look out for her." There was only that one time when he'd screwed up. Surely that night didn't negate all the good things he'd tried to do over the years.

Or did it?

"You've done a lot," Dylan conceded. "But all she's ever really wanted was for you to love her."

Mack straightened in surprise. His brother

37

would say that *now,* after all the pressure he'd been under to stay away from her? "I *couldn't* love her," he said. "She was only sixteen when she came into our lives. I was twenty-five. And our father was married to her mother!"

"I know," Dylan said with a sigh. "I've felt bad for you both from the beginning. And I've always admired you for not taking advantage of her feelings. You had to have known how much she adored you — there was no way you could miss it. She followed you around like a lost puppy, tried to get close to you at every opportunity. I'll never forget one night I went into the kitchen to eat, and she told me dinner was gone. But then you came home and I found out the food wasn't gone — she'd just saved all that was left for you."

Dylan chuckled at the memory, but Mack couldn't laugh. Natasha had made her feelings plain, all right, and, Lord help him, he'd managed to keep his own feelings under control for many years. But all the wins didn't matter; he'd succumbed in the end — and Lucas could be proof of that.

Did Natasha get pregnant without telling him, and then marry someone else? Once he'd learned of the pregnancy, he'd tried to ask her, but she'd insisted the child belonged to Ace — and if they were happy together, he couldn't get in the way of that.

"I've got to go." Mack was suddenly anxious to get off the phone. Today, everything his brother said seemed to upset him. "We're in a store."

"Okay. I'll talk to you later. Give Natasha my love."

"Sounds like you two stay in touch."

"So . . ."

"I guess you can do that yourself." After he disconnected, he regretted the curtness of his response. If not for Dylan, he would've been put into foster care when he was just a boy. He loved and admired his oldest brother more than any man in the world.

Besides, the way he'd acted just now would only confirm that Dylan had hit a tender spot. But Mack had always been torn when it came to Natasha. The way he'd met her, and her young age at the time, had set them both up for a tug-of-war that had left him facing something he'd never anticipated.

"Are we done with this shit?" Lucas asked, once again hitting one of the racks with his sword.

Mack couldn't help smiling in spite of being all twisted up inside. What a little hellion. "I wouldn't be surprised if you *are* my son," he muttered to himself and started going through the windows.

It felt nice to have a break from Lucas. As much as Natasha loved him, it was so much harder to deal with her own emotions while she was also trying to make sure he was happy, well cared for, entertained and shielded, as much as possible, from the more difficult aspects of the divorce. She'd thought her ex would help more, but the divorce had brought out the worst in Ace. Determined to be free to focus on his own life, he was pretty much expecting her to take care of Lucas, even when it came to child support, since he didn't have a job. His wealthy parents were helping him get by, and she had no one to lean on until she could get back on her feet, but he didn't seem to care whether she had money, even though it wasn't just she who would suffer if she couldn't buy groceries.

She supposed she shouldn't be *too* critical of him when it came to money matters, however. After all, she'd been the primary breadwinner. It made sense that he'd expect her to take care of herself. But he knew that she was struggling, and he knew why. That should've made a difference.

40

He just didn't care. That was the bottom line. And she suspected he preferred she be the one who had to babysit so she wouldn't have the opportunity to find someone else.

Little did he know, she didn't want to get into another relationship. She'd never marry again, never risk her peace of mind or her financial well-being, let alone her heart. She was so done with that. Since she was sixteen, she'd tried to give Mack everything she had, and he hadn't wanted it. So she'd tried to give Ace everything she had left. And it hadn't been enough.

She refused to keep trying, to wind up as a carbon copy of her mother, who'd been with so many different men over the years that Natasha couldn't even remember them all.

Exhausted, she stopped sweeping and rested her head on her hands. How many "fathers" had she had? Some of her mother's lovers had only been around for a few weeks, and yet Anya had insisted Natasha call each one Daddy. It was a pathetic attempt to draw the man in and get him to commit. But it never worked — at least, not for long. J.T., Mack's dad, was probably the longest relationship she'd ever had, and that was because he was in prison for the first part of the marriage.

41

Natasha was going to live her life differently — with some dignity — even if it meant being alone.

All she wanted to do was collapse into a chair, but, drawing a deep breath, she summoned the energy to finish sweeping. She had to keep putting one foot in front of the other and appreciate all the little things. That was how she'd get through this dark time. In this moment, she could clean without having to worry about Lucas getting near the rat droppings or trying to escape out the front gate, where he could get into the street. That was something.

Thank God.

Actually, she could thank Mack. He was the one who was helping her — the only one who'd come to her rescue. That meant it would be difficult not to be *too* grateful to him. Having his support when she felt so lost and broken would naturally soften her heart toward him. He always did things like that, things that made her believe he cared.

He probably *did* care to some degree, or he wouldn't do anything, but she had to remember that it wasn't in the way she'd always wanted him to care. She couldn't let the nice things he did cloud her judgment. No way would she put her son through anything remotely similar to what she'd been through as a child. The only father Lucas knew was Ace, and it was going to stay that way.

She'd opened the windows to air out the place, so she could hear the car when Mack and Lucas returned. She wished the errand had taken them longer, wished for an additional couple of hours in which she could take a nap. But at least she'd had ninety minutes of silence in which she'd been able to accomplish a few things.

"Mom! We're back!" Lucas yelled as he came running up the steps and into the house, letting the screen door slam behind him.

"Were you able to find the right window?" She turned, expecting her son to rush into her arms, but he had his hands full, and he was so eager to reach her that he nearly tripped.

"No, but we got you these!"

He was holding a bouquet of red and white tulips. Her favorite.

The sight of them — the simple beauty of them — made her throat grow tight.

It was the exhaustion, she told herself. She hadn't gotten enough sleep for months, and it was beginning to bring her emotions to the surface.

Afraid Mack would be able to tell that

she'd choked up for no reason, she was careful not to look at him when he came in.

"Thank you," she told Lucas as she took the flowers. "They're beautiful."

Her son smiled proudly. "Uncle Mack said you used to plant them in the front yard when you lived with him."

She'd forgotten about that. She'd tried to add a few feminine touches to the all-male home — had cooked and cleaned and planted flowers to spruce up the place — in an attempt to repay them for taking her and her mother in. They'd basically been homeless. What would've happened to her if Mack and his brothers hadn't done that? Her own mother had been too caught up in getting her next fix, whether that was a man or the drugs she used, to keep a roof over their heads or even notice what her daughter needed.

Mack was carrying a bag of groceries in each arm, which he put on the kitchen counter. "We couldn't find the right size of window," he said to her, "but I'm going to check online. You hungry? I got stuff to make sandwiches."

She was starving. She hadn't had anything to eat today except the carrots Lucas had refused to finish from the sack lunch she'd given him on the drive. But she didn't want to rely on Mack in any way, not more than she could help it, at least. "No, I'm fine. I ate on the drive," she lied and pretended to be completely uninterested in what he'd purchased as she searched for a container for the flowers.

There were a couple of dusty old mason jars in the pantry. She rinsed one out and carefully arranged the flowers before putting them on the counter with the groceries. She had to admit, the splash of color lifted her spirits. As insanely busy as she'd been, she hadn't stopped to admire a bouquet of flowers in . . . forever. With summer coming on, she'd all but missed spring.

As she set to work cleaning the kitchen, Mack made her a sandwich anyway. He used a plastic fork to spread the mayonnaise and mustard and put the finished sandwich on a paper towel on the counter.

Since she was hungry, and it would go to waste if she didn't eat it, she took it and sat on the floor, where she could use the wall to support her back while she ate.

The sandwich was made with sourdough bread and filled with thin layers of honey ham, and she'd never tasted anything better. She hadn't quite finished when a bottle of beer came into focus. She'd been enjoying her food so much she hadn't realized

Mack was standing over her, trying to hand her a drink. "Hasn't been in the fridge long enough to be cold quite yet," he said, "but it tastes okay."

This time she didn't even try to refuse. He'd already popped the top.

Once she finished her sandwich, she just sat there, slumped against the wall, watching him play with her son while slowly drinking her beer.

"You all set?" he asked, after she was done, and offered a hand to help her up.

Surprisingly, she'd regained some of her strength. Who knew a sandwich could make such a difference? But she still had a problem with the fact that she was once again relying on Mack Amos. The last time she'd accepted his help, she'd fallen so deeply in love he'd ruined her for all other men.

But she was going to be much smarter this time.

They needed to get far enough on the cleaning that they could unload the beds, at least, so they'd have somewhere to sleep tonight. Telling herself that his touch did nothing for her, she let Mack haul her to her feet.

THREE

After being awakened by Lucas at three in the morning and getting him back in bed, Natasha couldn't drop off again. Pulling on a cardigan over the gray silk tank top and matching shorts she'd received at her bridal shower almost seven years ago, she slipped down the stairs and past Mack, who was sleeping on the old couch from the den, to go outside and sit on the front steps, where she could gaze at her new town and feel the cool breeze rustling the leaves of the maple tree taking up most of the front yard.

So much had changed in her life. And in such a short time. Only eighteen months ago, she'd been getting her credentials and negotiating contracts with the various health insurance companies that were popular in LA, signing a small business loan for financing and investigating medical record software so she could run her office as efficiently as possible. She'd also been spending a great deal of time with a commercial real estate agent, searching for the perfect location for a pediatrician. Instead of buying into an existing practice, or purchasing the practice of a doctor who was retiring, she'd chosen to start out on her own. She'd been eager to set the tone for how her patients would be treated from the very beginning. Even though Los Angeles was a big city, she wanted to offer small-town care, the kind where a doctor took a greater interest in getting to know her patients and maintained a lasting relationship with each one.

She'd expected her first few years to be tough, knew it would take time to build a practice, and cash flow would be a challenge. Being a doctor wasn't only difficult when it came to getting through school and paying back a mountain of student debt. Insurance companies took so long to pay after she'd seen a patient. And it was difficult to collect from people who left the office without taking care of their share.

But she'd known the challenges she'd face and had still been optimistic, especially when, in her first three months, she'd outpaced all her projections. She'd thought she was going to make it, that she would continue to grow and become an important part of the community — had never dreamed that something she couldn't have planned for, something unforeseen, would bring her down.

When it could've been so many other things — why was it *that*?

She sighed as she leaned back and stared up at the sky. If not for Maxine Green, she'd probably be back in Laguna Beach, giving babies their immunizations and helping sick kids get well before going home to Ace and Lucas at night. Her marriage could've withstood her success; it just couldn't withstand her failure. Ace wasn't capable of supporting her, financially or emotionally. He'd always relied on *her* to support *him,* and she'd done her best to play that role — until she just . . . couldn't.

The screen door creaked and she twisted around to see Mack. He was barefoot, like she was, but wearing shorts he'd made himself by cutting the legs off a pair of sweatpants. They rode low on his narrow hips, and he wasn't wearing a shirt, so she could see his well-muscled torso — something that would be better for her *not* to see.

Besides being only half-dressed, his hair was mussed from sleep, but he didn't seem remotely self-conscious. She'd never known him to be self-conscious. Vain, either. That was part of his appeal. He was just himself, always. With thick, curly hair he often let grow too long, a prominent chin and jaw — one that sported a five-o'clock shadow almost immediately after he shaved — eyes that somehow saw the best in everything and a pair of dimples that gave him a megawatt smile, it was sometimes difficult for her to look away. His teeth weren't quite straight, and one of his incisors had a slight chip, but even those imperfections added to the overall character of his face.

Damn him, she thought, wearily. After everything she'd been through, she should not be feeling the same old attraction.

She supposed some battles she'd have to fight forever.

"Having trouble sleeping?" he asked.

Mustering what she could of her defenses, she wrapped her cardigan tighter around her. "Lucas woke up. He was disoriented, what with being in a new place. After I helped him find the bathroom, I couldn't go back to sleep. What about you? What are you doing up?"

He sat on the step beside her. "He must've come downstairs after you took him to the bathroom."

"He woke *you*?" she asked in surprise.

He lifted a hand. "It's fine. He's on the couch. I'll take his bed when I go in. At least he's back to sleep."

"His bed will be way too small for you. I'll move him. I'm sorry." She'd have to risk waking Lucas again when she carried him upstairs; it wasn't as if Mack had many options. Other than boxes, the beds and that couch were all they'd brought in. By the time they'd cleaned the house, they didn't have the time or energy to haul any more.

"He's quite a kid."

She was glad Mack liked Lucas, couldn't help wanting him to. "A handful," she acknowledged. "But I never dreamed he'd bother you. The divorce has him missing Ace, I guess."

She'd never seen Luke take to someone so quickly. Of course, it would be Mack.

His sidelong glance gave her the impression he had something weighty to say, something beyond the parameters of what they'd discussed since he'd come to LA. Afraid for what that might be, she stiffened, but when the intense expression left his face and he turned away, she could tell he'd decided not to go forward with it and relaxed.

"Must be tough to deal with what your nurse did," he said instead. "Is that what

51

keeps you up at night?"

She generally avoided talking about this, as well. It was too fresh, too painful. But with Mack, she preferred this topic to some of the others he could've chosen. At least this had nothing to do with *them*. "Part of the reason."

"What's the rest?"

"The divorce. The loss of my practice. Having to move and work as a school nurse after all the effort I put into becoming a doctor. Take your pick." She frowned, feeling the terrible burden of regret, which somehow grew heavier at night. "But mostly what my nurse did."

"I've never heard of anyone doing anything like that before. You must be devastated."

"There are so many emotions zinging around inside me I don't know how to cope with them all, so I try to ignore the crushing pressure on my heart. I have a son who's depending on me. I can't give way."

"You're going to be fine," he said. "You'll get over this."

"Maybe *I* will, but what about the family who lost their little girl? I doubt they will. I became a doctor because I wanted to help people, especially children. To think that my nurse would purposely harm my patients . . ." She squeezed her eyes closed as she remembered all the times she'd had to call an ambulance to her office, not realizing that Maxine was capable of doing the things she'd done — and then the worst day of her life, when the child she'd been trying to save didn't survive. "That's just . . . beyond my understanding."

He rested his elbows on his knees. "I don't get her motivation. What did she have to gain?"

"Attention. The adrenaline rush of causing the alarm. Feeling important and in the thick of it. In some misguided way, I believe she wanted to put these children in danger so that we could then be praised for saving them. That's the closest I can come to explaining, after reading everything I can find on Munchausen by proxy."

"So she was doing you a favor," he said sarcastically.

"She painted it that way once I confronted her."

"That's crazy. I don't know how she lives with herself."

"I don't, either. After what's happened, I can barely go on."

He nudged her knee with his own. "What's that supposed to mean?"

She would've said nothing and let it go at

53

that, but she felt obligated to clarify. She knew he was especially sensitive to any reference to suicide. His mother had killed herself with pills when he was just a little boy, and he'd been the one to find her. Natasha hadn't been intimating that she'd do anything like that, but because of his background, she could see why his mind might automatically go in that direction. "It means I can't help feeling responsible."

There. She'd said it. What she felt in her heart but had been terrified to say for fear just speaking the words aloud would establish them as fact. Had she been more aware, more diligent, more intuitive — instead of focusing so much effort and energy on her crumbling marriage — maybe she would've recognized what was going on much sooner. And that could've saved little Amelia Grossman's life.

Mack took her hand. "Listen to me, Tash. It wasn't your fault."

"How do you know?" she asked as she stared glumly down at their entwined fingers.

"Because I know you."

That simple answer caused the tears that'd been lurking just below the surface all day to well up again. Guilt and doubt ate at her constantly, especially on long nights like this one, when she was prone to blame herself for the divorce, too. After all, she'd known from the beginning that she didn't love Ace nearly enough to make that kind of commitment. She'd just been grateful someone wanted her, and that smacked so much of her mother it made her sick. "I wish I would've wised up sooner," she said softly. "You'd never expect . . . never think . . . that someone you know and like . . ."

He squeezed her hand. "You had no clue and you put a stop to what she was doing as soon as you learned."

That wasn't good enough. She'd been too late for one child, and she didn't know if she could live with that. She wanted to tell him so, but the words jammed up in her throat.

Desperate not to allow herself to lean on Mack for the emotional support her own husband hadn't been able to give her, she pulled her hand away under the guise of wiping an errant tear. "We had to call an ambulance to my office *four times* in the first eight months my practice was open."

"I'm guessing that's a high number of emergencies?"

"For dealing with routine office visits, yes. I kept racking my brain for the cause. At first, I thought it might be a strange allergen from the tenant improvements. We had new carpet and paint put in when I leased the space. After I ruled that out, I thought maybe a weird virus was going around, and we were unwittingly passing it from one child to the next because our cleaning service wasn't being thorough enough. So I started sterilizing the place myself every night, which only put me home later and caused that much more friction between Ace and me. I never dreamed what was happening could be purposeful, that it could be Maxine. She seemed so nice, so normal, so innocent. She'd cry whenever we had something go wrong, and *I* would have to comfort *her*!"

"That's evil," he mumbled. "How was she doing it?"

"She was using a muscle relaxant, one that's effective in small doses and very hard to detect, and that would send the child into cardiac arrest."

"Where was she getting it?"

"From my own medicine stash, which is even more disturbing. But the closet was locked, and I was the only one with a key. Plus, I checked those shelves constantly. None of the medications appeared to have been tampered with and none were missing."

"So what was going on?"

"She'd stolen my key, had her locksmith roommate make a copy of it and replaced it before I even noticed. He testified in court that he duplicated it for her because she said she needed it — didn't even question why. My attorney thinks he was hoping to curry favor with her, thinking he might get lucky."

"But you said none of the medications were missing."

"They didn't *appear* to be missing. Succinylcholine is a clear liquid that comes in a vial. She'd used a syringe to draw it out before filling the vial back up with water. It wasn't until after the Grossmans lost their eighteen-month-old daughter that I overheard a *Dateline* episode Ace was watching about a nurse who killed his love interest with the same thing." Her stomach hurt as she remembered that night. "It was late, and I was trying to clean up the kitchen. I hadn't been to work in several days. After Amelia, I closed the practice for a week, couldn't even go in. But I got in the car that night, drove over to my office and tore that closet apart using a magnifying glass to examine every bottle and package. That's when I found the needle marks."

"I'm so sorry."

The anger and betrayal Natasha felt, along with everything else, made her grit her teeth. "I wish to God I'd never hired her, wish her application had never crossed my desk. I felt sorry for her, if you can believe that, because she was alone in a new place. She wanted to come over to my house all the time — now I think she wanted to *be* me — and I allowed it because I was trying to be a friend."

"Just hearing about it is enraging." He shook his head. "How'd you meet her? Where'd she come from?"

"Pennsylvania. She answered my ad, told me she'd recently been through a rough breakup — wanted kids but her ex wouldn't hear of it — was tired of the cold winters back East and wanted to move to California. And she came with a glowing recommendation from the hospital where she'd worked before, so . . . how was I to know?"

"They liked her at that hospital?"

"Not really. It came out in court that they'd had several babies die under her watch. They were being sued by some of the parents and didn't want to risk more trouble. So they asked her to resign, and she agreed as long as they gave her a recommendation so that she could move on."

"They knew she was dangerous and gave

58

it to her anyway?"

"They had their suspicions. But they didn't have proof. They just wanted to be rid of her. And I relied on their recommendation. Her background check came back clean, and there wasn't anything in her file that told me she might be dangerous."

"You should sue the hospital."

"That's what everyone says. And I've thought about it. But it would take a lot of time, energy and money — and if I win, it would be the hospital that would pay, not the people who are responsible."

"Don't tell me they still work there."

"No. They've been fired. I could sue the hospital anyway, of course, but do I really want something that terrible consuming so much of my life? Those things aren't quick. And there's no guarantee I'll win, even if I go through the agony." She preferred to bring an end to that chapter of her life as soon as possible — cut away the negativity and move on. "I've decided it'll be better for me, and Lucas, if I just start over."

He scrubbed a hand over his face. "Well, you did everything you could. The death of that child is on the person who gave her the recommendation, not you. No other doctor could've seen her coming."

"That's what I keep telling myself." She

59

swallowed hard. "I just wish I could believe it."

He put his arm around her, but she was so tempted to lean into him that she leaned away instead, and he let his arm drop.

They sat in silence for several seconds. Then he said, "I'm sorry, you know."

She could tell by his tone and manner that he was now broaching an entirely different subject. "I don't want to talk about us."

"Okay, but . . . . can I just say one thing?"

"No."

"Come on, Tash. *You're* the one who never came back, not for good."

Only because she couldn't take the soul-crushing rejection. Because she was determined to build a meaningful life instead of sticking around Whiskey Creek with her heart in her hand, hoping he'd eventually see her differently. She refused to beg for a man's love the way her mother did; she'd seen how far that had gotten Anya. "If that's the way you see it, I'll take the blame."

"I'm not blaming you. I'm . . . I want you to know how sorry I am that —"

"You don't owe me any apologies," she interrupted, too afraid to let him finish. "You've done a lot for me over the years, and I'm grateful." He'd also smashed her heart into a thousand tiny pieces over and over again, which had eventually caused her to marry someone she shouldn't have, but she wasn't going to try to explain how he'd triggered that cascade of bad decisions. Mack couldn't love her the way she'd always loved him. Period. End of story. Given that, nothing else mattered.

"I know I've hurt you, and I feel terrible about it," he said. "That was never my intention. I've always wanted you to be happy, tried to look out for you."

"I've just been through the worst year of my life," she said. "I can't deal with this right now, okay?"

The reedy sound of her voice must've gotten through to him. He pursed his lips as he studied her. "All right."

"I'm getting tired." She covered a fake yawn. "I think I'll go in and move Lucas so that we can get back to bed. See you in the morning."

He didn't answer. Neither did he follow her inside.

After the screen door shut, Mack sighed. Natasha wouldn't trust him. In the three days they'd been together, she'd been careful to show her appreciation for his help, but she remained wary of anything too reminiscent of where they'd been before.

He couldn't blame her. He'd let her down. But whenever he looked at the past, he couldn't see how he could've done things any differently. Except for that Christmas seven years ago when his desire for her had simply overcome his restraint, he'd been as circumspect as he could be, especially considering how difficult it had been almost from the start.

She'd been only sixteen when he met her, and yet she'd let him know right away that she wanted him. He'd thought it was a childish crush, at first, but she never wavered. And when he started to feel the same attraction, he became alarmed. He didn't want to be the kind of lech who would move in on a sixteen-year-old! Besides, he and his brothers had let her and her mother come live at the house to help Tasha get through school, which would've made a physical relationship with her even more predatory — as if he was taking advantage of the fact that she didn't have a mom decent enough to look after her properly.

He'd never admitted his true feelings — to anyone, especially her. He'd resisted even when she came into his room right before she left for college and told him she was in love with him and wanted to give him her virginity. Although she'd been nineteen at the time, technically an adult, he'd refused because he'd been thinking of what was best for her. In his mind, nineteen was still too young. Not only was his father still married to her mother at the time, he'd known if he took her to bed, she wouldn't leave. She'd stay in Whiskey Creek to be with him, and he wanted her to have the opportunity to experience more of life, to see what was outside their small town before she tied herself down to him or anyone else.

He cursed under his breath at the memory of how difficult that night had been. But even if there hadn't been such an age difference between them, he couldn't do anything that would embarrass or humiliate his brothers. He wasn't going to make it any harder for them to live down the stigma of what their parents had done. If not for Dylan, Aaron, Rod and Grady, he didn't know where he'd be. His older brothers were the ones who'd always looked out for him. They'd all warned him to stay away from Natasha. And he'd listened — until that night in Whiskey Creek when he'd finally succumbed. After that, he'd freaked out because he couldn't believe he'd crossed that line, and while he was trying to come to terms with whether or not he could allow himself to take what he wanted, she'd gone back to seeing Ace.

"Damn it," he muttered and scrolled through the photos he'd saved on his phone. They were pictures of Lucas that Natasha had sent to Dylan periodically and Dylan had shared on their brothers' group chat. Mack had saved every single one of them, because it was the only way he could watch Lucas grow without running the risk of screwing up Natasha's life again.

Until this opportunity arose.

He wasn't sure how things would go while he was here. What'd happened in the past had created too many scars. But now that Natasha's life had already been disrupted, he wasn't leaving until he learned about Lucas.

And if it was what he thought it was, he was definitely going to be part of his son's life.

FOUR

Lucas woke up at seven. Of course. Natasha groaned when she heard his voice. She wasn't ready to get up and face the day, but just when she thought she had no other choice — like every other morning since she'd become a single parent — she heard a much deeper voice coming through her bedroom door.

"You can sleep a little longer, Tash. I got Lucas."

Mack. The man she'd dreamed about all night. She'd almost convinced herself that having him with her the past three days was merely a dream, too.

"It's okay." The rasp in her voice forced her to clear her throat so she could speak clearly. "I'll get up. We have a lot to do."

"There's no rush to unpack. You have a whole week before you start work. We'll be done by then."

But they needed to return the truck before

they incurred yet another charge. And she hated living out of boxes, not knowing where anything was. For her own peace of mind, she had to get organized as soon as possible. That was the only thing that might make her feel as though she'd regained control of her life. "No, Lucas will be hungry," she said. "I need to get him something to eat."

"I'm sure I can manage to feed him while you grab a couple more hours."

She was tired enough to attempt a trade. "If you'll feed him breakfast, I'll make us all a nice dinner. Does that sound fair?"

"You don't have to pay me back for every little thing I do," he grumbled.

In *her* mind, she did. She didn't want to feel indebted to him. That would only undermine her strength and determination where he was concerned, and she needed to maintain her position, remain on guard, now more than ever.

Otherwise, she might wind up making another catastrophic mistake — like allowing herself to get hurt yet again.

Letting her eyelids slide closed, she retreated from the light slanting into her room. She'd get out of bed in fifteen minutes, she told herself.

She could hear Lucas, down in the

kitchen. "Can I have some Fruity Pebbles?"

"Fruity Pebbles!" Mack replied, as though her son had suggested eating worms for breakfast. "Why would you ever want to eat those?"

"Because they taste good," Lucas said.

"They're fine for wimps, I guess. But you don't want to be a wimp, do you?"

"No, I want to have big muscles, like you!"

"Then you should eat a better breakfast. How about some oatmeal with bananas?"

"*Oatmeal?*" her son repeated, clearly not excited by that suggestion.

"With bananas," Mack reiterated, as if that should change everything. "Surely you like bananas."

There was a slight pause, as though Lucas was thinking it over. "How many bites do I have to take?" he asked at length.

"Ten, to be exact. You need to take ten big bites a day. Can you count that high?"

To be exact? If she wasn't so tired, Natasha would've chuckled at the bullshit Mack was selling her son. But he was doing it for a good reason, and she was glad that he was taking the job of caring for Lucas so seriously. She knew Luke would be safe in Mack's hands, and that made it even harder to drag her butt out of bed.

"Of course I can count that high," Lucas

said, slightly affronted that Mack wasn't more aware of his capabilities. "I'm *six*. I can *read,* you know."

"I had no idea you were so smart," Mack told him, acting shocked.

"Want me to show you?"

That was the last thing Natasha remembered. She couldn't say if Mack agreed to hear Lucas read or whether Lucas showed him.

The next thing she knew, Mack was knocking on the door. "Tash? Someone's here to see you."

Startled, she sat up so quickly she felt dizzy for a moment. She'd dropped off in spite of her decision to get up. How long had she been out?

She grabbed her phone from where it was charging on a box next to the bed to check the time. It was after noon. She'd slept for five hours since Lucas had gotten up this morning. "Shit!" she whispered and sprang out of bed. "I'm sorry, Mack," she said, louder. "I never meant to go back to sleep, let alone zonk out until lunchtime."

"It's fine," he said. "You needed the rest."

"Where's Lucas?" she asked, slightly alarmed that she couldn't hear him.

"He's in the kitchen, having a peanut butter and jelly sandwich." He raised his voice so that Lucas could hear, too. "Or he will be after he finishes his carrots, right, buddy?"

"All done!" her son cried out. "Can I eat my sandwich now?"

She should never have left Mack babysitting all morning. But she couldn't dwell on that right now. He'd told her that someone was at the door. Was it the internet company? She didn't think they were scheduled until tomorrow.

"I'll be right out," she said and pulled on some cutoffs and a fresh Namaste T-shirt from her overnight bag before pulling her hair into a ponytail.

A draft of warm air, coming in from outside, hit her as she approached the door, which Mack had left standing open.

"Hello," she said when she saw a red-headed woman, about ten years older, through the screen.

"You must be Dr. Gray," the woman responded.

Natasha opened the screen door and noticed a picnic basket at the woman's feet. "Yes."

"I'm Camilla Ricci. I own Da Nonna, the Italian restaurant down the street. Aiyana Turner — Buchanon since she got married; I always forget that — planned to visit and welcome you in person, but something has come up that means she won't be able to get away today. She asked me to bring you dinner, so that you wouldn't feel so alone in your new house." She lifted the basket to hand it over. "Welcome to Silver Springs."

Natasha could see why she'd set it down. It was too heavy to hold for long. "That's very nice of her. And you," she said. "Thank you."

"You're welcome. Aiyana's excited you're here, and I hope I'll have the chance to get to know you, too."

"You said the name of your restaurant is Da Nonna?"

"Yes, but it's not entirely mine. I only own half of it. My mother and I took over for my grandmother, once she passed. That's why we changed the name to Da Nonna. It means *Grandma's place.* But that's the only change," she added proudly. "We still use all of Nonna's old recipes."

"It sounds wonderful. I'll stop in once I get settled. But I don't want Mrs. Buchanon to have to pay for my dinner. Let me get my purse." Natasha didn't have a lot of cash, and her debit card had been declined at the U-Haul place, but she was hoping there'd be room for this meal.

"Don't bother," the woman said, stopping

her. "Aiyana's already taken care of it. And she'd be mad at me if I let you pay instead."

"This is . . . such a nice welcome." When Natasha put the basket down and opened the lid, the scent of garlic, onions and basil permeated the room. "There's even a bottle of wine in here."

Obviously curious, Mack walked over, and that was all it took to distract Lucas from his lunch. He followed Mack and leaned up against Natasha while Mack sorted through the basket. "Wow," he said. "Looks delicious."

"This must be your little boy," Camilla said.

"Yes. His name's Lucas. Can you say hello to Mrs. Ricci, Lucas?"

"Hello," he mumbled shyly.

"What a cutie." Camilla jerked her head to indicate Mack. "Looks just like his father, doesn't he?"

For a moment, the whole world seemed to stand still. "Mack isn't Lucas's father," Natasha said, oddly breathless, her heart in her throat. "My ex still lives in LA. Mack is . . . um . . . just a family friend who's helping me move."

Camilla's face went as red as her hair. "Oh! I'm sorry. Aiyana made it sound as though you weren't bringing your husband

71

with you, but when I saw —" she gestured toward Mack "— and then Lucas, I assumed . . ."

Her words faded away when she realized she was only making things worse. "I have to go," she said and hurried back down the walkway.

Mack didn't move or speak as Natasha closed the door, and he didn't offer to help when she lifted the basket into the kitchen. "Looks like we'll have a great dinner," she said, infusing as much enthusiasm into her voice as possible in an attempt to direct attention away from what'd just occurred. She'd always told herself and everyone else that Lucas belonged to Ace. But the truth was she didn't know for sure — didn't want to know, either. Although she and Ace hadn't been exclusive when she'd returned to Whiskey Creek and spent that crazy night with Mack, she had slept with him before then, so chances were good Lucas belonged to Ace.

But sometimes when she looked at her son, she saw Mack's likeness herself.

Lucas scrambled up on a chair Mack must've brought in and shoved the paper towel that held his sandwich aside so he could see inside the basket. "Are there any treats?"

72

"There's some tiramisu, which is dessert."

"Tira . . . what?"

She forced a laugh while watching Mack from the corner of her eye. "Never mind. You wouldn't like that even if I could give it to you. I packed some snacks, so you don't have anything to worry about. Speaking of which, we'd better finish unloading the van. I'll just go brush my teeth first."

Her mind was racing a million miles a minute, and so was her heart as she got out the toothpaste. *It'll be okay.* Even if Lucas wasn't Ace's son, Mack couldn't be mad at her. He'd never followed up after their night together. Not the way she'd wanted and needed him to. At the time, she'd fully believed he wouldn't want to know.

She heard movement behind her and wished it was Lucas, but she could tell by the heavy tread on the stairs that it was Mack. He came up and leaned against the bathroom doorjamb, watching as she brushed her teeth.

His eyes never left her as she rinsed and dried her mouth. Finally, she answered the question she knew was burning uppermost in his mind. "It's not possible."

"You'd tell me?"

She dried her hands and tried to slip past him, but he caught her by the shoulders,

73

which wasn't hard to do since she only came up to his chest, and searched her face so thoroughly she could scarcely bring herself to meet his gaze. "Of course I would," she lied. Things were what they were, and she was going to leave them that way. Lucas had a father; there was no reason to confuse him. And if she was wrong about the genetics, it didn't matter. It wasn't as if her mistake was costing Ace anything. She was taking care of Lucas herself. He wasn't even paying child support. "Do you mind?" she said when Mack still didn't step aside.

"Can we talk about the circumstances and timing?" he asked.

What was she going to do? She'd gotten over him, moved on with her life. She refused to open her heart or her mind to anything from the past. "I've already told you — no."

"No, you don't want to talk about it? Or no, it's not a possibility?"

"Both."

"Damn it, Tash," he muttered, but he let go of her and moved out of the way.

It was difficult not to watch Lucas even more closely as they unloaded the truck. Mack didn't want to put Natasha through anything else. Her life had been rough, and he'd inadvertently caused some of that pain. But did that mean he had to accept what she said without proof?

When she caught him studying Lucas, who was playing in the truck while they unloaded, he got back to work and lifted another box out of the moving van. "Where do you want this one?" he asked.

She seemed worried about what he was thinking and feeling, but she didn't address it. He could tell she was too afraid — and that only made him more suspicious.

She peeked inside the flaps. "I'm sorry — I forgot to mark it. Looks like it goes in the bathroom."

After she grabbed a different box, she followed him inside, and they made one trip after another until they'd managed to empty the van.

"Now I just need to put all this stuff away," she said. "Moving is such a nightmare, isn't it?"

He didn't reply. She was trying to act as though that incident with Camilla Ricci had never occurred, but he couldn't get the woman's words out of his head: *Looks just like his father, doesn't he?*

"Mack?"

"I'll take the truck back to LA," he said.

She nibbled at her bottom lip as she eyed

75

him warily. "And then what?"

He came closer to her, so that he could lower his voice. "I'm going to buy an in-home paternity test."

The blood drained from her face. "Why?"

He pointed at Lucas, who was busy taking toys out of a box they'd brought in. "That's why."

The gravity in his voice somehow drew Lucas's attention, and he hurried over. "Me, Uncle Mack? Are you talking about me?"

Mack didn't answer. He was too focused on Natasha, who didn't seem to know what to say.

Lucas tilted his head back to look up at him. "Uncle Mack, are you mad?"

Mack pulled the boy close enough to be able to give him a reassuring pat. "No, I'm not mad. What happened was my fault."

"What'd you do?" he asked.

"I made a mistake. But I'm hoping your mother will give me the chance to fix it."

Natasha covered her face.

"Come on, Tash," he said. "You know I would never have left you high and dry with a kid."

She rubbed her forehead as though she had a spot on it she was trying to remove.

"Let me get the test," he pressed. "Hiding from it won't change the truth."

"It'll change other things," she mumbled. "But now that you suspect, you'll do it anyway."

"I'd rather have your permission," he said. "And I would rather you not hate the idea of it quite so much."

She dropped her hands. "Damn it, Mack. I could've moved here myself. You didn't have to come. Then that woman wouldn't have said what she did and — and this probably would never have happened."

She couldn't even have rented the moving van without him. But he didn't point that out. This wasn't about helping her move and they both knew it. She was scared. If he was Lucas's father, it would completely rewrite her child's story, change one of the most important aspects of the boy's life, which would be hard on Lucas and would certainly necessitate a difficult conversation with her ex-husband and his family.

Those were no small things.

"I've wondered from the beginning," he admitted. "I would've asked you eventually, even if . . . if Camilla Ricci hadn't said anything." He lowered his head to catch her eye, since she was now staring at the floor. "I've just been working my way up to it."

"I know," she said with a sigh. "You almost asked me last night."

His stomach filled with butterflies at the prospect of gaining proof of what he'd long suspected. Was he a father? What would it feel like to know for sure? "So you're okay with my getting a paternity test?"

She blinked rapidly, giving him the impression she was on the verge of tears. "Where will you get one?" she asked without specifically answering.

"I researched it online. They sell them at Walgreens."

"Walgreens," she echoed faintly. "It's that easy."

"These days, yes."

"How long does it take to get the results?"

"After we swab our cheeks — they need the mother's DNA, too — and mail in all samples, it'll take the lab only a couple of days before we can get the results online. So . . . from start to finish, including shipping, I'd say a week."

She rubbed her palms on the front of her cutoffs, a nervous gesture he'd seen her do many times before — and one that drew his attention to her legs. She'd always had magnificent legs.

"Are you sure you want to do this?" she asked. "Once we know, we can't un-know. There will be no going back. And if what we suspect turns out to be true, your broth-

78

ers will find out about that night seven years ago. Your father will, too. *And* my mother." She drew a deep breath. "Maybe we should rethink this."

She didn't mention her ex, but he knew she had to be imagining what the results might mean for him, too. That their son didn't belong to Ace would not be an easy thing to explain to him, especially after so long. And what would she tell Lucas?

"I've spent seven years thinking about it," he told her.

"Thinking about what?" Lucas piped up.

"Thinking about *you*," he replied and felt his heart melt as he lifted the boy into his arms and received a spontaneous hug.

FIVE

Mack left right after dinner. Natasha let Lucas help her unpack the kitchen, but once she got him into bed, she spent the remainder of the evening pacing. Was she facing yet another big upheaval?

If the paternity test came back positive, and Mack moved to Los Angeles, he'd be close enough to visit Lucas. Which meant he'd become a fixture in *her* life, too. There'd be phone calls to coordinate visitation, and he'd come to the house to take their son and bring him home. Maybe he'd even stay over once in a while. And she'd have to be amenable. How could she not be accommodating after everything he'd done for her?

And yet . . . how would she cope with having Mack back in her life? With having the man she'd always wanted to love *her* love her son instead?

Her phone began to ring. She could hear

the vibration on the counter. Grabbing it, she checked the screen. Dylan was trying to reach her. She didn't hear from him often, and they'd spoken recently, so she wondered if he was calling because he couldn't get hold of Mack.

She pressed the talk button as she went out onto the front porch, where the katydids were singing and the air was cooling off as it grew late. "Hey, Dyl."

"Tash, how are you?"

She sank onto the top step. Dylan was like a big brother to her. She loved him but also resented the fact that Mack had always put Dylan and his other brothers first, that he'd chosen to abide by their sense of propriety over being with her.

But Mack and his brothers were especially close and incredibly loyal to each other. They'd had to be to survive. So she supposed she should've expected that she would never quite be one of them — and yet, because they'd taken her and her mother in when they were homeless, she would be off-limits in a romantic sense. "Hanging in there," she said. "What about you?"

"The same. It's crazy busy at the shop."

"That's a good problem to have. How're Cheyenne and Kellan?"

"Great. Chey's now a beekeeper. We have a colony in our backyard. Not sure if I mentioned that the last time we talked. And Kellan is enjoying summer until football practice starts next month."

"He's growing up fast."

"He sure is," Dylan said. "How's the move?"

"I'm managing." She decided not to mention Mack. She was so used to Mack downplaying any attention he gave her that she'd made a habit of doing the same.

"From what I hear, you didn't get a very good divorce attorney."

Mack must've shared that recently, because even he hadn't known much about her divorce until a couple of days ago. "She did her job."

"Not according to Mack. He insists you got fleeced, which makes me feel terrible. I offered to help. Why didn't you take the money and get a decent lawyer?"

Because she didn't want to go even deeper into debt. And when she accepted their help, she fell more firmly into the "sister" category, something she'd been fighting ever since she'd fallen in love with Mack. Yes, along with her mother, they'd taken her in for three years when she was in high school. But they'd been adults at the time; she was the only minor. She hadn't been raised with them or by them. And she would've traded everything the Amos brothers had ever done for her if only it would also have changed the nature of her relationship with Mack. She'd wanted him *that* badly.

But what they could've had together was in the past, she reminded herself. She wasn't going to let her obsession with Mack dominate her life anymore. She'd made that decision when she married Ace, had cut all emotional ties — the ones she could cut, anyway. Now that she was divorced, and Mack was coming around again, it could get difficult. She wasn't stupid. But she was determined to guard her heart and not wind up the brokenhearted young woman she'd once been. She would do anything to avoid that. "Because I didn't want to fight," she said. "I just wanted out."

"I can understand that, but now you have to pay spousal support? That's bullshit. Why can't he work?"

That Ace made no real effort to support himself grated on her, as well. The men she'd admired most — the Amos brothers — worked hard. But when she'd been negotiating the divorce, she'd been so consumed with grief over the loss of Amelia Grossman that she hadn't had the strength or the presence of mind to make sure that their finances and belongings were divided fairly. She simply hadn't cared enough about physical objects and money to stop Ace from taking advantage of her. A *child* had been lost. "It's only for the next three years."

"*Only?*" he echoed, clearly perturbed. "What about all the student debt you're carrying? Do you have enough to get by?"

She hoped he hadn't been told she'd been unable to rent the moving van. "I'll be fine, Dyl."

After a slight pause, he said, "Would you tell me if you needed anything?"

"Of course."

He sighed. "Since I'm not there, I can only take your word for it. But Mack will be closer to you now. I guess he'll make sure."

"Los Angeles is an hour and a half away. Mack and I won't even see each other."

She knew that statement was dependent on Lucas's paternity, but he didn't. Even still, he said, "Oh, really."

"Yes, *really*," she said, irritated by the skepticism in his response.

"Okay." He backed off, but she could tell it was only to placate her. "By the way, I saw your mother last night for the first time in a long while."

Natasha wanted to continue to insist that Mack wasn't going to be a big part of her life — only as much as she *had* to allow if it turned out that he was indeed Lucas's father. But with Lucas's paternity still up in the air, she decided that now was not the time to keep going after that. "Where was she?" she asked, allowing herself to be distracted instead.

"Are you ready for this?"

She sat up straighter. The simple answer was no. Her mother had always been an embarrassment, had chosen the exact wrong thing to say or do in almost every situation. "That's ominous."

"She was at my father's."

"You're kidding."

"I'm not. I think they're seeing each other again. She might even be living there."

She shook her head. "They'd be stupid to get back together. It came to blows there at the end." And she knew her mother was at least as much to blame as J.T. Anya could get abusive when she drank.

"Not only do they fight like cats and dogs, neither one of them will stand up and be responsible for themselves. But they aren't the type to learn from past mistakes, or they'd both be in a much different situation right now."

"You deserved a better father," she said. "You all did."

"And you deserved a better mother. But you've got us, so who needs her," he joked.

"I can't thank you enough for everything you've done." She was truly grateful, had no idea what would've become of her without them. And yet . . . she knew all too well that having her life intersect with the Amos brothers — Mack in particular — had been as much a curse as it was a blessing.

It was an hour after Natasha had hung up with Dylan and gone back inside to unpack her bedroom that her phone went off again. Rocking back on her heels from where she was crouched in front of the dresser, putting away her clothes, she reached up to get her phone.

It was Ace.

"Oh great." Her ex-husband was the last person she wanted to talk to, but she knew it wasn't reasonable to think she could cut him out of her life entirely. That would require some time, possibly a lot of it.

Taking a moment to find her center, she answered. "Hello?"

"You make it to Silver Springs okay?" he asked.

As if he cared. He knew she'd have Lucas

and would be loading and driving a big truck — something she had no experience doing — and yet he hadn't offered to lend a hand. "Yeah. Everything's fine."

"How'd you do it?"

"What do you mean?"

"Don't tell me you moved all by yourself."

He'd been hoping she'd need him, that she'd call and ask for his assistance so that he could show her what she'd be missing out on in the future.

Sometimes he was *so* transparent. He may have asked for the divorce, but he hadn't really wanted it. He'd threatened to leave her to shock her into lavishing him with more attention and apologies for what they were going through. After all, *she* was the one who'd hired Maxine Green. Nothing bad would've happened had she not done that (he said). Instead, his threat to dissolve their marriage — at a time when she was going through so much in other regards — had broken the last of her loyalty and commitment, and she'd realized she wasn't happy, either. "No, I had someone help."

"Who?"

"A friend." She was reluctant to give him Mack's name. She knew he'd say something sarcastic. She'd made the mistake of telling him about Mack — not everything but some

87

of it — and he'd never forgotten or let it go. Although she'd since tried to act as though Mack had never been anything more than a childish crush, he'd thrown Mack up to her again and again, whenever they got into an argument. *What? I can't compare with the great Mack Amos? I'm not the man he is?*

He wasn't. But she'd never said that. She'd revealed too much that night, after they'd both had several glasses of wine, and he would never let her take it back.

"What can I do for you?" she asked. They'd already agreed that he'd pick up Lucas a week from Friday. So why was he calling now?

"It's not what you can do for me. It's what I can do for you," he announced.

That would be a first. She was being sarcastic herself, but he had to be the most selfish person she'd ever met. "I don't understand."

"I ran across something of yours. Something I'm pretty sure you'll want back."

Natasha couldn't imagine what that could be. Some of Lucas's baby pictures? She'd want those, but Ace would never give them to her. Just to be spiteful, she doubted he'd even allow her to make copies. Could it be a piece of her jewelry? She'd never owned anything of much value. She had the locket

Mack had given her at her high school graduation. Other than that, she didn't have any jewelry she particularly cared about. Her wedding ring had been the only thing Ace had ever given her. It'd been expensive, but his parents had paid for it, and she'd already pawned it for $2,500 to be able to stay afloat until she could get on her feet again. "What is it?"

"A box of your childhood pictures and stuff."

She got up and walked over to the window. He had that box? The pictures in it were the only ones she had from when she was little. Her mother wasn't much for hanging on to things — she'd been too transient — so Natasha felt lucky to have that much. "How did that wind up in your stuff?"

"I have no clue."

"Where'd you find it?"

"In an even bigger box with my yearbooks and other things I took out of the attic. You must've stuck it in there after we got married and forgot about it."

That was plausible. She'd been so busy trying to be a wife and mother while finishing med school, and then fulfill her residency, she hadn't given much thought to anything else. She'd been trying to outdistance her past, not dwell on it. "I'm sorry about that."

"No problem. Would you like me to drive it out to you tomorrow?"

Absolutely not. She didn't want to have any unnecessary contact with him.

She considered asking him to mail it instead, but she doubted he'd go to the trouble. And if he got the impression she didn't want to see him, she wouldn't put it past him to toss it all. He was bitter about the divorce, far more so than she was, even though he was the one who'd first wanted to call it quits.

"Sure. That'd be great," she said. But then she thought of another solution. It wasn't perfect, but it was better than having Ace come to Silver Springs.

"Actually, my friend's in LA returning the moving van right now. If you'll just set it out on the stoop, I could ask him to swing by and pick it up. Would that be okay?"

"Him?" he said.

She winced. "Yeah."

"Who is it?"

"No one you've met."

"What's his name?"

"Does it matter?"

"I just want to know his name," he said.

It sounded as though he was getting upset, so she relented. "It's Mack, okay?"

90

"Mack *Amos*? From the family of rowdy boys who raised you?"

"They didn't *raise* me. They let me and my mother live with them for three years so I could finish high school."

"Oh, that's right. That's when you fell in love with the youngest one."

"Nothing happened with Mack when I was living there, and you know that."

"Because you were too young, and he was too honorable."

Hearing the sarcasm in those words, she ground her teeth. "He was."

"Is that why you've never gotten over him?"

Thank God she'd never told Ace about the night she'd spent with Mack over Christmas. She'd never felt as though she owed that to him. As far as she knew, he'd been seeing other women during the same period. "I've told you before — that was just a childish crush."

"Really? Because sometimes I wonder if Mack Amos is the reason I could never really break through."

"Let's not start this," she said. Ace always complained that she was too aloof, too hard to engage, too indifferent to him, even though she'd tried hard to be otherwise. "I gave our marriage everything I had."

91

"No, you didn't. You held back. You didn't even care when I asked for a divorce."

"I've been very fair with you all along, including the divorce. I gave you everything you asked for, even though I could've gotten out of spousal support. I don't have an income right now myself, not until I start my new job."

"Your earning potential is a lot greater than mine, since I was the one to make the sacrifice of staying home with Lucas."

Sacrifice? It was hard not to laugh. He hadn't stayed home to do her any favors. He'd done it so that he could game 24/7. But she decided not to say that. Why let this argument escalate? "Whatever. I still gave you what you wanted."

"Out of guilt. Not love."

"Not guilt," she insisted. "I never did anything *that* wrong. So, please, just put the box out and let my friend pick it up."

"Your friend. Sure, why not? He can come by. Give him my address and tell him the box is here waiting for him."

Something in his voice made her uneasy. "You'd be stupid to mess with Mack, Ace."

"Oh yeah? Is that a warning?"

"Just a heads-up."

"You think he could take me?"

Easily. But she didn't want them to wind

up in a fight, and she hadn't told Ace that to make him feel inferior. "No. He's not part of this. He's just helping me move."

"Then what are you worried about?"

What *was* she worried about? Although Ace could get angry and say some stupid things, he'd never been violent. She'd had almost no contact with Mack since they'd married — certainly not the type that should make Ace think Mack had interfered in any way. Besides, they were divorced. She could hang out with whomever she pleased. "Nothing. Never mind. So you're putting it out?"

"Yep. Right now."

She figured she'd talk to Mack, see what he thought. If he wasn't comfortable going there, she'd drive over as soon as he returned so that someone would be home with Lucas through the night. As much as she'd tried to outdistance her past, she hated to risk losing her personal items for good, when she had so little from her childhood to begin with. "Okay, thanks," she said and disconnected so that she could call Mack.

He answered on the first ring. "I just got the truck back," he announced. "Heading your way now."

"Have you already left the LA area?"

"Not quite. Why?"

"My ex-husband has a box of pictures and other stuff that means a lot to me. It's all I have of my childhood, and I'm afraid of what he might do to it if I don't get it from him right away. I know it's late, so I feel bad asking, but he said he'd set it outside if —"

"You want me to grab it? Of course. Where does he live?"

Mack acted like it would be no big deal. And it shouldn't be. Maybe she was reading too much into Ace's response. Mack had nothing to do with their marriage falling apart — other than existing. "I'm a little hesitant to give it to you," she admitted.

"Is it that far?"

"It shouldn't be. It's Burbank, but he was acting strange on the phone. I'm afraid he might give you a hard time just because you're helping me."

"Why would that be any of his business?"

"You know how messy divorces can be. Old feelings, resentment."

"Well, if there are any hard feelings, I think it's better that I pick it up instead of you."

"Except I don't want him to start anything."

"I'm not worried about that."

94

Should he be? She hesitated while weighing it all out in her mind. No. It should be no big deal. Mack was already in LA. If Ace set out her memorabilia, he could grab it and the two men wouldn't even have to see each other.

"I've already turned around," Mack said. "Text me his address."

She crossed to her bed and dropped onto it. "Okay. I'm probably worried for nothing. You'd only be picking up a small box."

"Right. I've never even met this man. Why would we have a problem?"

"Exactly." Feeling better about the whole thing — and hoping she could get her pictures and other mementos before something happened to them — she provided Ace's address.

SIX

The porch light was on, giving Mack the impression Ace was expecting him, but he couldn't find a box, a bag or anything else at the front door. He considered calling Natasha to ask for Ace's phone number — he knew Ace had roommates and didn't want to wake the whole household by pounding on the door if he didn't have to — but he was afraid Natasha had fallen asleep, and if he disturbed her she'd be up for the rest of the night.

After checking one more time around the stoop and nearby bushes, he lifted his hand to knock, but the door opened before he could make contact.

"You must be Mack."

A tall, slender man stood there in a tank top, cutoffs and flip-flops, someone who looked like the quintessential Southern California surfer, with gleaming teeth, a deep tan, a leather necklace and bleached bangs that were so long he had to keep flipping them out of his eyes. "Yeah, I'm Mack," he said, instantly wary. Something wasn't right: he could tell. What kind of game was Ace playing? Why hadn't he just left the box outside, as he'd said he would? "And you're Ace, right?"

"That's right."

In an attempt to be polite, Mack stuck out his hand, but Ace wouldn't take it, so Mack said, "Can I get what I came for?"

"In a sec. First, I have something I'd like to say to you."

Mack took a step back. He could hear the suppressed emotion in Ace's voice. "What's that? Because I don't think there's anything *to* say. We don't even know each other."

"For one thing, I'd like to hear you say you've never slept with my wife."

That was a loaded question, one Mack knew he had to handle carefully. He couldn't categorically deny any sexual contact with Natasha. What if Lucas turned out to be his? How would he explain that? He hadn't touched Natasha since she'd been married, but clarifying would give away that he had touched her before. "I don't see why that's any of your business — not at this point."

"She lived with you and your brothers for

three years when she was only sixteen. I can't believe none of you tapped a piece of ass that fine and that accessible."

Mack felt his muscles bunch but told himself to keep a cool head. "As you've mentioned, she was only sixteen. I was twenty-five. Sleeping with her would not only have been morally wrong, it would've been a crime."

"And you're claiming that stopped you? When she was dying to fuck you and her mother was always so stoned she had no one to look out for her?"

Even Ace's choice of words were inflammatory. "We were there to look after her," Mack said, keeping his tone measured.

"You expect me to believe you didn't do anything with her before she turned eighteen? You're lying, and that's why she's so screwed up she can't love anyone but you."

"I didn't touch her when she lived with us," Mack reiterated. "It wasn't like that." But there were certainly moments when the situation nearly got away from him. The harder he'd tried to keep his thoughts and desires under control, the harder she'd tried to make him change his mind. Sometimes she wouldn't close her door all the way when she was changing, if she knew he was the only one at home, or she'd purposely walk back to her room after a shower in nothing but a towel. Even when his brothers were around, she'd brush up against him at every opportunity. She'd kept him so sexually frustrated he'd slept with a lot of other women, just to satisfy that urge. By the time she'd moved out at nineteen, it had been all he could do not to give her exactly what she was asking for — until they'd both had their fill.

But, somehow, he'd managed to restrain himself for seven more years. It wasn't until that Christmas, when she was in her twenties, that he hadn't been able to deny himself.

"You're so full of shit," Ace scoffed.

"Look, is there a point to this?" Mack asked. "Because it's late, I've got a long drive ahead of me and I'd just as soon be on my way."

"Actually, I do have a point."

"And that is . . ."

"Lucas is my point."

The hair stood up on the back of Mack's neck. "Your son?"

"That's just it. *Is* he my son?" Ace asked, his eyes sparking with tightly leashed fury.

"Far as I know." Mack wasn't about to say anything more, not if he could help it. First, he had to establish Lucas's paternity.

Then they could figure out a way to deal with the results.

"You're saying you don't think he could be yours?" After reaching inside the house, Ace held up a small journal, which he opened and began to read aloud. " 'God, I'm tired. And I have a big test coming up. I need to concentrate, and yet I can't quit thinking about Mack finally stripping off our clothes and pressing inside me. Nothing in my life has ever felt so good. I didn't want to come, because then I knew he'd come and it would all be over. But it was impossible to hold back. I've never had a night like that one. The only problem is, I'm not sure what I'm going to tell Ace. Do I stay in the relationship — or get out of it?' "

"That's enough," Mack grumbled.

Ace sneered at him but seemed to be choking up at the same time. "Do you want me to give you the date of this entry?"

"No." He already knew the date. It had been two days before Christmas over seven years ago. He hadn't been able to forget that night, either.

"That stupid bitch lied to me!" he cried. "She told me she loved me. I never knew she'd been with anyone else, not after I started seeing her. I assumed a pregnancy meant the baby was mine."

Mack winced. "To be fair, I don't think she knows any different."

"She had to have known there was a possibility!" His voice had been rising all along; now he was shouting. "Tell her I don't want anything to do with her ever again. Tell her I will *never* even look at Lucas, never come near him, never be his dad. She used me. She used me because she couldn't have you. And now she's wrecked my life," he said and slammed the door.

Natasha would never have purposely used Ace or anyone else. She wasn't the type. She must've thought she loved him enough to make it work — to create the family she'd always wanted and never had. Or she wouldn't have married him. But Mack still felt partially responsible. The way he'd responded to that night had been wrong. He was sorry for that, but he couldn't change the past. So what did he do now? And, more specifically, how did he react in this moment? Ace still had Natasha's journal and pictures, and he obviously wasn't planning on giving them back.

Mack stood on the stoop, trying to decide if he should risk a fight by pushing the issue. He wanted to, but even if he banged on the door, he doubted Ace would answer.

"What a mess," he muttered as he returned to his truck.

Once he was behind the wheel, he called Natasha.

Her voice was thick with sleep when she answered. "You okay?" she asked.

"I'm fine."

"Did you get my stuff?"

"Um, ran into a small wrinkle there."

"What happened?" Her voice was much clearer now. The surprise had woken her up.

"Ace is a little upset."

"Why?"

"Apparently, he found an old journal inside your box of pictures."

"A journal?"

"Yep."

She went quiet. Then she said, "Oh. My. God."

"Yeah."

"He read it?"

"He did." Mack didn't add that he'd read it aloud to him, as well.

"And? Did it get ugly between you?"

"Not too bad, but he says he wants nothing more to do with you or Lucas."

This declaration was met with silence. After she'd had a chance to process it, she said, "He doesn't want to wait until we find out for sure?"

"He was upset, didn't seem concerned with proof. He may come back later and demand it, but we should have the results by then."

"I should've burned that journal," she said, so low he could barely hear her.

"Don't be too hard on yourself," he said. "You've been through a lot. You're physically and emotionally exhausted."

"Yeah, I am," she admitted. "And as nice as you've always been to me, I wish I'd never met you."

She disconnected and Mack let his head fall onto the steering wheel. He couldn't believe this had to happen, especially before Natasha could get back on her feet and feel strong enough to take another blow.

He started the engine and was about to head back to Silver Springs. But he couldn't let Ace keep Natasha's pictures. Once they were lost, they'd be gone for good. And she already had such a meager endowment from her childhood.

Putting the truck back in Park, he released his seat belt and got out. As far as he was concerned, Natasha and Lucas would both be better off without Ace. The dude could get the hell out of their lives if he wanted to, but he wasn't going to hang on to Na-

103

tasha's belongings just to spite her.

As Mack stalked up the walkway, he saw the curtain move in the front window. Ace had been watching him. Good. Now he could open up and hand over her stuff, or Mack would bang on the door until he did. "Listen, I know you're pissed off," he called through the panel. "Maybe you have a right to be. What's happened hasn't been good for any of us, and I'm sorry if I'm to blame. But I can promise you that Natasha has never tried to hurt anyone. She's not that kind of person. When she married you, she must've loved you and believed Lucas belonged to you. So give me her things, and after I take a paternity test, I'll let you know the results. Fair enough?"

The door shuddered beneath a violent blow. "You can go to hell!" Ace shouted.

"The two of you are divorced," Mack reasoned. "You have no right to keep her pictures. You have no use for them."

"I'm going to burn them," he announced. "That's what I'm going to do, because it's what she deserves."

"No, you're not," Mack said. "There's no way I'll ever let you get away with that. So just give them to me and I'll go."

Another male voice entered the fray, someone they'd apparently disturbed with

104

their argument: "Shut up! What's going on? I'm trying to sleep!"

"It's nothing," Ace called back. "Mind your own damn business!"

"Hey, help me out here," Mack shouted. "Ace has his ex-wife's baby pictures, and I'm here to get them. That's it. Once he gives me those, I'll be gone and you can go back to sleep without all the racket."

"I'm about to call the police," the man threatened.

"There's no reason to get the police involved," Mack responded. "Just hand me her things."

"Get the hell off my property!" Ace shouted.

"I'm not leaving until I get those pictures," Mack said. "Go ahead and call the cops, do whatever you've got to do, but you're going to have a problem with me as long as you try to hang on to Natasha's things."

The door flew open and a much larger man than Ace — larger than Mack, too — loomed in the opening. "Get the hell out of here!" he growled.

Mack felt his hands curl into fists. "Sorry, I can't do that. I'm not going, which leaves you two choices — you can try to make me, or go ahead and call the cops."

The guy glared at him before turning to

Ace. "Are you being a spiteful little bitch? Do you have some of your ex-wife's pictures?"

An argument ensued between them, but right in the middle of it, the guy must've realized that what Mack wanted was by the door, because he shoved a small box into Mack's chest. "Here, these look like what you want. Take 'em and get out of here," he said and slammed the door.

Mack quickly dug through what he'd been given. Sure enough, it was photographs of Anya and Natasha when Natasha was young, a painting she'd done as a child, her birth certificate, a small jewelry box he and his brothers had once given her for Christmas and a few other things. The journal Ace had read wasn't in there. He must've set it somewhere else, somewhere his roommate didn't notice, but Mack supposed he was lucky to have gotten as much as he did.

Deciding to accept the compromise, he carried the items he'd recovered back to the car. I have most of your stuff, he texted to Natasha, but he didn't get a response.

Natasha woke up before Lucas, pulled on a light dressing robe and went down to see if Mack had gotten home. She'd been so upset about Ace finding her journal and reading what she'd written that she'd never expected to be able to fall back to sleep last night, certainly not before Mack arrived. She did toss and turn and stew for a while, but she'd been so exhausted that she'd eventually drifted off in spite of that. Relocating had taken all of her energy. And she'd been through so much with Ace — over the past year, in particular — she was growing immune to the upset. This was just more of the same.

Except for what it might mean for Lucas. She felt terrible for her son. Had she not kept that journal, and the paternity test Mack was about to take came back negative, Ace would never have had to know there was a possibility that he wasn't the father. Now he'd try to punish her for what she'd done with Mack, try to paint it as a betrayal when it was really just a case of bad timing. Even then, it wasn't as if she'd tried to trap him. *He'd* been the one who'd wanted to get married. He'd pressed her for months until, after Lucas was born, she'd finally relented.

Mack was asleep on the couch. Despite what she'd said to him last night, she was relieved to see that he was safe — and that he had returned in spite of her harsh words.

With a sigh, she raked her fingernails

through her hair and went back upstairs to the bathroom. She had to shower and go over to New Horizons. Last night when she'd emailed Aiyana Buchanon to thank her for sending the dinner from Da Nonna, Aiyana had asked her to stop by the school this morning, take a quick tour and check out the nurse's office to see if she was going to need any supplies that Aiyana could order before she started, and she'd agreed. Since she'd interviewed via Zoom, and had never actually visited New Horizons, she was looking forward to seeing the campus.

The hot water pounding down on her sore muscles felt so good it was difficult to get out. The old house had its problems, but water pressure wasn't one of them.

She'd just finished putting on her makeup and drying her hair, which took forever because it was so thick, when Lucas stumbled into the bathroom.

"Where're you going, Mommy?" he asked, still half-asleep as he squinted up at her.

She crouched to give him a hug. "To work."

"What about me?"

"My boss would like to meet you, so I'm taking you with me. Go potty while I make breakfast. Then I'll lay out your clothes."

"Can I stay here with Uncle Mack?"

"No. Uncle Mack was up late. We need to let him get some rest."

"But . . . will he still be here when we get back?"

After what she'd said to him, Natasha wasn't sure. As much as she understood she'd be better off, in some ways, if he left, there was a part of her that dreaded the moment he drove off.

Damn her traitorous heart.

"I think so."

"You don't know?"

Last night Lucas had asked, over and over again, when Mack would be back. She knew he wasn't going to be happy when Mack went away and felt as though she needed to prepare him for that moment. "No, I don't know, and we can't put any pressure on Mack, okay? He won't be staying long. You need to remember that and not get too attached."

Leaving him in the bathroom, she went to put on her red dress, which she paired with a white belt and heeled sandals. She stared at herself in the mirror, discouraged to see how the dress hung on her. It used to fit so nicely. But she didn't have time to worry about how skinny she was getting.

After pulling her hair back, she squirted on some perfume and went down to make pancakes. That was when she found the small box containing her pictures sitting on the counter.

Apparently, Mack had been able to reclaim her memorabilia after all. The journal wasn't there, but as she sifted through the photographs she would've lost without him, she couldn't help regretting what she'd said on the phone last night. There was no reason he'd had to take her in when she was younger, no reason for him to provide the money she'd needed to get ready for college, no reason to stay in touch to keep her from feeling too lost and homesick that first year, no reason to come to LA to help her move or reclaim her pictures.

But he'd done all of those things.

Damn it. He always did this to her — made it impossible for her to hate him.

"Can I have strawberries on my pancake?" Lucas asked.

"We don't have any strawberries. How about peanut butter?"

"Okay."

Mack woke up at eight thirty, just as they were getting ready to leave. "What's going on?"

"I have to meet my boss and take a tour of the school."

"You can leave Lucas here with me, if you

110

want. I can watch him."

She thought of the paternity test he'd said he'd bought last night and felt a frisson of fear. What would it mean if Lucas *was* his? "No, that's okay. Aiyana told me I could bring him, that she'd like to meet him." She grabbed her purse and started digging through it for her keys.

"My truck's parked behind your car. Just take it." He got up and grabbed his fob off the counter and tossed it to her.

"Okay. Thank you." She gestured at the box filled with her pictures. "How'd you manage that?"

He scrubbed a hand over his beard growth. "I just insisted on it."

She lowered her voice. "And you left Ace in one piece?"

He glanced at Lucas. "Of course I did."

"Thank you. I appreciate it."

"No problem."

She grabbed Lucas's hand to lead him out, but as soon as they'd descended the porch steps, she turned around and led her son right back inside. "Mack?"

He'd opened the refrigerator. At the sound of his name, he closed the door so they could see each other. "Yeah?"

She felt an unnerving wave of tenderness as she looked at him and tried to convince herself it was just gratitude. "I'm sorry."

He studied her for several seconds before he responded with, "So am I."

SEVEN

The wrought iron arch over the entrance to the school read New Horizons and reminded Natasha of the arches she'd seen at the entrance of various cattle ranches.

"Where are we going?" Lucas asked as she turned in.

"To my work," she replied, even though she'd already told him that two or three times.

"You work *here*?"

"Now I do."

"This is where you take care of sick babies?"

"Not babies but bigger kids."

"Like me?"

"A little older than you. The students here range in age from middle school to high school."

"Oh." They watched a boy's PE class play basketball as they drove by. The turnoff for the administration building, marked with a black-and-tan sign, came halfway around the loop that circled the entire campus.

"Will I go here when I get bigger?" Lucas asked.

Because she knew it was a school for troubled teens, Natasha said, "I hope not."

It wasn't difficult to find a parking space. Although the school was open year-round, half their students went home for the summer. Aiyana had said that now would be a great time to start because the school wasn't running at full capacity, which would give Natasha a chance to ease into her job before things got busy in the fall.

After she helped Lucas out of his car seat, Natasha hitched her purse up higher on her shoulder and led him inside, where they found a short, stout woman seated at a desk behind the front counter. "I'm here to see Aiyana Buchanon," Natasha explained when the woman looked up.

"Oh, you must be Dr. Gray."

"Yes, and this is my son, Lucas."

"It's a pleasure to meet you both." The placard on the desk gave her name, but she volunteered it anyway. "I'm Betty May. I've been here at the school almost since it opened."

"Looks like a great place to work."

"It is — because of Aiyana and the way

she runs it." She winked. "Let me tell her you're here."

Expecting to wait a few minutes, Natasha was about to take a seat in the reception area when Betty returned. "She's ready for you. Right this way," she said and gestured toward the corner office.

Aiyana didn't look much different than she had on the screen of Natasha's laptop — except that Natasha could now ascertain her height. Barely five-one or five-two, she was diminutive, with skin the color of café au lait and long black hair she wore in a braid down her back. With her kind eyes and warm smile, she was easy to like. "I'm glad you're here," she exclaimed as she came around the desk. The bangle bracelets on her wrist clanged together as she reached out to take Natasha's hand, which she clasped in both her own. "Welcome."

"That dinner you sent over last night was something special," Natasha told her. "Thank you again for that. It was such a nice surprise."

"No one makes Italian food quite like Da Nonna's," she said, and her long skirt puddled on the carpet as she squatted down to address Lucas. "And who is this handsome young man?"

Lucas could be shy with strangers, especially when directly addressed by an adult, but he showed no signs of that with Aiyana. "I'm Lucas."

"Lucas!" Aiyana repeated. "What a nice name. How old are you, Lucas?"

"Six."

"Will you be starting first grade or second grade in the fall?"

"First."

"He has a late birthday," Natasha explained. "He missed the cutoff and had to wait until he was six to start kindergarten."

"It's probably better for him to be on the older side than the younger side anyway," she remarked and returned to her desk to get a ring of keys out of her top drawer. "Let me show you your office. Then I'll take you around campus."

"I've been looking forward to seeing it all."

Aiyana made Natasha feel right at home. As difficult as everything else had been recently, being around someone like her felt almost like falling into a mother's embrace — the kind of mother Natasha had always wished she had. Aiyana had such a way with people that Natasha couldn't help being grateful she'd answered Aiyana's ad for a medical professional, even if she was overqualified. At least she'd found a soft place to land. Maybe here she'd be able to pull her life back together.

Her office wasn't large, but it was sufficient — about what she'd expected — and Natasha was surprised to find it well stocked. "Looks like I'll have everything I need."

"If not, all you have to do is ask," Aiyana said.

"Thank you." As she closed the cabinets and drawers, a poster that hung on one wall — the picture of a louse, magnified to such a degree it looked like a monster from a science fiction film — caught Natasha's eye. She'd had head lice in second grade. She'd scratched her head so hard and so often her teacher had finally sent her to the school nurse. Without Nurse Seamus shampooing her hair with the expensive medicated shampoo and painstakingly picking out all the nits even a fine-tooth comb couldn't strip off her hair shafts, she might've become even more of a pariah. She'd already been largely ignored, as if she didn't matter or have anything to offer, because she couldn't come to school on time, in clean clothes or even with a lunch.

Following her gaze, Aiyana said, "If you don't like that, feel free to take it down. This is your office. You can personalize it any way you'd like."

117

"Thank you. I think I will take it down." She could put up rules about sharing hairbrushes and touching another student's hair without scaring those who found themselves in the same situation she'd been in at seven. Had she seen that magnified louse back then, it would've given her nightmares to think she had such vicious-looking creatures crawling around in her hair.

The rest of the buildings and landscaping were clean and well maintained. She knew from what Aiyana had told her during their interview that, although New Horizons was a private school, it did receive some public funding. Aiyana worked closely with both the foster care system and the court system to try to provide a safe environment for teenagers who hadn't received the proper love and care at home and were acting out because of it. She'd started the school with just the boys' side before expanding to include a separate girls' side a few years ago, and she'd adopted eight of her students — mostly grown men now. Her youngest would be leaving for college this fall.

"Many of the kids who come here have been neglected or abused in some way. Some of their stories are heartbreaking," Aiyana was saying as they made the trek back from the gymnasium to the administration building.

"I'm sorry to hear that," Natasha said, especially because she could relate. Her mother hadn't been abusive in a physical sense — at least, not terribly. But Anya had often been emotionally abusive, and she'd certainly neglected Natasha, which was why, once she met them, the Amos brothers had tried to step in to help.

As they meandered back, they talked as comfortably as if they were old friends, and the immediate connection made Natasha feel coming to New Horizons might turn out to be a blessing. She loved the gentle, healing atmosphere. Maybe she'd be working as a nurse, and she wouldn't make as much as she could as a doctor, but the money would be steady, she wouldn't have the cash-flow challenges she'd faced before, which had put so much stress on her and her marriage, and she could still do a lot of good. She'd always wanted to make a difference. That was the reason she'd become a doctor — that and to make sure she didn't wind up like her mother, with nothing to show for her life.

"Thank you for this opportunity," she said to Aiyana. "I know it couldn't have been an easy decision to hire a doctor when you were looking for a nurse. You must be at least a little worried that I won't be fulfilled and you'll just have to replace me in a few months."

"I admit the thought that you might move on rather quickly crossed my mind," Aiyana said. "But when you responded to my ad, I recognized your name, and once I went online to figure out why, I knew you were just the person for the job."

"*What?*" she cried with a startled laugh. "Learning what happened to me didn't scare you away?"

"Why would it scare me away? *You* weren't responsible."

"Not directly. But don't you wonder whether I could've figured it out sooner? If, had I been more vigilant, I could've saved little —" Her throat tightened to the point she couldn't speak.

"Are you okay, Mommy?" Lucas asked.

Natasha swallowed hard and managed to say, "Yes, I'm okay, honey."

"No," Aiyana said, earnestly. "I didn't wonder any such thing."

"Because . . ."

She stopped, so Natasha and Lucas stopped, too. "Because I saw you on the news."

Natasha didn't know which segment she was referring to. There'd been several sta-

120

tions that'd come out. She'd spoken to the media because she'd wanted to make parents and other doctors more aware of what could happen. There were other people out there like Maxine, and they needed to know what to watch out for. Anyway, in whatever interview Aiyana had caught, she'd been so shocked and devastated that it must've come through.

"Besides, why would a brand-new doctor allow someone to harm her patients, even through negligence? When it would ruin everything she's worked so hard to establish — all those years of getting through school and the tremendous expense of setting up a practice?" Aiyana shook her head as she started walking again. "No, I knew you had to have been as much a victim of Maxine Green as your patients were, and I didn't want to make it possible for the harm she did to continue on and on."

Natasha struggled to hold back tears. The fact that Aiyana had so easily seen past the stigma and was willing to give her a chance made her emotional. She supposed it didn't help that, these days, she was always on the verge of tears. "So you hired me."

"That's right. And I'm glad I did." She smiled. "Because I like you already."

Natasha turned her face away so that Ai-

121

yana wouldn't see her wipe her eyes. "Thank you," she said softly.

"LA's loss is Silver Springs' gain," Aiyana joked.

Natasha drew a deep breath as she lifted her head and, once again, surveyed the campus. "I think I'm going to like it here."

They were almost back to the administration building when Aiyana pulled her to a stop. "Natasha, before you go, I wanted to apologize for Camilla's blunder last night. She called me from the car after she left your place, afraid she'd put you in an awkward position. I hope that's not the case."

Natasha saw nothing but compassion in Aiyana's eyes, so she said something she probably wouldn't have said to any other stranger. "It was a little awkward. Mack and I have a long history, and . . . and we've always cared about each other very much, so . . . it sort of raised the question."

Aiyana frowned. "I hope he didn't get angry."

"No. He demanded a paternity test, but he would've done that eventually anyway."

"What's a paternity test?" Lucas asked, shading his eyes against the sun as he looked up at her.

"Just a way to see if you're genetically

linked to someone else," she replied.

He wrinkled his nose. *"What?"*

She'd known that explanation would be indecipherable to him, which was why she'd used it. "Never mind."

Aiyana seemed thoughtful. "Which way do you want it to go?"

Natasha wasn't sure how to answer that question. Given Ace's behavior the past twelve months, it would be nice to know she wouldn't have to deal with him indefinitely. If he wasn't Lucas's father, she could send him a check each month for the next three years and be done with him. If he got too difficult, she might even take him back to court to get rid of the spousal support — make him work for his own living. The thought of that brought a certain amount of relief, especially because she believed Mack would be a good father. He took care of those he loved, and she'd al-ready seen how interested he was in Lucas, had watched them interact in a positive, healthy way.

But she didn't want to switch fathers on her child if she didn't have to. Even if that didn't cause Lucas to struggle now, it could leave a nasty scar, especially if Ace bugged out as if he'd never really meant a thing.

"That's hard to say."

"Who's the better person?" Aiyana asked.

"There's nothing wrong with either one of them," she replied, just in case her son could understand even a portion of what they were talking about. But she knew in her heart there was really only one answer to that question: Mack.

Mack expected Natasha to be somewhat depressed when she got home. She was taking a big step down, going from being a pediatrician with her own practice to working as a school nurse, but he was surprised to see a smile on her face when she walked through the door.

"Your meeting must've gone well," he said, turning away from the frame he was tearing out so that he could replace the broken window.

She stopped, obviously taken aback by the demolition. "What are you doing?"

"The landlord dropped by. He said he ordered the window right after you leased the place and stuck it in the garage for safekeeping until he could get over here to install it."

Lucas, excited by what Mack was doing, hurried over to play with the tools strewn at his feet.

"Where in the garage?" she asked. "I didn't see it when I parked in there."

Using the claw part of the hammer, Mack pried out the sill of the old window, which had so much dry rot it was turning to sawdust anyway. "It was wrapped up in padding and cardboard behind the trash cans."

"So where is my landlord?" she asked. "Why isn't *he* installing it?"

"He's got to be eighty years old, didn't look strong enough to lift it, let alone put it in. So I said I'd do it."

"And he let you, even though he doesn't know you? He doesn't care that you're tearing out part of the wall?"

"I *have* to tear it out. Wood's bad." He stopped working long enough to look over at her. "So? How'd it go at the school?"

She put her purse on the counter. "Really well. I like the woman I'm working for. And I'm excited to have the chance to make a difference in the lives of kids who really need the time, energy and love I'm willing to invest. Because I was an outcast growing up, too, so different from all the other little girls at school who were clean and well cared for, I'm thinking I should be able to understand a little of what these poor, broken kids have endured."

He remembered how angry she'd been at the world when she and her mother moved in. At sixteen, she'd used more profanity

125

than they did — and with five brothers growing up mostly without parents, their language had never been good. Dylan was constantly trying to get Natasha to quit swearing — he'd tell her that the way she talked didn't sound like a young lady — but she'd just tell him to fuck off. It used to make them all laugh, but Mack secretly admired how tough she was for being so small and vulnerable and how hard she worked around the house and the auto body shop. She was determined to earn her place in the world and pay them back for their "charity." But she refused to allow them to tell her what to do otherwise. She wouldn't alter the language she used, the clothes she wore or the friends she hung out with.

"Why are you smiling?" she asked.

He wiped the nostalgic expression off his face. "No reason."

She narrowed her eyes. "Tell me."

"I was remembering what you used to be like."

"Don't remind me. I had a huge chip on my shoulder. I know."

They all did, he thought, as he grabbed Lucas by the back of his shirt to stop him from carting away the hammer he'd put down. "I admired you," he admitted.

"Because you didn't know me when I was

the little girl no one wanted to sit next to. Consider yourself lucky that you didn't come into my life until I was old enough to get the lice out of my hair."

"What's lice, Mommy?" Lucas asked, picking up Mack's new screwdriver.

"I hope you never have to find out," she told him. "Or if you do, that I'll catch it here at home, and you won't be embarrassed at school the way I was."

That her mother hadn't taken proper care of her had always made Mack angry. He wished he would've been around to protect her sooner. "You're right — I didn't know the little girl whose mother would routinely forget her at school, or send her to class without even combing her hair. By the time I met you, you had most things figured out." He hid a smile. By then, she'd been determined not to need anyone, was willing to take on the whole world by herself if she had to. He'd never forget her getting into a fight with a boy at school — one that turned physical — because that boy said something about "the dirty Amos brothers" she lived with. Their reputations weren't any better than hers. Plenty of people had gossiped about them, tried to insinuate that she was sleeping with them all, but he and his brothers had looked out for each other, done what they could for Natasha, too, and somehow they'd gotten through those difficult times, some of which he actually remembered fondly. Not too many kids messed with him; they knew better than to rile up the Amoses. And Natasha had proved herself one of them that day.

"I was so angry," she said. "Sometimes I'm *still* angry — and have to talk myself down. Since my mother isn't capable of living a productive life, it's a waste of time to expect more than she can deliver. Once I realized I would never have the mother I wanted, or the father, either, I've done a lot better."

She was so damn smart. "I still don't know how you graduated from high school, let alone college and med school. The odds were stacked against you, but you've done amazing things."

"I *thought* I was going to do amazing things — until last year," she grumbled.

"Last year takes nothing away from what you've achieved. You're no stranger to hard times. You'll get past this." He started to saw through the Sheetrock and two-by-fours that held the rest of the window frame in place. "By the way, the internet company's come and gone. You're all hooked up."

"That's wonderful. Now we'll have Disney

Plus and a few games to entertain Lucas while we unpack."

"Has your mother shown much interest in Lucas?" he asked.

"Not really," she replied and gave Lucas some of his toys as she moved him out of Mack's way. "Occasionally, she'll call and want to talk to him, or she'll send him a little something, but she doesn't make a great deal of effort. You're not surprised by that, are you?"

"Sadly, no."

She went over to get the leftovers out of the refrigerator. "You hungry? There's still some pasta."

"You go ahead, unless you'd like to wait for what I have coming."

"What's that?"

"Lasagna. Should be here by one."

"You bought more food from Da Nonna's?"

"Yes, and don't pretend you aren't glad," he teased.

She scowled at him. "I'm going to have money again soon."

"I don't mind picking up a few things."

"*I* mind," she said. "I feel terrible about it."

Only because she hated to take help from him — or anyone else. "Don't waste your time with that." If Lucas was his son, he should've been providing for him all along anyway.

She went into the bedroom and came back in a pair of white shorts and a yellow T-shirt. Her hair, which she'd curled for her meeting earlier, was now tied up in a messy bun. He loved it like that, but he was trying not to notice how beautiful she was — or what it had felt like that night at Christmas seven years ago to finally surrender to the desire she evoked.

He'd been ignoring a lot of things since coming to LA.

"Has Dylan told you that he thinks our parents might be getting back together?" she asked as she opened a box marked "kitchen" and started to unpack it. "He thinks Anya's living at J.T.'s again."

Mack wiped the sweat from his face with his forearm. "You've got to be kidding me."

"I wish I was."

He started to push the broken pieces of the frame he'd removed into the corner so that it would be easier to keep Lucas out of it until he was done. "Won't last."

"I agree."

Her phone went off as he measured the length of wood he'd have to cut for the new window casing.

130

"Speak of the devil," she said.

"It's your mother?"

"Yeah."

He heard her say hello right before Lucas perked up.

"It's Mimi? Mama, is that Mimi?"

As Lucas hurried over to speak to Anya, it occurred to Mack that if the boy lost Ace as a father, he'd lose a set of grandparents, too. Lucas wouldn't be able to count on Anya and J.T. for anything — just as Mack and his brothers and Natasha had never been able to count on them.

Mack wondered how much contact Lucas had with Ace's parents and how the outcome of the DNA test might affect those relationships.

After Natasha finished letting her son talk to Anya, and was in the middle of a conversation herself, Mack was tempted to take Lucas into the bathroom and swab his cheek. He wanted to send in the paternity test as soon as possible, to finally get an answer. But he didn't want to make her feel as though he was trying to strong-arm the whole thing. After what she'd been through, he could have a little patience, wait until she was ready to deal with the situation and felt she could cope with the outcome, whatever it was.

"Stop. Don't say that." When he heard the volume of Natasha's voice escalate, he turned around to see what was going on, but she had her back to him.

"You don't know what you're talking about," she continued. "Because *I* know . . . Quit it! I'm not going to be that stupid. You're wrong. I promise you, I will *never* fall in love again. I don't care . . . Seriously? That's why you're getting back with him? Sex is such a lousy excuse. They have toys for that . . . No, I won't. I have no use for a man, and you should've learned your lesson by now, too. Stay away from J.T. You'll only cause each other more pain — and while we're talking about this, it's not fair to lean on his sons the way you do . . . That's so untrue. You take whatever they'll give you . . . Oh yeah? They're the ones who moved you last time, remember? And they gave you your car. Who knows what else they've done that I haven't heard about . . . It's not like they'd tell me . . . I'm aware of that, Mother — I know they've done a lot for me, too. They've done a lot for both of us. That's why we need to get out of their way and let them go on with their lives . . . I didn't ask him to come! I'm fine on my own, and I've told him that . . . No, I don't need anybody."

After she hung up, Natasha made a sound of frustration and shoved her phone in her back pocket.

"I take it they *are* getting back together." Mack couldn't help being stung by what he'd heard. So much of that conversation had been about him. But he was doing his best to pretend otherwise.

"Yes. It's unbelievable," Natasha responded, oblivious to the fact that he knew she'd been using him as her best argument against getting with a man.

Or maybe she *did* realize that he would be able to decipher the conversation. After all, she hadn't made it hard. She just fully believed he didn't care enough about her to mind.

"Talk about not learning from her mistakes," she went on. "She insists it will work this time, but she's lying to herself, and I'm tired of hearing the excuses she gives when she makes yet another bad decision."

Natasha had said that he and his brothers had done a lot for her. That was nice. But he also knew that *he* was the man she didn't need, the one who'd hurt her so deeply she preferred a sex toy. "Not every relationship is doomed," he said.

"No, just every one of mine and my mother's," she responded. "I don't know when she's going to make herself stop wanting what she can't have."

"The way you have," he said.

"Yes, the way I have," she responded and marched down the hall.

Lucas gave him a quizzical look. "Mimi makes her *so* mad."

Mack would've laughed at the boy's exasperated response. The expression on his face was funny. But it was tough to laugh when it felt as though Natasha had just shoved a knife in his chest.

EIGHT

When would Mack be leaving? Natasha wondered as she tried to sleep that night. As much as he'd helped — with everything from packing, moving and driving to buying groceries, babysitting and replacing the broken window — he made life so much more difficult for her on an emotional level. When he was around, she couldn't let her guard down for an instant, had to watch where her eyes wandered, be careful of even incidental contact. She had to police her thoughts, too, so that she wouldn't start to dwell on what it'd been like to make love with him. Those memories were so potent. If they hadn't been, she would never have felt the need to write about that night, and then there would have been no journal for Ace to discover.

She'd dated plenty of men in college, and yet she'd never even recorded their names. But Mack had always been different. She'd continued to write about him even during her first year of marriage, which had been far more difficult than she'd ever anticipated. That journal had helped her cope with the longing and the loss, and the fact that she'd never stopped missing him.

Ace had to feel betrayed, though. And now that he'd read her journal, she felt completely exposed. Although she'd never had any inappropriate contact — or conversations — with Mack after she got married, she hadn't been able to stamp out her feelings for him. And now that the curtain had been pulled back on her heart, she felt like such a fraud, as though the failure of her marriage was indeed entirely her fault, just as Ace had claimed throughout the divorce.

Climbing out of bed because she couldn't sleep anyway, she wandered quietly around the house for the next few minutes, surveying the progress they'd made moving in via the moonlight streaming in the windows. It wouldn't take much longer to get settled. She should be ready by the time she started work at New Horizons. Having the move behind her would be nice. No doubt Mack would be gone by the time she went to work, too, so she could focus on rebuilding her life.

The ironic thing was that she'd thought

she'd *finally* managed to relegate what she'd felt for him to the past when all hell broke loose thanks to "Nurse Ratched." Now here she was, seeing him again, being with him.

Wanting him.

She glanced at his sleeping form on the couch. *What's wrong with me? Why can't I get over him?* Squeezing her eyes closed, she shook her head. She would not make the same mistake again. She'd learned her lesson.

Taking a deep breath, she opened her eyes and ran her fingers over the casing of the new window. He'd done a nice job. He was good with his hands, could do almost anything.

She admired so many things about him, which didn't help.

Her phone dinged upstairs in her bedroom. Apparently, she'd forgotten to turn it off, and the sound came across as abnormally loud in the silence. To stop it going off again, she hurried up to retrieve it. But she'd forgotten to plug it in to charge and had to turn on the light to find that it had fallen on the floor and must've been kicked under the bed.

She thought maybe it was her mother again. Their conversation hadn't ended well. Anya had hung up on her. And her mother was often up late, which wasn't surprising for someone who typically slept all day.

But the text Natasha had received wasn't from Anya; it was from Ace.

God, I'm tired. And I have a big test coming up. I need to concentrate, and yet I can't quit thinking about Mack finally stripping off our clothes and pressing inside me.

She cringed as she recognized those words. He was texting what she'd written in her journal.

Should she respond? Apologize? Attempt to explain?

What good would it do? Before she said anything, she needed to find out, for sure, if he was Lucas's father. At this point, even if he was, she wasn't convinced he'd continue to be the parent he'd been in the past. Maybe he'd use the confusion over Lucas's paternity as an excuse to duck out on their son, to be free to start completely over. She got the impression it would be easy for him to blame her and move on, which was weird. Didn't he love Lucas?

Poor kid . . . Had she messed things up for her son, too?

She jumped when her phone dinged again.

She'd been so caught up in her own thoughts and in what she was reading that she'd forgotten to silence it, even though that had been her original intent. She took care of that but couldn't help reading the new text that had come in, even though she knew it would upset her.

Nothing in my life has ever felt so good. I didn't want to come, because then I knew he'd come and it would all be over. But it was impossible to hold back. I've never had a night like that one.

Really? Ace wrote. You've never had a night like that one? What about the first night we slept together, you coldhearted bitch?

She hadn't meant to hurt him. She hadn't meant to hurt anyone. She'd been trying to move on with her life and be normal — get married and have a family like other people. I'm sorry, she wrote, unable to hold back. I never meant for you to see that.

I'm glad I did. Now I know that our marriage was bullshit from the start.

She felt chilled, and her head was pounding. But she figured it was all the drama — emotional pain presenting itself in a physical manner. It wasn't bullshit, Ace. I gave it everything I could.

Oh, right. I'm just not as lovable as Mack. Is that it?

That isn't it, she insisted.

Did you cheat on me?

No. Never.

I don't believe you.

It's true.

You're a lying whore. God, I hate you. I wish I'd never even met you.

His words felt like bullets tearing into her flesh. She was shaking as she stared down at her phone, couldn't seem to stop. But neither could she look away. She kept thinking about how terrible it must've felt for him to read what she'd written about Mack.

"What is it?"

Mack must've heard her phone go off or her movements around the house, because he'd come up and was shoving his hair out of his eyes as he walked into her room wearing nothing but a pair of basketball shorts.

Swallowing hard, she let the hand holding her phone drop. "N-nothing."

"I can see that you're about to cry."

She *was* about to cry, but she couldn't tell him why. She was terrified he'd see what Ace had sent — not the "I hate you" and "lying bitch" parts but the parts where he quoted her journal. She didn't want Mack to know her response to that night, how badly she'd wished he'd follow up and pursue the kind of relationship she'd always wanted with him. "No, I'm fine. It's okay. It's going to be . . . f-fine," she said, as if the mere repetition would make it true — or at least more convincing.

"Give me your phone," he demanded. "Let me see what's going on."

She clutched it to her chest. "No!"

"Is it your mother?"

She shook her head.

"Ace?"

"He — he's angry. That's all. He has a right to be angry. Anyone would be angry."

Mack didn't seem sympathetic to him. "*How* angry? What's he saying?"

"Nothing. I can handle it."

"Then why are you trembling?"

"I'm not. I'd better . . . get back to bed," she said. "I'm sorry if I woke you."

"That's not a problem. But I hate that you won't tell me what's going on."

"Like I said, I'm tired. That's all. For some reason, I'm not . . . f-feeling very well," she said and grabbed the wastebasket just in time to throw up.

Natasha didn't get sick very often. She didn't even have seasonal allergies. But she'd been under a great deal of stress for a long time. So maybe it wasn't any wonder that her immune system would struggle.

For the next twenty-four hours, she couldn't keep anything down. Even after she quit throwing up, she felt drained — too weak to get out of bed.

Fortunately, Mack was there to take care of Lucas, because she couldn't have done it on her own. During the few minutes here and there that she was awake, she could hear them talking or playing, which both soothed and worried her. She could rest assured that her son was happy, safe and well. She trusted Mack with Lucas in that way. But her son was spending too much time with the man she'd always loved, despite all her efforts to *stop* loving him. She was afraid Lucas was getting attached, and that he'd suffer for it the way she had, but there wasn't a damn thing she could do about it.

Whatever she'd caught was too virulent to enable her to get out of bed.

Late Saturday afternoon, she could hear a show droning on in Lucas's room when Mack came in carrying a bowl of soup on a cookie sheet he was using as a tray. "How're you feeling?" he asked as soon as he saw that she was awake. "Any better?"

"I've quit throwing up," she replied. "So there's that."

"How do you know? You haven't eaten anything."

"I'd rather not test it," she joked. "My stomach's too tender."

"I'd take you to a doctor, but you *are* a doctor, so . . . is there something else we should be doing to get you well?"

"Nothing. Rest and plenty of liquids."

"What about a painkiller?"

"Not on an empty stomach." She frowned at the chicken noodle soup in the bowl; it didn't look the least bit appetizing. "Thanks for the food, but, like I said, I'm not ready to eat."

"You need to try. I have to get something down you. You haven't eaten anything since Thursday."

"It's been that long?" She knew it had, but it sounded worse when stated that way.

"I've heard doctors make the worst patients. Now I know it's true."

"Fine. I'll take a few bites. Where's Lucas?"

"Watching a panda movie on the television we bought today."

"Why'd you buy a TV?"

"Because you must've given yours to your ex along with everything else."

"Lucas could've continued to use my iPad."

"You needed a TV."

She glowered at him. "No, I didn't. I don't care about TVs."

"I can tell." He set the tray to one side so he could adjust the pillows to make it easier for her to sit up. "You look completely spent."

"I'm not surprised. I don't remember ever being so weak. I'm sorry if you're dying to get home and I'm holding you up. I'm sure my strength will return soon."

"I'm not in any hurry. I rarely take off work. I figure Dylan owes me as much time as I need. Besides, my dad has been a little more reliable lately, so he's been helping out again."

He dipped the spoon in the soup and tried to feed her, but she gestured weakly at her lap. "Just set the cookie sheet here. I'll do it."

He did as she requested and watched as she summoned the energy to take her first bite. "What do you think's wrong with you?" he asked, looking worried.

"The flu, I guess. I don't know."

"You're a doctor, and that's the best you can do?"

"If you understood how many viruses are floating around at any given moment, you wouldn't be surprised."

He watched her struggle to take another bite and moved as though he was tempted to help, but she held up a hand, proud of herself when she managed it on her own.

"Aiyana called yesterday." He gestured at her phone. "I saw the call come in."

She remembered the texts Ace had sent right before she threw up for the first time. "And my ex?"

"He's been texting you. He's getting pretty pissed off that you won't respond."

"What's he saying?"

When Mack hesitated, she rolled her eyes. "Tell me. I know you read them."

He looked like a little boy who'd been caught with his hand in the cookie jar. "I couldn't resist," he said, and then that endearing expression morphed into a scowl. "I knew the bastard was up to something."

"Up to what?"

145

"Trying to hurt you as much as possible. I get the impression that's been his goal for some time."

"That's what divorce looks like," she said, letting her head fall back. "Please tell me you didn't respond."

"I may have said a few things . . ."

She felt her eyes widen. "From *my* phone? As me?"

"From *me.* I have his number now, too, so he'd better be careful."

"You stole his contact information from me."

"I figured you'd want me to have it." His grin went a little lopsided. He was completely unrepentant, but she didn't complain. She was too weak to care about what he said to Ace.

"Okay, whatever. I guess that bridge has been burned anyway."

Mack lowered his voice. "He's being a complete asshole about Lucas, too. That's the part I don't understand. Lucas is an innocent child. He hasn't done anything wrong, and it's not fair to try to punish you by hurting him."

"Ace is hurt himself," she tried to explain.

His lip curled in contempt. "He's a big baby — that's what he is."

She opened her mouth to try to make Ace

146

sound more sympathetic. She thought that was only fair, didn't want to be that bitter ex who was always complaining about the person she'd been with.

But on second thought, she realized Mack was right. Ace had always felt sorry for himself if things didn't go his way, tried to blame his unhappiness on others and looked for excuses as to why he could never do his part. So she didn't bother defending him. "I feel gross. I need a shower."

"It takes you fifteen minutes just to shuffle down the hall when you have to go to the bathroom. I don't trust you to be able to stand up long enough for a shower. How about a bath instead?"

Grateful that she didn't feel as though she was going to throw up what little soup she'd eaten, she nodded. "That'll work."

"Great. I'll fill the tub."

She slumped back onto the pillows. "Can you take the soup to the kitchen?" she asked before he could leave. "I can't eat any more."

"You barely touched it," he complained but lifted the tray off her lap.

"I'm more interested in brushing my teeth and having that bath."

She almost drifted off again before he returned. It'd been weeks since she'd been able to grab a solid night's rest, and now she couldn't stay awake for thirty minutes at a time.

"It's ready," he announced from the doorway. "You all set?"

"I think so." Except that she wasn't fully dressed. "I'll make my way down there in a minute."

"I'll help you do it now."

She hesitated. "Then . . . can you hand me something to put on?"

He did as she requested and turned away while she wiggled into a pair of shorts. But she swayed as soon as she came to her feet and would've fallen if he hadn't scooped her into his arms.

"I got you," he said.

Grateful for his steadiness and strength, she let her head rest on his shoulder as he carried her into the bathroom and didn't even try to stop him when he stripped off her clothes and lowered her, naked, into the water. He'd always taken care of her when he was around. On some level, it seemed perfectly natural.

"You're scaring me," he said when she looked up at him before letting her eyelids slide closed.

"I'll be okay. Believe it or not, I'm through the worst of it." She heard the breathless quality to her own voice and couldn't remember ever being quite so sick. "Can I . . . can I get my toothbrush?"

He put some toothpaste on the bristles and handed it over, and she managed to brush her own teeth. But she was even more exhausted afterward — as if she'd used up what small amount of energy her body had been able to store while fighting this illness.

He sat on the closed toilet seat, watching her, but after she was finished with her toothbrush, and he'd rinsed it off, she said, "I'm fine. You don't have to stay."

He didn't move. "I've never seen you like this. I'm not leaving you."

Since she didn't feel capable of getting out of the tub by herself, let alone walking back to the bedroom, she didn't argue with him. She rested for a few minutes before she started trying to wash her long hair, but her arms felt so rubbery she couldn't get the shampoo out of it without taking breaks every couple of minutes to rest, so Mack took over. Kneeling on the floor next to her, he rinsed her head and put on some conditioner.

It felt good to get clean. But it felt even better to have Mack's hands on her. Especially when he started to scrub her body. At first, he was careful to keep the soap between her and his palm as he washed her feet, her legs, her stomach and, finally, her breasts, but those simple actions were somehow still erotic. After all, it was him. The longer he scrubbed, the slower his movements became. He even stopped once when his thumb accidentally brushed her nipple.

Natasha felt every swipe, but she was too sick to have a problem with anything that made her feel better, and this definitely made her feel better. It wasn't just his touch; it was the care. She'd felt isolated and alone for so long, was constantly striving to give love to her husband, her son and her patients, but she'd been running on empty.

She watched Mack's face as he worked, saw a muscle flex in his cheek when he returned to her breasts. He had to be enjoying her bath as much as she was, because he certainly wasn't in any hurry.

After he washed her shoulders and neck, which he rubbed for several minutes to ease the soreness, he let go of the soap — and when he touched her again, it was with his bare hands. He watched her as carefully as she watched him, and she guessed he was wondering if she'd accept the change.

When she didn't stiffen or resist, his hands

slid through the lather he'd already created, going over what he'd already washed, including her breasts — only now he let his palms and fingers slide slowly over her nipples before working his way back down her belly. Whatever part of her he touched felt immediately better. The gentle pressure he used even eased the soreness in her stomach. She was enjoying what he was doing so much she couldn't help closing her eyes and only opened them when he moved steadily lower, slipping one hand between her legs as though he was tempted to focus on an even more sensitive area.

She gave him a look to let him know *that* would be going too far, and he grinned as if to say it was worth a shot and moved on.

By the time he finished, the water was growing tepid, and she was so relaxed she could barely keep her eyes open. She felt him pour clean water over her to rinse her off. Then he helped her out of the water, wrapped her in a towel and carried her back to her room, where he got her a clean T-shirt to put on before she dropped into bed and, once again, welcomed the dark void of sickness-induced sleep.

Mack closed Natasha's door on his way out, then stood in the hall as he let go of a long breath. That bath he'd given her was . . . *wow.* He hadn't felt that much sexual desire in a long time. But Natasha did something to him no other woman could, and it didn't seem to matter how hard he fought it.

He checked on Lucas, who was holding his favorite toy — the sword he'd taken to the home improvement store — while watching TV. "You ready for a snack, buddy?" he asked, but Lucas was too engrossed in his program to hear him, let alone answer, so he figured the kid was okay.

By the time Mack had cleaned up dinner, Lucas came out of his room, so Mack pretended to let him help fix the screen door, which hung at an odd angle and squeaked every time someone opened it. Then they played hide-and-seek in the backyard and Lucas watched as Mack knocked down all the cobwebs in the garage, so that Natasha wouldn't have to deal with them. As tough and determined as she'd always been — working every bit as hard as the rest of them at Amos Auto Body at only sixteen — he knew how she felt about spiders.

"Look," Lucas said as he examined a daddy longlegs that was wobbling on its threadlike legs as it hurried to escape the swish of Mack's broom. "He's so cool!"

Mack couldn't help chuckling. "I used to like spiders when I was a kid, too. I liked snakes even more and used to catch water snakes in the creek behind my house."

"Can I see one?" he asked eagerly.

"Sure. I'll catch you one someday."

After they went in, Mack checked on Natasha, but she seemed to be sleeping soundly, so he backed quietly out of the room and read a stack of books to Lucas before putting him to bed.

It was after ten when his brother Rod called. Mack saw the call come in while he was entertaining himself watching sports clips on YouTube.

" 'Lo?" he said, propping up his pillow as he leaned back on it.

"Hey, man, have you heard the news?"

Mack was mildly surprised by the intensity of Rod's voice. This particular brother was pretty mellow, especially since he got married and became a doting stepparent to India's daughter. "What news?"

"About Kellan."

"Don't tell me he got injured at football practice," Mack said, sitting up at the sound of his nephew's name. He'd always been particularly close with Dylan's son.

"No. Nothing like that. He ran away last night."

Mack came to his feet. "He . . . *what*?"

"He ran away."

"But that doesn't make any sense. Dylan and Cheyenne have never had any trouble with Kellan. What happened?"

"I don't know. Neither does anyone else here. When Cheyenne got home from her friend's house a few hours ago, she found a note on his bed that said he was running away and not to look for him."

Mack couldn't imagine his nephew writing that. "Doesn't sound like anything Kellan would do."

"Right? It's taken everyone by surprise. So . . . you haven't heard from him?"

"Not a peep."

"Damn. We've been searching everywhere. I was hoping you might be able to tell us something."

"Why would he call me? I'm not even in town."

"Doesn't matter. He adores you. All the kids in the family do."

Mack had spent a lot of time with his nephew. He went to most of Kellan's games and hung out with him sometimes on Saturdays, throwing a football to him, taking him to Tahoe to go skiing during the winter or just sitting around, watching sports together. "Well, I haven't heard from him," Mack reiterated. "But there must've been something that set him off."

"Dylan claims there was nothing. Cheyenne says the same. They're freaking out."

Mack could understand why. This behavior was so uncharacteristic of their son. "He's not answering his phone?"

"Not for any of us. Can you try him?"

"Of course."

Mack disconnected and hit Kellan's picture on his list of favorites, but the call transferred to voice mail on the first ring. He sent a text message, too, but he didn't expect a response. He was pretty sure Kellan had turned off his phone.

"Did you get hold of him?" Rod asked eagerly, in lieu of a hello, when Mack called back.

"I'm afraid not," Mack replied.

"Damn it! What's going on? Where the hell is he?"

"Have you checked with his friends?"

"Dylan and Cheyenne are going down the list. Meanwhile, Grady and I are driving around town, looking for him at the places he likes to go."

Whiskey Creek wasn't a big town, but it would still be hard to find someone through such a random process. "I can't imagine you'll have any luck without some clue of where he's at."

"We have to do *something*," Rod said. "I've never seen Dylan like this — not in years, anyway."

Mack could only imagine what Dylan had to be feeling. Kellan meant so much to him. "Things like this don't just pop up out of nowhere."

"This one did. When are you coming home?"

"I don't know yet."

"You should come as soon as possible. You have always been Dylan's favorite. And you're the one who's closest to Kellan, too — other than Dylan. If we find him, and he refuses to come home, maybe you'll be able to talk some sense into him. He obviously has some sort of problem with his parents, or he wouldn't have run away."

Mack shot a glance down the hall. "I don't know if I can come right now. Natasha hasn't been feeling well."

"What's wrong?"

"She says it's just a virus, probably the flu, and she seems to be through the worst of it. She hasn't thrown up all day, but —"

"Then she'll be fine. Come home. I think it would mean a lot to Dylan. He's always loved you more like a son than a brother."

Because Mack was the baby of the family.

He'd been just a child when Dylan had had to take over as the patriarch of the family. In many respects, Dylan *was* a father to him.

Mack drew a deep breath. Not only had Natasha stopped throwing up, her fever was gone. He could tell that when he'd bathed her, was pretty sure she was through the worst of it. The fact that she was finally sleeping so well was another sign.

After everything Dylan had done for him, he felt he needed to be there to support his brother. "Okay," he said. "I'll leave first thing in the morning."

The next time Natasha woke up, she felt better. Lucas was in bed for the night, so the house was quiet when Mack brought her some more soup.

Neither of them mentioned what'd happened in the bathroom. Natasha figured they never would. With Mack, it had always been better to ignore those types of things — the times she'd caught him staring at her with naked desire; the kiss she'd given him the night before she left for college and the explosive way he'd reacted, as though he'd take her right then and there; the night they'd shared during Victorian Days years later. After all, the fact that he'd bathed her

157

wasn't a big deal. Maybe he'd gone a little further than anyone else would have, and she shouldn't have let him. But the stronger she got, the more capable she would be of taking on the mantle of being a divorcée with a child to raise on her own and a career to rescue. The last thing she needed was more unrequited love, and she knew it.

She was almost over the flu or whatever she had. She figured one more day and she should be back on her feet.

"You look a lot better," he said, sounding relieved as he settled the cookie sheet on her lap like he had before.

"I'm getting there."

"I hope Lucas doesn't catch whatever it is."

"I hope neither of you do."

While she ate, he crossed his arms and rocked back in the chair he'd put next to her bed, and she wondered what he was thinking. She could tell he had *something* on his mind and guessed it wasn't about her bath. After they'd made love all those years ago, he'd completely ignored the fact that it'd ever happened, other than one awkward attempt to broach the subject after he heard she was pregnant, so she figured that was how he'd handle the bath, too. The bath was subtle by comparison, probably didn't rate. But it had been just what she'd needed — a little TLC — and she couldn't help being grateful that she could have *someone's* care at a time when she had no one to rely on.

"I swabbed Lucas's cheek," he said, out of the blue.

She gripped the spoon she was using a lot tighter. "And? Did you send it in?"

"Not yet. I need to get your DNA, too, remember? And I was reluctant to mail it without your okay. I know you must be scared about . . . about how it could change things. I just wanted to be sure you were ready. I'd rather you not be upset if it turns out that Lucas is mine."

She kept her gaze fastened to her bowl. "Will *you* be upset?"

"No."

She couldn't help looking up. "But then your brothers will know we . . . Well, they'll know. Or . . . what are you thinking? Are you thinking we'll just continue to call you Lucas's uncle?"

"That's what he calls *them,*" he said.

"Exactly. Then they won't know anything has changed. That might actually be the best thing for him."

He frowned. "We'll wait to get the results before we decide what to do."

"Okay."

He put his chair back down on all four legs. "Do you believe Ace will really walk away even if I'm not Lucas's father?"

She drew a deep breath. "I don't know. He's always been a quitter."

"A quitter?"

"Yeah. If things get tough, he quits. He's quit almost every sports team he's ever belonged to, every solid job he's had and our marriage. So I wouldn't be surprised if he gave up on being Lucas's dad, too. Because of that journal, he can walk away from all responsibility and blame me for doing it. That would be the easiest route for him."

Mack rubbed his chin. "I knew I didn't like him."

The soup was warm and, thankfully, gentle on her stomach. That she was hungry and actually welcomed food indicated she was getting well. "What have you said to Ace since I got sick?"

"Not a lot. I'm just keeping him honest."

She arched an eyebrow at him. "That's cryptic."

"I told him to keep his name-calling and guilt-inducing bullshit to himself. You have enough to worry about. I don't want him bothering you, especially because I have to leave in the morning."

She let her spoon dangle between her bowl and her mouth as she looked over. She'd told herself she'd welcome the day he left. It was the only way to stop the longing — or lessen it — so she was surprised to feel such bitter disappointment. "Okay." Unable to take another bite, she set her spoon back in her bowl. "Thanks for . . . everything. I owe you a lot, and I'll get you paid for the truck and the groceries soon."

"Forget about it. You don't owe me anything."

"Of course I do."

"If Lucas is mine, I owe you a lot more than you owe me. Is it okay if I go ahead and swab your cheek?"

She nodded and he went out to get the kit. *If Lucas is mine . . .* Those were words she'd never expected to hear him say. "Will you give me the link where I can go to find the results of the DNA test?" she asked when he returned.

Using what looked like an extra-large Q-tip, he took the swab. "I'll call you."

"Just in case you don't."

His eyebrows came together. "Natasha, I didn't call before because —"

"You don't have to explain," she broke in, determined not to let that night in Whiskey

Creek further disrupt her life. "Just give me the link, and then it's okay if you forget."

"No problem." He slipped the swab in its vial. "I'll text it to you."

"Thanks." She cleared her throat. "Did you tell Lucas you were leaving, or . . . ?"

He shook his head. "Didn't have the chance. He was asleep before I got Rod's call."

"The auto body shop's getting too busy to go on without you?"

"That's not it. Kellan's run away."

"Dylan's son? Why?"

"I don't know. I need to go see what's happening."

She chuckled mirthlessly.

What?" he said, looking confused.

"Nothing." She just found it ironic that he tried so hard to be a brother to her instead of a lover, but when it came to any real family involvement, she was still very much an outsider. He had to know more about Kellan than he was saying.

"You finished?" he asked, gesturing at the soup.

She nodded.

He lifted the tray but didn't walk out right away. "Will you be okay if I leave?"

"Of course," she said with greater conviction than she felt. "I'm almost well. I should be fine by tomorrow morning." At which point she'd wake up and Mack would be gone. She wondered how Lucas was going to react.

"Then I'll see you again soon." He bent and kissed her forehead.

"Sure thing," she said as he went out, but if the DNA test came back such that Ace was Lucas's father, it would probably be years before she saw Mack again. He'd return to Whiskey Creek, get caught up in his own life and the family business, and forget about the new location in Los Angeles — forget about *her*.

After all, he'd always let her go easily enough before.

But she wanted Mack to leave, didn't she?

Absolutely. Then she could get on with her life. She hoped he never looked back.

Because she wasn't going to be sitting around waiting for him.

NINE

"Mack's *gone*?"

Natasha woke to that question. Before she could answer, the mattress jiggled as her son climbed onto the other side of the bed. She hadn't heard Mack leave, but the fact that he'd said his goodbyes last night had warned her that he wouldn't be around when she got up.

Lucas didn't have the benefit of that foreknowledge. For him, it'd come as a nasty surprise.

"Yeah." Her mouth was so dry she had to wet her lips before she could continue talking, but she was feeling better. Thank God for that, because she needed to fix Lucas breakfast.

She wondered what she would've done without Mack to help her through the worst of her illness, but shoved that thought away. He deserved her gratitude, but gratitude only made things that much more difficult for her. It was anger that provided strength and determination. And she was going to need determination as she forged ahead and built a new life here in Silver Springs.

"Where'd he go?" Lucas asked.

The whine in her son's voice only made her own disappointment more acute, even though she was trying not to attribute a certain despondency to Mack's departure. "He went home. He doesn't live here, honey. It had to happen eventually."

"But he said we'd go to the park today. That he'd teach me how to play ball. Is he coming back?"

She wasn't sure how to answer that question. If Mack wasn't Lucas's father, she didn't think he'd bother. But she couldn't say that — not to Lucas. "How about *I* teach you something?"

"Baseball?" he asked skeptically.

"When I feel better. For now, I'm just going to teach you how to protect yourself so that you don't get hurt."

He looked down at his knees. "I'm not hurt."

"I know. And the only way to avoid it is to lower your expectations."

"What?"

"If you don't expect Mack to stay, you won't be sad when he leaves."

Lucas wrinkled his nose. "Can you just tell me when he's coming back?"

Her son wasn't old enough to understand the concept, but it was a good reminder for her. "One day," she said, planning to put him off for a week or two until he eventually forgot the charismatic man who'd helped them move.

His shoulders slumped. "Why didn't he tell me he was leaving?"

"He didn't know, honey. Something came up."

Her phone began to buzz. She was going to ignore it, but Lucas scrambled over to answer it, and she didn't bother to stop him. "Yes . . . She's sick . . ." she heard him say. "I don't know . . . Want me to ask her? . . . Just a minute." He handed the phone to her. "The lady we met at the school wants to talk to you. Can I go watch my show?"

He loved *Ben 10.* "Yes." Mack had told her that Aiyana had called, but Natasha hadn't attempted to get in touch. She'd been too ill.

She accepted the phone from Lucas as he ran out to turn on the TV. "Hello?"

"I'm just checking on you," Aiyana said. "Mack called me a few minutes ago to say that he had to leave town unexpectedly. He asked me to make sure you were okay while he was gone."

While he was gone? She had at least a fifty-fifty chance that he wasn't coming back. "He called *you*? How did he even get your number?"

"He called the school, and I happened to be in my office, so I answered. He was hoping I'd look in on you tonight, and I plan to do that, but I was wondering if you need me earlier."

"Don't put yourself to the trouble," she said. "If you come over here, you might only catch what I've got. Besides, I'm starting to feel better."

"Are you capable of caring for Lucas?"

"We can muddle through."

"Will you call me if that isn't the case?"

"I will."

"If you need to put off coming to work until Tuesday or Wednesday, that would be fine."

"I'll keep that in mind, but it shouldn't be necessary. Really. I should be back to normal tomorrow."

"I hope so. Mack said he left you some food you can warm up in the microwave, but if that isn't enough, or something else comes up, just let me know."

"I will."

"See you in the morning, then — unless I hear from you sooner."

As Natasha hit the end button, Lucas said, "Can I eat?"

"Of course." Taking a deep breath, Natasha summoned the energy to drag herself out of bed. She had to use the walls for support, but she managed to stuff her feet into her fluffy slippers and shuffle all the way down to the kitchen — only to realize that Mack had opened the blinds on the front windows, which looked out on Main Street, and she wasn't wearing anything except the overlarge T-shirt he'd helped her put on after her bath.

She was exhausted by the time she'd gone up to put on some more clothes and gingerly navigated her way back to the kitchen, but at least the nausea was gone. She was leaning against the counter cooking oatmeal when she heard her phone go off in her room. "Shoot. Luke, will you go up and get Mommy's phone, please?"

Surprisingly, he pulled away from the TV. "Okay!"

As she heard him run upstairs, she was grateful he was old enough to help her, to a degree. She wondered if Aiyana was calling back to insist on coming — until she heard him answer and say, "Hi, Grandma . . .

168

Yeah. We're at our new house . . . It's old and it stinks and me and Mack had to bury a skunk that died in our yard . . . What? *You* know Mack? No, he's gone now . . . I don't know where . . . She's cooking breakfast . . ."

The prospect of speaking to her mother-in-law — Grandma was Ace's mother and Mimi was hers — sent a jolt of nervous energy through Natasha. Heartened by necessity, she straightened and put out her hand. "Luke, give me the phone, please," she said. No way did she want to let Ace's mother pump her son for information.

When she'd first married Ace, she'd liked and admired her in-laws. They were everything she'd thought she ever wanted to be — educated, affluent and involved in the community, with lots of friends. Not only that, but they'd been together forever and never failed to put their two children before everything else. Ace had had it all growing up.

But her relationship with them had deteriorated along with her marriage, and she believed it was the way Ace had talked about her. After all, he complained about everyone and everything else; why would she be the exception? Although she didn't know exactly what he'd said, she guessed he'd made it sound as though she put her career before him and Lucas, that she was too busy to give him the time and attention he deserved, and that she shoved all the mundane tasks, like housework, cooking and childcare, onto him.

But if she had to earn their living, it was only fair that he do *something,* wasn't it?

As she took the phone from her son, she couldn't help recalling the disgusted look her father-in-law had shot her the night Ace had mentioned that he'd soon be helping to build her practice by running the front office. She could tell Blake thought she was trying to "wear the pants in the family." To him, if a woman took the lead in anything, she was overstepping.

But it wasn't as if she'd ever taken advantage of Ace. He went surfing and golfing with his college buddies all the time. And he wouldn't miss a football or basketball game. She'd never realized just how many sporting events there were on TV until she married him. One was always blaring in her living room. He'd had poker nights with friends and played disc golf with their neighbor and tennis with his brother, all while she was working to cover their bills and start a practice.

Her pulse kicked up as she brought the phone to her ear. "Hello? Peggy?"

"I hear you've already made the move," Ace's mother said. "Are you unpacked?"

Natasha thought about how sick she'd been but didn't bother to mention it. "Not yet."

"I'm sure it won't take too long."

"It shouldn't." She couldn't yet tell whether this was going to be one of *those* conversations — the ones where she had to ignore all the subtext — but she had an inkling it would be. Lately, they all seemed to be that way. Her in-laws were angry with her, too, and while they tried to cloak it beneath a polite veneer and a pretense that they weren't going to choose sides, Natasha could tell that wasn't true. They supported their sons whether their sons were right or wrong, and although Natasha had thought that was wonderful, at first, she now saw how it had enabled Ace and his brother to become lazy, indolent crybabies.

"Especially if you have help," Peggy added. "Who's this . . . Mack person Lucas was talking about?"

She gripped the phone tighter. Sure enough, this was going to be one of those conversations. Peggy already knew who Mack was. She'd heard Lucas say as much before he handed her the phone. "I've mentioned the Amos brothers to you before.

171

It's thanks to them I was able to graduate from high school, remember?"

"Oh, yes. They let you and your mother live with them while their father was in prison for a few years."

"They did."

"And how, exactly, have you thanked them?"

Natasha was tempted to hang up. She didn't want to try to justify her actions, especially because she hadn't been committed to Ace when she slept with Mack. But these people played an important role in her son's life, and she didn't want to alienate them if there was any way to avoid it. "I haven't done anything specific, but I'm grateful to them," she said. "I'll always be grateful to them."

"Is that why you had sex with Mack?" she asked.

That was much more of a direct hit than usual. As Natasha had suspected, Ace must've already gone to his parents with the latest. "That isn't why, no," she said and was proud of herself for keeping her voice steady.

"Then why did you do it?"

Lucas was watching his show again, but Natasha turned away from him and lowered her voice, just in case. "I was with Mack before Ace and I were in a committed relationship, Peggy."

"Before you got married, you mean."

"Before we agreed not to see other people," she clarified. "Is there a point to this?"

"I'm just trying to understand how it could be that we don't even know — *after six and a half years* — if Lucas is our grandson."

Natasha wasn't feeling strong enough for this.

An acrid odor alerted her that she'd let Lucas's oatmeal burn. Swallowing a curse, she shoved the pan off the stove. "We'll find out soon enough," she said.

"That's all you've got to say?"

"Yes, because explaining how it happened won't do any good. You'll just twist it to make me look bad."

"I don't need to twist anything," she spit and disconnected.

Natasha sagged against the counter. This wouldn't be happening if she hadn't lost track of that journal. She should've destroyed it. But even now, if she had hold of it, she wasn't sure she'd be able to do that. There were things in there she didn't want to forget — details about what Mack had said or done that she'd saved up because they were some of her greatest treasures.

"Ew! It stinks again," Lucas complained.

Natasha grabbed the pan of burnt oatmeal, stuck it in the sink and filled it with water. She had to clean it out and make more, had to get her son fed, because if there was one thing she'd learned, it was that the world didn't stop turning just because she was down and out.

Her phone lit up with another call. This one was from Mack, but she felt so raw inside she knew she couldn't talk to him without breaking down, so she let it go to voice mail.

When Mack couldn't get Natasha to answer, he called Aiyana, who assured him that she must be in the shower, where she couldn't hear her phone. Aiyana had just talked to her and indicated she was okay, which relieved some of his concern, but he hated to leave while Tash was sick. He'd almost turned around three or four times. He would have, except that he was also worried about Kellan. They'd finally found him at a buddy's house, but he refused to come home — said he'd just run away again if they made him.

Because Mack was closer to Kellan than anyone else in the family — all of Mack's brothers were married with their own fami-

174

lies, except Grady, who swore he'd never marry — he was hoping he could get Kellan to talk to him. Even if he couldn't, Mack owed Dylan so much he felt obligated to rush home and do what he could.

Wishing he could be in both places at once, he glanced at the DNA kit he'd packaged up, which sat in the seat beside him. Once he dropped that in the mail, he'd have only a few more days to wait before he received an answer to the question he'd been wondering about since he learned that Natasha was pregnant. They'd used birth control the first couple of times they'd made love, but he'd only had two condoms in his wallet. After that, they'd opted for the withdrawal method — definitely not the most reliable form of birth control.

He always felt a jolt of testosterone when he thought of that night. He'd never spent twelve hours quite like that, had never made love so intensely or so recklessly. He'd been drinking at the Christmas festival, but that had only lowered his resistance enough to get things started. He'd been clearheaded within an hour or two — knew exactly what he was doing — and yet he couldn't stop. All those years of resistance had simply exploded.

She was still the standard by which he

measured every other woman.

His phone rang. He assumed Natasha was returning his call, but it was Dylan.

"You on your way?" he asked as soon as Mack answered.

"Yeah. What's going on?"

"Kellan's at Jeremy Rinehardt's house."

"So when's he coming home?"

"Not today. Jeremy's parents are acting really weird — as if they feel they have to protect him from *us*. It's pissing me off so badly it's hard to stop myself from going over there and breaking down the door."

Suddenly, Mack knew he was doing the right thing by going home. Dylan had calmed down a great deal since he'd gotten married. Cheyenne had made him whole, happy. But he'd had to fight to survive from a very young age — literally, since he'd had to supplement their income as an MMA fighter in those early years — so Mack believed he *would* break down the door if he had to. "Don't do that," he said. "Getting yourself thrown in jail isn't going to help Kellan."

"I may have a reputation from when I was younger, but I've barely even raised my voice to him. What could Kellan have told them to make them think we're the enemy?"

Mack was at a complete loss. Dylan was

the best dad in the world — he knew because Dylan had essentially been *his* dad. Maybe Dyl had been younger and wilder back then, but his determination and drive had enabled him to accomplish as a teenage boy what a lot of grown men wouldn't have been able to do. He was barely eighteen when their father went to prison and he had to take over the auto body shop, not to mention getting in the ring on weekends, just to make enough to feed and clothe his four younger brothers. It didn't make it any easier that they'd been as wild, unruly and hard to manage as he was. "I can't imagine."

"They won't even let us see him."

Mack felt his muscles tense. "Unless they have evidence of abuse, they can't deny you access to your own child. Maybe you should call the cops."

"No. I've never called the cops in my life. I had too many brushes with the law when I was younger to consider them my friends."

The chief of police back then had had it out for them. It was no wonder Dylan was hesitant to ask them for help. "Come on. Chief Stacy's long gone."

"Bennett's not much better. And old grievances die hard, I guess. Cheyenne's afraid it'll only make matters worse, anyway. She says we need to try to work it out on our own first."

"But if the Rinehardts won't let you see your son . . ."

"They said they're willing to set up a meeting, but Kellan needs some time before that happens."

"Time for what?"

"That's the thing. I don't know. I told him he couldn't hang out with Denny the other night, but Denny's a big pothead. I don't want my son getting into that."

"You think that's the reason he ran away? Because he couldn't hang out with Denny?"

"What else could it be? But even if he's mad about that, fathers have a right to say no when they think it's best."

"So how long are the Rinehardts going to make you wait?"

"They said to give them until tomorrow."

At least that wasn't long. "I'll try Kellan's cell in an hour or so. See if he'll talk to me. I don't want to call too early."

"Okay. Let me know what he says."

"I will."

"This is nuts, man."

"Yeah. I never saw it coming. But we'll work it out. Don't worry."

"Right. Sure." Dylan sighed into the phone. "How'd things go with Natasha?"

Mack once again eyed the paternity test

in the seat next to him. "Good."

"I know you wanted to stay long enough to scout out an expansion location in LA, but I appreciate you coming home. Kellan's always loved you. I can't imagine he won't talk to you."

"We'll see. How's Cheyenne holding up?"

"She's scared. We both are. Kellan's always been a good kid. We don't understand what's going on — why this is happening."

Dylan had already lost his mother and, for all intents and purposes, his father, since J.T. had never been the same after her suicide. Dylan didn't want to lose his son, too. Mack had the same background. He understood the fear that went with loving someone so much. Although he hated to admit it, he knew what he'd experienced as a child was part of what'd caused him to act the way he had with Natasha. She was the only woman who could threaten his heart to that degree, which was why he tried so hard to keep her at an arm's distance. All the other things they had going against them just gave him valid excuses. "You need to be careful not to do anything that will give the Rinehardts the impression that they have any reason to protect Kellan," he told Dylan.

"If there's something wrong with our son, we'll handle it. It's family business."

"Not everyone sees it that way. This could be some . . . misguided attempt to do the right thing."

"I don't care. They'd better not push me any further," Dylan warned and hung up.

Mack checked the time. It was only nine o'clock on a Sunday. He wasn't going to start blowing up Kellan's phone quite yet.

He called his other brother Grady, who answered on the first ring. "What's up, man?"

"I heard about Kellan," Mack said. "What's going on?"

"Beats the hell out of me. I thought he was happy. I didn't know they had problems."

"Neither did I."

"How'd you find out?"

"Rod called me."

"Yeah, he's just as shocked as we are."

"And Dad? Could he have something to do with this?"

"Doubt it. Dad says crazy shit to everyone, but I think we all pretty much ignore him these days."

"So this came out of nowhere."

"Seems that way."

"Have you checked with Aaron?" Aaron

no longer lived in Whiskey Creek, but he was only two and a half hours away and brought his family back regularly to hang out on weekends or holidays. Aaron was married to Cheyenne's stepsister and was closest to Dylan in age. He also had a son three years older than Kellan. The two cousins had always been close. "Maybe Wyatt can tell us what's going on in Kellan's mind."

"We've asked Wyatt. He hasn't heard from Kellan and Kellan won't answer his calls."

"That's weird."

"*Really* weird. He won't pick up my calls, either. Have you tried to reach him?"

"Not today." Mack was hoping to get some indication of what could be wrong before he talked to Kellan, so he'd know how to approach him. "I doubt he's up this early."

"I hope you can get hold of him. Dylan's going crazy."

"I know. I just talked to him."

"Oh yeah? Where are you now?"

"On my way home."

"How was Natasha?"

Mack didn't mention that she had the flu. He felt too guilty leaving her. "As good as could be expected after a divorce."

"Just be glad *you* didn't marry her," he

181

said. "Imagine what it would be like to have her mother in our lives permanently."

Mack shifted uncomfortably. His brothers had never been supportive of him having a romantic relationship with Natasha. And they had some valid concerns. The way she'd come into their lives. The age difference. The fact that they'd all be put in a bad position if the relationship didn't work out.

But deep down he knew it wasn't any of those things that'd stopped him, at least not later, when she was older and they made love after bumping into each other during Victorian Days. The intensity of that night had frightened him, made him unwilling to follow up. He knew that, with Natasha, he wouldn't be able to get away with risking just part of his heart. She'd demand the whole damn thing.

He frowned at the DNA test that kept drawing his eye again and again. Did he dare mail it? What if Lucas was his son? What would he do then?

TEN

Mack was expecting to get Kellan's voice mail just like last time, so he was surprised when Dylan's son answered.

"What's up?" Mack said.

"Not a lot," Kellan replied. "You still in LA?"

The boy sounded down. There was no doubt about that. But *why?* "I'm on my way home right now."

"Are you still going to move there?"

"I'm seriously thinking about it."

"Will you take me with you?"

Mack felt his eyebrows shoot up. Where was this coming from? "Aren't you a little young to move out of your parents' place?"

"I could live with you."

"You know I'd take you in if you ever needed it," Mack said, passing a slower-moving vehicle in front of him. "But why would you want to leave Whiskey Creek and all your friends when you have a great home already?"

"Because I can't stay here."

"Why not?"

"Have you talked to my dad?"

"Yes. He's worried sick about you."

Silence.

"Kellan? What's going on?"

"Does he know?" Kellan asked.

Mack detected tears in his nephew's voice. "Know what?"

"That I'm not his son?"

Mack's heart nearly stopped. Cheyenne loved Dylan so much; there was no way she'd cheat. "Of course you're his son."

"I'm not," he said firmly. "And I have the DNA results to prove it."

Mack turned down the music that was playing. "What are you talking about, bud?"

"You know my friend Josh?"

"Yeah."

"He looks *nothing* like his father, who's a big jerk anyway. They fight constantly. So Josh thought that maybe he belonged to someone else."

"What does that have to do with you?"

"I'm getting there. He talked me into taking a DNA test with him, so that he'd know what the results *should* look like. We both swabbed our cheeks. Then we told our fathers that we needed them to swab theirs

184

for a science project and sent it all off to the lab."

"They let you do that?"

"Yeah. It was easy."

"How'd you pay for it without a credit card?"

"Josh's older half brother has one, and Josh gave him cash for his and mine."

"Josh paid for yours."

"Yeah. He has lots of money."

"Where does he get it?"

"He sells dope."

Mack winced. "I don't think I'd mention that to your dad."

"You mean *Dylan*?"

"Come on, Kellan —"

"Come on, what? Josh shares fifty percent of his DNA with his father, and I share only twenty-five percent with mine."

Mack wasn't sure how to respond. He'd just swabbed his own cheek, might soon be dealing with DNA results that threatened to change a lot of things in his own life, but he wasn't that educated in this sort of thing. "I've never looked into it, but maybe those ratios fluctuate or . . . . or differ between people."

"That's not how it works," Kellan said, adamant.

Mack didn't think so, either, but he'd

185

been grasping at any possible explanation. Kellan *had* to belong to Dylan. Who else could he belong to?

"I've looked it up on the internet," Kellan was saying. "I also emailed my biology teacher from last year. Twenty-five percent is the amount of DNA I would share with a grandparent or an uncle — not a father."

Holy shit. "But . . . you look exactly like Dylan!"

"I look like an *Amos,*" he clarified, "because I have Amos DNA. I'm related to Dylan. But he's not a close enough match to be my father."

Mack had to pull off the road. This was so shocking and upsetting that he needed to get out of his car, move around. "There has to be something wrong with that test," he said. "Maybe the sample you got from Dylan wasn't large enough or . . . or it was too degraded because the package got hot in this warm weather or . . . something. Or they messed up in the lab."

"If there'd been no match at all, maybe we could blame it on one of those reasons. But the fact that there's a twenty-five percent match indicates that Dylan is related to my father. My biology teacher said so."

This was going to *destroy* Dylan. That was Mack's first thought. Then the meaning of that 25 percent match hit him — *really* hit him — and he stopped dead in his tracks. An Amos who was a brother or a father to Dylan had to be Kellan's father? *What the hell?* "There's more to being a father than donating sperm," Mack heard himself say, desperate to do all he could to keep the family together until they could get this sorted out. "No matter how you were conceived — and I don't pretend to understand what's going on here — Dylan's loved you since the day you were born. He'd die for you, and you know it. You and your mother mean everything to him."

"I love him, too." Kellan's voice broke, and he had to clear his throat to be able to continue speaking. "But . . . who's my real father? That's what I want to know."

Mack couldn't answer that question. He had no idea — and he was afraid to find out. "Does it really matter?" he persisted.

"It matters to me," Kellan replied, now defiant. "I'm not coming home until I know."

"Kellan —" Mack started, but Kellan had already hung up.

"Shit!" Mack yelled to the miles and miles of countryside surrounding him that was mostly filled with dairy farms. Dylan was waiting for him to call and report on this conversation with Kellan, but how was he going to tell Dylan *this*?

He wasn't. Not until he could sit down with his brother face-to-face.

It was after noon when Natasha got up off the floor, where she'd been playing with Lucas, to get a drink and found the money Mack had left for her. It was right in the middle of the table, partly tucked under one of her potted plants. She probably would've noticed it sooner, but she hadn't been paying attention to much of anything — other than her son. She and Lucas had made all kinds of creations out of clay and building blocks, had watched a movie and read a stack of books. Even if she hadn't been recovering from the flu, she'd needed a day like this, where she could focus almost exclusively on her child and simply enjoy being a mother. So, after Peggy's call, she'd turned off her phone. She hadn't wanted to hear from her in-laws again, or Ace or her own mother. She hadn't even wanted to hear from Mack.

But she was beginning to wonder about Kellan and whether they'd found him.

"What's that?" Lucas asked.

Natasha hadn't heard him follow her into the kitchen. She'd been too caught up in her own thoughts. "Mack's money," she replied.

"Why'd he leave it here?"

"To be nice." And to make sure she had what she needed. There was a note beside it, written in Mack's chicken scratch writing, which she read aloud. " 'Use this for whatever you need. See you soon. M.' "

When she fanned out the bills, Lucas's eyes went wide. "That's a lot!"

There were quite a few twenty-dollar bills, which gave her the impression that Mack had visited an ATM right before he left. The amount suggested the same, because it was the maximum amount allowed by most ATMs — five hundred dollars.

Lucas scrambled up on a chair. "What're we going to do with it? Can we buy toys?"

"I think he left it for emergencies, bud."

"Just one toy, then? Can I ask him? *Please?*"

"I'm afraid not," she replied, chuckling. "We don't ask Mack for toys. And we don't use his money unless we absolutely have to."

Slightly relieved to have some cash on hand, she put the money in her purse. But then, feeling the need to thank him and see if he'd learned anything about Kellan, she powered up her phone.

"There you are," he said when she called. "Where've you been? Sleeping?"

"No. Lucas and I have just been chilling together, playing games and watching a movie."

"Are you feeling any better?"

"I am."

"That's good. I've been worried."

She'd learned not to put *too* much weight behind statements like those. "Are you home yet?"

"Not quite. But I will be soon."

"Have you heard anything more about Kellan?"

He hesitated before he said, "Nothing definitive."

"You still don't know why he ran away? Was there an argument at home? A punishment or something? What triggered it?"

"Things are . . . unclear right now. I'm hoping to figure it all out after I hit town."

She could tell by his voice that he knew more than he was saying. "Oh, I see."

"What?" he said.

"This is 'family business,' which makes it none of *my* business."

"No, not at all. It's just . . . sensitive."

She cared about Dylan. Like Mack, he'd done a lot for her, so she couldn't help feeling a little left out. But the Amos boys

190

always looked after each other first and foremost. "It doesn't matter. I'm just calling to thank you for taking care of me while I was sick, and for leaving me with some money. I'm embarrassed that I need it, but I'll Venmo you as soon as I receive my first check."

"Keep it. You're going to need your first check for other things by the time it arrives."

"No, I'll pay you back." She tried not to remember his hands moving over her soapy breasts, but it was impossible. Since she'd started feeling better, her mind had gone back to that experience in the tub again and again, especially that moment when his hand had slid down between her thighs before she gave him the look that made him withdraw it. The mere fact that she was excited by those memories meant she had to get him back out of her life. She couldn't move forward if she was always longing for something — or someone, in this case — from the past. "Did you drop off the paternity test?" she asked.

"Not yet," he replied. "Because of everything that's going on with Kellan, I didn't want to take the time to find a post office when I can just drop it off after I get home."

She glanced back at her son, who was using a plastic dinosaur to break apart the Lego structure they'd built. "It's not too late to change your mind, you know," she said into the phone.

"About the test?" Mack asked.

"Yes. It's a big decision. You should take some time to think about it. I mean . . . once you know, you can't not know. And a child's a lifelong commitment."

"I would never expect you to shoulder more than your share of the responsibility."

He sounded offended that she'd even suggest it, but she had to think about how she could best get back on her feet. And now that she'd relocated and she was getting over the flu, she felt it would be wise to move on from here without his involvement. "That's just it," she said. "I don't want you to act out of a sense of obligation. After everything you've done for me, I'd rather not continue to be a burden. That night at Victorian Days was my fault. I know that. You've always been careful to avoid anything physical. So I've got this. Even if Ace bugs out, Lucas and I will be okay."

"Tash, I'm mailing the test. We'll know in a few days."

He sounded tired but resolved.

Closing her eyes, she sank into the closest seat. "You could be opening Pandora's box."

"I understand that. But I wouldn't want to be the kind of man who would hide from the truth — not *this* truth."

So he was going to do the right thing.

She wished she could be happy about that.

Mack went straight to his brother's house. Dylan had been calling and texting, demanding to know what was going on, and although it hadn't been easy, Mack had held him off by saying they'd discuss it when he arrived.

Well, now he was here, and he knew what he was going to face. He'd never had to cross Dylan, had never wanted to, either. It wasn't so much that his oldest brother was a force to be reckoned with — although there was that. Mack couldn't bear to hurt the man he loved more than any other. And he knew what he had to say would devastate him.

The door of Dylan's house flew open as soon as Mack pulled to the curb, and Dylan came charging out.

"Here we go," Mack muttered as he cut the engine and got out.

"What'd Kellan say?" Dylan demanded. "What's going on?"

Mack held up a hand. "Before I tell you anything, I need to talk to Cheyenne."

Dylan gaped at him. "What? *Why?*"

"Because I need to speak to her first. Please. Just . . . trust me on this."

Dylan was so worked up he couldn't quit moving. "Trust you? Nothing about this is making any damn sense. What could you need to say to her that you can't say to me?"

Cheyenne appeared in the doorway, and Mack could tell, even from where he stood on the walkway, that she'd been crying. "Have you heard anything?" she asked, looking fearful as he approached.

"I talked to Kellan this morning, Chey."

"Why would Kellan answer the phone for you when he won't pick up for any of the rest of us? We don't even know what we've done wrong."

"Mack and Kellan have always been close," Dylan replied, trying to comfort her.

"Can you take a ride with me?" Mack asked, focusing on Cheyenne.

She cast a worried glance at her husband. "Without Dyl?"

"I'll be okay. Go with him," Dylan said. "The sooner we get to the bottom of this, the better."

Dylan gave him a look over his wife's head that said he was banking on all the love and trust they'd developed over the years, and Mack nodded to indicate he was well aware that he held Dylan's heart in his hands and would remain mindful of that.

By the time he'd started his truck, Cheyenne had her seat belt on, but she also had her arms folded so tightly she looked as though she was trying to hold herself together.

It was difficult to leave Dylan standing in his front yard, but Mack didn't feel as though he had a choice.

"Do you know what I'm going to say?" he asked gently, once they were a block or so away from the house.

Her gaze remained fastened on some imaginary point straight ahead of them. "I hope not," she murmured.

He studied her profile. "Kellan knows," he said.

She squeezed her eyes closed, but that didn't stop a tear from slipping out and rolling down her face. *"How?"*

"He took a DNA test — mostly on a lark, which is the crazy part."

She made a strangled sound, probably trying to hold back tears. A DNA test meant there was no wiggle room, no way to lie out of the situation or make it more palatable to the individuals it affected.

Mack drove straight out of town. He was looking to get away from all the buildings and people, so he could pull over and they could talk without worrying about being seen or interrupted. "Who's Kellan's father?" he asked.

She didn't answer. Her gaze fell to her lap and she sniffed as tears continued to drop from her chin.

"Chey, I know it's one of us. So does Kellan. The DNA test showed that Dylan was a brother — or a son — to Kellan's real father."

"A son!" she snapped, surprising him by speaking up right away. "It certainly wasn't J.T.!"

"Thank God," he said, but he hadn't really thought it was. "Who, then? Rod?"

She shook her head and dashed a hand across her cheeks.

"Chey? Who was it?"

"Aaron," she finally responded with a sigh.

"Aaron!" That was the last name Mack had expected Cheyenne to give him. Aaron and Dylan hadn't become close until the past ten years. Because Aaron was only three years younger than Dylan, it'd been most difficult on him to have his older brother take over when their father went to prison and try to control his behavior and tell him what to do. They'd fought so often back then. There were times Mack thought they might kill each other. He'd automatically assumed it had to be another one of his brothers — and Cheyenne had always seemed to get along best with Rod. They were always teasing each other.

"He didn't want to do it," she said. "I mean, he didn't want to do it behind Dylan's back. But . . . I didn't want Dyl to have to know. I just . . . couldn't bear to put him through anything more than he'd already been through."

That sounded an awful lot like an affair. But how could she have had an affair with her own sister's husband? Actually, she and Presley weren't related, but they'd been raised together. "So . . . was it just a onetime thing or . . . ?"

His words fell off. He couldn't even say it. But she knew what he meant.

"We never *slept* together," she snapped, looking suitably horrified by the mere suggestion.

Mack sagged in his seat. He felt stupid for having asked, but he was also relieved by her response. She'd been faithful, at least. He wasn't going to have to break his brother's heart in that way. Or Presley's, either. "Then . . . what happened?"

Her throat worked as she swallowed. She was obviously still wrestling with her emotions. "Dyl and I were trying to get pregnant when . . . when I found out that he wasn't capable of fathering a child." She spoke haltingly, wiping fresh tears as they fell. "I didn't want him to feel as though . . . as though he'd let me down in any way. He would've taken the news hard, as a personal failing, if he couldn't give me a child. So . . . I decided I wouldn't put him through that."

Mack could scarcely believe what he was hearing. This was the best-kept family secret in the world. He'd had no inkling whatsoever. "You came up with another way to get a baby."

"Yes."

"What about Presley?"

"My sister was the one who helped me."

"In what way?"

"Presley had moved back to town, and she and Aaron were just starting to see each other again. But she felt sorry for me and managed to convince him to make a . . . a genetic contribution so that Dylan and I could have a child and the DNA would be as close to Dylan's as possible."

Mack dug around in his glove box to get a napkin he could give her. "Does that mean he went into the doctor's with you? It was official?"

"No." She blew her nose. "That would've

198

cost money. I didn't dare create any kind of a paper trail."

Mack blinked several times as he tried to imagine how this had all come to pass. "So . . . how'd it work?"

"We did it ourselves — at Presley's. He donated in one room and I inseminated in another."

"And that *worked*?" Mack was almost as surprised by that as all the rest.

"All we needed was a turkey baster," she said.

He pressed three fingers to his forehead. "I'm not even going to ask what that is."

"There wasn't anything nefarious between us."

"What about Wyatt?" Kellan was Wyatt's half brother, not cousin? That was mind-blowing. And Aaron was Kellan's father. Mack tried to think of the interactions he'd witnessed between the two of them, which had always seemed perfectly normal. Aaron was a caring uncle, but Mack had to hand it to him. He'd truly given this child to Dylan, which had to feel weird.

"He was too little to understand what was going on," Cheyenne explained. "He has no clue. No one else knows."

"Except Kellan," he pointed out.

She wrung her hands, twisting the napkin

up at the same time. "I knew it might come to this, if . . . if he ever needed a kidney or bone marrow transplant or other medical emergency. I was willing to take that risk because . . . what were the chances of that happening? I never dreamed he'd take a DNA test," she added. "Not at fourteen."

"They weren't so prevalent when you artificially inseminated yourself."

"No." She covered her face with her hands. "Oh my God. What am I going to do?"

"You're going to have to tell Dylan," he said.

ELEVEN

Mack let the engine idle as he waited for Cheyenne to get out. Dylan was no longer outside, but he must've heard Mack's truck, because the door swung open again as soon as he pulled up, and Dylan filled the threshold as his wife crossed the yard. Mack had asked Cheyenne if she wanted him to come in to help break the news, but she'd declined his offer, and he understood why. This was something she needed to do herself. It was probably the most sensitive conversation they'd ever have.

He waved at Dylan, who was so intently focused on his wife that he didn't seem to notice. In any case, there was no response.

Mack pulled away in spite of that and headed toward home, where he lived with Grady. They were the only two brothers left in the house they were raised in. They paid rent, but since there was no longer a mortgage, they used the money, by consent of all five brothers, to cover the expenses on their father's small house. Neither Mack nor Grady wanted J.T. to live with them. J.T. preferred having his own place anyway, so that they wouldn't "get involved in his affairs." He didn't like them criticizing his drug use or his laziness, but he sure didn't mind them paying for his living. He worked part-time and earned some pocket money but considered what they gave him his due for starting Amos Auto Body in the first place, even though it hadn't been worth much when he went to prison, and it was their hard work that'd turned it around.

That sense of entitlement was irritating after how terribly he'd let them all down, but Mack couldn't think about that right now. He was too worried about what was happening to the man who'd raised him.

The post office came up on his right, and he turned in as he'd been planning to do all day, swung around to the parcel receptacle and rolled down his window. If he'd ever considered *not* having this test performed, what he'd experienced this afternoon had quashed the temptation. He had no desire for Lucas, when he was older, to come knocking on his door, hurt and angry that Mack hadn't cared enough to be part of his life. As hard as it would be to change fathers on the kid now, Mack believed it was better to do that than let him live a lie. There'd be less rage to contend with later. Hopefully, there'd be less emotional damage, too.

He reclaimed the package he'd shoved under his seat before arriving at Dylan and Cheyenne's, stared at the label for several seconds, then dropped it inside.

There. He'd done it. There was no turning back.

Aaron called as he was driving away. Mack considered letting it transfer to voice mail. He knew his second-oldest brother would want to talk about Kellan and wasn't convinced it was his place to divulge what he'd learned. But Cheyenne was busy with Dylan, so she couldn't alert him to the fact that their secret was out, and Mack thought it might be smart to prepare Aaron, in case Dylan showed up at his house. "Hello?"

"It's me," Aaron said.

Mack drew a deep breath. This day was beginning to feel interminable. "I know. What's up?"

"When I called Dylan earlier, he told me Kellan might've spoken to you. Is that true? Do you know what's going on?"

Aaron was asking about his *son,* not his nephew. And he knew that. The idea was so strange Mack could hardly wrap his mind around it, but after fourteen years, maybe Aaron was used to the weirdness. "I talked to him, yeah."

There was a slight pause, then, "What'd he say?"

"I don't know if I should tell you."

"Why would it be a secret?"

Because of the ramifications. Although some part of Aaron had to be wondering if this was the day he'd always feared. How would he feel about everyone knowing that he was Kellan's true father? How would Aaron's son, Wyatt, and his two younger sisters react to learning that Kellan was their half brother instead of their cousin?

How much damage would this do to the family? Should they try to contain it, despite Kellan finding out?

Mack was convinced it would be smarter to continue to keep it a secret. It would certainly be better for Dylan and Cheyenne. Aaron and Presley, too. But how would they do that? Kellan knew. He could tell anyone he wanted. He could announce it to the world — and at fourteen he might not see the danger of doing exactly that.

"I'd rather let Cheyenne fill you in," Mack said.

"*Cheyenne?* Why not you or Dylan?"

He was beginning to catch on. "You

204

haven't guessed by now?"

"I'm afraid to guess."

Poor Aaron. Mack couldn't help feeling sorry for him. This wasn't going to be easy on him, either. "Kellan took a DNA test, bro."

No response.

"Did you hear me?"

"Yeah, I heard," he replied.

"Cheyenne's breaking the news to Dylan right now."

Aaron swore.

"I'm sorry," Mack said.

"I was afraid of this," he responded. "I told Cheyenne and Presley that it would get out eventually. Secrets always do. But it's been so long . . . I thought we were in the clear."

"This doesn't have to change anything," Mack said, trying to do a little damage control. "Everyone still loves each other. That's what counts. Love, not genetics."

"Don't kid yourself," Aaron said, sounding defeated. "This will change everything. Dylan will never be able to look at me the same way again. I wouldn't be surprised if he started to hate me, even though I only did it so that he could have a kid — to give back just a little for everything he's done for us."

205

Mack eased off the gas. He didn't want to arrive at the house and have Grady confront him when he was still on the phone with Aaron. "It must've been hard all these years, watching Kellan grow up, knowing you were his father."

"No. It's been surprisingly easy."

Taken aback by his answer, Mack turned off the music that had already been playing so low it was barely audible. "How?"

"It felt good to think I was able to give Dylan something for a change. And he didn't know about it, so he didn't have to feel grateful to me. I've considered it the best gift I've ever given to anyone. Until now."

"You've never regretted it?" Mack said. "Even for a minute? You've never looked at Kellan and wished you could tell him the truth?"

"No. It's been too rewarding to see the happiness he's brought Dylan. Dylan has loved being a dad now that he's not fighting such a huge battle every day just to scrape by, like he had to do with us. Dylan adores that kid."

Mack had never expected Aaron to be the one to make such a sacrifice. For all he denied the difficulty of it, Mack couldn't believe there weren't times when he felt a twinge of regret. Kellan was large and athletic, with a good chance at a football scholarship. He was also smart, handsome, gregarious and well-liked. So was Wyatt, Aaron's oldest, but a child would be a difficult thing to give someone else, especially in a situation like this one, where Aaron had a front-row seat to watching Kellan grow up, and no one else, except Cheyenne and Presley, knew the truth. When Mack saw it from that perspective, he had to agree that it was a beautiful gift, and he felt terrible to think the happiness it'd brought Dylan was going to be destroyed. Genetics shouldn't matter — not when there was so much love involved. "He loves him even more than he loved us."

"And I don't want that to be taken away from either one of them," Aaron said.

"Dylan could never stop loving him. But the truth will be hard on him. He might get angry and show up at your house. Who knows? We've been through a lot as a family, but this is a first."

"It'd be a mistake to let everyone else know," Aaron said.

"I agree."

"I'm driving over to make sure this doesn't get out of hand. I should talk to Dylan. Maybe I can help convince him that our intentions were good."

Mack could see his house just down the street and pulled over to give himself another moment on the phone. "Maybe you should approach Kellan first. Tell him you'd like to explain what happened and why. See if you can't get him to calm down. If you can manage that, it'll go a long way toward helping Dylan get through this."

"I'd be happy to, except he won't take my calls," he said, clearly exasperated. "You're the only one he'll speak to."

"Then text him. And give Dyl a chance to absorb what's happened before you confront him and Cheyenne. That would be smart, too." Dylan and Aaron's interactions — at least, in the past — had been so volatile. Mack thought they could both use some time to let their emotions settle, so that they didn't revert to the rocky relationship they'd had in the past.

"Okay."

"Let me know how it goes."

"Mack?"

"Yes?"

"If we hadn't done what we did, Cheyenne would never have been able to have a child of her own. She could've been artificially inseminated with a stranger's sperm, but then Kellan wouldn't have been related to

208

Dylan at all. After the sacrifices he made to raise us, Chey, Presley and I wanted him to see part of himself in his child. I guess that sounds crazy now, but it made sense at the time."

"I understand. It was a case of what he didn't know wouldn't hurt him."

"Yes." Aaron sighed heavily. "Except now he knows."

Dylan stared at the floor. What he was hearing didn't seem as though it could be real. Had he fallen into some sort of alternate universe? He'd spent fourteen years thinking that Kellan was his son. Kellan had spent every moment since he was born believing the same thing.

"Dyl?"

He could hear the tears in his wife's voice. She'd been crying since before she even told him. He'd never seen her so upset. But he couldn't react, couldn't comfort her as he normally would, *couldn't move.*

She knelt down beside him. "Dyl, I'm so sorry. Please forgive me. I didn't want you to have to know."

She'd said Aaron, his *brother,* had fathered their son. He thought back, trying to remember what his relationship with that particular brother had been like when

Cheyenne got pregnant. Aaron had always been so full of resentment. Had he agreed to do what he'd done as a way to hurt Dylan? To get back at him for the things Dylan had had to do to carry the family through those lean years when he was the only thing standing between his siblings and foster care?

No. He couldn't believe that. He and Aaron had had their run-ins. But as difficult as their relationship had been, Aaron would never purposely hurt him. Not in this way. If he was angry, it was obvious. He didn't sneak around. Cheyenne wouldn't try to hurt him, either. So why did it feel as though they'd just ripped his heart out of his chest?

Or . . . maybe that wasn't fair. Maybe they weren't responsible for the pain — only the shock. The pain came from the reality of the situation. He couldn't have given Cheyenne a baby without *some* help. And Cheyenne had made it so that he hadn't even had to ask or acknowledge that fact.

Why had he never questioned how they got Kellan? Although he hadn't realized it back then, he knew now that he couldn't have children. After Kellan was born, they'd tried for years with no results. But Cheyenne claimed she was happy with just the one child — that it was fine — and he'd believed her and the doctor when they'd told him that Kellan must've been a miracle baby.

Pinching the bridge of his nose, Dylan drew a steadying breath. He doubted the doctor would lie just to preserve his feelings, which meant even the doctor didn't know how Cheyenne had conceived. Although Cheyenne had just explained it to him, he'd only been able to comprehend a few words here and there. Aaron and Cheyenne hadn't slept together — it had been nothing sordid like that. He'd caught that much, and he believed it without question. But that didn't change the fact that he wasn't Kellan's father.

"Please, Dyl," she said. "I'd do anything to stop the pain this is causing you."

Anything. She'd already gone to pretty great lengths to preserve his feelings. Should he be grateful?

If she hadn't done what she'd done, they wouldn't have had Kellan.

"I love you," she whispered fervently. "So does Kellan. That will never change. No matter what. You're such a good man. You could never lose either one of us. I hope you know that."

It felt like he was awfully close to losing Kellan right now. The poor kid had to be as shocked and confused as he was. No wonder he'd run away!

He managed to cover her hand with his. But that was the most he could do. Then he stood so that he could get his keys.

"Where're you going?" she asked, sounding scared as she followed him into the kitchen.

"Out," he replied simply.

"Where?"

"For a drive." He gestured to stop her from coming any closer. "I just . . . I need some time, Chey. Give me a chance to work through this."

She covered her mouth and choked back a sob as he stalked past her, but she didn't cling to him. "I understand," she managed to say between hiccups from crying. "I love you."

"Right. I got that," he said and walked out.

Mack had just made himself a burger for dinner when he texted Cheyenne to see how things were going with Dylan. He didn't know if she'd have the chance to see his message. If she was still talking to Dylan, she wouldn't be paying any attention to her phone, but he was worried, and he knew Aaron was, too. Because Kellan hadn't reacted to Aaron's text, Aaron didn't know what to do — whether to finish driving over, so he could try to talk to Dylan, or wait until he received some word from Cheyenne.

Mack guessed Aaron was probably going to turn around when his phone rang again. Cheyenne.

"Mack?" she said as soon as he answered.

"Yeah. Did you get my message? How's it going?"

"Not too good." She broke down but managed to continue, "Dylan walked out a few minutes ago."

Mack gripped his phone that much tighter. "Walked out?"

"He said he needed some time."

"Where'd he go?"

"I don't know." She sounded drained. No doubt she was after such an emotional day.

"How upset was he?"

"That's hard to say. He didn't really react, just listened to me tell him what happened. Then he stood up and got his keys. I'm guessing he's more hurt than angry, which is killing me. I can't stand to think I did this to him." She sniffed. "But I was trying to protect him. Barring a medical emergency, I believed he'd never have to know."

"You couldn't have seen this coming," he

said. "For what it's worth, Aaron still believes you made the right choice."

"How?" she gasped.

"No way could Kellan have been as much Dylan's son as he has been — and still is — if Dylan knew from the beginning that Aaron was the one who'd fathered him."

She sniffed again. "Aaron said that?"

"He did."

"Thank God. I thought he might hate me, too."

"Dylan could never hate you, Chey," Mack said. "So . . . you haven't heard from Aaron?"

"He sent a text saying he was almost to town."

Apparently, he hadn't turned around. "What about Presley?"

"She called to say it would all be okay. I just wish I could believe her."

"She's right," Mack said. "It's just going to take some time to wade through this and sort it all out."

"I hope you're right. Listen, if . . . if you hear from Dylan, will you let me know?"

"I will." Where had Dylan gone? Mack finished his meal so that he could go drive around town and, hopefully, find his big brother. He wanted to make sure he was okay. But as soon as he grabbed his keys, he received a text that let him know exactly where Dylan was.

I'm out front, it read. Do you have a minute?

Dylan waited for Mack to get in and put on his seat belt before driving away. He didn't speak immediately, and neither did Mack. Mack was waiting to give his brother a chance to sort out his thoughts and say what he needed to say.

"Does Grady know about Kellan?" Dylan asked, breaking the silence, but not until after they'd reached the middle of town.

"No," Mack replied. "I didn't think it would be wise to tell him. In my opinion, the less people who know, the better."

"How many people does that encompass?"

"You, Cheyenne and Kellan, of course. And Aaron and Presley."

"That's it? You haven't told anyone else?"

"No. I have spoken to Aaron, however."

"What'd he have to say?" Dylan's jaw was tight, his words clipped.

"He's upset."

"*He's* upset?" Dylan echoed.

"Yeah. He never wanted it to come to this. Said it ruins the best gift he's ever given you. Nothing has made him happier than watching you with Kellan, Dyl, knowing how much you love him. To think he was able to be part of that, well, he said it felt pretty damn good."

When Dylan didn't respond, Mack knew those words had hit him hard. If that hadn't been clear, the single tear rolling down his cheek would've made it obvious. Had Dylan assumed his younger brother would be glad the truth was finally out? That he'd be gloating?

"Dyl, you know how much pride Aaron has. It was hard for him to let you take over and be in charge when we were younger. He resented you and challenged you at every turn. Made what you were trying to do that much harder. But you never gave up on him, never let him go into the system, and you could have. Now that he's older, he realizes what a Herculean effort taking over for Dad really was and how much he owes you — how much we all do. I guess he felt making it possible for you to have Kellan was one way he could repay you for some of that."

No response.

"Aaron didn't say this part," Mack continued, "but I believe it allowed him to feel more like your equal. I think that's why you two started getting along so much better about that time. Part of it was basic maturity. You were both settling down. But part of it was knowing he could love you enough to give you something that would mean everything to you."

Dylan didn't speak. He was too busy trying to blink back tears.

"Don't blow up your marriage, or your relationship with Kellan or Aaron, because of this," Mack said. "I know it must've come as a blow. I can't say it was fair that they didn't tell you. But I can't say they were wrong, either."

Dylan gaped at him. "You don't think they were wrong?"

"No, not really. In my book, it was a judgment call. Some people think a lie is a lie is a lie — and every lie is bad. Maybe to those people life is black or white. But that's far too simplistic a view for me. I see too many shades of gray for that to adequately reflect reality. Cheyenne did what she did because it was the only way to make having a child free and easy for you. Does that make sense? And I'm not talking about doctor bills. She didn't want you to feel the disappointment of being unable to give her a child, not after everything you'd already been through. Aaron didn't want that, either. And he was trying to arrange it so that you wouldn't feel indebted to him for stepping up to make it happen. He certainly didn't want to make things awkward, to have to worry about you watching him more closely than the rest of us for fear he might try to assume a different role with Kellan than that of uncle. They did it for so many reasons, Dyl. But the biggest was love. Everything else fits under that umbrella."

He watched Dylan's throat work as he struggled to swallow.

"Isn't that what matters most?" Mack asked. "Not *what* they did but *why* they did it? From what I've seen, Aaron hasn't treated Kellan any differently than Rod's kids. He *wanted* you to have Kellan. He still does. Kellan's actual DNA means nothing, but even if it did, you're closely related to him — because of Cheyenne and Aaron."

The silence stretched once again. Eventually, Dylan cleared his throat. "So what am I supposed to tell Kellan?"

Mack stared out the window. They'd left Whiskey Creek and were on Highway 49, which passed through so many of the historic mining communities of the gold rush almost two centuries ago. If they continued, they'd run into another small town very similar to the one where they'd both been born and raised. "I think you tell him exactly what happened and why. What other choice do you have?"

Dylan cleared his throat again. "And if he still won't come home? What if he asks to go live with Aaron?"

That was a terrible thought. But Kellan was just a child. And he was hurt himself. He could make the situation worse without even realizing what he was doing. "I hope he won't do that, Dyl. I hope he knows what he has in you. We did. Most of the time, anyway. But even if he doesn't, Aaron would never allow it. *You're* Kellan's father. It might not seem like it now, but Kellan will get over this — and the better you take it, the better he'll take it. Treat it like it's no big deal. That you love him, regardless, and that's what's important. Because it is."

Dylan drove without speaking for several minutes. Then he said, "Life is crazy. You know that?"

"Yeah, I know," Mack said. "It can be tough. But you're tough, too. You may be older than the MMA fighter who pulled us all through the darkest time of our lives —" he grinned "— but I don't think you've gone soft quite yet."

Dylan arched a challenging eyebrow at him, and Mack chuckled. "There you go," he said.

"Just wait until you have a child of your own," Dylan grumbled.

Knowing he might already have a son, Mack glanced away. "Yeah, well, when I do, I hope I'm half the dad you are."

"You're kidding, right?" Dylan said. "I made so many freaking mistakes with you guys. I was barely eighteen. I had no idea what I was doing."

"Every dad makes mistakes. You came through for us. You were immovable in your love and loyalty. That was what we needed most. And that's what Kellan needs right now."

Dylan reached over and squeezed his shoulder. "Thanks, man."

TWELVE

Aaron's truck was parked in front of the house when Dylan got home. His brother had driven almost three hours from Reno, where he ran their second Amos Auto Body location, even though he had to be up early to open the shop.

As soon as Dylan let himself into the house, both Aaron and Cheyenne came to their feet, and Cheyenne rushed across the room, her worried gaze searching his face — probably for any hint of forgiveness. "Dyl?" she said. "Are you okay?"

He nodded.

"I'm so sorry," she said.

He put an arm around her, drawing her close. He wasn't sure how he felt about what they'd done, but he knew Mack was right. They loved him, and they meant well. And since, in his mind, fairness meant judging by intentions and not actions, he had to take their good intentions into consideration. "It's going to be okay," he said as she buried her face in his chest. "We'll figure it out."

Aaron didn't say anything until Dylan looked at him.

"I'm sorry, bro," he said. "We just wanted to make you happy."

"I know." Dylan sighed. "So . . . what do we do now?"

Aaron's chest lifted as he took a deep breath. "We wait until Kellan calms down enough that we can talk to him."

"Have you tried to reach him?"

"I have. Several times. I thought . . . I thought if I could convince him of the truth — that this doesn't have to change anything — it might make you feel better."

"But . . ."

Aaron shrugged. "He won't pick up for me, either. Once Cheyenne knew I was coming, she let me know where he's staying. I drove by, but it looked as though they were settled in for the night, so I decided not to risk upsetting him any further by banging on the door."

"Probably a wise decision. The Rinehardts have agreed to let us see him tomorrow. The high-handedness of them deciding when it would be appropriate for us to see our own family member sort of pisses me off — that they feel they should have any say in this thing — but I'm holding my tongue, not saying or doing anything until I get to talk to Kellan tomorrow."

Aaron shifted uncomfortably. "Do you want me to stick around for that?"

Dylan studied his younger brother, taking in the tall, muscular yet wiry body and the rugged face that was so much like his own — and Kellan's. "Do you *want* to be present?" It was a difficult question to ask. Was he going to have to share his son with Aaron from here on out?

"No," he said immediately. "Not at all. He's *your* kid, Dyl. But I'll stay if you think it will help."

Suddenly, Dylan felt like he could breathe again — for the first time since Cheyenne had dropped the bomb that Kellan wasn't his. Maybe Mack was right. Maybe the DNA results didn't matter all that much. They'd been living under the same circumstances for fourteen years. The only difference was that he now knew how Kellan was conceived, and it wasn't as he'd thought. So maybe he could put his life, which had seemed shattered only a couple of hours earlier, back together again — providing he could convince Kellan to see the situation in the same way. "No," he said. "I think we got it."

"If not — if you need me to say something to him that would back you up in any way — let me know."

Dylan's phone vibrated in his pocket. He pulled it out, hoping that he'd finally received a text from Kellan, but it was Presley.

We all love you.

Aaron's wife had sent that. Nothing else. Just that. And he was glad. It was so much easier to keep it simple.

"You'd better get home to your own family," he told Aaron.

"Okay." Aaron pulled his keys from his pocket. "Listen, Dyl. I know this probably won't make the situation any better, but for what it's worth, I'm sorry. It must seem as though we purposely set you up for a terrible fall. But we believed it would be so much better for you if you didn't have to know."

Having Cheyenne's body pressed against his, her arms holding him tight, felt so familiar and so comforting that the shock and numbness Dylan had been experiencing since she told him began to ebb away.

They'd been happy together; he'd be stupid to let this come between them. "Would you have ever told me?" he asked, curious to see whether Aaron had been tempted.

His brother shook his head adamantly. "Are you kidding? I wish you didn't have to know even now."

Somehow, in spite of everything, Dylan chuckled. "We've had to deal with some weird situations, you and I."

"That's true. But we're brothers, and we'll always be there for each other. It might not seem like it, but that's what this was about, Dyl."

Letting go of Cheyenne, Dylan clasped Aaron's hand and gave him a brief man hug. He'd always found it strange that it was more awkward for him to be demonstrative with Aaron than his other brothers, but it was what it was.

And now he knew it wasn't likely to change.

Mack's phone went off bright and early the next morning. Hoping it wasn't more bad news about Kellan or Dylan, he fumbled to answer and managed to hit the right button. What he couldn't do was talk without sounding hoarse. " 'Lo?" he croaked.

"Mack?"

It was a child's voice — but his caller was too young to be Kellan. "Lucas?" he said.

"Can I buy a toy, Mack?"

Yes, it was Lucas. Mack recognized the voice. Scrubbing his free hand over his face, he sat up against the headboard. "What kind of toy, buddy?"

"One at the store."

His eyes felt like sandpaper, and this call had interrupted some desperately needed sleep. So that he'd be available in case something happened with Dylan, Aaron, Cheyenne or Kellan, he'd sat up watching a movie with Grady last night. But he couldn't help laughing. "Where's your mom?"

"In the shower."

His mind immediately conjured the image of Natasha lying naked in the tub as he rubbed her soapy body — and suddenly he felt much more alert. "Can I talk to her?"

"No!" he said. "She'll get mad at me."

"For . . ."

"Calling you. She told me I couldn't."

"I won't tell her," Mack said. "Just give her the phone, and I'll bring you a surprise when I come back."

"You will?"

"I will."

"You promise?"

Mack laughed again. "I promise." He

226

could hear Lucas running upstairs. A door opening. The water running.

"Mommy?"

"What, sweetheart?" Natasha's voice was surprisingly clear when she responded, but she didn't give Lucas a chance to answer before she asked, "Did you finish your breakfast?"

"No," he replied. "I don't like oatmeal."

"You ate it for Mack."

"It had bananas in it."

"I put bananas in this, too," she said, clearly exasperated. "You have to eat some of it, or you're going to be hungry at day care today."

"I don't want to go to day care! I don't like day care!"

"It'll be fun. You'll see. There will be other kids to play with. My boss knows the owner, says it's a great place."

"Why can't I go with you?" he asked, sulkily.

"Because I have to work, remember?"

The water went off. Afraid that Lucas had forgotten about him, Mack almost hung up so that he could call back, but then Natasha said, "What are you doing with my phone?"

"Mack wants to talk to you."

"What?"

"Mack's on the phone."

"This early? You didn't call him, did you?" she added, her voice suddenly stern. "We talked about this, Lucas. That's Mack's money we found on the table. We're not going to buy toys with it — we're going to give it back to him."

"He *wants* to get me a present," Lucas said.

"Oh, he does," she said with a laugh. "We'll see about that. Give me the phone.

"I'm sorry," Natasha said when she came on the line. "I told him it wasn't polite to ask for things, but —"

"He's six, Tash. Life is simple to him. He asks for what he wants. It's fine. Maybe we should all do that."

"Oh yeah?" she said. "And what would *you* ask for?"

He didn't have to think about it for long. He'd ask for another night like the one he'd spent with her during Victorian Days. After giving her that bath, making love to her was all he could think about. But he knew she'd be shocked to know that — shocked to know just how much he'd struggled to stay away from her through the years. "For you to forgive me," he said.

There was a slight pause. He'd taken her off guard. "There's nothing to forgive," she said at length. "What are you doing up so early?"

He didn't tell her that he hadn't been up until Lucas called. "Just wanted to check in. See if you're feeling well enough to go to work."

"I am. That was a terrible bout of the flu, but it's gone now. Thank God. I hope you don't come down with it. How're you feeling?"

"Fine."

"Is everything okay at home?"

He was tempted to tell her about the turmoil last night. It wasn't that he didn't trust her. It was that he'd already told Dylan he hadn't said anything to anyone else and wanted that to remain true. "Yeah."

"You going to the shop today?"

"Maybe this afternoon."

"Must be nice to have the luxury of deciding when you want to work," she joked. "It hasn't always been that way."

"You would know. You helped us build Amos Auto Body back in the day." He'd had so much fun when she lived and worked with him. But she'd flirted with him shamelessly, making him want things he couldn't have. He couldn't remember a time when he *didn't* want her. Although he'd tried hard to generate some genuine interest in the other women he'd dated, he'd never felt quite the same about them. Natasha's memory overshadowed everything else.

"It's my first day," she said. "I can't be late. I'd better go."

"Can you take Lucas to the store after work, so that he can buy a toy with the money I left?" he asked.

"No, I can't," she replied. "I told him not to ask you."

"He didn't ask."

"You already admitted that he did."

"Fine. I get it. You have to teach him the right things. I'll bring him something when I come back instead."

"You mean *if* you come back."

"I'm coming back. Have you heard from Ace?"

"No, but his parents called me yesterday."

"And?"

"Let's just say they aren't pleased. But I didn't expect them to be. Did you mail that . . . um . . . test?"

"I did."

She didn't respond.

"It's going to be okay," he said. "Either way."

"Maybe for *you* it'll be okay. I'm screwed, regardless."

"Tash —"

"I have to go," she broke in. "I'm running out of time."

"Okay." He said he'd call later and hung up, but he knew she was right. Her life would only get more difficult, no matter who Lucas's father turned out to be.

"Hello? Natasha?"

Natasha blinked and returned her attention to the crowded cafeteria, where she'd been having lunch with Aiyana, Aiyana's son Eli, who helped run the school, Aiyana's other son Gavin, who took care of the grounds and maintenance, and several teachers, including Cora, Eli's wife. Instead of utilizing a staff lunchroom, most of the teachers ate with the students. From what Natasha could tell, they enjoyed it — treated the kids almost like their own children. The love and acceptance demonstrated at this school was remarkable, especially because Natasha knew some of the kids did everything they could to prove they didn't deserve love in the first place.

"Yes?" She focused on Aiyana, who'd been the one to address her. "Sorry. My mind was wandering."

She'd been thinking about her conversation with Mack this morning. He insisted that he was coming back. Could it be true?

Would he return even if he wasn't Luke's father? And what would she do if she had to see him very often? How would she ever grow content with being alone if he was always there to remind her of what she was missing?

"I was just wondering how your morning went," Aiyana said. "I heard you were sort of thrust into the fire when Rand Jenson cut his knee."

"Yes, I wasn't expecting to encounter so much blood on my first day," she joked. "It required seven stitches, but I made the sutures so small the scarring should be minimal. He'll be fine, as long as he keeps it clean. He's going to check in with me day after tomorrow to let me take a look at it. I gave him a tetanus booster, too, just to be safe."

"I didn't hear about this," Gavin said. "How'd he cut it?"

"Trying to climb up on some chairs here in the gymnasium to put up that poster." Aiyana tilted her head to indicate the one advertising the Popsicle and sports day reward for everyone who maintained a 3.5 GPA this quarter.

Gavin's eyebrows shot up. "He fell?"

"He did. Hit a metal piece on the corner of the bleachers," Aiyana said. "Mr. Banks told him to use the ladder. He was just being funny, trying to show off for the other members of the student council, and Mr. Banks didn't see what was going on until it was too late."

"Tough lesson," Cora muttered.

"I'm glad it wasn't his head that he split open," Aiyana said. "I'm also relieved that we didn't have to send him to the hospital — and that's only because we now have a *doctor* on staff." The way she saluted Natasha made Natasha smile. Aiyana was obviously trying to recognize her accomplishments and make her feel valued. She suspected Aiyana did the same with the teachers and students — tried to make *everyone* feel valued and appreciated. But what she'd said made Natasha a little self-conscious. She preferred not to make a big deal about being a doctor and not a nurse. She didn't want those who might not have clued in to the fact that she was *that* doctor, the one whose nurse had caused the death of a baby, to realize who she was and why she no longer had a practice of her own.

"There's nothing like diving right in," Eli quipped.

"It wasn't a big deal," Natasha mumbled.

Cora put down the single-serving milk carton she'd been drinking out of. "I hear you have a little boy."

Relieved at the change of subject, Natasha nodded. "Lucas. He's six."

"I have a girl that age and a boy two years older," Gavin said. "We should get them together for a playdate."

"That'd be great. I live on Main Street, so we don't have any other young families nearby."

Natasha couldn't help liking Eli, Cora and Gavin. They seemed friendly, easygoing. "Sounds great." She gave Gavin her contact information before she got up to stack her tray.

The bell went off, and the students flooded toward the exit. Natasha didn't have to be back in her office at any specific time. She just had to be on campus and available, in case she was needed, so she hung back and let everyone else go first. Aiyana, who was also waiting, pulled her aside.

"I wanted to tell you that we'll be getting a new student soon," she said. "His name's Austin Forester, and he's fifteen."

Since Natasha didn't know any of the students yet, besides the boy who'd cut his knee and a girl who'd started her period and needed feminine hygiene products and a little reassurance, she didn't understand why Aiyana would call her attention to this new student. But she smiled and nodded. "Okay. Will he be one of our boarders?"

"Yes."

"It's so early in the summer. Isn't that an unusual time to take in a new boarder?"

A pained expression claimed her employer's face. "Not at this school. That's the problem. Austin's been removed from his home and is now a ward of the state. So he's going to need all the love and care we can give him."

Natasha tucked her hair behind her ears. "I'll be happy to do my part."

"I know you will. I just wanted to warn you because . . . he'll have some scars and other injuries I'll need you to take a look at."

Natasha's lunch suddenly sat heavy in her stomach. "You mean he's a victim of abuse."

"Yes. We see that more often at this school than you would at any other, of course. And from what I hear, his case is . . . rather severe."

Natasha felt herself tense. "I'm sorry."

Aiyana squeezed her arm. "So am I. But we'll take care of him."

After the death of the Grossman child, Natasha was terrified of losing another patient. Working at New Horizons seemed like the perfect stopgap in so many regards, but could she handle what she might see here? Would it be too much for her?

Or would it give her the opportunity to truly help children as she'd intended from the start?

THIRTEEN

Dylan didn't think he'd ever been so nervous. He knew he'd have to persuade Kellan, who could be just as stubborn as he was — after all, he was an Amos and Aaron was arguably the most stubborn among them — that they could still be a family. And as if that didn't promise to be difficult enough, he'd have to do it with the Rinehardts, who were people he no longer liked, looking on. He'd never been one to share his private business. But he had to do what he had to do, and if he'd realized anything through this, it was that he'd do whatever it required to get his son back.

"You ready?" Cheyenne murmured as they parked in front of the house.

He leaned forward to see around her, wondering if the Rinehardts were gazing out their front window, watching them, right now. The sun was reflecting off the glass, so he couldn't tell. "Yeah."

"You think Kellan will talk to us?" she asked. "He's been pretty resolute. Hasn't accepted anyone's call, except for Mack's."

Kellan had even ignored Aaron, but that actually made Dylan feel better instead of worse. Although Kellan didn't yet know it was Aaron who'd sired him, Dylan couldn't help fearing that Kellan would suddenly decide he wanted to go live with his "real" father once he learned who that was.

Fortunately, the way Aaron had acted last night had convinced Dylan he'd never allow it, that he'd insist on being just an uncle and tell Kellan he had to deal with the parents who were raising him.

Dylan got out, shoved the car keys in his pocket and stalked around the car, where Cheyenne joined him. After smoothing her dress, she squared her shoulders and slipped her smaller hand in his.

When he kissed her knuckles, she looked up at him, startled by the gesture but also clearly relieved. He knew showing his commitment would make her feel better, but he needed that contact and reassurance, too. They would hold tight during this storm, would not break apart and lose each other — no matter what.

"Thank you," she murmured. "Thank you for forgiving me."

"How could I not?" he muttered. "You know how much you mean to me."

Even though she smiled at his response, he could see there was still plenty of apprehension in her eyes. "Everything will be okay," she said.

She was trying to convince herself as much as him. "Whatever happens, we'll deal with it together."

They didn't have to knock. Mr. Rinehardt — Carl — opened the door just as they reached the top step. "Come on in," he said.

Dylan dipped his head politely, but he didn't say anything, and he didn't reach out to shake hands. He couldn't quite forgive Carl for treating him as though it was necessary to act as a mediator between him and his child. It was offensive, but Dylan had to acknowledge that he was a little more sensitive to that sort of thing than most people. He'd been judged and gossiped about for most of his life.

"Kellan? Your parents are here," Carl yelled, and Maggie, Carl's wife, came into the living room.

"Hello." She smiled, but that smile wilted almost immediately. No doubt she could tell he didn't appreciate the way she and her husband had stood between him and

Kellan. "Would you like something to drink?"

Cheyenne squeezed his hand, silently pleading with him to remain civil. "No, thank you," she said. "As you can imagine, we're pretty anxious to see our son."

"Of course." She glanced at her husband. "Maybe you should go get him."

Once Carl left, Maggie gestured toward the sofa. "Would you like to sit down?"

That was the last thing Dylan wanted to do. He preferred to take his son so he could speak to him in private. Tell him how much he loved him and that they could get past this. But knowing it would be smarter to play along, at this point, he followed Cheyenne's lead and perched uncomfortably beside her.

Carl reappeared. Kellan, head bowed, came into the room behind him.

"Have a seat, Kellan," Carl said. "Do you want anything to drink, buddy? A soda?"

Dylan felt his muscles bunch at the other man's solicitous tone. He was acting as if *he* was the one looking out for Kellan.

"Naw." Kellan peered up at them from under his bangs, but his gaze skittered away as soon as he met Dylan's eye.

"Can we have a minute?" Dylan had told himself he wouldn't try to take control of this meeting, that he'd let Carl and Maggie run the show. He didn't want to risk Kellan refusing to talk to them and going back into the nether regions of the house. Dylan knew he wouldn't be able to stop himself from tearing the place apart until he found his son.

Carl looked at his wife, and she looked back at him. "Well, we thought we'd —"

"I just really need to talk to my son," Dylan broke in, coming to his feet. "He means everything to me, so the past few days have been incredibly upsetting. I hope you understand."

"But . . . he tells us he's not even your son," Carl said with an accusatory glance at Cheyenne that further enraged Dylan.

"It doesn't matter what that DNA test indicated. He's mine. He's always been mine, and he'll always be mine."

"He said something about it being one of your brothers who must've —"

"Can I please talk to him?" Dylan broke in again, more forcefully this time.

Looking flustered, Maggie stood up. "Of course. Come on, Carl."

Carl turned his attention to Kellan. "Do you need me here, buddy?"

Dylan felt his jaw tighten until he thought it might shatter, but, fortunately, Kellan shook his head and the odious Rinehardts left the room.

"Kellan, first of all, I'm sorry," Cheyenne said. "I want you to know that nothing . . . inappropriate has ever happened between me and *any* of your uncles. Aaron donated the sperm that was used to artificially inseminate me. That's all. I wanted to use DNA that was as close as I could get to your father's, and Aaron was kind enough to agree to help me."

"So you didn't sleep with him," he said, sullenly.

"No, of course not," she cried. "I've always been true to your father, never wanted anyone else."

"Why didn't you tell me?" he asked.

"I didn't see why you needed to know," she replied. "Even your father didn't know."

This made Kellan sit up. "*You* didn't know?"

"Not until last night, when your mother told me."

His jaw dropped. "And you're not upset? You're not mad?"

"I was," he admitted. "It was . . . a shock. A leveling blow. But . . ."

"What?" Kellan prompted, his gaze now fastened on Dylan's face.

"I realized that it's love that binds us

242

together. And love isn't dependent on DNA."

Kellan dropped his head into his hands. Dylan suspected it was to hide tears, so he got up and went over to kneel beside him. "Kellan, listen to me. I was telling the truth a minute ago when I said that you're mine and you'll always be mine. My heart could never bear it if you weren't."

Kellan dropped his hands, letting Dylan see his eyes, which were, sure enough, growing red and puffy. "I don't want what I've learned to be true," he said. "I've always been proud to be your son. I love you more than anyone in the world. I always have."

"Then come home," Dylan said. "Our lives don't have to change."

"You don't think it's any big deal that you're not my real father? That it's . . . that it's Wyatt's dad? *Uncle Aaron?*"

Dylan squeezed his shoulder. "He's just the donor. I'm your father in all the ways that count the most."

Cheyenne knelt beside Dylan and took their son's hand. "Kellan, I did what I did because I knew how badly your father wanted a child, and that he couldn't have one the regular way. I should've told him, but —"

"She knew it wouldn't make any difference to me," Dylan said. That wasn't the real reason she hadn't told him, but he felt it was all Kellan needed to know. "So . . . does it matter to you? Are you going to kick me to the curb now that you know?" He attempted a grin and was heartened when Kellan gave him a watery smile in return.

"Does Uncle Aaron know that I know?"

"He does now," Dylan replied.

"What'd he say about it?"

"He's leaving it between us, as he should."

Carl poked his head into the room. "Everything going okay in here?"

Dylan gave his son a pained look. "Is there any way you could tell Mr. Rinehardt that we got this? And come home, so we can discuss it in private?"

When Kellan nodded, Dylan couldn't help pulling him into his arms. "I've missed you," he said and was relieved when he felt his son's arms tighten around him.

"I've missed you, too," he said. "Let's go home."

Mack had gone into work earlier than he'd planned. Since Dylan needed the day off, he'd figured he might as well help out, rather than make Grady and Rod limp by without either one of them, and was glad he did, because once he arrived he learned that

J.T. had called in sick. They had other, hourly workers, but they also had so much business they could barely keep up. They'd established such a good name in the auto body industry that they were getting customers from as far away as Sacramento and the Bay Area.

"You heard that Kellan's home, right?" Rod asked as he strolled into the front office, where Mack was manning the front desk.

Mack shoved the stack of invoices he'd already processed into the appropriate cubbyhole and started to straighten up his workspace. "No. When did that happen?"

Rod put some money into the vending machine, and Mack heard a *thunk* as a soda landed in the bin. "I had to text Dylan about a car I'm working on, and he told me."

"I'm glad Kellan's home." Mack had known Dylan and Cheyenne had a meeting with Kellan and the people Kellan was staying with this morning, but he hadn't heard how it went. He'd been curious, but he hadn't wanted to bother them if they were still dealing with everything. This was a good sign.

Rod popped the top of his Coke and sauntered over. "Why'd Kellan run away?

245

Do you know?"

Mack shuffled things around on the desk again. "Dylan didn't say?"

"Nope. Just told me not to worry about it, that everything was going to be fine."

"You know how Dylan is," Mack said, purposely avoiding eye contact. "Family business is family business."

"But family business doesn't usually exclude *us.*"

"Kellan's his kid. It's natural that he'd be protective."

"Guess so." Rod took a long drink of his soda. "By the way, Grady said you're going to open an Amos Auto Body in LA. That true?"

"I'm thinking about it."

"*Seriously* thinking about it?"

"Very seriously."

"Why now? You've been talking about opening your own shop for years."

Mack shrugged. "I have the money. I'm willing to take the risk." He could stay in Whiskey Creek and continue getting paid a monthly salary, along with receiving a fifth of the profits on the business at the end of each year. He was making good money; it was difficult to walk away from such a reliable income. Dylan got two shares, since none of them would have a business without him, but Aaron didn't take a share now that he owned his own location, so Mack received 20 percent even though they split the money between only four brothers. Owning his own location would mean that, just like Aaron, Mack would have to pay a nominal amount each month for the franchise. But he'd get to keep whatever profits the location garnered, so he could potentially do a lot better than he was now. The choice had worked out well for Aaron, which was encouraging. Bottom line, if the economy held, and he found a good location with the right demographics, he'd be better off to own his own shop. However, if the economy tanked, or he didn't choose well, he'd be better off to stay right where he was.

It was a tough call, but he now had added incentive to try to make it all work . . .

Rod leaned up against the counter. "What made you choose LA?"

"What do you mean? It's a huge market. We've talked about it being a good candidate before."

Rod gave him a skeptical look. "Natasha has nothing to do with it?"

Mack shoved his hands in his pockets. "Maybe she does."

"That's what I thought," his brother said with a laugh.

Suddenly defensive, Mack stiffened. *"What?"* He was getting tired of his brothers teasing him about Natasha. He'd put up with it for years.

"Now that she's available again, you want to be closer to her?"

"If that's the case, it's *my* business. Do you have a problem with it?"

Rod sobered. "Whoa. Are you pissed off?"

"No, I'm just tired of everyone having something to say about Natasha."

His brother studied him carefully.

"What are you doing?" Mack asked. "Why are you staring at me?"

"Something's changed," he replied. "What is it?"

Mack immediately thought of Lucas but grumbled, "Nothing's changed."

"Did you sleep with Natasha while you were there?"

"No!" he snapped, but he'd certainly wanted to. He couldn't remember a time when that wasn't a temptation.

"For years, I've watched you go out with one woman after the next, without any real interest in any of them. But you've always felt something for Natasha."

Mack was tempted to continue to deny it. He didn't want to hear Rod's opinion or his advice. But he was pretty sure Lucas was his, and if that was the case, there'd be no more hiding the fact that he'd always had a romantic interest. "So what?" he said.

Rod blinked, probably surprised that he'd admit it. "Does she know how you feel?"

"She just lost her pediatric practice and her marriage — basically at the same time. She's trying to recover. I don't think she's concerned with what I feel."

"Oh, stop. She's *always* been concerned with what you feel," he said with a grin and crushed his can, shooting it like a basketball into the wastebasket behind the counter. "You can get her back if you really want her." He grew more serious. "But make sure you really want her. It wouldn't be fair to break her heart again."

Mack felt his jaw sag, but Rod didn't give him a chance to respond before he walked out.

His brother was right. He didn't want to hurt her. That was the *last* thing he wanted. And yet he wasn't sure he could let himself fall as hard as he knew he could fall with her.

He checked his phone. Ever since he'd mailed that DNA test, he'd been on pins and needles. He couldn't help wondering if Natasha was also nervous, which brought her to mind for probably the millionth time since he'd left Silver Springs. Since he still didn't have any customers in the lobby, he sent her a message.

How's your first day at work?

So far, so good, she responded. I like the people. Aiyana, Eli, Gavin, Cora. Everyone's been great, except for one teacher who showed up at my office after lunch.

What'd she want?

It was a he. He was aware of what happened with Maxine Green and wanted to chat about it.

Frustrated by how long it took to text, Mack called her. "What did this male teacher have to say about your demented former nurse?"

"He kept assuring me that Amelia's death wasn't my fault, but that almost made me more uncomfortable, because it suggests that there are people out there who think it was. I mean, I know she worked for me, which places some of the blame on me, too, but he doesn't have to keep reminding me of it."

She was talking softly. Mack guessed she

didn't want her voice to carry through the whole administration building. "What was his name?"

"Roger Burns."

"How old is he?"

"Close to our age, I guess."

He didn't say anything about the nine-year spread. She always acted like it was nothing. "He married?"

She hesitated. "What does that have to do with anything?"

"Just curious." Mack could see a customer parking in the lot and knew his short reprieve would soon be over. "How'd you get rid of him?"

"A girl came in with a migraine who needed to lie down. I got the impression he would've kept rambling on about it, even in front of the student. But I said I needed to focus on my work."

"So he finally left?"

"After he asked for my number."

"In front of the girl?"

"Yes! I was shocked."

Mack wasn't. Natasha was gorgeous. What man wouldn't want her number, no matter who was around? "Did you give it to him?"

"No. I'm doing everything I can to save my career, and I have a son to raise. I'm not the least bit interested in dating."

She'd made that clear. "I'm glad he's gone," Mack said.

"So am I. What's the word on Kellan?"

"He's back home and all is well."

"That's good. Did you ever find out why he left?"

"He got mad because he couldn't hang out with a guy named Denny. It was stupid, but you know teenagers." Mack hated lying to her, but he had to keep his word. "Have you heard from the day-care place? I know Lucas was worried about going there."

"He's okay. They sent me a picture of him playing, which was reassuring."

"Can you forward it to me?"

She seemed startled. "Why?"

"Because I'd like to see it, too."

"Don't worry. Like I said, he's fine." She covered the phone while speaking to someone else. "I have a student here," she said when she came back on the line. "He's diabetic and needs to test his blood. I have to go."

Mack said goodbye and hung up. He had to help the customer who'd come in to pick up a convertible BMW, anyway. Fortunately, it was finished.

Mack had him check the car to approve the work, pay and sign the papers.

The man was just walking out when

Mack's phone dinged. He pulled it from his pocket to find a picture of Lucas playing with a couple of other kids on a large rock.

"What're you looking at?"

Mack had been so preoccupied he hadn't realized that Rod had come back inside.

"Nothing."

"It must be something. I've never seen such a dreamy smile on your face."

Mack scowled. "What're you talking about?"

"Let me see what it was." Rod reached out, but Mack knocked his hand away.

"Fuck off," he said, jokingly, but he shoved his phone back into his pocket at the same time. There was no way he wanted Rod to know he'd been looking at a picture of Lucas.

FOURTEEN

Despite knowing that Mack had mailed in the DNA test and they would soon have the results, the week passed quickly for Natasha. The stress of having a new job and dealing with the unfamiliar had kept her too preoccupied to be able to dwell on that. She had checked the link Mack had given her daily. But it was Friday and nothing had been posted so far. Maybe the lab was behind, or shipping had taken longer than expected . . .

She was about to check again — even though she'd already tried right before she left for work — when Aiyana rapped on her open door and stepped into her office. "Hey, how's it going?"

Natasha didn't currently have any students who were convalescing from a headache, having a wound cleansed or checking blood sugar, which had been the bulk of what she'd treated so far. Trying to grow more

254

comfortable in her new office and situation, she'd been using the time to reorganize her supplies. "Good."

"How was your first week?" Aiyana asked.

"It went well," Natasha told her. "Rand Jenson's knee seems to be healing without any infection, and he was my most serious case."

"I'm glad to hear that. We're lucky to have you. I hope you're happy here."

Natasha smiled. "Of course I am. You're wonderful to work for. You should know that."

"Oh, I have my detractors just like anybody else," she said with a chuckle. "But I'm glad you're not one of them. Any big plans for this weekend?"

Ace was supposed to pick up Lucas tonight, but she hadn't heard from him. She'd tried calling him twice, so that she'd know whether to pack a bag — and what to tell Luke when she picked him up from day care — but Ace hadn't responded. She hadn't been able to reach his parents, either. She was afraid they'd written Luke off along with her. She could see them doing that. They were vengeful and would try to punish her, even if it hurt them — or Lucas. "That sort of depends on my ex," she replied. "It's his turn to take Luke, but I

255

haven't been able to get hold of him, so I'm not certain he's coming."

Aiyana glanced over her shoulder at where Betty May was working at her desk. "Did you get the results from that . . . um . . . test we spoke about?"

Her boss was so easy to talk to that Natasha had told her the whole situation last night, when they were the only two people left in the building before going home. She doubted Betty was listening to their conversation, but she appreciated Aiyana's discretion, all the same. "Not yet. We're still waiting."

She lowered her voice. "Well, I hope your ex-husband won't disappoint Luke, regardless. After all, he's just a child."

"The way Ace acts, you'd think he was just a child, too." Natasha rolled her eyes. "I guess I sound bitter, huh? I told myself I would never be *that* kind of divorcée, but I'm definitely sliding in that direction."

"Sounds like he might be giving you reason." She smiled tolerantly. "When's Mack coming back?"

Mack had kept in close touch. Natasha had been surprised by how often she'd heard from him. He'd texted her various things — pictures of his brothers acting goofy or a car they'd done a particularly good job of fixing. Since she'd once worked at Amos Auto Body herself and could appreciate the skill it required to be good at that type of thing, she liked seeing what they were doing. Besides the fairly frequent messages, he'd also called her almost every night. She hated how much she was starting to look forward to hearing his voice. "I don't know. He hasn't said. I think he's waiting for the results before deciding what to do."

"I see. Well, I'll be thinking of you this weekend. And if you get lonely or want to talk, give me a call."

"Thank you."

Aiyana started to leave but turned back. "I've noticed that Roger Burns has been coming into the office quite often this week, and you seem to be the draw. Is that okay?"

Natasha didn't know how to respond. Roger hadn't been unfriendly. But she did prefer he leave her alone. "He knows about Maxine Green," she said simply. "That's usually what he wants to talk about."

Aiyana peered more closely at her. "I can't imagine you want to discuss that."

"No . . ."

"I see. I'll ask him to give you some space, so that you can get settled in."

"I don't want to put you in an uncomfortable position —"

257

"It won't. I'll be diplomatic," she said with a wink, and Natasha let it go because she believed if anyone could say something like that nicely enough, it would be Aiyana.

"Thank you."

Aiyana left and Natasha checked her phone before she finished reorganizing her supplies. She told herself she was hoping to hear from Ace. For Lucas's sake, she was. But he hadn't attempted to return her call. Neither had he responded to her messages.

She was, however, inordinately happy to find another text from Mack.

Any word from the asshole you divorced?

She'd told him last night that she hadn't heard from Ace since the whole journal debacle. None. I think he means to stand me up. I'm not sure what to tell Luke.

Tell him that I'm coming tonight, and I've got the surprise I promised him. ;)

You're coming back to Silver Springs? Does that mean the results are up?

Her stomach tightened. Had she missed them?

Not yet. The lab is back East, and it's so

258

late now I'm thinking they won't post anything until Monday. But it's okay if I come anyway, isn't it?

"Say no," she told herself. "Put him off somehow." But she couldn't do that, not after all he'd done for her — and how excited Luke would be to see him. If Ace was going to let her son down, a visit from Mack would certainly help take away the sting. Luke hadn't stopped talking about Mack all week.

Of course, she wrote. But I thought you were working today. When would you leave?

As soon as I get off. It's only a six-hour drive. If I leave at five, I'll get there at eleven.

Won't you be too tired?

I'll be fine.

What was the rush? Why wasn't he waiting until tomorrow? Did he have to be back on Monday? How long will you be staying?

A few days. I need to find a good location for an Amos Auto Body shop since I wasn't able to do that before. Now that Kellan's home and all is well here, I might as well start putting out some feelers.

He was still thinking of going through with that? She was afraid he was making decisions based on the assumption that Lucas was his.

But she was excited anyway; she couldn't help it.

I'll make up the couch.

Great. See you soon.

When Mack arrived, he found the porch light on. He hadn't been able to get away from Whiskey Creek as soon as he'd planned — it'd taken longer than he thought to finish up a few items at work so that he wouldn't have to rush back. That meant it was after one when he finally pulled into the drive.

When he'd texted Natasha to let her know that he was going to be late, she'd said she'd leave the door unlocked for him, but he hadn't been willing to let her take that risk. He'd insisted she hide a key instead — a decision he regretted since he was having trouble finding it. By the time he discovered which rock she'd put it under, she must've heard him prowling around the place, because she let him in.

"Sorry to wake you," he whispered as he hefted his duffel bag over his shoulder and slipped through the opening.

"It's okay," she said. "I hadn't dropped off yet."

"Not tired?"

"I was just . . . too caught up in my thoughts."

"Any word from Ace?"

She sighed. "No. He didn't come. Can you believe it? Poor Lucas."

"What a jerk," he muttered.

As she shut the door, she accidentally brushed against him, coming close enough that he could smell the womanly scent he'd always associated with her, and he felt his body react. That he was tired and had spent much of the drive dwelling on how exciting it had been to touch her in the bath undermined his resolve. It didn't help that she'd answered the door in a tank top, without a bra, and in what he assumed were a pair of pajama shorts but could easily have been underwear. When he put down his duffel bag to embrace her, and she slipped into his arms to give him a customary welcome hug, his hands went around her waist to hold her against him instead of letting her go.

"All I've been able to think about is you in that damn bathtub," he admitted, his mouth next to her ear. "And that night during Victorian Days in Whiskey Creek."

She didn't say anything, but she didn't pull away, either.

He kissed her neck — once, twice, three times, working his way up. She still didn't step away, and he allowed himself to press his lips to her temple as he slid his hands under her shirt to touch the smooth, warm skin of her back.

"I — I have your bed ready," she said, but the last thing he wanted to do was let go of her and sleep on the couch.

"Natasha?"

Her eyes seemed troubled, torn when she tilted her head back to meet his gaze. "What?"

He watched her face as he slowly brought his hand around to cup her breast, saw her lips part when he moved his thumb over her nipple. "I want to make love to you."

She didn't say anything.

"If you don't want that, you need to tell me now, because —" he closed his eyes "— I can't seem to stop on my own." He'd been thinking about her too much, talking to her too much, missing her too badly this week — so badly that he'd come back as soon as he could.

"It's just sex, right?" she whispered. "You sleep with plenty of other women. Besides, it's nothing we haven't done before."

He was pretty sure she was trying to minimize what they were feeling, make it as casual as possible. But he was too caught up to focus on subtleties. "Is that a yes?" he asked, so hungry for the taste of her that he pressed his lips to hers before she could even answer. He figured if she was going to refuse, she wouldn't allow him to kiss her, or she wouldn't respond to his kiss. But she made no attempt to stop him, and she definitely participated.

She accepted his tongue at the perfect moment, and he groaned as she offered him hers.

Then it was like Victorian Days all over again. Intense and immediate. She pulled off his shirt, and they nearly knocked over a chair on their way to the bedroom.

She locked the door so that Lucas couldn't walk in on them before helping him pull off his jeans.

"I've never wanted anyone so badly," he admitted when her hand closed around him.

She looked up, her gaze challenging, but she didn't say anything. He told himself that that was okay; her touch was enough. This time, he hadn't been drinking, but she made him so drunk on desire he couldn't think of anything but pressing inside her.

Once he'd finished stripping off her clothes, he turned her toward the window so that he could study her bare body in the moonlight. He recognized the size and shape of her breasts, the smooth plane of her belly, the flare of her hips. He'd already memorized every detail. This, like the incident in the tub, was just a chance to become reacquainted with the image he'd carried in his head for so long, the same one he'd recalled thousands of times.

Lowering his head, he took her nipple in his mouth. It'd been over seven years since he'd last done this. The pent-up desire from years of denial, both before and after that incident, made him feel like the character in *Chocolat* who gave up chocolate for Lent but finally couldn't bear it any longer, broke down and ate everything in the chocolate shop.

She gasped as his tongue moved over her and began to tremble, which made him rock-hard.

"You're so beautiful, Tash," he said. "Tell me you want to feel me inside you." He'd thought the fact that she wasn't saying anything wouldn't bother him, but her silence was becoming noticeable. It was so different from last time. Then she'd told him he was the only man she'd ever loved, served her heart up on a platter. And what bothered him now was that he'd hurt her so badly afterward she wasn't going to give him even the slightest access to her heart. "I want to hear you say it," he added.

"No," she said.

He hadn't expected her to refuse. And it surprised him that she sounded so resolute.

He lifted his head. "Do you want me to stop?"

Her throat worked as she swallowed. "That's up to you."

He could tell she was enjoying herself. So what was going on? "Tash?" He felt his eyebrows jerk together. "What do you mean? Is this okay?"

"Of course," she replied. "I obviously want it, too."

He lowered his voice as he let his forehead rest against hers. "But you won't say you want me."

"No."

"Fine." He nipped at her neck and bit her hard enough that it would probably leave a mark. But, for some strange reason, he wanted to leave a mark, something he could see in the morning to remind him of this night. "I'll *make* you say it."

"I won't do it," she insisted.

"We'll see about that." Lifting her in his arms, he put her on the bed. "You say you don't need a man? That you prefer a sex toy?" He settled himself between her knees and started to kiss his way down her stomach. "We'll see if a sex toy can do this."

Natasha grabbed handfuls of the bedding on either side of her so that she wouldn't fist her hands in Mack's hair, the way she wanted to. She'd never had a man do what he was doing, not in quite the same way, and the pleasure was so intense she couldn't help writhing beneath him. She was addicted to him. Everything he did seemed to be better than anyone else.

But right when she was on the cusp of what promised to be the greatest climax of her life, he stopped and lifted his head. "Do you want more?" he asked.

He thought he had her. She was so close — of course she would want more. But she refused to tell him what he wanted to hear, wouldn't give in, even now.

"Come on," he said when she just glared at him. He attempted a grin. "All you have to do is make it a little more personal."

Squeezing her eyes closed so she would

no longer see his handsome face, she shook her head.

"Why not?" he asked.

She could understand his surprise. This wasn't how things had gone last time. She'd told him anything he'd wanted to hear and probably a lot more. But she couldn't do that again. She could no longer be that open, that trusting, that vulnerable. She had to remove the power he held over her, at last, so that she could take control of her own heart and life and come out victorious for a change. "You can stop . . . if you want," she managed to say above the pounding of her heart.

When he didn't respond, she opened her eyes and thought she saw some real disappointment on his face. But she knew he couldn't care that much. So she remained resolute and prepared herself, in case he pulled away.

Fortunately, he didn't. With a curse that suggested he couldn't stop even if he wanted to, he put on a condom and pressed inside her, and the pressure and friction of just a few thrusts was all it took to throw her over the edge. She gasped as her body began to spasm, and he surprised her again by pausing to kiss her forehead and each cheek throughout the climax.

"God, you're stubborn," he complained as he began to move again, but she just closed her eyes and tried to pretend he was someone else, anyone else, so that she wouldn't feel the tenderness that threatened to pry her fingers off the precipice of emotional safety to which she clung.

This was just physical, a mutual use, she reminded herself. She'd needed the release. It'd been a long time since she'd had sex with anyone, even Ace. But it didn't matter how good it felt. It was ultimately meaningless, even with Mack. He'd already proved that he looked at sex that way. She wasn't going to be the stupid fool her mother was by believing the way to a man's heart was through a strong climax no matter how many times her partner proved that his affection didn't last longer than it took to have one.

When he finished and she felt his body tense as he came, she couldn't help tightening her embrace, if only slightly. That she'd shared this intimate experience with him was somehow meaningful in spite of all her self-talk. He'd always meant the world to her. He probably always would. She just couldn't allow herself to think about it too much.

"Are you okay?" he asked as he rolled off.

"I'm fine." She wanted to reach out and pull him close to her, to hold him while they fell asleep, but she resisted the urge.

That would be crossing the line.

Mack woke up three hours later. Natasha was still sleeping, so he wasn't sure what had disturbed him until he heard someone in the bathroom.

Lucas was up.

Because he felt terrible that Ace had disappointed the kid, he slipped out of bed, pulled on his jeans and crept out of the bedroom so he wouldn't bother Natasha.

Sure enough, the light was on in the bathroom.

He rapped lightly on the door, which stood halfway open, and poked his head in.

"Mack!" Lucas cried, seeing him in the mirror.

Mack put a finger to his lips. "Shh. Your mom's sleeping," he said, but as soon as Lucas was finished, he swept the kid into his arms.

"I'm so glad you're here! Did you bring me something?" he asked.

"I did."

His eyes went wide. "What is it?"

"Do you want to see it now?"

He nodded vigorously.

"Okay, but it's still nighttime. Will you go back to bed afterward, if I show you?"

He nodded again, and Mack carried him down to the living room. "Wait right here," he said before going out to get the box from his truck.

"It's so big!" Lucas exclaimed as Mack carried it in. "What is it?"

Mack set it down so that Luke could see the picture on the front. "It's your own basketball hoop — and it's for indoors, so you can have it in your room."

"Yay! I don't have one of those!" He rushed over to take a closer look. "Will you get it out for me?"

"In the morning. I'll set it up for you, and we can play with it."

"Thanks, Mack!" he said and hugged Mack's leg.

"Sure thing, buddy." Mack lifted him up, and Lucas put his arms around Mack's neck instead.

They stood like that for several seconds with Mack holding him and rubbing his back. He was feeling . . . He hated to put a name to the emotions that were going through him. So he ultimately refused to think about it and carried the kid back to his room.

"Will you lie down with me for a few

minutes?" Lucas asked when Mack tucked him in.

Mack smoothed his dark curly hair off his forehead. "Sure."

As Mack lay next to him, Lucas showed him that he could spell some simple words. He did some math, too — addition or subtraction problems Mack gave him — before he finally drifted off to sleep, at which point Mack let himself out of the room.

Mack knew he should go to the couch to spend the rest of the night. Natasha had made it up for him. But the thought of her naked in bed was too much of a temptation.

After he let himself back into her room and peeled off his jeans, he climbed under the covers and drew her body up against his.

"What are you doing awake?" she murmured sleepily.

"Lucas got up."

"He okay?"

"Yeah. Don't worry. I got him back to bed." He kissed her, thinking that would be it, but she not only returned the kiss, she rolled to face him, and the next thing he knew, he was inside her again and her legs were locked around his hips.

271

FIFTEEN

When pounding on the front door woke Natasha, she realized two things at once: Mack never made it to the couch, and she had company.

With a yawn, she lifted her head. Mack seemed to be sleeping through the racket. She wasn't surprised. He'd always lived with at least one brother, was conditioned to noise. She remembered what the Amos household had been like when she lived there. It had been nothing short of chaotic.

She needed to answer the door before whoever it was woke Lucas. But as she got up and grabbed her robe, she caught sight of the clock on her makeshift nightstand. Surprisingly, it was after nine — not as early as she'd thought.

As soon as the time registered, she had little hope that Lucas would continue sleeping, and sure enough, she heard his voice the very next instant. "Mommy? Can I answer the door?"

Since she was coming, she gave him permission so that whoever it was wouldn't knock again. Maybe Mack, at least, could sleep a little longer.

But as she started down the stairs, she heard a voice that made her blood run cold. "Who owns the truck in the drive, Lucas?"

Ace's mother! "Peggy?" Natasha said before Lucas could answer, tying the belt on her robe as she hurried down the last few steps. "What are you doing here?"

"It's our weekend with Lucas, isn't it?" she asked as though Natasha should've been expecting them.

Spotting Mack's T-shirt on the floor, Natasha used one foot to kick it to the side before Peggy saw it and rested her hands on her son's small shoulders to keep him next to her. With her hair falling about her face in a tangled mess, she had no doubt it was apparent she'd just rolled out of bed, which would make her look lazy in comparison to her in-laws, who were always up at the crack of dawn. Not only had Peggy had her hair and nails done recently, she also had her makeup on and her clothing looked as though it'd just seen an iron, even though it was supposed to be casualwear.

Fortunately, Blake wasn't standing beside

273

her. He was still behind the steering wheel of their large Mercedes sedan. It sat at the curb in front of the house, and he kept lowering his head to look at them.

"It's not your weekend. It's Ace's weekend," Natasha clarified. "But he never came last night."

Peggy was tall, which made it easy for her to look down her nose at Natasha. "Because he couldn't," she said simply.

He couldn't? Or he *wouldn't*? Were Peggy and Blake, once again, stepping up to do something one of their sons should've done? From what Natasha had seen since marrying into the family, they filled in a lot. "But he didn't even return my text messages or my phone calls," she said. "He didn't tell me you were coming."

"Can you blame him for ignoring you?" she asked. "Can you imagine what he must be going through after learning you had an affair with your *stepbrother*?"

Natasha tried not to let a sudden burst of anger make her hands tighten on Lucas's shoulders. He didn't need to be privy to an argument. "First of all, I never had an affair with anyone," she said, keeping her tone as measured as possible. "I was loyal to your son throughout our marriage. And second, Mack isn't my stepbrother. He's not related to me in any way. We didn't even meet until he was twenty-five."

"His father married your mother, didn't he? What about that part? And the part where you were just sixteen when you went to live with him?"

"What, exactly, are you accusing me of?"

To her credit, Peggy's gaze dipped to Lucas, who was staring up at her, transfixed by the pique in her voice, which wasn't something he'd heard very often. Peggy went to great lengths to be the ideal mother to her boys and grandmother to Lucas, typically tried to pretend all was well even when it wasn't — like when Natasha's marriage to Ace began to crumble. "I'm saying we're extremely disappointed in what we've learned. That you could mislead us the way you have —"

"I never misled anyone," Natasha interrupted. "Ace and I weren't exclusive until several months into my pregnancy. If you'll remember, he was still seeing his ex-girlfriend, Rhonda Coates, until I was nearly four months along."

"Doesn't matter," she insisted. "You should've told him you'd been with someone else around the time Lucas was conceived."

In Natasha's mind, it hadn't mattered.

She and her baby came as a package. Any man she married would have to accept them that way. And Ace had been the one pursuing her. It wasn't as if she'd been trying to convince him to make that commitment. "He never asked. I admit the thought crossed my mind, but I figured some things were better off left unsaid for the sake of our marriage, which fell apart anyway, but —" Natasha heard movement behind her and whipped around. When she saw Mack coming down the stairs, wearing only his jeans and a steely look on his face, she felt her heart sink.

"Do you want a weekend with your grandson or not?" he asked Peggy. "Because if you do, I suggest you go back and wait in your car, and we'll bring him out when he's ready."

Peggy gaped at Mack, her mouth opening and closing twice with only a short puff of air coming out each time. It was obvious that he'd just climbed out of bed — and the way Peggy's gaze suddenly focused on Natasha's neck, she could guess it was Natasha's bed.

Natasha wished Mack would've let her handle this, but she knew none of the Amos brothers ever shied away from a fight. They always had each other's back — and, if she was around, they had hers, too.

"So you're together, then?" Peggy asked when she finally found her voice. "Or just screwing each other like you've probably been doing since you were sixteen?"

Natasha was stunned Peggy would say something like that in front of Lucas. So many retorts went through her mind, but Mack answered before she could. "It sounds like you might be a little too upset to take Lucas this weekend," he said. "Why don't we plan it for another time?"

"What'd you say?" Peggy asked, so shocked her voice squeaked on the last word.

"You heard me. I won't have you making derogatory comments about his mother. Let us know when you're willing to behave in an appropriate manner."

Natasha doubted Peggy had ever been criticized for being inappropriate. She considered herself a modern-day authority on good manners.

"Come on, Lucas," Peggy said. "Get your stuff. We're leaving."

Mack stepped around Lucas. "Maybe you didn't hear me."

"Natasha?" she said, ignoring him. "Don't tell me you're going to allow this."

"Of course I'm going to allow it," Natasha

said. "Because Mack's right. I haven't done anything wrong."

Lucas wrinkled his nose as he looked up at them. "So I'm staying here with you? Are we going to play with my new basketball hoop, Mack?"

"We sure are," Mack said, and Natasha sagged in relief when Lucas seemed perfectly content with that, because Peggy couldn't have hurried away from them any faster if they'd been holding a gun.

The closest coffee shop, a place called The Daily Grind, was busy, but Mack had said Natasha would feel better just getting out of the house, and he was right. He'd put the basketball hoop up in Lucas's room while she showered, and they'd all left together about an hour after their confrontation with Ace's mother.

"You okay?" Mack asked once the barista had called his name and he'd put Luke's hot chocolate in front of him before handing her the coffee she'd ordered.

"I'm fine." She slid her phone under the table so that he wouldn't see the text that had just come in from Ace, who'd said he couldn't believe she'd treat his mother so poorly and that she couldn't deny them the right to see Lucas — it was in the custody agreement. She wasn't going to mention it to Mack. She figured she'd deal with it later, didn't want this thing between her and her ex to turn into all-out war.

Mack seemed to measure her response. "Are you mad at me for getting involved when Ace's mother came this morning?"

She was more angry at herself for going back to bed with him than anything else. He was the only man she'd slept with, besides Ace, in eight years. Why had she done that? Why him? There were other men who would probably be interested, if she gave them a chance. Mr. Burns had been hemming and hawing the last time he'd stopped by her office as if he'd been looking for the opportunity to ask her out. Instead of making it easy for him, however, she'd complained to Aiyana that he was bothering her.

Once again, she tried telling herself that last night had been strictly physical, that it didn't matter, but it was difficult not to dwell on the way he'd touched her. He'd been tender, attentive, fully engaged. She couldn't ask for a better lover. Was that why she couldn't forget the taste of his kiss and the pressure of his arm looped casually and yet possessively around her while they slept?

She swallowed a sigh. She'd promised

herself she'd get over him, that she would no longer allow him to take ownership of her heart.

Sleeping with him definitely wasn't the best way to achieve that.

"Tash?" he said, still awaiting her response.

"I'm not mad," she said. "I'm just . . . worried." Fortunately, Lucas was treating the spoon from his hot chocolate like it was Superman, flying around the table, and wasn't paying attention to their conversation. But she lowered her voice anyway. "I don't want to deprive Lucas of his grandparents. They're so *normal.* The kind of grandparents I always wished I had."

He took a sip of his own coffee. "I understand that. But they were taking advantage of the fact that those familial relationships mean so much to you. Peggy was out of line, Tash."

She had been unkind, but . . . "They're hurt and shocked that Lucas might not be . . . you know."

"A blood relative?" he said, filling in with something Lucas wouldn't be likely to understand.

"Yes. You have to admit that what they've learned recently would be a nasty surprise. And the possibility that Lucas might not be . . . you know . . . is my fault, not theirs."

"Your fault *and* mine," he clarified. "But you and Ace weren't exclusive when we were together. You've already made that clear to them." He shoved his cup aside as he leaned closer. "Look, it's nice of you to view the situation from their perspective, but is it too much to ask that they show you the same courtesy? The past year has been hard on you. You don't need them making it worse."

Her phone vibrated, signaling another text, but she knew who it was probably from and didn't dare look at it. "I just wish the lab would hurry and post the results. Once we know for sure, everyone can figure out their place in Luke's life and . . . and we can all begin to heal." Then Mack could move on, if he wasn't Luke's father, and she wouldn't be faced with the constant temptation he posed.

"Can I have more whipped cream?" Lucas asked.

He hadn't drunk any of the hot chocolate. It probably wasn't the sweet kind he was used to. He just liked the whipped cream.

Natasha opened her mouth to say that it was too busy to approach the register again, but Mack took the cup and wove to the front.

As soon as he left, she braved a glance at her phone. But what Ace had written this time made her feel as though someone had just punched her in the stomach.

She was still gaping at his spiteful words when Mack returned.

"Something wrong?" Mack asked.

She quickly jammed her phone into the pocket of her shorts. He'd returned much quicker than she'd expected. "No, ah, no. Nothing," she mumbled, but she could barely think straight, let alone speak coherently.

"What is it?" he asked, clearly concerned.

She shook her head. "It's fine."

"I can tell something's wrong." He reached out for her phone. "Let me see what it is."

Lucas had whipped cream on his nose when he clued in to the conversation. "Are you okay, Mommy?"

She managed to wipe her son's face. "Of course, honey. Enjoy your hot chocolate. That was nice of Mack to go back and get more whipped cream."

"Natasha . . ." Mack said.

She couldn't meet his gaze for fear he'd read what she was feeling all too easily. "What?"

"Is it the Grays? What are they saying?"

Knowing he'd keep after her until she told him, she finally relinquished her phone.

When he read, his lips were barely moving. Lucas wouldn't be able to make out the words. But she'd already seen the text, so she knew what he was saying. You stupid whore. I don't know how I could ever have loved a baby killer like you.

Mack shot out of his chair. "I'm going to break this fool's jaw."

"What, Mack? What'd you say?" Lucas asked, obviously startled. "Whose jaw?"

Natasha wanted to reassure her son that Mack didn't mean what he'd said, but she was too busy trying to hold back tears. The death of Amelia Grossman had been the hardest thing she'd ever been through. She *still* agonized over it — blamed herself for not seeing that something was missing inside of Maxine that other people possessed. For holding back just because she didn't want to accuse someone who might be innocent, especially of such a heinous crime. For not catching those faint needle marks in that vial sooner.

If only she'd figured out what was going on before Maxine had been able to use that medicine to harm another child . . .

Ace knew every detail. He'd witnessed her pain. He was trying to hit her where it would hurt most.

And he'd succeeded.

"I — I need to use the restroom," she said and nearly bumped into a stranger in her hurry to escape the table. She couldn't let Mack show her any sympathy. It would only make it that much more difficult to maintain her composure.

It wasn't until she'd spent several minutes in a bathroom stall, trying to calm down, that she realized she'd left her phone with Mack.

Mack didn't think he'd ever been so enraged. He could tell Natasha had been deeply hurt that a man she'd once loved, and lived with for so long, could launch such a horrible accusation. He was tempted to follow her into the women's restroom to make sure she was okay, but he couldn't leave Lucas at the table alone. Using her phone, he texted Ace instead. This is Mack, he wrote. If you want to hurt somebody, why don't you try to hurt me?

He got no response, so he dialed Ace's number.

Ace didn't pick up; his voice mail did.

"Hey, it's me, you little coward," Mack said, leaving a message. "Don't try to call or text Natasha until we get the results of the DNA test. We'll let you know what they are. Then we'll decide who has the right to do what."

"Where's Mommy?" Lucas asked as Mack punched the end button with much more force than necessary.

"She went to the bathroom, remember?" Because he was so agitated, he led Lucas outside, where he paced back and forth in front of the coffee shop, trying to blow off steam.

Lucas shaded his eyes against the sun as he looked up. "Is Mommy crying?"

"No, I . . . I think she had something in her eye," Mack said.

"Oh." He took Mack's hand and walked back and forth with him, mimicking Mack's expression and movements. It was so darn cute, but Mack was too upset to enjoy it.

"Can we go home and play basketball now?" Lucas asked after they'd made several passes and Natasha still hadn't come out.

Mack checked her phone, hoping Ace would respond. But nothing came in. "Soon, little buddy."

When Natasha finally emerged, she was wearing a pair of sunglasses she must've had in her purse along with a fake smile. "All set?"

She started toward the car, as if that

would be that, but Mack caught her by the hand as she passed him. When his arms first went around her, she stiffened, as though she wouldn't allow it, but it didn't take more than a few seconds for her to crumble against his chest. "I did everything I could for Amelia," she said, starting to cry again. "But maybe he's right. How did I not see it sooner? How could I have ever let something like that happen?"

"You didn't let anything happen," he said. "No one would expect to run into someone like your former nurse. Ignore him. Don't give him the power to hurt you."

He sneaked a peek at her phone. Still nothing.

"What'd you say to him?" she asked when she pulled away.

"I told him we'll figure it all out after the results come in."

She nodded as if that was fair and wiped her cheeks as her gaze settled on her son. "I hope he's not a Gray," she said.

Mack unlocked her car. "So do I."

SIXTEEN

Natasha could hear Mack talking to Dylan,
even though she was upstairs in Lucas's
room, scraping the flowery wallpaper from
the old plaster walls. Luke had gone down
with Mack. He followed his new hero
everywhere. But they'd both been helping
her before Mack's phone rang — if you
could call what Lucas was doing "helping."
When Mack had suggested they spend the
rest of the weekend fixing up the place,
she'd suspected he was doing it to keep her
mind off Ace and his parents. That was nice
of him, but she couldn't imagine he'd want
to spend his time off doing physical labor,
so she'd tried to talk him out of it. She'd
told him she could manage it alone, or they
could do it next time he was in the area. He
was the one who'd insisted. He'd even
contacted the landlord to get the approval.

Finished with the small area she'd been
working on, she grabbed the spray bottle at

her feet so that she could squirt the next section with stripping solution. She was tired and wanted a break, but she needed to give the solution time to soak through the paper and dissolve the glue underneath.

"Is Kellan doing okay?" she heard Mack ask as she put the bottle back down and sank onto the plastic they'd used to cover the floor to rest. They'd pushed all the furniture into the center of the room, so she only had a four-foot swath, but it was enough.

"That's good . . ." he went on. "How's Cheyenne dealing with everything? . . . Any more word from the Rinehardts?" He laughed. "I bet. I'd feel the same . . . But did they agree to keep their mouths shut since that's what's in Kellan's best interest? . . . That's good, at least . . . No, I haven't talked to him recently. Have you? . . . That's all he said? . . . Aaron's so funny. That sounds like him . . . What? . . . No, Grady has no idea. Neither does Rod . . . I'm not going to tell them, and I highly doubt Aaron will ever say anything, either. If he's kept the secret this long, I'm sure you can trust him . . . I think things can just go on as they've always been, unless Kellan decides to open his mouth . . . Oh, I'm glad he feels that way . . . . Okay. I hope that's the case . . . On Tuesday, unless you need me sooner . . . All right . . . Natasha? She's great. So's Lucas. She's upstairs, but he's right here. Want to talk to him? . . . Hang on."

Natasha was lying on her back, staring up at the ceiling, as she heard Lucas get on the phone with Dylan. "I'm working," he announced. "Yeah. I'm a big boy now. I play basketball. And soccer. And baseball. Like Mack. You can? . . . You want to come over and play with my new basketball hoop? . . . Okay! You can sleep in my room . . . No, Mack doesn't sleep there. He sleeps with Mommy."

Natasha had let her eyes drift closed as she listened. But as soon as she heard her son say *that,* she sat up and clamped both hands over her mouth. Lucas had just told Dylan that she and Mack were sleeping together?

Mack took the phone immediately and said what had to have been an awkward goodbye while she held her breath, waiting to see what he'd do next.

"I sleep with Mommy?" he echoed, presumably questioning Lucas.

"Don't you?" her son said, sounding uncertain and completely clueless as to why that would be the wrong thing to say.

Mack laughed. "God, I can't get away with anything."

"Did I do something wrong?" Lucas asked.

"No. Don't worry," he replied and made Lucas squeal in delight just before Natasha heard them coming up the stairs.

When Mack appeared in the doorway, he had to duck to get into the room because he had Lucas on his shoulders.

She got to her feet and navigated around the furniture. "What'd Dylan have to say?"

"Are you asking the reason he called?" He cocked an eyebrow at her. "Or do you want to know how he reacted to what Luke just told him?"

"Both."

"So you heard that."

"Yeah."

"Dylan was returning my call. I wanted to make sure all was well with Kellan now that he's been home for a day or two."

Luke saw his basketball on the floor and wanted to get down, so Mack set him on the floor and he took his basketball and ran into the hall to throw it down the stairs.

"And? Is it?" Natasha asked.

"Sounds like it."

"How'd he react to what Lucas said?"

They could hear Lucas hurrying down the

stairs to retrieve his ball. Mack hitched a thumb in his direction. "That kid catches a lot more than we give him credit for. You know that? He's smart, like his mother." He grinned. "But it doesn't really matter. If he's mine, Dylan and my other brothers are bound to find out we've been together at least once, right?"

"So it wasn't too awkward?"

"I didn't say that," he said with a laugh.

"How'd Dylan react?"

"He didn't. Not yet."

"Meaning . . ."

"He'll say something eventually."

"What do you expect that to be?"

"A warning to be careful with your heart, since he cares about you, too."

"That's ridiculous!"

"What's ridiculous?"

She scowled at him. "You don't have to be careful with my heart. I'm not a child anymore. I can take care of myself. Besides, I know the difference between sex and love." There was no way she wanted Mack to feel trapped even if they did share a child, wouldn't marry him, even if he offered. She'd been through enough, wasn't about to spend the rest of her life wondering if he would've made a different decision had Lucas belonged to Ace.

When Mack didn't respond, she turned to see him watching her. "What's going on between us?" he asked. "Is it just sex?"

"That's right." She'd chased him for so long, she wasn't going to do it anymore. She'd be a fool to fall into that same old trap of wanting something she wasn't going to get. In his defense, losing his mother the way he did, and his father, had made him careful who he loved. It was possible he *couldn't* love her, or anyone else, because of his own fear of loss. So it was stupid to set them both up for more disappointment. She had her education, her career and her son. That was more than enough. She was going to rebuild her life such that she wasn't begging for *anyone's* love or attention.

"Friends with benefits — who might share a son," he said.

"We might share a son, but Luke and I don't come as a package deal," she clarified. "You're free to continue on as you've always been, regardless of what the DNA test says. It doesn't matter to me anymore."

The levity fled his face. "That sounds an awful lot like *I* don't matter to you anymore."

She thought of how desperately she'd loved him when they'd been living under the same roof. Back then she'd firmly believed he felt something, too. But now that she was an adult, she could see that she must've seemed like a mere child to him. And then, after Victorian Days, he'd shied away from the intensity, the commitment — and the stigma. "Not in that way. I'll always care about you, of course. I'm grateful for —"

"All that I've done," he broke in. "I know. You've told me that many times."

"It's true. But what I felt back then, when . . . when we first met, that's gone. And I'm sure you're glad. It must've been embarrassing *and* annoying with your brothers teasing you all the time," she said with a laugh.

He didn't speak right away. When he did, he said, "I didn't mind."

"Well, either way, you don't have to worry about that anymore, because it's all behind us."

"Okay," he said but acted so distant for the rest of the day that he barely spoke to her. He certainly didn't touch her.

After they finished stripping the rest of the wallpaper in Luke's room, cleaned up the mess so that Luke would still be able to sleep in there and had pizza for dinner, they were both exhausted. But she thought Mack might visit her bed. After all, she'd let him know, in no uncertain terms, that there were no strings attached. That had to be welcome news to a confirmed bachelor like him.

But after he read several books to Lucas and finally got him to sleep, he didn't cross the hall. He went downstairs to the couch.

Mack had been expecting to hear *something* from Dylan. He knew his brother wouldn't let what Lucas had disclosed slide. As the oldest in the family, he felt too responsible for Natasha. So Mack wasn't surprised to see a text from Dylan come in just after eleven.

Is it true about you and Tash?

Mack sighed as he read those words. Did he deny it?

No. He'd never lied to Dylan before. He wasn't going to start now. Yes.

Yes? No explanation? Can you call me so that we can talk about this?

I can't talk — not while I'm here.

You realize Natasha's fresh on the heels of a rough divorce.

I do.

And? Do you think sleeping with her is smart? She's been through a lot. I don't want to see her get hurt again.

I'm not going to hurt her.

How do you know? She's always had a thing for you. And I haven't seen you in ONE serious relationship.

That doesn't mean there won't be a first. Natasha had been the only woman who could ever really threaten his heart. Apparently, his brothers hadn't caught on as much as he'd thought. Or they'd just forgotten what it was really like in the old days.

Don't get involved with Natasha, Mack. Not right now. Give her some time to get over her losses.

That was probably good advice, but there were extenuating circumstances his brother didn't know about. This isn't the first time we've been together, Dyl.

His brother's answer came right away: Please don't tell me that sort of thing was going on when she was living at our place!

You mean when she was underage? Thanks for giving me absolutely no credit.

If I remember right, she was nineteen by the time she graduated. That's old enough.

She was still too young for me, and I knew it. Plus, the circumstances. You know what I mean. I didn't touch her back then.

When have you been together long enough since?

During Victorian Days seven years ago.

Mack could hear Natasha getting ready for bed upstairs, remembered her talking about keeping their relationship strictly physical. But he knew she wasn't built that way. What she'd witnessed growing up, what she'd lived through, had instilled a strong desire to be everything her mother was not. He believed it was that drive that had propelled her — a girl with no prospects — all the way through med school.

He felt his phone buzz: But Lucas is almost seven. Wasn't she married?

He decided to keep his answer simple. No. She'd been dating Ace for a couple of months, but they weren't exclusive when we ran into each other at the celebration.

So do you care about her?

Of course.

But not the way we care about her.

How was he supposed to answer that question? He'd always love the girl he knew, but he was just getting to know the woman she'd become. It's been years since she lived with us.

Exactly. So how the hell is it moving that fast?

Because of their history. He'd never had to fight his desire for any woman quite as hard as he'd had to fight his desire for Natasha. Which was why he was relieved that he'd managed to do the right thing back then. At least when he'd screwed up she'd been much older.

And now . . . it was a relief to finally give in, to enjoy everything he'd denied himself. But was it more than that?

He scratched his head, blew out a sigh

and quit trying to keep what was going on a damn secret. Dyl, Lucas might be mine.

WTF???? Are you kidding?

No. He was born nine months after Natasha and I were together.

And you've never said anything?

I wasn't sure, and I didn't want to cause problems in her marriage. But I'll find out soon. I took a paternity test last week.

When will you get the results?

Any day now.

Does Natasha's ex-husband know about this?

He does.

Why would you tell him before you have the results?

It's a long story.

He must be pissed.

He is.

So if Lucas is yours, are you going to assume the role of his father?

Of course. Why would I let anyone else take my place?

What about Ace?

It's sticky, I admit. But we'll figure it out. First we have to get the results. Then we'll take it from there.

And I thought *I* was caught up in some drama.

You were, no question. How's that going?

A lot better. It's taken some reassurance, but Kellan seems to be moving on as if it's no big deal. It's helped that Aaron hasn't contacted him since he came home. He's left it all to me, and I think that's made Kellan realize that nothing is going to change. I'm still his dad and Aaron is still just his uncle.

I'm glad.

So now you might have a son.

Looks that way.

And he's Natasha's.

Yeah.

Wow. Life can get complicated. Will you see him on weekends or what?

I'm trying not to get too far ahead of myself.

You must've thought about it.

I'll do whatever I have to do to see him.

Is that why you're suddenly getting serious about opening an Amos Auto Body in LA?

It's certainly a consideration.

Will you be relieved if he's not your son?

No, I'll be disappointed, he wrote and was surprised to realize just how much.

The next day, they decided to drive to the

beach. They had to wait for the walls to dry in Lucas's bedroom before they could paint, anyway. And although Natasha wanted to peel the wallpaper from the master, too, she preferred to finish one room before moving on to the next. She figured she'd do that herself, after Mack was gone. If she was going to be single for the rest of her life, she had to get used to being self-reliant.

Besides, she wanted Mack to have some fun during his time off. She knew how hard he worked when he was at home.

She made a picnic to take with them while he taught Lucas how to shoot a basketball. Then they got in their swimsuits, packed some sunblock and sand toys in addition to the food and set out for San Buenaventura State Beach, about twenty minutes away.

It was a hot day, one in which everything and everyone seemed to be moving sluggishly, and the horizon shimmered with heat waves.

Diving into the sea was refreshing. They played in the surf with Lucas for almost two hours before dropping onto their towels to watch him dig in the sand.

Hoping her skin would get a little color — she'd been indoors so much while going through school and starting her practice — Natasha covered her face with her beach hat while allowing the sun to dry her off and chase away the chill of the water. She didn't mean to fall asleep but quickly grew drowsy. She'd been up so many nights since everything had gone wrong at her medical practice. With someone she trusted as much as Mack there to help keep an eye on Lucas, this felt like the first time she'd been able to truly relax in a long while.

She woke up to Mack putting sunblock on her. "You're getting roasted," he explained.

The heat was making her brain sluggish, too. "I'm sorry. I didn't mean to drift off completely. Is Lucas okay?"

"He's fine. He can't go anywhere even if he wanted to. I've buried him in the sand."

"Look, Mommy," Lucas cried. "I can't move!"

She leaned up on an elbow and shaded her eyes. Lucas's head was the only part of him sticking out of the sand, but she could tell Mack hadn't buried him deep. He could get free if he really wanted to. "Did Mack do that? I might have to get him back for you."

A devilish glint entered Mack's eyes. "How do you propose to do that?"

She grinned. "I have my ways."

He nudged her to get her to roll over.

302

When she did, his large hands spread lotion on her neck, shoulders, lower back and legs, pausing almost imperceptibly as he pushed the cream up under the edge of her bikini bottoms. She knew he was trying to keep her from getting burned, but his touch made her catch her breath.

She could tell he wasn't unaffected himself.

"I'm getting the impression you regret sleeping on the couch last night," she joked.

He gave her a dirty look as she rolled back over to face him. "Really? You're going to make fun of me? Because I made that sacrifice for you."

She laughed. "For *me*!"

He tossed the bottle of sunblock on the towel as he sat down again. "Yes. I'm trying to protect our relationship."

She watched Lucas wiggle and break through the sand before chasing a seagull about ten feet away. "Oh, is *that* what you've been doing."

"One of us has to," he grumbled.

"Who says?"

He scowled at her. "What do you mean?"

She took the sunblock and got up on her knees to put some on his back. "We're both adults. Now that we've set some ground rules, I figure it's no big deal if we make love whenever we want."

"You're not worried about where that could lead?"

Once she was finished rubbing in the sunblock, she gripped his broad shoulders and leaned around to kiss him. She wanted to go on kissing him. That was definitely a warning sign. But she chose to ignore it. Maybe she was being reckless, but her life had been so difficult lately. Surely she could grab this little bit of happiness and enjoy Mack while he was around. "Not really. The way I see it, we could have the best of both worlds."

He'd returned her kiss, but she could tell he was wary of this new direction. "All the fun, none of the commitment," he said.

"Exactly. Lucas already told Dylan that we're sleeping together. So we don't have to worry about your brothers finding out."

His gaze moved down the length of her. He seemed tempted — but something was holding him back.

"What's wrong?" she asked. "Are you afraid this offer is too good to be true?"

"I'm afraid we'll wind up enemies. That's what I'm afraid of."

"How? As long as we're up-front, honest and kind, we should be fine. We truly care about each other. We can protect that."

"Those are just words, Tash. A sexual relationship always comes with risks."

"But we've slept together before."

"Not regularly. You've seen how Ace is behaving."

"Ace and I were married."

"Doesn't matter. He's hurt and he's jealous. That's how people act when they feel those things."

"You would never behave like that."

"And yet none of the women I've slept with in the past are part of my life now. That tells you something, doesn't it? Those kinds of relationships are hard to maintain. They either go somewhere — or they fizzle out. Someone always gets hurt."

"Well, we know it won't be *you*," she said with a laugh.

"That's the problem," he said. "I definitely don't want it to be you."

She knew he was protective of her. He'd proved that time and again. But was he being completely honest with himself? There'd been times when she could swear he'd wanted more from her, too. The way he made love to her was too intense for there not to be some level of emotion.

Maybe she wasn't the only one running scared.

She got up and started unloading the

basket, so they could eat. "Fine. If you're not interested, there are other men out there." With that, she gave such a bright smile to two guys who were striding past that one bumped into the other as he did a double take.

"Be careful, Natasha," Mack growled.

Seeing Mack, and the dark scowl on his face, they hurried on, but she'd made her point.

"*What?*" she said, widening her eyes in mock innocence.

He glowered at her. "You're playing with fire."

Lucas was exhausted after spending most of the day at the beach. He was taking a nap, so the house was quiet, except for the shower. Mack could hear the water running, but he was trying to ignore it.

He'd decided not to let his relationship with Natasha get out of control. That was why he'd slept on the couch last night. They still had so much to consider. The DNA test that had yet to reveal Lucas's biological father. Whether Mack would be able to find the right place to open an Amos Auto Body location and move closer. How, if they started seeing each other, they'd break the news to their families. Mack had told Dylan, but he knew Dylan wouldn't say anything to anyone else, and when the others eventually found out, they wouldn't be happy about this coming back up. They'd seen him go from woman to woman for so long they'd be too worried about how it would end, because this would affect someone they knew and loved, too.

For the first time ever, he'd be breaking code — going against what everyone felt was best for the family.

Then there was everything Natasha had experienced the past couple of years. He didn't think getting together was a risk they should take right now. She was so hurt and angry. When she talked about their attraction being only physical, there were moments when he believed she wouldn't think twice about hurting him in return — no matter how many times he apologized for the past.

But the sound of that shower, knowing she was in there naked, was driving him mad. The tension between them had been so palpable on the ride home that they'd barely spoken. After the way she'd challenged him on the beach — not to mention seeing her in that bikini all day — he could scarcely think of anything except getting his hands on her again. It didn't help that his mind kept returning to that moment when she'd leaned around and kissed him as though it didn't matter who saw, even Lucas. Because of the way they'd met, he'd always felt as though he had to keep his desire for her a secret. It was something he had to control, something he had to deny, something he'd always felt a little ashamed of, since he knew it wasn't a good thing for either one of them — at least, it hadn't been in the past. So to be that open, to kiss right on the beach in front of other people, was a heady experience. It made him feel as though she belonged to him after all — something he'd always felt deep down anyway.

So was he really going to miss this?

No.

When he opened the bathroom door, he wasn't sure she could hear him above the water. But she definitely knew he was there when he slid the curtain back. From the second she saw him, she watched him warily as the water continued to run down her body in rivulets.

"Are you still trying to decide whether you want to be in here?" she asked.

"No," he said and stepped in with her, clothes and all.

SEVENTEEN

Natasha had goaded Mack into continuing the physical aspect of their relationship. If she regretted this later, it would be her own fault. But right now, she didn't care about later.

If the DNA test results came back on Monday, and it turned out that Ace was Lucas's father, at least she'd have this weekend with Mack before his role in her life dwindled back down to an occasional text. This weekend might be all she ever had; she might as well take what she could get.

He stripped off his swim trunks. The way his T-shirt, now soaking wet, stuck to his skin made it slightly more difficult. But as soon as his clothes lay in a heap at their feet, they were forgotten as he brought her naked body against his.

"What is it about you?" he said, clearly not happy that he couldn't resist her.

"I could say the same about you," she

replied defiantly.

His hands curled around her ass, pressing her more tightly against his erection, and his mouth met hers. They kissed so deeply they were both breathless by the time he lifted his head. "No one kisses like you do," he said. "No one feels like you do. No one drives me half as crazy as you do."

Natasha discounted his words in the heat of the moment. He'd made similar declarations when they'd been together during Victorian Days. Still, it felt good to hear those things. He could no longer refuse her, and that provided some small satisfaction. After all the years of tug-of-war between them, his resistance was finally beginning to fray.

"Glad I can return the favor," she said. "So . . . are we going to talk all day? Or are you going to give me what you've got?"

She felt the muscles in his shoulders bunch beneath her hands as he lifted her against the shower wall. "Is this what you want?" he asked as he pressed inside her.

It was exactly what she wanted, but she said, "I guess it'll do."

They weren't being nearly as nice to each other as they'd always been before. She got the impression he was angry and frustrated — with himself, if not with her — because he took her hard and fast, grunting with each powerful thrust.

Since she was angry and frustrated herself, she welcomed the raw physicality, as well as the intense emotions that seemed to be driving him. She was feeling some pretty intense emotions, too. She bit his shoulder and then his lower lip just hard enough to hurt, and he swore, but he didn't withdraw. He seemed as willing to battle this out as she was.

She'd never made love in such a hungry, desperate fashion — not with him or Ace — but the fact that Mack was a little out of control made it that much more exciting. It probably wouldn't have been if she trusted him any less, but she knew he'd never really hurt her, just as he knew she'd never really hurt him. On some level, they loved each other. They both knew that. It was just difficult to define how.

She came so quickly it surprised her, especially because her climax was as exaggerated as everything else. When she cried out, startled by the strength of it, he covered her mouth with his as though he'd swallow the sound, take everything she had to give, even that.

She could tell he was close to climax himself. But she couldn't let him come. He wasn't wearing a condom.

When she pushed him away, his chest rose and fell rapidly as he tried to catch his breath. She got the impression he wouldn't have been able to withdraw in time, but he didn't complain about her making him stop at the worst possible moment. Neither did he try to touch her again. He just stared at her with the most troubled expression she'd ever seen in his eyes.

She got the impression she'd finally cracked through his defenses — was finally getting a glimpse of why he refused to let her get too close to him. It wasn't an issue of love; it was an issue of trust. The Amoses didn't trust easily. And Mack, who'd lost his mother at such a vulnerable age, was determined not to suffer like that ever again. He was afraid of what she'd have the power to do if he ever really let her inside his head and his heart.

She decided then that she was going to win this war between them if it was the last thing she did.

Pushing him up against the tile, she licked the water running down his neck, his chest, his torso and his hip as she moved lower — expressing everything she felt but couldn't say using action — and heard him moan as she sank to her knees and took him in her mouth.

Natasha was making dinner when Mack came up behind her. He didn't touch her. They were trying not to be too physical in front of Lucas. But she could tell that he wanted to. Their experience in the shower had changed him. He'd quit holding back. Although Lucas had gotten up from his nap almost as soon as they'd turned off the water, and she'd slipped out of the bathroom as though she'd been in there alone and distracted her son with a snack so that Mack could get out without being seen, she knew from now on that she and Mack would probably have sex whenever they had the opportunity. They wouldn't be able to stop themselves. They were becoming more and more familiar with each other in that way, more and more conditioned to the fulfillment that intimacy provided.

She was pretty sure this change — the snapped restraint — was what Mack had been warning her about on the beach. He'd been trying to tell her that if they didn't stop letting themselves cross that line, they soon wouldn't be able to keep from crossing it, and if an intimate relationship didn't work out for them in the end, they might later regret the loss of the friendship and support they'd always given each other before.

And he could be right. But how did she turn away what she'd always wanted, even if she didn't know if it would last?

"What time is Lucas going to bed?" he asked.

She knew why he wanted to know. The shower had been an incredible encounter, but it hadn't lasted nearly long enough. He wanted more, and she was just as anxious for night to come. "He doesn't normally take a nap — not anymore — so I don't expect him to go to bed too early."

"Damn."

She chuckled as Lucas, who was pretending to ride a horse, galloped up the stairs into his room. "I take it you're not sleeping on the couch tonight," she murmured, putting her spatula on the counter as she turned to face him.

His gaze lowered over her. He was undressing her with his eyes — didn't even bother to hide it. "I'm mad that I slept there last night."

Rising up on tiptoe, she licked his bottom lip. "Yet you think what we're doing is a mistake."

His hands went around her waist as

314

though he'd draw her back to him, but Lucas threw the basketball down and came after it, and Mack let go of her. "Even if it is, that ship has sailed."

"Want to play with me, Mack?" Lucas asked, once he'd reclaimed his basketball.

"Sure, buddy," Mack told him. "In a minute." He nudged her. "Where's your phone?"

She reclaimed her spatula. "I don't know. It's around here somewhere. Why?"

"I want to see if Ace has had anything to say. You haven't heard from him, have you?"

"I haven't checked since we've been home." She went back to stirring the ground beef she was browning for tacos. "But I hope I haven't heard from him. I hope I haven't heard from his parents, either. Although I admit their silence is a little ominous. What if they're getting a lawyer?"

"It's the weekend."

"That doesn't matter. His parents are very well-connected. They probably have half a dozen attorney friends they could call."

"Still, I doubt they'd do that. They're probably letting Ace take the lead — at least, that's what they should do. After all, he's not a child. And I'm assuming they're all smart enough to know that they should wait until the results are in before they make those kinds of decisions."

"Maybe you're right. Ace only picks fights he knows he can win, so he might be holding off."

"Is that why he hasn't responded to my messages?"

"I wouldn't be surprised." She doubted Ace would ever willingly tangle with Mack. She'd said too much about Mack and his brothers through the years. He knew they weren't likely to put up with much.

While looking for her phone, Mack came close enough to her to lower his voice. "Did you love him, Tash?"

She knew he was talking about Ace, so she didn't ask him to clarify. "I tried," she replied.

"But . . ."

She'd loved Mack instead. She'd always loved Mack, and all the self-talk in the world couldn't seem to change that. "I did my best. It just . . . didn't work."

"There it is."

She turned to see him pointing at her phone on the far counter. "Anything?" she asked when he walked over to pick it up.

"Nope."

"Good."

"You think he'll give us trouble even if —" he jerked his head at Lucas "— you know . . . he technically shouldn't? After all, he raised him for six years. I doubt *I* could walk away at that point, regardless of the DNA results."

"I've been wondering that myself."

"What's your guess?"

"You love more fiercely than he does." Which was why Mack rarely allowed someone into his inner circle. He was careful about the people he loved because he stood by them through thick and thin. All the Amos brothers were like that. When they fell, they fell hard.

Ace, on the other hand, seemed to slip in and out of love quite easily. And no one could rely on him, even his parents. From what Natasha had seen while they were married, he just manipulated them to get whatever he wanted. "You'd hang on. But I'm not convinced he will. Lately, he hasn't shown a great deal of interest in being a father — although it could be that he's just hoping, if I have to babysit all the time, I won't be able to go out and meet someone else."

Mack put down her phone, took the ball from Lucas and showed him, once again, how to dribble. "You told me *he* asked for the divorce."

"He did. But I think it surprised him

when I agreed."

"He thought you'd fight him?"

"He threatened divorce whenever he couldn't get his way. He knew how badly I wanted our marriage to succeed, so he used its potential failure as a weapon against me. It usually worked. But the last time he tried that trick, I threw up my hands and said, 'Do it.' "

"How'd he respond?" Mack asked.

"He tried to convince me that he didn't really want out after all. But by then I was done. Whatever we'd had was gone. I could no longer continue to fight for something that wasn't fulfilling to begin with."

Mack's own phone went off. He pulled it from his pocket while Natasha began to stuff the tortillas with meat. "This is interesting," he said.

"What is it?" she asked.

He walked over to show her. "Grady just sent me this picture."

She frowned as she looked down at the screen. Grady had stumbled upon their father making out with her mother at the local bar and taken a short video of them, which he was apparently sending to a group text that went to all five Amos brothers, along with the message, Unbelievable . . .

A message from Rod came in while she

was looking at it. Oh God. That's trouble.

Natasha sighed. She always felt awkward when her mother did something embarrassing. She could see why Mack and his brothers weren't excited about J.T. and Anya getting back together; Anya had given them plenty of reason to be leery of her. But even after all the years she'd been dealing with her mother, Natasha felt torn. Anya was, after all, her only blood relative — at least, that she had any contact with — and it was almost impossible to root out the loyalty that inspired. "Maybe it'll work this time," she said. "There must be some reason they keep getting back together."

Another text — this one from Dylan — popped onto Mack's screen. The timing of it, and what he'd written, made it seem as if he was responding specifically to what she'd just said. Can anyone say codependent?

At least they were as hard on their no-good father as they were her no-good mother.

"Their relationship is a drug- and alcohol-fueled frenzy," Mack said. "Maybe it's been too long since you've witnessed one of their fights."

"They got along surprisingly well the first few years, when I was around. But they were still living with you when I went away to

319

college, and that's when it all went bad, so I imagine you saw a lot more than I did."

He whistled. "They got vicious with each other."

"I'm sorry that she won't move on. I've told her and told her not to lean on you guys, but now that *I* don't have anything to give her, she's probably circling back, looking for another place to get what she needs —"

"Hey." He caught her by the arm. "She's responsible for what she does, not you."

She bit her lip as she tried to examine her feelings. "My head tells me that, but —" she groaned "— it's always been so humiliating being her daughter." Especially when it came to the Amos brothers, because Natasha cared so much about them and their opinion, and her parasitic mother had taken advantage of them for so long.

"I know," he said and kissed her temple. "But it's no reflection on you. Look at what you've accomplished. And you did it even though you didn't have the support most kids do. You're a doctor, Tash. A freakin' *doctor!* You made it through a decade of incredibly difficult challenges to achieve your dream. And you did it on your own."

"Not on my own," she argued. "You and your brothers helped give me a start when

320

you paid for some of my living expenses that first year at college, not to mention my plane fare to get there in the first place. You even bought me some decent clothes. I want you to know how much I appreciate it, and that I'm sorry I screwed it all up by hiring a psychopath for a nurse —"

He shot her a quelling look. "Let's not talk about that murderous bitch anymore."

"Bitch? Did you say *bitch,* Mack?" Lucas asked.

He ruffled her son's hair. "I said *witch.* Like the kind that casts spells." He lifted his gaze back to her. "Anyway, what that nurse did does not take away from what you've accomplished. I'm *so* proud of you."

She didn't know how to react when he said stuff like that. While it was flattering, it sounded a little too much like what a brother might say to a sister, and she'd always been terrified that Mack would classify her, once and for all, as "family," even though she'd never felt anything remotely platonic where he was concerned. With the way they'd met and her age at the time, it would be easy for him to consider her out of bounds. No doubt his brothers wished he would.

But no matter what happened, they always

came back together.

They just couldn't seem to stay that way.

Aiyana Buchanon called Natasha after dinner to talk about a boy they had coming to the school this week. From what Mack could tell overhearing Natasha's side of the conversation, the child had been abused or something, so to give Natasha the chance to speak freely, he'd volunteered to put Luke to bed. What she was dealing with sounded important. Although he could hear the drone of her voice as she sat out on the porch steps, he couldn't make out the individual words, and for that he was glad. As a pediatrician, especially one working for the kind of troubled kids who attended this school, Natasha would have to deal with such things. He knew, with her inherent kindness, she'd be good at it. But since there wasn't anything he could do to contribute to the situation, he preferred not knowing the dirty details. Hearing about it would just make him mad.

"Mack?" Lucas said as he cuddled up close.

"What, buddy?"

"Are you my friend?"

Mack couldn't help smiling at how adorable his child was — if Luke was his child.

322

He'd been trying not to assume too much, but he was beginning to feel attached. "Of course I am."

"Will you *always* be my friend?"

Mack cleared his throat. They might soon learn that they were a lot more than friends. "I hope so."

Apparently, Lucas wasn't satisfied to only lie next to Mack. He kept wiggling, trying to get more comfortable, and after he finished moving around, he was halfway on top of Mack. "Can we play basketball again tomorrow?"

"Sure."

"In the morning? When I wake up?"

"Probably tomorrow night, after we all get home."

"Home from where?"

"Your mother has to work, so you'll be at day care."

"But I don't want to go to day care!" he protested. "I want to stay with you!"

"I won't be here, bud. I have to go to LA."

"For what?"

"To meet a commercial real estate agent."

"What for?"

"She's going to help me find something I'm looking for."

"What are you looking for?"

He laughed. The questions just kept coming. "A place to run my business."

"What's a business?"

"I fix cars that have been wrecked or damaged."

"Oh," he said, as if he finally understood, even though Mack doubted he did.

"Mack?" Lucas said again.

"What?"

"Can I go with you?"

Mack supposed it probably wouldn't be a big deal if Lucas came along. The agent he was meeting would make a sizable commission if she showed Mack a location that he ended up leasing, so he couldn't imagine she wouldn't be accommodating. "Maybe."

"Does maybe mean yes?" he asked.

Laughing again, Mack said, "That's an age-old debate among men. As one dude speaking to another, I'd advise you to assume it means no."

"What'd you say, Mack?"

"Never mind," he said.

"So . . . can I go with you?"

"You're going to make a very good salesman, you know that?"

"What's a salesman?"

"If I can take you with me tomorrow, you'll meet one."

"Okay."

Lucas fell silent. Mack thought he might

finally be going to sleep, but a few seconds later, he lifted his head and got very close to Mack's face. "I love you, Mack," he whispered, spontaneously.

Mack had no defense against the sweetness of this declaration. He'd done everything possible to protect his heart from Natasha. But he realized in that moment that he was completely vulnerable to Luke, because he'd fallen in love, too. Mack wanted to protect him against anything and anyone who would ever hurt him, and that instinct was so strong it surprised him.

It also frightened him. Obviously, he was breaking his own cardinal rule and starting to care too much.

After that, Lucas continued to talk, speaking again and again just when Mack thought he might be drifting off. It took a while, but once he did fall asleep, the one thing that kept going through Mack's mind was Lucas's young voice piping up in the dark room: "I love you, Mack."

Although fate hadn't been kind to Mack during his own childhood, if it had conspired to bring him the chance to know he was Luke's father while there was still time to be involved in his young life, he'd consider himself far luckier than most. If Natasha had stayed with Ace, it could easily have gone a different way. It wasn't as if Mack would ever have done anything to mess up her marriage. He'd assumed she was happy.

The DNA test results should be up tomorrow.

Briefly, he thought of how he'd feel if he didn't get the answer he was hoping for, but, shoving that from his mind, he slipped out of bed, pulled the covers up and kissed Lucas on the temple.

EIGHTEEN

When Natasha woke up, the sun was hitting the sheet she'd tacked over the window, which looked out on an alley below and the dumpsters from the commercial businesses on either side of her, but there was no noise. It was early yet. Although she could've used more sleep, she was glad to have a few minutes while Mack was still passed out to enjoy lying on his chest. Last night they'd made love again, much more gently and slowly than they had in the shower. It was particularly memorable because it was somehow different from any of the times before — there was less lust and more of something else. But she was afraid to try to define what that "something else" was for fear she'd imbue it with too much meaning.

Assuming Mack felt more than he did was what had always gotten her in trouble.

Forcing her mind away from the memory of last night, she reminded herself, once again, to take what they were doing in stride. She'd agreed to keep it physical, and she was going to stand by her word. Something was better than nothing, especially now, when she was so broken and lost and lonely. Maybe he'd stick around long enough that she could get back on her feet.

What would he do if it turned out that Lucas belonged to Ace? Would he decide there was no reason to move to LA? Stop visiting? Would even the physical part of their relationship be over? Six hours was a long time to drive for sex when he could so easily find a woman in Whiskey Creek or nearby Sacramento. It wasn't as if he'd ever had any trouble getting laid.

"Did I miss the alarm?" he mumbled, one arm curving to hold her more tightly against him.

Fear of what this day would hold made her so nervous she wouldn't be able to eat, not until the butterflies in her stomach settled down. Maybe Mack had been able to feel her fear and dread, and that was what woke him, because she'd been so careful not to move. "No. It hasn't gone off yet."

He scrubbed his free hand over his face. "Then what are you doing up?"

"Thinking."

"About . . ."

"Bella."

He covered a yawn. "Who's Bella?"

"That woman you brought home one night — just before I left for college."

She felt him tense. "I don't remember her," he said. Then, more gruffly, "Why are you thinking about her, anyway?"

Because it was a good reminder, a way to keep what was happening between them now in perspective. "I feel sort of bad for what I did to you both back then, and I don't think I've ever apologized."

He hesitated as if he didn't really want to go down this path but wound up saying, "What you did to us?"

"You probably never realized it, but I sat outside your bedroom door for probably an hour, listening to every sigh and moan, and cried."

"I *didn't* know that," he said softly. "I'm sorry."

"Don't apologize. I had no business invading your privacy like that. I'm embarrassed about it now. Here I was, this girl who wouldn't even have had a home without you, thinking you owed me some kind of fidelity."

"You never had the kind of love you needed."

"You offered me love. I just wanted a different kind." After all, he was the one who'd helped her with her homework, taught her how to play chess when the catty girls at school were excluding her, tried to teach her how to cook, even though he was much better at grilling, and drove her to dance lessons for the whole of one year. He was also the one who'd given her his computer for college and helped pay for her flight when she left. Her life would've gone so differently without him. She certainly would never have become a doctor. "Anyway, poor Bella. The next morning, she tried to shake my hand when you both came up for breakfast, and I told her, 'I'm your worst nightmare. You touch me, you'll draw back a stub.' Remember that?"

She thought he'd laugh with her, but he didn't. "I remember how bad your language was. That's what I remember."

"Yeah. But I didn't care. I was aching to flip off the world."

"You were angry. We were all familiar with that feeling."

"That's no excuse," she said. "Because of me, Bella stormed out. I'm sorry if I messed that up for you."

He grimaced. "I didn't even know her. I was drunk when I brought her home."

"And you were making a statement, trying to get me to back off. I just . . . wouldn't let go." She hadn't been able to figure out *how* to let go. But she was older and wiser now. She knew that marriage wasn't all it was cracked up to be — just a long series of compromises and struggles as two people attempted to get along, to get by, to overlook, to forgive and to ignore pet peeves and other irritations. She was much better off on her own. By keeping it light and easy, enjoying each other when they were both interested and moving on when that was no longer the case, she'd never have to worry about going through another divorce. And she'd be less likely to expect anything from Mack that could result in disappointment — whether he was Lucas's father or not.

"We have a lot of history together," he said.

"I can't believe you put up with me. She might've been 'the one' if I hadn't screwed it up for you. I did so many crazy things. Maybe you won't remember this, either, but not too long before that, I showed up in your bedroom late one night. You tried to tell me to leave, but —"

"You whipped off the T-shirt you typically wore to bed — one of my T-shirts — and stood there, almost completely naked."

"I thought I could tempt you beyond your

ability to resist, I guess." She smacked her forehead. "So dumb! Instead of being tempted, you scrambled out of bed to pick up that shirt and make me put it back on." She made a sound of disgust. "God, I was an idiot."

"Do we have to talk about these things?" he asked.

"You don't want to?"

"No. I feel terrible that I hurt you. I just . . . I couldn't have felt good about myself if I'd taken what you were offering. I hope you know that. You were the first of any of us to get the grades you got and have the kind of opportunities that would afford. I knew you could be anything, and I wanted you to have the chance to go out and experience life, see the world."

"And yet . . . here I am, divorced, bankrupt and without my practice."

"Through no fault of your own. Everyone faces setbacks. What you're going through now — it's just temporary."

"I hope so." The alarm went off, and she leaned across him to turn it off. "I'd better get up. New Horizons has that new student coming in today." She'd told him about Aiyana's call last night.

"Troy Mason?"

"Yeah. I'm anxious to meet him and to

332

make sure his injuries have healed."

She started to slip away from him, but he caught her arm. "Would you mind if I took Lucas with me today?"

"To LA?"

"Yeah. He really doesn't want to go to day care."

"It's not easy to work with a six-year-old in tow, Mack."

"I won't be working, just driving around to see various potential locations for the new shop. I can manage."

Shoving her tangled hair out of her face, she drew a deep breath. "Should we check the lab website?"

"My phone's in the other room," he said immediately. "I'll do it later."

"We can use my phone." She gestured at the box that doubled as a nightstand, but he didn't reach for it.

"Can we wait until after we get home tonight?"

He was nervous, too. She could tell.

Maybe he was right. Maybe it would be smarter not to look until they had more time to deal with the results, just in case. She didn't want to start the day off with bad news any more than he did. She was still trying to get used to her new job — and the fact that she was now sleeping with

333

Mack on a regular basis, at least for however long he'd be around. "Okay."

"So you don't mind if I take Luke with me today?" he asked as she got up and put on her robe so that she could go into the bathroom and get showered.

She wouldn't let her own mother take Luke, but she trusted Mack much more than she did Anya. "He'd love that."

As if on cue, Lucas opened the door. "I'm ready to go, Mack," he said and had his school backpack on even though he was still in his pajamas.

After Natasha left for work, Mack sat down with Lucas, who was still finishing his breakfast.

"Aren't you going to eat, Mack?" Luke asked, eyeing his plate.

Mack had made egg burritos while Natasha got ready so that she'd have something besides coffee for breakfast, but his own burrito sat untouched. He was too uptight to be hungry.

"In a minute." His pulse raced as he got out his phone and navigated to the lab's website. He'd told Natasha they'd check the results later. He'd meant it at the time and felt guilty for going ahead without her, but he *couldn't* wait. He had to find out before she did so that he'd have a chance to react to the news — whatever it was — on his own.

"What are you doing, Mack?" Lucas asked, disappointed that he couldn't get more of Mack's attention. "Are you playing a game?"

Mack reached over to wipe the refried beans from Lucas's chin. *I'm trying to find out if I'm your father,* he thought. But all he said was "No, I'm not playing a game. I'm checking something. Give me a minute, okay?"

Once the website came up, Mack looked over at Lucas, who stared right back at him, for several seconds. Then he took a deep breath and logged in.

The results were there, along with a rather lengthy explanation on how to interpret them.

Mack skimmed the fine print. If what he saw wasn't clear, he could go back and read all that. For now, he couldn't wait to get to the bottom line, which he found on a locus/allele sizes chart that had "Child" at the top of one column, "Mother" at the top of a second column and "alleged FATHER" at the top of a third. There were a lot of numbers under each heading that didn't mean anything to him. But below all that, it said "Interpretation" and listed the combined paternity index as zero.

He blinked. *Zero?* As in there was zero chance that he wasn't Luke's father? Or zero chance that he was?

He didn't have to search very far for clarification. The conclusion was right below the paternity index, and six words immediately jumped out at him: ". . . is excluded as the biological father."

Excluded. He let his phone drop to the table with a clunk and rocked back.

"You dropped your phone," Lucas said.

Mack couldn't even respond.

"Is something wrong?" the boy asked.

"No," he managed to say. But that wasn't true. Everything was wrong.

Lucas belonged to Ace.

Natasha had come into the break room to get some more coffee but left her empty cup sitting on the counter while she stared at her phone. She was contemplating logging into the lab's website. She'd told Mack she'd wait to get the results with him tonight, and she wanted to keep her word. It had been a busy morning, which made it easier to put the paternity test out of her mind. But the afternoon had been much slower, and she was getting tired of waiting and wondering and worrying.

If she peeked, would there be something to indicate that someone had already logged onto the website? And even if there wasn't, would she be able to act sufficiently surprised later on?

"Hello, how are you today?"

She turned to see Aiyana walk into the room. "I'm doing good. You?"

"Better now that Troy Mason is here, safe and in good hands. How'd his exam go?"

"I did a few X-rays on the arm he said was injured by his stepfather. It looks as though his most recent break was a scaphoid here." She indicated the bone in her wrist that she was talking about. "It's a break that rarely heals without surgery. But it looks as though he got lucky. His wrist healed fine. And I couldn't find any other broken bones or injuries — not recent ones that need to be treated."

"That's a relief." Aiyana washed her hands in the sink. "Thanks for checking him out."

"No problem." Natasha filled her cup and added a splash of cream. "I was worried about him, too. A broken bone that doesn't receive the proper treatment can result in an infection or even permanent deformity, so I was anxious to get a peek at it."

Aiyana checked the doorway as though

she wanted to be sure they weren't about to be interrupted. "I've been thinking about you all weekend. How'd the DNA test turn out?"

"I don't know yet."

"The wait must be nerve-racking."

Natasha glanced at the clock. It was nearly two. "It shouldn't be much longer."

Aiyana gave her arm a gentle squeeze. "Don't look so worried. It'll be okay."

Natasha feigned a smile. "Of course," she said, as though she believed that to be true, and was about to follow Aiyana out of the room when her phone went off.

It was Ace. No doubt he wanted to know what they'd found.

In an attempt to be as pleasant as possible, in hopes that she could get them back on the right track of at least treating each other more civilly, she decided to answer. "Hello?"

"Is he mine?" he asked without preamble.

A teacher came into the break room. Hoping for more privacy, she lowered her voice and went back to her office. "I don't know yet."

"From everything I've read on the internet, it doesn't take that long to get the results, Tasha."

Relieved to find that she didn't have any

students waiting for her, she closed the door after she went inside. "They might be posted," she admitted. "I've just . . . I've been too busy to check."

"Well, I'm tired of waiting. Can't you at least do me the courtesy of taking five seconds to pull up the website?"

This meant a lot to him, too. For more than six years, he'd believed Lucas was his. She felt bad for what he must be going through and agreed that it wasn't fair to draw it out any longer. "I'll log in and call you right back."

He hung up without so much as a thank-you, but she ignored that and called Mack. "Hey."

"How's it going?" he asked.

"Good. Troy Mason is going to be fine. I gave him a thorough examination this morning, and he has no permanent injuries."

"I'm happy to hear that."

"Did you and Lucas find a location for the shop?"

"Not yet. The Realtor had a conflict and had to reschedule."

"So what have you been doing?"

"We've been painting. Luke's room is done. Looks great."

"That's nice. But I feel bad that I wasn't

there to help."

"Don't. It was easy. When will you get off?"

"In an hour and a half. But . . . Ace just called." She was afraid if she didn't hurry and get to the point they'd be interrupted.

"He's looking for the results," Mack guessed.

"Do you think we should go ahead and see if they've been posted?"

He didn't answer right away.

"Mack?"

"I already did, Tash," he said. "This morning."

"But . . . you made it sound as though we'd do it together."

"I know. I'm sorry. I did that because . . . well, because I needed you to hold off and give me the chance to look first — to react to the news on my own."

She supposed she could understand that. She was used to the idea of having a child. This was new to him, could change his life drastically. But . . . "Why didn't you call me once you knew?"

"I figured we'd talk about it tonight."

If it had been what they were hoping for, Mack would've let her know. Why would he have had to wait to tell her that Luke was his? "He belongs to Ace," she guessed.

"Yeah." He cleared his throat. "But that's not *bad* news, you know? It'll create less confusion for him. It'll get your in-laws to calm down and continue to be loving grandparents. It'll mean that the visitation schedule you just set up in your divorce won't have to be redone. It . . . it's probably the best way this thing could've worked out."

She sank into her seat. He didn't sound convinced, but she could tell he was trying hard to convince her. She hoped the results would at least be easier on Lucas, as Mack had said, because she believed he'd missed out on having a much better father. Ace was so selfish, so caught up in his gaming addiction. And now he was on the hunt for another woman. This wasn't what she'd wanted to hear, but DNA didn't lie. She had to accept what was. "Okay," she said once she'd summoned the energy necessary to respond. "I'll let him know."

"Tash?"

She gripped the phone tighter. "What?"

"That doesn't mean I can't love him, too."

No, but it meant Mack probably wouldn't — not any more than his other brothers loved Lucas, anyway. Mack had said that he hadn't gone out with the real estate agent today, that she'd had a conflict. But Natasha couldn't help wondering if this was the real reason. Was it that he no longer had sufficient motivation to take the risk of moving and starting his own location? "Of course it doesn't," she said, pumping so much false cheer into her voice she was afraid she'd gone overboard. "I'm sorry, but . . . I have to go. Someone just came into my office."

It was a lie. She was still alone. But she was afraid if they kept talking she'd end up revealing just how disappointed she was. If Mack was Lucas's father, she had no doubt he would've stayed in much closer touch.

Now her situation was unlikely to change.

She'd still have to cope with visitation with Ace and his family.

She'd still have to stand strong and rebuild her life on her own.

And, on top of that, she'd have to let go of Mack much sooner than she'd anticipated.

But that was okay, she told herself. She wouldn't crumble. She'd let him go with a smile and walk away with her head held high.

When Natasha got home, Mack's bag was packed and sitting in the drive by his car. Now that they knew what they knew, she'd expected him to leave soon, but that he wasn't even going to stay for dinner hit her hard.

Drawing a bolstering breath, she summoned what emotional fortitude she could muster after the very difficult conversation she'd had with Ace on the drive home and got out of the car. "All packed up?" she said, as though it wasn't a surprise at all, or even an unwelcome event.

He lifted Lucas into his arms and gave him a hug. "Yeah. I'm sorry to rush out of here, but something's come up at home."

"The shop is always so busy. I'm sure Dylan needs you back."

He seemed surprised she'd agree with him so readily. "He does, actually. There's a problem and . . . and my father can't work. Dyl can't get by without both of us for long."

"What's going on? Don't tell me J.T.'s on another bender."

When she'd been living with the Amoses, there were weeks when J.T. would disappear and no one would know where he went. He wouldn't go to work. He wouldn't come home. Even her mother had no idea where to find him. Then the cops would pick him up. Or he'd eventually show up under his own power, looking unkempt and smelling like alcohol.

"I'm not sure exactly," he said.

Because she was struggling to hold herself together, and she believed she already knew why he was leaving, she didn't feel much concern for his father. But it would've seemed strange if she didn't at least pretend to be worried. So she pulled Lucas into her own arms, taking what small consolation she could get from his brief hug before he started wiggling to get down. "What else could it be?" she asked.

"Let me get home and figure it out. I'll give you a call as soon as I understand what happened."

So it was like the situation with Kellan. She was to be excluded. "Okay," she said. "I hope he isn't hurt."

Mack didn't address that comment. "I made some spaghetti. It was a little early to feed Lucas dinner, but I thought I might as well make something so you wouldn't have to."

Head high, she reminded herself. *Smile bright.* "That's very nice of you. Thank you. I'm sorry if I held you up."

"I didn't have to wait long." After throwing his duffel bag into his truck, he fished out his keys. "I'll talk to you soon."

Lucas started to cry. "I don't want Mack to leave," he said. "He's my best friend."

It probably felt like he was his only friend. It sort of felt that way for Natasha, too, but she kept telling herself it was because they were new here. Things would improve. She had to believe that.

Mack ruffled his hair. "I'll be back. You be good, okay?"

"No," Lucas said, his bottom lip sticking out in an angry pout. "I won't be good."

Mack laughed. "I swear, if I didn't know better, I'd still think he was mine."

"We'll get through this," Natasha whispered in her son's ear under the guise of kissing his cheek. Then she tried to distract herself by thinking of some useful aphorisms and other encouraging thoughts. *When the going gets tough, the tough get going . . . What lies behind us and what lies ahead of us are tiny matters compared to what lies within us . . . I knew this was coming eventually. Better to get it over with and be done with it.*

Mack caught her chin and brushed his lips over hers. "Don't worry about anything, okay?"

She couldn't force any words past the lump in her throat, so she nodded and wished he'd just leave so that she wouldn't have the added burden of trying to pretend.

Something must've betrayed her, however,

because he hesitated for a moment and stared into her eyes before he said, "I love you. You know that, right?"

She swallowed hard so she could speak. "Oh, I know. I love you and your brothers right back. Be safe."

He gave her a funny look, as though he found that to be a strange response. Maybe it was a strange response for someone she'd been sleeping with. But he fell in both categories, and if he could switch between them so blithely, so could she.

With a final wave, he got in his truck and took off, and it wasn't too long after that Ace and his parents arrived. They banged on her door and insisted they should get to take Lucas home for a week, since she "blew their weekend" and caused them so much pain and suffering.

Natasha was hanging on by such a thin thread she didn't even argue. She figured she *did* owe them a week. Maybe more. Nothing she did seemed to be right.

She packed her son's clothes like some kind of automaton, handed his small suitcase over to her ex-mother-in-law and let Ace transfer the car seat from her car into his parents' Mercedes sedan.

"I used to think the world of you," his mother said. "But now that I know what

you're really like, I feel sorry for my son —
and Lucas, too."

"What you did is unforgivable," Ace
added.

Again, she didn't respond. She just bent
to kiss her son on the head. Then she sank
onto the porch steps and watched as Ace
led him away.

NINETEEN

Mack drove as fast as he dared. A cop pulled him over just after he hit Interstate 5 and gave him a speeding ticket, but he didn't slow down. He had to get home, had to figure out what was going on, because he couldn't believe what Dylan had told him. Surely something else had happened, which was why he hadn't said anything to Natasha. He didn't want to tell her what he'd been told. He preferred to get back to Whiskey Creek and make sure it was true — that there were no other possibilities.

Although he'd tried to call Dylan, he hadn't been able to reach him or any of his other brothers. Why wasn't anyone picking up? Had J.T. *died*?

Mack wondered how he'd feel if his father was gone. J.T. had been a pain in the ass for so long. Would Mack secretly be glad that he no longer had to deal with him? Or would his father's death hit him harder than he'd ever imagined? They had such a complicated relationship. On the one hand, Mack felt some empathy for J.T., who'd fallen apart after their mother's depression and subsequent suicide, turned to alcohol and ended up knifing some guy who was heckling him in a bar. J.T. wasn't himself when he did that, so as shocking and terrible as that act was, the incident itself was forgivable. It was more the way that night and his subsequent years in prison had changed J.T. The man who emerged when he was released couldn't cope with *any* responsibility or stress, would barely work, even to support himself, and hung out with drug abusers like Anya. It was as if Mack's only remaining parent had become a child.

That reversal had been weird and uncomfortable, especially to Mack. As the youngest, he was probably the one who'd looked up to J.T. the most. Dylan was clearly the patriarch of the family now, the one they all respected, but J.T. was still their father.

On the other hand, there was *some* love left, wasn't there?

Mack didn't know, couldn't honestly say yes to that question, which made him wonder what kind of man *he'd* turned out to be.

To avoid being alone with his thoughts, he

tried calling Dylan again — with the same result. Dylan's voice mail came on, but instead of leaving another message, he called Cheyenne and was relieved when she picked up.

"Hey, what's going on?" he asked as soon as he heard her voice.

"J. T.'s in pretty bad shape." The solemnity of her response scared him as much as her words.

"He'll pull through, though, won't he?"

"Hard to say," she replied. "He's lost a lot of blood. The doctors are doing what they can."

This was serious, all right. "Where was he shot?"

"In the chest. The bullet barely missed his heart and collapsed a lung."

"Do we know how it happened?"

"Nothing's very clear at the moment."

It hadn't been clear before, either. Dylan had contacted him only an hour or so before Natasha came home to say that he'd received a call from the police department telling him that he'd better get over to the hospital because his father had been shot. He'd had no other details, except that it was a woman who'd requested an ambulance, which led him to believe that J. T. and Anya must've had one of their epic fights.

"Where's Dylan and everyone else?"

"At the hospital."

"I've been trying to reach them."

"There's no cell service in that wing, for whatever reason. You only got me because everyone's starving. I left to get some food."

"You don't really think Anya did this, do you?"

"I can't say for sure. So far, all we've heard is what the paramedics told us."

"Which was . . ."

"A woman called 9-1-1 who sounded hysterical. Said J.T. Amos had been shot and was dying on the floor. She told them to come quick, but by the time they got there, the door was standing open, there was a gun on the floor near him with blood on the handle and he was alone."

"Did the caller identify herself?"

"No. Wouldn't give her name. Just kept screaming for them to come. But who else could it be?"

"He's been with other women now and then."

"True, but no one has been a bigger part of his life since prison than Anya. They were seeing each other again. And surely you remember how they used to go at each other when they were angry. We've been afraid that one of them would get hurt. We just . . ."

never dreamed it would be quite *this* bad."

Had Natasha's mother killed his father? "Where would she get a gun?"

"Dylan thinks it was your father's."

"J.T.'s a convicted felon. He can't own a gun."

"He can't own one *legally.* There's a difference, right? Anyway, someone came into the shop a few weeks ago and told Dylan J.T. had been brandishing a Glock 9 mm at some party and acting tough. But when Dylan confronted him, J.T. swore up and down that it belonged to someone else at the party and he'd only been looking at it."

"He accepted that?"

"Your father's an adult. What more can Dylan do?"

"That's true, I guess. But where would J.T. get it in the first place?"

"You know the kind of people he hangs out with. He probably traded drugs for it."

Sadly, Mack could all too easily see that happening. "So where is Anya now?"

"We don't know."

"No one's heard from her?"

"Not yet."

"Has anyone tried to reach her?"

"I don't think anyone has any interest in talking to her. We're leaving that to the police for now."

The police. If Anya was responsible, she could go to prison. And if J.T. died, she might be there for quite some time.

"Is Natasha very upset about all this?" Cheyenne asked.

"I haven't told her about it yet," he replied.

"Why not?"

"Because she's already had a terrible year. I'm still hoping we'll find out that it *wasn't* Anya, that it was someone else."

"Who else could it be?" Cheyenne sounded surprised.

"Maybe the owner of the gun decided he wanted it back and Anya just came upon the scene. You never know."

"I'm pretty sure it was Anya, Mack, and if I'm right, you won't be able to keep it from Natasha for long."

"I don't need long," he said. "Just a day or two. I don't want to say anything to her until we know if Dad will survive and if it really was her mother who shot him."

"I think you're grasping at straws, trying to believe that it could be anyone else, but I understand why you're doing it. You've always been so protective of Natasha. When will you be home?"

He let the part about Natasha go and

glanced at the clock on his dashboard. "I still have five hours." Which seemed like an eternity. He wished he was there *now*.

"Okay. We'll see you when you get here. Just . . . be careful. It's been a rough week, what with this happening on the heels of Kellan learning what he did. Dyl doesn't need any more upset."

Mack had suffered his own share of disappointment, thanks to the results of the paternity test. But he was trying not to dwell on that. "How's Kellan now that he's been home for a few days?" he asked.

"Seems to be okay. Dylan's good at navigating rough water — he's had a lot of experience at it, as you know — so we should be fine as long as you don't say anything to anyone."

"Chey, I would never tell a soul."

"Even Natasha?" She sounded worried, if not downright skeptical. "Because that's how it starts. One person tells someone they trust, who tells someone they trust, and so on."

"I haven't said a word to Natasha or anyone else — and I won't."

He heard her breathe a sigh of relief. "Thank you."

"Of course."

"I'm at the restaurant," she said. "I'd better go."

As they said their goodbyes and disconnected, Mack pulled off the interstate for gas. He wanted to call Natasha, to reassure her. He knew hearing her voice would also reassure him. She probably believed he'd bugged out on her just because he wasn't Lucas's father. But if he called, he'd say too much. First, he needed to see what he could do to straighten out this mess and try to soften the blow.

Instead of breaking down and calling her anyway, as he was tempted to do, he navigated to his photographs on his phone while waiting for his tank to fill and brought up a picture of her and Lucas — one he'd taken on the beach.

God, she was beautiful. He'd fallen in love with her years ago.

And now he knew, in spite of everything, that hadn't changed.

The pump shut itself off with a deep *glug* as he made that photograph his wallpaper.

Natasha didn't know what to do with herself. Being suddenly alone without Mack or Lucas, when she'd expected to be with both of them tonight, made her feel sort of bereft. But she refused to mope around all night.

To make sure she couldn't, she put on the summer dress that fit her best, piled her hair on top of her head and drove over to a bar she'd heard some of the teachers talk about at school.

From what she could tell, The Blue Suede Shoe was a popular place to hang out, even on a Monday. The parking lot wasn't as crowded as she suspected it would be on weekends, but it was over halfway full, which felt hopeful. She needed to be around people. To hear their voices. To listen to some music. To start making friends in the community. To forget the brief flash of hope she'd had for that paternity test and believe that all would be well eventually — even without Mack — if only she kept marching forward.

And yet, after she arrived, it was difficult to get out of the car and go inside. She was a stranger in Silver Springs — one who didn't want to talk about who she was, whether she was in a relationship or what she did for a living, all topics that would naturally come up when introducing herself to others.

Thinking she might've made a mistake trying to get out of the house for the evening, that she wasn't ready for this after all, she started her car. But as she was looking to back out, she spotted two men in her rearview mirror and realized she recognized them. It was Eli and Gavin Turner. They'd just climbed out of Eli's truck and he was turning back to lock it.

If she could walk in with them, she'd feel much less conspicuous.

Quickly shutting off her engine again, she got out and waved to get Eli's attention because Gavin was looking down as he strode beside his brother.

"Hey," Eli said when he saw her. "How are you?"

Gavin's head popped up and he said hello, too.

"I'm good." She attempted a smile even though she couldn't remember ever feeling quite so low. "Just . . . hoping to get out and meet a few people, but it's hard to walk into a place when you don't know anyone, so I'm excited to see a couple of familiar faces."

"There's no need to be self-conscious," Gavin said. "It's totally casual here."

"And you can hang out with us," Eli added. "Gavin and I come to play pool or darts every couple of weeks. Sometimes some of our other brothers join us."

She gazed up at the neon sign — a pair of blue shoes — that was blinking on and off above the door. "Do your wives ever come with you?"

"Sometimes," Eli said. "Our mom would've taken the kids so that they could've joined us tonight, but they were both doing other things."

"Where's your son?" Gavin asked. "Were you able to find a babysitter?"

"His father has him this week," she replied.

He gave her a sympathetic look. "I bet it's hard to get back into the swing of things after a divorce."

"Yes. It's a strange new world being single again."

It was too dark to see Eli's expression clearly, but she got the impression he was confused. "I thought I heard my mother say you were seeing someone."

"She was probably talking about Mack. But he's just a family friend." She could've added that Mack was more like a brother to her. But since it wasn't true, and she'd always rebelled against that, she wouldn't do it even to stop people from expecting them to get together.

"I see." They reached the entrance and Eli held the door for her and Gavin.

The inside was even more dimly lit, but she'd been expecting that and was grateful for the darkness.

"Can I get you a drink?" Gavin asked as they approached the bar.

She'd fed some of the spaghetti Mack had made to Lucas, but she'd been too despondent to eat herself. She didn't want to drink too much on an empty stomach, but she figured she could have one.

"Sure." She got a gin and tonic; they each got a beer. Then Eli and Gavin drew her into some billiards. The two brothers wagered on just about every aspect of the game, and although they offered to let her in on it, too, she didn't bet. She did, however, buy the next round of drinks and indulged in a Greyhound simply because she was starting to feel happier and didn't want to let reality intrude too soon.

"How about another game?" Eli asked when Gavin barely edged him out, winning the money.

She was so terrible at pool that she declined. She'd spent almost every waking moment for the last thirteen years pursuing a medical career, hadn't spent much time hanging out in bars. "No. I'm happy to watch."

Because the alcohol was making her lightheaded, she was considering sitting down to listen to the music and study the people

359

around her when she spotted someone else she recognized.

Roger Burns was walking toward her.

"Hi," he said as soon as he was close enough to make himself heard.

Normally, she wouldn't have been happy to see him. She avoided him at the school. But she'd had enough to drink that her defenses weren't what they usually were, and it was nice to bump into someone else she knew — someone who wasn't already married and had enough interest in her to make her feel not only welcome but wanted in this strange place. "I don't mean to interrupt your game —" he started, but she cut him off.

"Oh, I'm not playing anymore."

Eli and Gavin greeted him, which made her feel even more comfortable. They all knew each other; they all worked together.

"I normally don't get out on a school night," he told her. "But since I was finished grading papers, I figured I'd grab a drink. How's the move going?"

She didn't want to think about the move, because then she'd think about the man who'd helped her move and had just finished painting her son's room. "Fine." She set her glass on the closest table. "Would you like to dance?"

He looked taken aback but quickly set his beer aside, too, and led her onto the dance floor.

The steady beep of a heart monitor sounded in the otherwise quiet hospital room. Mack sat near his father, who was attached to all kinds of medical equipment. It was just the two of them; his brothers had gone home. They had families to worry about and/or they had to work in the morning, so Mack was the logical choice to sit up with J.T. through the night. He'd agreed to call the others if their father took a turn for the worse, but Mack was hoping that wouldn't happen. The doctor had said, barring anything unforeseen, like an infection, J.T. had a decent chance of surviving.

Mack wondered how long it would be before J.T. could talk and tell them what had happened. The police hadn't yet located Anya. He'd called them just a few minutes ago to check. And she wasn't picking up her phone. He'd tried her at least ten times, but Officer Howton, one of the better officers on the force, told him that her phone had been found in J.T.'s house, which wasn't comforting. That, if nothing else, proved she'd been there, and very recently.

He closed his eyes to give them a rest and

was drifting off when his phone vibrated in his pocket. After his father's surgery, they'd moved J.T. into a section of the hospital where there was cell service — which came as a relief since it was frustrating to be cut off — but Mack didn't want to talk in his full voice in case it would disturb J.T. right when he most needed the rest.

Straightening his leg to be able to dig out his phone, he saw that it was Grady and left the room before answering.

"What's going on?" he said once he was in the hallway. "What're you doing up so late? You were supposed to go home and get some sleep. You told Dyl you'd open the shop tomorrow at seven."

"And I will. But I'm too pissed off to sleep right now. I've been driving around, looking for that bitch, Anya."

Mack winced at his brother's response. Whatever courtesy they'd extended to Anya was gone. She'd bitten the hand that fed her, and that was so disloyal and unappreciative that his brothers would never forget it, never offer her help or protection again. "The police will take care of her, Grady."

"Fuck the police!" he said, instantly enraged by Mack's more tempered response. "Since when have they ever done anything for us? Even if we had a better relationship with law enforcement in this town, they aren't going to waste their time if it gets too difficult. And it might already be 'too difficult.' If she's left the area, it's not as if anyone on the force is going to go after her. They're going to clock out when their shifts end and go home to their families."

Mack and his brothers had a deep distrust of the authorities, especially in Whiskey Creek. What with J.T. going to prison and Dylan taking over when he was young, hotheaded and defiant, they hadn't had the best interactions with the law. They'd been dealing with a small force to begin with, and the old chief had tried to make an example out of Dylan, so there'd been a lot of friction over the years. "They won't have to go anywhere. If we all just bide our time, she'll come back."

"Why would she come back and risk going to prison?"

"She lives here."

"Doesn't matter. Now that she's shot Dad, there's nothing for her here except possible arrest. She's on disability, so she doesn't have a job to return to. She rents a room in a house filled with other druggies and doesn't have many belongings — none she couldn't replace. She could easily drive off in that rattletrap piece of shit she owns — which is ironic because she wouldn't have a vehicle at all if we hadn't provided it for her — and head to Sacramento or LA, someplace much bigger than here, where she could dye her hair and drop out of sight. But I won't let that happen."

Mack swallowed a sigh. His brothers were always quick to defend the family. That was how they'd survived. And even though J.T. had caused a lot of what they'd been through, he was one of their own. "Don't worry. I think Dad's going to make it."

"She's not going to get away with this, even if he does. Call Natasha and tell her if she hears from her mother she'd better contact us immediately. After all, we've done more for her than Anya has, at least in the past fifteen years. We —"

"Grady," Mack broke in.

"What?" he said, sounding surprised to be interrupted.

"Don't *ever* threaten Natasha."

This statement was met with silence. Then Grady said, "Wow. You sound pretty adamant. But you'd never choose her over us . . ."

"I don't know what happened," Mack responded. "So I'm reserving judgment. But even if it was Anya who shot him, Natasha had nothing to do with it."

"Oh shit," Grady said. "You're in love with her, aren't you. That's what the past couple weeks have been about. Now that Natasha's divorced, you're going after what you've wanted all along."

"So?" Mack said.

"Really, Mack? It's got to be her?" Grady cried. "*Why,* for God's sake?"

"Because she's the only woman I've ever loved," he said and disconnected.

Natasha danced until she was breathless and her feet hurt. And just for good measure, she had another drink. She couldn't remember a night when she'd forgotten about medicine and her family and acted as if she didn't have a care in the world. She'd needed just that, but she had to work in the morning, so she couldn't let go entirely. Around eleven, she told Roger she had to go home and allowed him to drive her since she knew better than to get behind the wheel. She could walk to The Blue Suede Shoe to reclaim her car in the morning. It wasn't that far. She'd just have to leave thirty minutes earlier.

Roger had been a congenial companion. He'd danced with her, talked with her, laughed with her. And he hadn't brought up her background even once. She was relieved about that, hoped they were through with that subject forever.

Once he pulled into her drive, he mentioned coming in for a final drink, but she knew he was hoping for more than she'd ever be able to offer him. He was lonely, wanted a relationship. And he'd been interested in her from the beginning. But she'd never really loved anyone other than Mack, and she wasn't going to make the same mistake she'd made with Ace by settling for less. She'd rather be single for the rest of her life.

"I'm sorry," she told him. "But I think we'd better call it a night."

"As long as I leave by midnight, we should get enough sleep to be able to work tomorrow," he said, pressing her.

She rested a hand on his arm to show that she was trying to be as gentle as possible. "I'm not open to a relationship, Roger. I don't want to give you false hope."

He seemed surprised by her honesty. "You're not attracted to me?"

"That's not it at all," she replied. "You're a very nice man. It's just that I'm in love with someone else."

"Your ex?" he guessed.

366

"Sadly, no. I don't think I was ever truly in love with my ex. That was the problem," she said and got out of the car.

It wasn't until they'd both waved and he'd driven away that she realized there was a light on in her house. The sun went down so late during the summer that she hadn't even thought to turn one on when she left. She'd been too eager to find some way to get through what promised to be a very difficult evening.

Had Mack returned?

His vehicle wasn't in sight. There were no vehicles parked at her place.

She climbed up to the porch and peeked in through a crack in the blind.

She couldn't see anyone, but she thought she heard noises coming from within.

She pressed her ear to the door. Yes, she heard movement. What was going on? Someone was definitely in her house!

Heart pounding, she grabbed her purse, intending to get her phone so she could call 9-1-1, when she saw someone peering out the other window. With a yelp, she jumped back so fast she nearly fell down the stairs. Then she realized the face staring out at her belonged to her mother.

Since she'd dropped her purse, she picked it up as Anya unlocked and opened the door. "Mom! What are you doing here?" she asked. "And how'd you get in?"

"Luckily, I found the spare key."

Because Natasha had hid it where Anya had always hid hers — not that Anya had ever bothered to lock their house very often, when they had one. But . . . "Where's your car?" she asked, still confused.

Her mother looked pale and rattled herself as she stuck her head out and looked both ways down the street. "I parked it a few blocks away and walked."

Natasha was growing sober very quickly. *"Why?"*

Anya waved her in. "Because they'll be looking for it. Hurry and come inside, where we can talk."

"Looking for it," Natasha repeated. Who was her mother talking about? Why would she feel the need to leave her car and walk to the house? Natasha figured Anya must be having a paranoid delusion brought on by the drugs she took. She'd had episodes like that before.

But then she saw the blood on her mother's clothes and felt her heart drop to her knees. "Oh no," she whispered. "What happened?"

"I think he's dead," she said.

Twenty

Frightened by what she was both hearing and seeing, Natasha grabbed Anya by the shoulders. "*Who's* dead?"

"There was so much blood pooling around his body." She shuddered. "I've never seen so much blood. Oh, God!" she wailed. "He must be dead."

How Anya had managed to drive for so long — and find the new house — while in such a state was a complete mystery. "Mom, look at me," Natasha told her. "*Who* must be dead? What are you talking about?"

Tears welled up in Anya's eyes when she finally caught and held Natasha's gaze, and for a moment, she grew lucid. "J.T."

"How? What happened to him?"

"I don't know." She lifted her hands to wipe her tears, saw the blood on them and nearly swooned. "It wasn't me. *I* didn't do it."

Anxiety caused Natasha to raise her voice.

"Do *what*?"

Anya reacted as though it should be obvious by now. "Shoot him!"

Natasha felt her mouth fall open. "J.T.'s been shot?" The way Anya had been talking, Natasha had assumed he'd been in an accident or gotten in a fight. He had such a temper. Mack and the other Amos brothers acted as though he hadn't been that way before prison, but she hadn't met J.T. until after he got out, and the man she knew definitely had anger management issues.

Her mother's eyes glazed over as she crumbled onto the couch and began to rock back and forth.

Natasha stood over her. "Mom? I'm talking to you. How did J.T. get shot?" And did Mack know about his father? What about Dylan and the others?

No answer.

Kneeling, Natasha got right in her face. "Look at me! Tell me what happened."

She finally came to herself again. "I don't know. I — I can't remember."

"Then tell me what you *do* remember."

She began to wring her hands. "There's not much to tell. I came home and . . . and found him lying on the floor."

"You came home from where?"

Her mother didn't seem to have a response. The question itself alarmed her, which came off as odd as everything else about this.

"Where were you before you came home, Mom?" Natasha repeated.

"I went to get something."

"*What?* Groceries? Gas? Drugs?"

"Groceries."

She spoke as if she'd chosen from the list Natasha had provided, which gave Natasha the impression it wasn't true, but she was too eager to get the rest of the story to focus on that small detail. She just needed an anchor to get things started, would go back to that. "And then what?"

"I walked in and . . . and there he was in the entryway. I tried to lift him, to talk to him, to see what happened. But he was so heavy. *Too* heavy."

"If there was a lot of blood, how do you know he was shot? How do you know it wasn't something else that was causing all that blood?"

Anya shook her head. "Like what?"

"I don't know. He could've been in a fight, could've been stabbed —"

"The gun was *right* there. I saw it."

Natasha sat on the couch next to her while struggling to process what she'd learned.

"Please tell me you called for help right away."

"I did." She stared at some point across the room. "I called 9-1-1."

"And what did the paramedics say when they arrived?"

Fresh tears began to streak down her cheeks. "I didn't wait for them. I panicked and . . . ran. I was afraid they wouldn't believe me. That they'd think *I* did it."

A chill went through Natasha. "Why would they ever think that?"

"Because I was the only one there!"

"But running will only make you look more guilty!"

"I didn't shoot him," she said again. "You have to believe me, Tash. I would never do anything like that."

Natasha *wanted* to believe her. But could she even trust that Anya accurately remembered what had happened?

Part of Natasha — the part that sympathized with J.T. and Mack and his brothers — was outraged by the fact that Anya had left J.T. like that. But on the off chance that her mother was telling the truth, she deserved to have someone listen to her, didn't she? At the very least, her own daughter should do that. "When was this?"

"Earlier."

"When?"

Her mother got up and began to pace. "Do you have a cigarette?"

"Of course I don't. I'm a doctor."

"I'm shaking. I can't concentrate. I — I have to have a cigarette."

Natasha needed Anya to remain sharp and focused, and for that she was willing to forgo the whole "smoking isn't good for you" argument and simply accommodate her. "Do you have a pack in your purse?"

"I don't know where my purse is."

Natasha glanced around. "I don't see it. You must've left it in the car. We'll go look. But first, answer my question. When did you find J.T.?"

"I don't know!" she said, growing even more agitated. "About three o'clock, I guess. J.T. wanted me to . . . to go with him to watch Kellan at football practice. He was mad that I was going to make him late."

How did she know he was mad if he was already shot and bleeding on the floor when she got there?

Natasha hoped Anya had a good answer for that, that she'd spoken to him on the phone or something they could prove, if necessary. "Did you have an argument?"

Anya hesitated before she said, "No. I told

you. I found him on the floor when I got there."

Leaning forward, Natasha squeezed her forehead. Was J.T. dead? Had Mack been given the news that his father had been shot?

He had to know by now. She felt terrible for him. She knew he struggled to respect J.T., but he'd already lost his mother.

Why hadn't he called her? Why hadn't any of the Amos brothers called her?

The memory of the past few hours, drinking and dancing to loud music, flashed through her mind. Maybe they'd tried while she was at the club.

She felt damp, clammy even though it was plenty cool in the house as she reclaimed her small clutch, which she'd put on the counter when she walked in, and dug out her phone. Sure enough, she'd missed several calls. One from Dylan, one from Aaron, two from Rod, and there were multiple missed calls from Grady.

But none from Mack.

Feeling strange and a little shaky herself, she began to listen to the various voice mails.

Dylan: *Hey, Tash. Listen, I need to talk to you, okay? Call me when you can.*

Rod: *Have you heard from your mother? If*

so, can you please let me know where she is?

Grady: *Are you kidding me, Tash? We've been good to your mother. You know we have. And this is how she repays us? If you hear from her, you'd better give us a call and tell us where we can find her.*

Grady again: *Where are you? Why aren't you picking up? Avoiding me is only making me madder. I hope you know that. If she did this, she's going to prison. You can't protect her. Mack can't protect her. No one can protect her.*

That Grady would suddenly treat her like an enemy stung. *She* hadn't done anything wrong. She wasn't even sure her mother had. The only thing she knew for sure was that Anya had once again put her in a terrible situation.

She'd also missed a number of texts from the Amos brothers. Dylan: CM . . . Grady: Why aren't you answering? . . . Aaron: Tell me she didn't do it.

It was so late Natasha felt she might, without looking too bad, be able to put off returning their many calls and messages until morning. But time was ticking away and soon she'd have no excuse. If she didn't respond fairly soon, the battle lines would be drawn, and she'd find herself standing on her mother's side — against the men who'd protected her from Anya and Anya's lifestyle at a very critical point.

"Did anyone see you at the grocery store?" she asked. "Do you have a receipt? Anything to prove the time you were there?"

Anya seemed too flustered to be able to remember. "What about that cigarette?"

"In a minute. Do you have a receipt? Maybe in your purse?"

She stared at her bloodstained fingernails as though they didn't actually belong to her. "I don't know."

"Have you heard from Dylan or any of his brothers?"

"I don't have my phone. I — I must've left it behind."

"Left it *where*?"

"At J.T.'s."

"When you found him?"

"Yes."

The implications of that were not lost on Natasha. Dropping her head in her hands, she massaged her temples as she tried to think. If her mother really had shot J.T., Anya would have to pay the price. There was nothing Natasha could do to save her from the consequences. It wouldn't be right to even try, especially after all the Amoses had done for both of them.

But what if her mother was telling the truth? What if someone else shot J.T.? If she turned her mother over too soon, they might not look any further. Anya was the type of individual who made an easy scape-goat. There were plenty of people who'd gone to prison for something they didn't do, so it was certainly possible.

Although Natasha had been let down, disappointed, even disgusted by her mother's actions, being a drug addict who couldn't keep her life together didn't make Anya a murderer.

"We need to go to the car to get your purse." If she could find a receipt from the grocery store, maybe she'd have something to indicate her mother wasn't with J.T. at the time he was shot.

"Yes," her mother said in relief. "I need that cigarette."

She hurried for the door, but Natasha stopped her. "I'll get it. Just tell me where the car is and give me the keys. You can shower while I go."

Fortunately, Anya had the presence of mind to remember where she'd left her vehicle. At least, Natasha hoped it would be where she'd been told. She got her mother some sweats to change into for when she got out of the shower, walked down to the light and turned left for another eighth of a mile or so before finding the fruit stand with a small parking area her mother had described.

She couldn't help looking furtively over her shoulder again and again as she approached the car. It was so dark out, and there were no streetlights. She did have her phone, however, so she used the flashlight function to look around her and then inside the car.

It wasn't locked, even though her mother's purse was sitting on the passenger seat in plain sight. But had someone stolen it, they wouldn't have gotten away with much. Anya didn't have enough credit to get any credit cards; she relied exclusively on cash. And unless it was right after she got her disability check, she never seemed to have more than twenty bucks on her at a time.

The cabin light went on when Natasha opened the door, and she could plainly see dark brownish smears on the steering wheel, where her mother's hands had been, along with the gearshift. Bloodstains. They made her uneasy and desperate enough that she sat in the driver's seat, pulled her mother's purse into her lap and rummaged through it immediately, hoping against hope that she'd find a receipt from the grocery store or some other small shred of evidence to suggest her mother might be telling the truth.

Gum, cigarettes, makeup, pills — Natasha didn't even look at the label on the bottle because she knew she wouldn't approve and didn't need anything else to be upset about — some change, a ratty old wallet with very little money inside and a multitude of old wrappers and crushed receipts. Her mother's purse was full of those things and more, but there was nothing recent.

Yanking the purse strap over her shoulder, she got out so she could search the car.

She found nothing reassuring there, either. What she did find was a note from J.T. that had fallen between the seat and the console telling Anya that she had to move out right away because he'd met someone else — just the kind of thing that might upset someone badly enough to make them do something desperate.

"No way," she whispered.

Mack's eyes were so gritty he almost couldn't move them as dawn approached. His back and legs were stiff, too. He'd been sitting in the same uncomfortable chair all night, hoping his father might come around. But sticking it out for six miserable hours had been a waste of effort. While the equipment hummed, rattled and beeped, J.T. hadn't stirred. Chances were good he didn't even know Mack was there.

With a groan, Mack stood and stretched. He had a feeling this was going to be a long day. Last night, the shooting and its aftermath had seemed surreal. It'd been difficult to grasp that his father's life hung in the balance, that this wasn't something that could be easily fixed. He'd wanted to believe J.T. would pull through and be able to say who shot him and why, but after being up all night, watching a ventilator push air into J.T.'s lungs, Mack was beginning to understand that may never happen.

If it didn't — if J.T. died — then what?

Intending to go find a cup of coffee or get some food, he opened the door to step out into the hall and had to jump back to avoid colliding with the nurse who'd been checking on J.T. periodically through the night.

"How's your father?" she asked, her voice subdued in deference to J.T. and the patients in the rooms nearby.

"I don't know," he replied. "You're going to have to tell me." The sickly pallor of J.T.'s skin, his advancing age and his hard living had never been more apparent. Mack knew that much. J.T. looked like a cadaver already.

She gave him an encouraging smile. "The doctor should be by soon. Meanwhile, I'll check on him and let you know if I see anything new we should worry about."

They didn't need anything new; they had plenty of old things to worry about. But he understood that she was just trying to be nice. It wasn't as if she could offer him any guarantees. "Appreciate it." He scrubbed a hand over his face. "Is there a cafeteria in this hospital?"

"Down on one."

"Thanks." With a sigh, he pulled his phone from his pocket as he started for the elevator and was surprised to see that he'd missed a text from Natasha during the night. Apparently, he hadn't remained as vigilant and alert as he'd thought.

I'm sorry about your father. I hope he's going to be okay.

She knew. Who'd told her? One of his brothers?

Mack felt a flash of anger. *Grady?* He'd better not have been too hard on her.

Or had she heard from her mother?

To his knowledge, no one had found Anya yet. But it was possible that the police had picked her up — or whoever else might've shot J.T. — and he just hadn't heard about it.

He waited to respond until he could get off the elevator. But then he discovered that the cafeteria wasn't open quite yet and walked out into a courtyard to get some fresh air and stretch his legs. His initial response to what'd happened — trying to keep it from Natasha until he could get it figured out himself — seemed ridiculous now. Of course he wouldn't be able to keep this type of thing quiet for long. But he'd been hoping he could minimize this new drama, serve it up in a more palatable form. At a minimum, he'd planned to reassure her of J.T.'s well-being so that the consequences her mother faced wouldn't be nearly as bad.

But J.T. was lying in a hospital bed, fighting for his life, and Mack didn't know how to make that seem any better than it was.

So do I, but we don't know what's going on yet.

He waited fifteen minutes to see if she might respond but got nothing. It was early yet, though. He hoped she was sleeping and not just avoiding him.

He was about to go back in when Dylan called.

"How's Dad?" his brother asked.

"Hard to say," Mack replied. "Far as I can tell, there's been no change."

"Should I come over?"

"If you can. I'm dying to take a shower. What time do you need me at the shop?"

"You've got an hour or so. Grady's there, but he didn't get much sleep."

"He's furious that Anya has disappeared."

"So am I. That she would do this is just . . . unreal. Have you heard from Natasha?"

"No," he said because what she'd sent wasn't what Dylan was looking for anyway.

"Do you think she'll call us?"

"Have you tried to call her?"

"Several times. All of us have. But no one has gotten through to her yet."

"She'll respond."

"I hope so, because we can't cut her much slack on this one. If Anya shot Dad, and Natasha knows where she's at, she needs to turn her in."

"What if Anya didn't shoot Dad and is afraid that no one will believe her?"

"Come on, Mack."

The skepticism in that statement alarmed him. *"What?"*

"You know it was her as well as I do."

"No, I don't. And I don't think we should rush to judgment."

"You'd be rushing to judgment, too, if it wasn't for Natasha."

"Maybe, but still."

"That reminds me — how'd the paternity test turn out?"

The disappointment Mack had felt when he received the results washed over him again. That he was rumpled and tired and worried about this new problem didn't help. "He's not mine."

There was a brief pause. Then Dylan, his voice filled with honesty, said, "I can't say I'm sorry to hear that. See you soon."

After they disconnected, Mack stared down at the picture he'd selected for the wallpaper on his phone. Dylan might be glad Lucas wasn't his child. If things got sticky, it would make it easier for the Amoses not to have that wrinkle to deal with, and it had been Dylan's job to look out for the family for so long that anticipating and evaluating possible pitfalls came second nature to him now.

But Mack wasn't happy Lucas wasn't his son. He'd begun to want that above all else.

TWENTY-ONE

Natasha was too new at work to call in sick. Aiyana was understanding and kind enough that she'd probably be gracious, even if Natasha did beg off, but that was all the more reason not to do it. After owning her practice, she knew what it was like to be on the employer's side, and she didn't want to take advantage of someone like Aiyana. She guessed Aiyana's trust and inherent kindness was the reason she did so well with the broken boys she took under her wing. She was one of the few people Natasha had met who seemed to understand that love was the greatest healer there was, and she spread it around liberally.

Natasha left her mother sleeping in Lucas's bed and hurried back to the fruit stand. After discovering the letter that gave Anya motive to shoot J.T., she'd been loath to park Anya's car at her house. But she couldn't leave it at the fruit stand much longer. The owner might call the cops to report an abandoned vehicle, and Natasha didn't want to deal with the police. She'd decided to put the old Camry inside her garage until she could figure out what was going on — whether J.T. would recover, whether Anya was lying to her about what'd happened, whether she'd have to turn her own mother over to the authorities.

She was clammy with sweat by the time she'd moved the Camry and reached her Jetta at The Blue Suede Shoe so she could drive to work. She hated to show up at the school looking as though she could use another shower, but there was no way around that — not unless she was willing to be late. Everything had taken longer than expected.

She felt self-conscious as she walked into the administration building. It wasn't that hot yet, but she drew attention just for being new, and now she looked like a wilted flower even though the day had just begun. She hadn't slept much, had a headache from drinking at the club last night and was so worried about J.T. — whether he'd recover and how this latest development would affect his sons and her relationship with them — that she'd created sores on her fingertips from digging at her cuticles.

Eight hours. She could get through eight hours. She just hoped she didn't have any emergencies to contend with. During her residency, she'd been trained to deal with almost anything, and to handle it on very little sleep, but this went beyond rest. She didn't have any emotional reserves at the moment, either. She hoped the day would be uneventful and that she'd soon be able to get back to her mother, where, with any luck, she could get more coherent answers and a better idea of whether or not Anya had done the unthinkable.

"Good morning."

A male voice at the door startled Natasha, nearly causing her to drop her coffee. As she was coming into the building, she'd cast a wary glance at the office in the back corner and gotten the impression that Aiyana was out. Betty May was in the reception area, punctual as always, but she'd been so busy dealing with the throng of students waiting to get help with various schedule issues, appointments with the school counselor or forms for a field trip or after-school activity that Natasha had been able to scoot past her with barely a nod. She'd stopped at the break room so she could fuel the next few hours with caffeine and slipped into her office, where she'd been safe.

Until Eli had appeared, seemingly out of nowhere.

"Hey." She set her cup on her small desk so Aiyana's son wouldn't be able to spot her damaged cuticles. "How are you doing this morning?"

"Great," he replied. "Just wanted to check with you to make sure you were okay with what happened at the club last night."

Taken off guard, she blinked at him. "What was that?"

He checked behind him as if to make sure Betty May was still too busy to listen in. "My mother mentioned to me — maybe a day or two ago — that Roger was making himself a nuisance where you were concerned. So when he approached you last night, I didn't know whether to step in. You seemed to be enjoying yourself, which is why I didn't, but I thought I'd ask — for future reference."

"Oh, no. He's fine. You did the right thing. I needed a night out, and he was friendly and willing to dance."

"I wouldn't have thought twice about it, except —" he shifted uncomfortably "— when we left we saw your car was still in the lot, and . . . then I began to worry."

"I didn't go home with him," she said with a laugh. "He gave me a ride because I'd let

388

loose a little *too* much, if you know what I mean."

"Of course. I'm glad you were able to have a good time," he said with a kind smile, and she couldn't help thinking how much he sounded like his mother.

Grateful she'd made it to work in spite of the difficulties of the past twenty-four hours, she sank into her chair. She'd purposely avoided looking at her phone this morning for fear she'd find more messages from the Amos brothers. But she knew it would only provoke them if she put off responding for too long.

She sighed as she checked her messages.

No more calls or texts from Dylan, Aaron, Rod or Grady. They'd reached out, made it clear they wanted to talk to her. Now they were waiting to see what she'd do. The ball was in her court, so to speak.

The only new message she'd received was from Mack. He'd responded to what she'd sent him in the middle of the night when she couldn't sleep. She'd been hesitant to contact him. She'd known he could easily be awake, given what had occurred, and might try to call her if he realized she was up. Eventually, he, too, would ask where her mother was, and she wasn't ready to contend with that moment.

Fortunately, he hadn't asked yet. But now that she'd read his message, she almost wished she had talked to him. She was dying to get more information on how J.T. was doing, where he'd been shot and what damage had been done. As a doctor, she was especially interested in those details, so that she could form her own opinion on his chances of survival. But she was also longing to be part of their worry and their concern — as she would've been if it hadn't been Anya who was probably to blame.

So do I, but we don't know what's going on yet, he'd said.

That told her nothing, and she hadn't received anything else from him. Why didn't they know more by now? Was J.T. dying?

She tried to imagine what must be going through Mack's mind — through the minds of his brothers, too — and understood how betrayed and angry they must feel. She remembered how they'd reacted when Anya took her to meet them for the first time at a steak house in Sutter Creek. Anya had been so excited to get her hooks into them, so there'd be some benefit to having married J.T., she'd arranged the meeting before J.T. was even released from prison.

Although they'd been polite, Natasha had been able to tell they were far less excited to meet Anya than she was to meet them, and the way her mother had acted, as if she expected to be accepted as family right away, embarrassed Natasha. She'd sat at the table, sullen and angry and unable to eat, and somehow Dylan and the others had been able to understand the terrible position she was in as a young girl who had no control over the situation. Natasha honestly felt that, in the beginning, they'd put up with her mother for her sake as much as J.T.'s.

Then J.T. had gotten out after twenty years behind bars, and he'd had nowhere to go and no money, either, so the brothers had let him move in to the house, too. Natasha remembered being shocked by how entitled J.T. had acted. The house had been his in the beginning. Natasha understood that. But she didn't feel as though Dylan, Mack and the others owed him anything. Without their hard work while J.T. was in prison, there would've been nothing left. No house. No business.

"Damn it," she muttered as she straightened and restraightened her small desk. She owed them so much. But she was all her mother had. How did she turn Anya in without first making sure it was the right thing to do?

Because she was trying not to obsess about it until she could get home and speak to her mother once again, and she was missing her little boy, she sent a text to Ace.

How's Luke?

He didn't respond. But Ace was often up late, gaming, so he could still be sleeping. She assumed it was his mother who was taking care of Lucas and hoped she'd hear from Ace later. She needed a bit of reassurance. Everything in her life seemed upside down right now, including Ace's sudden interest in taking Luke for an extended visit. The paternity test and the threat of another man being Luke's father seemed to have made Ace snap out of his selfish preoccupation and apathy.

That might prove to be a good thing for Luke in the long term. Natasha certainly hoped so. But what did it mean for her?

An eighth-grade girl entered her office with an eye infection. Natasha treated that, then cleaned a large scrape on the leg of a boy who'd tried to show his buddies that he could free solo up the side of the gymnasium.

As the morning progressed, Natasha kept checking her phone but received no answer from her ex.

Ace was trying to punish her, of course. He was sulking and, no doubt, hoping to make the days he had Lucas as difficult as possible.

Could at least one thing go her way? she wondered. And then, as she was getting her purse before going to lunch, a text finally came in.

It wasn't from Ace. And she was relieved to see that it wasn't from Grady, either, although Grady seemed to be the Amos brother who was the most insistent that she get in touch right away.

It was from Mack: I know you're probably at work, and I hate to bother you there, but . . . do you know where your mother is?

Natasha couldn't continue to function normally, not in the middle of what was happening now. She'd thought when she moved to Silver Springs that most of the wreckage in her life would stay behind her, that she'd be able to settle in and rebuild. She hadn't expected to face yet another crisis, especially so soon, but this situation was serious enough that she went to Aiyana and told her privately that something had come up and she needed to take the rest of the week off.

As expected, Aiyana was understanding and supportive — so understanding and supportive that it brought tears to Natasha's eyes.

"This isn't about the paternity test, is it?" Aiyana asked, her forehead furrowed in concern when she saw Natasha's emotional reaction.

"No. That didn't turn out the way I'd hoped, but at least the man Lucas believes to be his father is really his father. That's a good thing for him, I guess. It wouldn't be easy to switch on him at this point."

"I suppose that's true. But something is obviously very wrong. His father isn't being . . . threatening or . . . or anything like that, is he?"

Natasha managed a wobbly smile. "No. He's not being *nice,* but he isn't the one who's causing this particular problem. This is . . . this is something else." She didn't want to go into it, didn't want her boss to know she had a mother like Anya for fear it would reflect badly on her. That had been one of the benefits of becoming an adult; she and her mother no longer traveled or lived as a pair, so she'd been able to escape the stigma of Anya's drug use and instability and build an entirely different kind of reputation for herself.

She also didn't want Aiyana to suspect she was one of those people who went from one emotional upheaval to another, or created a problem if one didn't exist. It was crazy that she'd lived such a consistent, uneventful life of study and professional pursuit for so long and then — *wham* — everything had crumbled around her and was still falling apart.

Fortunately, Aiyana didn't press for details. Maybe she could tell that Natasha wasn't yet ready to talk about it. "Well, whatever's going on, I wish you the best with it," she said.

"Thank you. I should have everything sorted out by Monday. I'm so sorry to do this to you, especially now, when I've barely started. I hope it doesn't make you question your decision to hire me."

"Of course not. We're not that busy here at the school during the summer, so we'll be fine. Take the time you need."

She thanked Aiyana, gathered her stuff and left forty-five minutes early, as soon as the bell rang signaling the end of classes.

She had a long drive ahead of her, and she still needed to pack.

Mack had managed to grab a few hours of sleep, but after checking on his father and learning that J.T.'s condition hadn't changed, he'd gone to the shop to help Grady and Rod stay on top of business.

Grady was working the desk today. Rod had insisted he stay away from the work going on in the back end. Grady had gotten even less sleep than Mack and was too bleary-eyed to do some of the detailing he usually did. So Mack had donned a jumpsuit and a mask, stepped into one of the paint stalls and painted a Dodge Charger a mustard yellow simply because the owner wanted to soup up his paint job, and a white Subaru that had been repaired after an accident.

He'd just pulled off his gloves and his respirator mask when Grady came out. "We closed for the day?" he asked.

"Not yet," Grady replied.

"It's after five."

"I know, but Chase Hallow called. He needs to pick up his truck tonight. I said I'd wait for him."

"When will he be here?"

"Ten minutes or so."

Mack stripped off his jumpsuit, hung it on a peg and used the sleeve of his T-shirt to wipe the perspiration from his forehead. "I can stay and take care of Chase. You head home and get some sleep."

"I'm not going home after this. I'm going to the hospital."

Mack pulled off his booties. "Dylan and Cheyenne have been there all day, and Aaron is on his way to spell them. Why not grab a few hours while you have the chance?"

"Because I can't sleep. I don't want to sleep. Not until I know Anya isn't going to get away with what she's done. Have you heard from Natasha?"

Mack had texted Natasha earlier, but he'd received no response. "Not yet. You?"

"Nothing. She knows what her mother's like. I can't believe she'd ignore us. That she wouldn't care about what her mother did to our father. That's why I'm so pissed off."

The memory of Natasha straddling him in bed, her hair tumbling down over her bare breasts as she moved, flashed through Mack's mind, and he knew he'd never be able to be impartial. What he felt for Natasha would eventually pit him against the brothers he loved so much. There was no way to avoid it. "It's not that she doesn't care, bro. She's in a difficult position."

"Yeah, well, so's Dad. He's the one fighting for his life, remember? Granted, he hasn't been much of a father to us, but he's got as much right to live as anybody."

"He's going to pull through," Mack said and hoped to God it was true.

"You don't know that."

"Well, he's still breathing, isn't he? It's too soon to dig his grave. So lighten up on Natasha, will ya?"

"Don't you care about Dad at all?" he asked.

"Of course I care," Mack retorted. "I'm just trying to give her the benefit of the doubt."

"No, you're not. You're already trying to protect her."

"Maybe I am. But what else can I do? Her mother hasn't been any better than our father, as far as parenting goes, but Anya's Natasha's only family."

"Anya's guilty of attempted murder — and the attempted part could go away any minute," Grady snapped and whirled around, slamming the door to the front office as he went back in.

Mack pulled his phone from his pocket and navigated to his messages. I take it from your silence that you DO know where she is, he wrote.

She says she didn't do it.

Mack frowned when he saw Natasha's reply. Would she tell you if she did?

TWENTY-TWO

Natasha rolled down her window, hoping the rush of air would keep her awake as she drove north. Interstate 5 served as a conduit between Southern California and Northern California, the two greatest population hubs in the state, but there was nothing on either side of her, except for long stretches of agriculture and giant dairy farms. The area between Bakersfield and Stockton certainly wasn't what a nonresident would picture when they thought of California. There were no beaches nearby, no large cities, no theme parks — just an occasional cluster of gas stations, fast-food places and a cheap motel or two huddled around an off-ramp.

Definitely lean pickings, Natasha thought as she pulled back onto the freeway after filling up with gas.

Given all the angst and the lost sleep, she was exhausted. She would've asked Anya to take a turn at the wheel, except she didn't trust her mother to be in any better condition — or to be able to battle through her fatigue the way Natasha could. All Anya had done since she arrived was sleep and, when she was awake, fend off Natasha's questions about J.T. by claiming she didn't remember.

Natasha slanted a suspicious glance at Anya, who had her head on a pillow wedged between the passenger seat and the door. Was she telling the truth? Did she *really* not remember? Or was it that she didn't dare say? She'd never been particularly violent, but she'd never been particularly honest, either. Mack had indicated that the fights between his father and her mother had been growing worse. Maybe Anya had been high when she arrived at the house and was so consumed with jealousy after J.T. asked her to move out that she —

Natasha purposely guided her mind away from what might've come next. She refused to imagine her mother shooting anyone, let alone Mack's father.

It was after six, but the sun didn't go down until nine this time of year. For now, it was still a fireball bearing down on her side of the car. She rolled up her window to make the air-conditioning more effective and because the dairy farm they were passing stank so badly she couldn't bear it.

Nothing but straight, flat highway lay in front of her. She risked a glance at her phone, which was on the console, wondering if there'd been any news with regards to J.T. From what she could tell, she had no missed calls or messages. Ace had never even bothered to respond to her inquiry about Lucas, which troubled her.

Figuring she'd deal with trying to get that relationship on a better footing when she got back, she tried to take some pleasure in the fact that he was unwittingly doing her a favor. This whole thing would only be worse if she had to worry about Lucas being involved in it.

An hour later, when she checked again, she noticed that her mother's eyes were finally open. Anya was staring dispassionately at the scenery, or lack thereof, flying past them.

"Feeling better?" Natasha turned down the radio, which she'd been playing extra loud in an attempt to stay alert.

"No," Anya said dully.

"Do you need something to drink? Eat? I bought you some chicken tenders when I stopped to get gas."

"I'm not hungry."

She had eaten hardly anything since she arrived, but Natasha could understand why.

She went through stretches like that when she was using heavily. Sleeping all the time was another sign. "Then can we talk?"

"No," her mother said, wearily, and closed her eyes again as though she'd go back to sleep.

"Mom, we need to use the time we've got."

"To do what?" she asked.

"To get prepared!"

"I don't want you to ask me again if I shot J.T. I don't know how many times I can tell you that I don't remember."

Before she'd said she *didn't* shoot J.T. It was the other details that were fuzzy. Now she couldn't remember that, either?

A fresh surge of anxiety caused the headache Natasha had been battling all day to pound even harder. "Why don't we talk about who might've done it, then? Is there anyone J.T. has been having trouble with? Anyone he hasn't been getting along with, other than you?" she added dryly.

Her mother gave her a dirty look. "He fought with everyone, Tash. Not just me. You know what he's like."

"Can you give me a name? Was there anyone in particular?"

She dug a pack of cigarettes from her purse, took one out and rolled down the window.

Natasha was about to stop her. She would not allow smoking in her car, even with the window down. But she didn't have to say anything. Anya cursed and rolled up the window almost right away. Apparently, she couldn't tolerate the smell of manure that enveloped them, even for a nicotine fix. "It would be easier to name someone who *did* like him," she said, leaving the cigarette dangling in her mouth, unlit.

"What about the other woman he's been seeing? *She* must like him."

Her mother removed the cigarette from her mouth and shifted to stare at her. "You found the letter."

Natasha scowled at the long, steady stream of traffic ahead of them. "Yes."

"Where was it?"

"In your car."

Holding her cigarette in her left hand, she flipped her lighter open and closed with her right. "And where is it now?"

Natasha had it in her purse, but she didn't know whether to hang on to it or destroy it. If her mother was innocent, she should destroy it so that it couldn't be used to incriminate Anya. But if Anya was guilty, Natasha would be destroying valuable evidence the Amos brothers might need to get a conviction. Since she couldn't figure out which was the right thing to do, she was hanging on to it for the time being, even though it frightened her so much she had to overcome the impulse to burn it almost every time she thought of it.

"We have to get rid of it," her mother said.

Natasha refused to look at her. She didn't want to see evidence of the fear she heard in her mother's voice, didn't want to react to it. Her natural protectiveness might lead her to do something that wasn't right or that she'd later regret. "We can't."

Anya gaped at her. "Why not?"

Natasha opened her mouth to try to explain her position but couldn't bring herself to reveal her doubt. "I left it back in the car," she said, lying instead.

"You didn't destroy it?" she asked in horror.

"I didn't know what to do with it."

"You know how it makes me look!"

"Then you should've destroyed it yourself."

"I wasn't in my right mind yesterday or I would have. I was . . . frantic, upset. All I could think about was that I needed to get to you. I'd just found the man I love bleeding to death in our house."

This reaction was at least slightly comforting. "You truly love J.T.?"

"Of course! Why would I still be messing with him after all these years if I didn't?"

"Do you know the woman he was seeing?"

"Which one?"

"He's been seeing more than one?" Natasha couldn't keep the surprise from her voice. In her mind, J.T. was no great catch. He did have a muscular build, which he was careful to maintain despite being disorganized in every other aspect of his life, because he liked to pretend he could compete favorably with his remarkable sons. He also had a high opinion of himself. Maybe more women than she would've thought were that easily fooled.

Anya finally put away the cigarette. "I don't think he's ever been faithful — not to me, anyway."

"Could it be that someone else got jealous?" Natasha asked.

"Maybe," Anya muttered, but she didn't seem particularly invested in the idea. Was that because she already knew it went down a different way? Or she was feeling too fatalistic to reach for this other scenario as a possible answer?

Natasha drove for a few more miles before trying to talk to Anya again. "What types of things did you and J.T. fight about, Mom?"

Anya sank deeper into the seat, as if she wished she could disappear altogether. "Do we have to continue with this?"

Was she worried about J.T.? Afraid he'd die? She hadn't articulated those concerns, but maybe that was why she wasn't coping very well. She claimed she loved him. It could be concern and fear and not regret and fear that had her acting like a cornered animal.

"I'm trying to understand, trying to learn enough that I can fight for you when we arrive," Natasha explained. "You understand that, don't you?"

"I don't think we should be going back in the first place," she spit, suddenly filled with some fight. "You're leading me right into the lion's den. You know that, don't you?"

Natasha swallowed hard. "We *have* to go back. We don't have any choice."

"Of course we do!" her mother argued.

"The man you supposedly love was nearly killed yesterday, Mom. He might die. Don't you want to go back to see him?"

She worried her lip.

"Mom?"

"Not if it means going to prison. He was breaking up with me for someone else, after all. I can't be that gullible."

"I'm hoping it won't mean prison or

anything like that." But she had to think of Mack, his brothers and J.T., couldn't only think of her mother. She loved them, too. Especially Mack, of course.

"I'm telling you it's a mistake," her mother reiterated.

Natasha feared her mother was right. Was she making the best decision? She didn't want to feel guilt and regret herself when this was all over. But what other choice did they have? "Staying at my house won't do any good," she said. "It's the first place they'll come looking for you. So what're our alternatives? You want to go on the run? Try to hide?"

"That would be better than going to prison! Dylan, Rod, Aaron —" she waved an arm for emphasis "— all of them are going to think it was *me*."

"It's still possible that J.T. will pull through and be able to tell us what happened. And I want to be there if he does. So . . . can you work with me? Please? Give me something to say until then, some reason for me to stand by your side when all the evidence seems to go against you?"

"I didn't shoot him!" she said, more emphatically.

"A few minutes ago, you said you don't remember."

"Maybe I don't. But I'm not the type of person who would do something like that, so . . . it couldn't have been me."

Natasha would accept that in a normal situation. But this wasn't a normal situation. Had that letter caused her mother to snap? "Were you upset about the other woman?" she asked.

"Of course I was upset about his other women, especially the one he was going to leave me for. J.T. was *my* man. Stephanie had no business messing around with him."

Natasha could hardly fault her for feeling that way. Wouldn't any woman? "You know her?"

"Of course. She's been hanging out with some of our friends the past few months." She sighed heavily and rolled her eyes. "Now I know why she's been showing up so often."

"What's her last name?"

"Vogler."

"Was this Stephanie Vogler the cause of most of the fights between you? Recently, I mean?"

Anya punched her pillow and rested her head on it again. "No. He doesn't love her, even if she thinks he does. The only woman J.T. has ever really loved is his dead wife. Every time he gets a little liquor in him, he

409

starts up about her. No one could ever make him as happy as she did. Blah, blah, blah. Definitely not what *I* ever wanted to hear. He compared us all the time, and, of course, I always fell short." She shot Natasha a sulky look. "He wouldn't have liked it if I did something like that to him — made him feel as though he wasn't good enough, would *never* be good enough. He was damn lucky to have me. Who else would put up with him?"

Natasha's phone rang but Natasha was trying to pass a slower-moving semi and couldn't take her eyes from the road.

"It's Mack," Anya announced.

Natasha managed to cut back into traffic and held out her hand. "Give it to me."

"No, don't answer it," her mother said, suddenly in a panic. "Stop the car. I have to get out."

"I can't stop here," Natasha said. "We're in the middle of nowhere."

"I don't care. I'm not going back to Whiskey Creek. It was a mistake to let you talk me into this. You said you would stand by me. You said you would protect me."

Her phone stopped ringing. "I said I'd do what I could as long as you were innocent," Natasha clarified.

Her mother reached for the door handle

410

as though she'd leap out, and Natasha nearly crashed trying to stop her. "What's wrong with you?" she asked, shaking from the adrenaline when she finally managed to pull the car safely to one side.

Anya was rattled, too. "I'm scared," she admitted, her eyes filling with tears.

Natasha didn't know what to do. Should she keep pushing her mother to return? Or give up and see what happened? She loved Mack. She loved his brothers, too. But this was her *mother*. All they'd ever really had was each other. Sure, most of Anya's problems were her own fault. If she lived a different life, she could change her circumstances. Instead, she was her own worst enemy and didn't seem to know how to change that.

Natasha could both hear and feel the semis whizzing past them on her left. The blast of wind that came off each one rocked her smaller Jetta, keeping her on edge. "We can go to Whiskey Creek and hope that will mitigate some of their anger, get them to listen to us and reserve judgment until J.T. comes around or the police can do an indepth investigation. Or we can go back to my house."

"Let's go back to your house," she said immediately.

"Okay, but if we do that, it'll *really* piss them off. And if they dig in and decide to come after you . . . well, I wouldn't bet against them, Mom. You know how capable they are. Not only that, but you wouldn't be able to stay with me. As I said, they'll look there first. And I couldn't go with you, wherever you go. I wouldn't even be able to talk to you on the phone. Or send you money. Because the police would be able to track all that. I have Lucas to think about. I can't allow this or anything else to negatively impact his life. I have to keep my house, my job, remain stable as much as possible."

"You want me to go back to Whiskey Creek."

"I don't know what I want at this point. I'm scared of making the wrong decision. But I won't be responsible for dragging you back in case it *is* a mistake." She drew a deep breath. "Only you know whether you shot J.T. What do you want to do?"

"That's the problem," Anya said, her voice barely above a whisper. "I *don't* know whether I shot him. I only know that I never *intended* to shoot him, that it never even crossed my mind. Surely that means something, doesn't it?"

Sadly, it wouldn't mean a lot if J.T. died and they couldn't come up with another suspect. Instead of answering, Natasha reached over to squeeze her mother's hand. "I know this isn't easy, but . . . what's it going to be?"

Mack was sitting in the hospital waiting room with his brothers and their wives when Natasha's text came in. J.T. had developed what the doctor called atelectasis — essentially his lung had collapsed again and there was some fluid buildup between the lung tissues and the chest wall. As a result, he was back in surgery, and they were all waiting to hear how it went.

No one had much to say. They were too morose after being up most of the night and working at the shop all day, and they were upset that J.T. had suffered a relapse. That it still wasn't clear whether he'd live or die made them even angrier with Anya — and Natasha, too, since they felt she wasn't being as forthcoming with them as she should be.

"Natasha and Anya are on their way," he said to the room at large, since he and his family were the only ones there, and breathed a sigh of relief that she'd finally responded to him. Just a few minutes earlier, Grady had been stalking around the room, cursing Anya's name, and he'd been complaining about Natasha, too, getting everyone riled up.

Mack believed that being able to talk to Anya in person and figure out what had happened might help, even if Anya was to blame for the shooting. His brothers craved justice. Knowing that she was no longer running away, that she would be held responsible for what she'd done, should bring them some relief and get them to calm down.

Mack wanted justice, too. He'd never liked Anya, had been angry with her for not taking better care of her daughter starting way back at the very beginning. But he worried about how hard it would be on Natasha to see the only family she had, besides Lucas, go to prison. She'd already been through so much, especially this year.

Grady had finally sat down, but his head snapped up as soon as Mack made the announcement. "How do you know?" he asked.

Mack couldn't help feeling some irritation that Grady was the first to pounce on his statement. "I just heard from Natasha."

"They're coming here — to the hospital?" he asked eagerly.

"I don't know. Her message says they're at a rest stop on Interstate 5 and will arrive in a couple of hours."

Grady came to his feet again. "Tell her to text me as soon as she gets in. I want to talk to her."

"I don't want you anywhere near her," Mack said. "I'll take care of it."

"What?" Grady cried.

Lifting his chin, Mack spoke more firmly. "I said I'll take care of it."

"I didn't ask you to take care of it," Grady retorted, raising his voice despite the fact that they were in a hospital and there were doctors and nurses striding up and down the hallway outside, as well as patients in nearby rooms. "*I'll* take care of it. Who appointed you official liaison with our stepsister, anyway?"

Grady was purposely trying to provoke him with that sister comment. "She isn't our stepsister, and you know it." His own voice sounded more steel-like than he'd intended, but he wasn't going to put up with Grady doing anything where Natasha was concerned, and he figured Grady might as well know it.

"Not anymore," Grady said. "But she was, whether you like it or not. She was our stepsister when we met her, and that's why we let her and her crappy mother move in and tried to help them. And Dad being shot is the thanks we get."

"Grady!" Dylan snapped.

"What?" Grady whipped around to face their oldest brother.

"We're all pretty pissed off — but we're mad at Anya, not Natasha, okay? And definitely not Mack. Let's keep some perspective on this."

Grady jabbed a finger toward Mack as he appealed to Rod, Aaron and the women in the room. "You know how he feels about her. You *all* know, right? He's in love with her. He's admitted as much to me. If we allow him to handle this, he'll probably let Anya drive right on out of here or try to protect her along with Natasha."

Mack felt his hands curl into fists as he stood. "What the fuck, Grady!"

Dylan scrambled to get between them, one palm pushed toward Grady and one toward Mack. "That's enough. We don't need this bullshit right now."

Mack glared at Grady and Grady glared back at him.

"Did you hear me?" Dylan said when neither of them spoke.

"You always take his side," Grady snapped and stalked out of the room.

Mack thought Dylan might go after him, but he didn't. With a tired shake of his head, their oldest brother sank back into his seat, and Cheyenne took his hand. Maybe, like Mack, Dylan was irritated by the way Grady had suddenly become their father's greatest champion. Normally, Grady was just as annoyed with J.T. as the rest of them.

The doctor filled the doorway, still wearing scrubs. "I was able to repair your father's lung," he said with a reassuring smile. "He's in recovery, but we'll be moving him to ICU shortly, where we can continue to keep a close watch on him."

"Can we see him?" Cheyenne asked.

"I think it would be better if you came back in the morning."

Mack was slightly grateful for the reprieve. He was hoping to grab a couple of hours of sleep before Natasha arrived. He wasn't sure where she'd be staying. Anya never had any money; she didn't get much from disability in the first place, and what she did get she spent on drugs. There was J.T.'s house, of course, but he couldn't believe they'd go there. No one had even been by to clean up the blood. They'd been dealing with too many other things. There were a couple of bed-and-breakfasts in the area, but Natasha hadn't even had enough room on her debit card to rent a moving van.

He'd left her five hundred dollars, though.

Maybe that was what she was using for gas and would use to get a motel, too.

He hoped she'd feel comfortable doing that. He wanted to offer up his place, but he knew she couldn't bring her mother to his house, not with the way Grady was behaving.

Be careful on the drive, and let me know as soon as you get here, okay?

He waited while his brothers and their wives gathered their stuff to leave, but he got no response, and when he looked up, Dylan was standing over him. "Don't let Grady get to you."

Mack felt like the baby of the family again for the first time in a long while. He laughed in spite of all the tension. "I'm fine, Dyl. Don't worry about me."

"I think —" Dylan started, but Aaron, Presley, Rod and his wife, India, interrupted him by calling out a final good-bye, and Dylan stopped to wave at them. Mack waved, too, before Dylan finished by saying, "I think Grady's still waiting for our father to be a father, if you know what I mean. If Dad dies, it takes that possibility away from him."

"Dad's never going to act like a normal

dad," Mack said. "Surely Grady knows that by now."

"Our brains may tell us one thing. But sometimes our hearts . . . Well, maybe it's easier for you to give up on that dream than it is for him." He squeezed Mack's shoulder. "Tell Natasha that —" he hesitated as he considered the message he wanted Mack to relay "— that we know none of this is her fault."

"I will," Mack said.

Dylan and Cheyenne told him to get some sleep and walked out, leaving Mack in the waiting room alone. He was tempted to call Natasha, but he knew she wouldn't pick up. He'd tried calling earlier. She probably didn't want to talk to him in front of her mother. He was about to text her again to ask where she was planning on staying when he realized that he could easily solve that problem for her.

How far away are you now? He sent her that message, and while he was waiting for her response, he switched over to the internet.

He'd just finished what he was doing when he got her reply.

No clue. We're in the middle of God

knows where. Had to pull over. I don't think my mother feels good.

Physically or mentally?

Both. The trauma and fear of this whole thing combined with withdrawal or a virus or something. She's slept almost since she arrived. Just waiting for her to come out of the bathroom so we can get back on the road.

Okay. Take it easy. There's no rush. But when you do get here, I got you a room at Little Mary's — Eve Harmon's B&B downtown.

You didn't have to do that.

But this way he'd know right where to find her. It's all handled, he wrote back. See you soon.

TWENTY-THREE

It was so late by the time Natasha arrived in Whiskey Creek that she didn't call Mack. She didn't want to wake him at nearly four in the morning. Besides that, she was ready to drop — couldn't handle anything else, not without first getting some sleep.

Her mother had gotten so sick on the drive they'd been stranded at a gas station somewhere along the highway for several hours. By the time Anya quit throwing up and had recovered enough to continue on, Natasha wasn't sure she'd be able to keep her eyes open long enough to finish the drive.

She took a NoDoz just to be safe and couldn't believe it when they finally pulled into the small gravel lot outside Little Mary's.

After dragging her luggage inside, she rang the bell at the front desk to get the key to their room.

It took several minutes for the night manager to appear. Natasha felt mildly guilty for making life more difficult for whoever this was, but the woman who greeted them didn't seem to be bothered by the disruption. As a matter of fact, she spoke almost *too* loudly and *too* cheerfully for Natasha's current frame of mind.

Natasha remembered Eve Harmon, the owner, who was now married and going by a different name. But she didn't recognize Eve's manager. Apparently, she'd been gone from Whiskey Creek for too long.

She got the key and managed to wrangle their luggage up the stairs. Of course their room would be on the second floor of a nineteenth-century Victorian that had no elevator, she thought, as her mother followed, zombielike, without even trying to help.

They both dropped into bed the second they got inside the room. Natasha didn't even bother to remove her clothes. She remembered being grateful for the fresh scent of lavender and the crisp cotton sheets right before she lost consciousness. Then she didn't so much as roll over, not until she heard someone banging on the door.

Assuming it was the maid attempting to get in to clean the room, she yelled to come back later and pulled the pillow over her head to block out the light streaming in from the window, but Mack's voice cut through the fog in her head.

"It's me."

Her mother didn't stir. Anya could sleep through Armageddon. So Natasha forced herself to get up, shoved her tangled hair out of her face and shuffled to the door.

Cracking it open an inch or so, she peered warily out at the man she loved so much it hurt. "Hey."

His eyebrows came together in apparent concern. "You okay?"

"Barely." She cleared her throat to rid her voice of the rasp. "It was a rough night — the longest drive of my life. Is J.T. still . . . ? Er . . . how is he?"

"Haven't been able to talk to him yet. His lung collapsed again last night, and he had to go back in for surgery, but I'm hoping he'll be able to recover now that it's fixed."

"I hope the same." She wished she could talk to J.T.'s doctor so she could gain a better understanding of what J.T. was facing and whether or not he'd survive. "What time is it?"

"Ten. What time did you get in?"

"Not until four. My mom got sick and couldn't quit throwing up."

"I'm sorry about that. I tried to let you sleep as long as possible, but I was afraid Grady would find you and . . ." He didn't finish that thought.

"And?"

"He's being an ass," he explained. "Dylan decided to close the shop today, so I know he's not at work, and yet, when I woke up, he was gone."

"You think he's looking for me."

"He's looking for your mother more than you, but . . . yeah. Or he's at the hospital. I decided to come over here first, just in case."

Of course it would be Grady who'd be the angriest among the brothers. He'd never been as accepting of her as the rest of them. Whatever friendship or love, if she could call it that, he'd offered had been somewhat grudging, although he seemed to like and accept her better at some points than others. "You told him I was bringing Mom back?"

"I told everyone last night when your text came in. I thought it might help them calm down to know your mother's not running away from this."

Still groggy, Natasha rubbed her face. "I can't really think right now. Let's set up a meeting with everyone for later, after I get some more sleep."

He tried to peer over her head. "Where's Lucas? Do you want me to take him with me?"

"Ace has him for the week."

"You took him to LA after how Ace has been acting? When he wouldn't even come out and pick him up for the weekend?"

"Ace and his parents came to get him as soon as you left. Within hours, as a matter of fact."

Mack frowned. "He's mad about the paternity test."

"Furious," she agreed. "But I have bigger things to worry about right now. At least I know my son's safe."

"He'd better be," Mack said. "Luke told me all his father does is game."

"That's true, but his parents are very responsible, and they're the ones who're probably watching Luke."

Mack looked tired and stressed himself. She could tell he wanted to say something to her — something he ultimately decided not to say.

"I'm really sorry about your father." She craved the comfort of his touch — the feel of his hand pressed to her back, his chest solid against hers as she rested her head on his shoulder — but left the door as a barrier between them.

425

"Thanks. I'll let you go back to sleep. What time do you want to meet?"

"This afternoon around three?"

"Where?"

"I'd suggest a restaurant or other neutral place, but I don't think we want this going on in public. So . . . your house?"

"Sure."

"No!" her mother moaned — suddenly coming back to life. "If you think I'm going to be there, I'm not. They'll crucify me!"

"We just want to figure out what happened," Mack said. "If we can prove it was someone else, this whole thing will go an entirely different direction."

"I agree," Natasha responded. "But I don't think it would be smart to have her meet with you and your brothers quite yet. They're too upset. It should be enough for them to know she's here, in case the police find incriminating evidence."

"She was the last person to see him, Natasha," Mack said.

"That doesn't mean she did it!" she retorted.

"Grady and the others are going to want to hear *her* say it, to have her tell them exactly what happened."

But Anya couldn't remember, and that meant she couldn't even defend herself. Natasha was hoping her mother's memory would return, or the police would find evidence that pointed to someone else. *Something.* And she needed to buy time to allow for that to happen. "I understand how it looks, Mack. But things aren't always as they appear. She loves your father. I know that much."

He seemed torn.

"Let the dust settle for another day or two until she can get well," she added. "I'll meet with your brothers today, but she's in no shape to come along."

"We just want the truth."

"But will you believe it when you hear it? Will Grady? Innocent people go to prison all the time. Please. Tell your brothers that, for today, it's just me."

When he didn't immediately relent, she knew he thought it was a waste of time and effort, that Anya was guilty.

She lowered her voice. "I know you care about me . . . in some way," she added. "Will you get them to back off a little?"

Closing his eyes, he blew out a breath before looking at her again. "Okay."

Judging by the number of vehicles clogging the drive and lining the road in front of Mack's house — the house along the river where she'd once lived herself — all the brothers were there. Natasha had purposely arrived a little late. She hadn't wanted to be sitting in the living room with Grady staring daggers at her while they waited for the others to arrive.

She didn't have to worry about that now, but she was still nervous. It was intimidating to face so many large and in-charge men, especially when they suspected her of being disloyal to them. It didn't help that she truly cared about them and wanted to remain part of their circle of friends, if not family.

At least she finally felt rested, she thought, as she parked behind a dusty black 4×4 with an ATV loaded into the back. After Mack left the B and B that morning, she'd gone back to bed and slept for another three hours, until she heard her mother in the shower. At that point she knew she needed to get up to make sure Anya had something to eat before she had to leave to meet with the Amos brothers. Anya had been so sick on the drive. She was probably feeling too weak to do much for herself. And they'd missed the breakfast that was provided along with the room.

Natasha knew she'd have to go out to get some food. She couldn't imagine Anya

428

would want to show her face around town for fear word of the shooting had already spread and there were other people who believed, like the Amos brothers, that she'd tried to kill J.T. The good citizens of Whiskey Creek had long looked down on her. They didn't especially care for J.T., either, but society in general was harder on women.

Natasha had to admit that the way Anya lived her life didn't inspire much respect, however — which made it difficult for her, too. Because of Anya, she'd always felt as though she was considered "less than" when she'd been living in Whiskey Creek.

Maybe that was why she'd had such a huge chip on her shoulder when she was younger, why she'd gotten tattoos even before she turned eighteen and piercings in places most well-adjusted girls did not.

She'd had to pay a lot to have some of those tattoos removed, didn't feel they would reflect well on her as a pediatrician. She'd let a lot of the piercings close, too.

Her phone buzzed. Taking it from her purse, she glanced down at the text she'd received before getting out.

Where the hell are you?

From Grady. She drew a deep breath and,

hoping the next hour wouldn't be as rough as she expected it to be, forced herself to approach the house.

The door swung open before she could reach the stoop. Mack had been watching for her. He gave her a sympathetic look as she drew closer, but she doubted even he understood how frightening his brothers could be. She'd always been glad to be on their side.

This was the first time that she wasn't.

"You look great," he said, his comment obviously engineered to encourage her.

She threw back her shoulders and managed a polite smile to go with the slight dip of her head, and he stepped back so that she could walk in.

Dylan immediately came forward to give her a hug, and she was tempted to cling to him. She felt bad about what'd happened to his father. She knew he and his brothers had been through enough where J.T. was concerned. They didn't need this. And Dylan was truly like a big brother to her. She craved his love and approval, and she was grateful to him for taking the lead when J.T. married her mother to see that she got the care she needed. "It's nice to see you," he mumbled, probably oblivious to how much that hug had meant to her.

She understood Dylan had also just set a precedent for how the others were to treat her and was grateful for that, too. They all looked up to him. Mack hadn't hugged her when she came in, but they'd been so intimate with each other they were afraid to touch in front of his family for fear they'd somehow be exposed.

Aaron and Rod followed Dylan's lead, and their wives gave her a quick embrace, too. She felt no animosity coming from any of them. But it was different with Grady. He sat in his recliner watching what was going on with a scornful expression, as if he was thinking, *I knew the apple wouldn't fall far from the tree.*

"Have a seat." Mack gestured at a chair that had been placed in the middle of the room, which made her self-conscious, but he pulled his own chair close, and she trusted him as much as she trusted anyone that he wouldn't let this get out of hand.

"Thanks for coming to town," Dylan said. "And for bringing your mother."

"Of course. I can't tell you how bad I feel about what's happened."

"Not bad enough to return my calls, evidently," Grady said.

"Grady," Dylan said, and she noticed Mack's heightened awareness, how stiff he

431

was beside her, the stony expression that came over his face whenever he looked at that particular brother.

"So what's your mother's story?" Grady asked, ignoring them.

She began to dig at her cuticles again, which hurt, but it gave her something to do with her hands. She felt so damn awkward, so unprepared to create the kind of excuses she knew her mother needed. "She says she found J.T. after he'd been shot, when she got back from running an errand. She saw all the blood, found the gun lying on the floor and picked it up, unable to believe what she was seeing, and —"

"Nice," Grady broke in.

They all looked over at him expectantly.

"That's a great excuse for why the police will find her prints on the gun," he explained.

She realized that her mother touching that gun wasn't a good thing, that it actually supported what they believed more than what she was trying to believe, even while she was saying it. But she was staying as close to the story her mother had given her as possible. "It's — it's conceivable that someone would really act that way. You wouldn't be thinking of evidence and fingerprints and all of that when you come upon a . . . a loved one in that condition."

"Of course," he said facetiously and made a rolling motion with his hand — a gesture for her to continue.

She tried to ignore him so that this meeting wouldn't go from bad to worse. "Then, when she realized what'd happened, and that it was real, she —"

"Didn't call the police?" Grady inserted.

Natasha met his chilling gaze. "She *did* call."

"Only to get an ambulance."

"Right," she admitted.

"And left before they could even get there," Grady said. "That's how concerned she was about Dad's life. Even if this story you're giving us were true, Natasha, even if she did only come upon Dad and wasn't the one to shoot him, she left the man she supposedly loves lying on the floor in a pool of his own blood and ran off to your house."

"Grady, lay off, okay?" Mack growled. "You're not making this any easier."

"Why should I make it easy for her to lie to us? Pretend I'm fool enough to believe this crap?" He came to his feet, and Mack shot up at the same time.

"You need to remember who you're talking to, that's all," Mack said.

Grady's chin jutted forward. "Oh yeah, I

forgot," he said, still facetious. "We're supposed to swallow this bullshit — let her mother murder our father — because you've fallen for our own stepsister!"

Mack launched himself at Grady, knocking over a chair in the process. India screamed for her husband to stop the fight as Mack took Grady to the floor, and Cheyenne and Presley scrambled to get out of the way.

"Mack, no!" Natasha cried. The last thing she wanted to do was come between him and his brothers. She knew how much they meant to him.

She would've tried to break it up herself, but Dylan and Aaron beat her to it. Fortunately, they pulled Mack and Grady apart before they could seriously hurt each other.

"What the hell's wrong with you two?" Dylan snapped. "I will not have you making things worse right now. Grady, you have to pull your shit together."

"What are you talking about? *He came at me!*" Grady's clothes were wrinkled from the brief scuffle and there was a trickle of blood rolling from his nose, which he wiped away with an air of impatience as he shot Mack a menacing look.

"You provoked him," Aaron said. "You were *trying* to provoke him."

"You're telling me you two believe this garbage?" Grady gestured at Natasha, making her feel even more self-conscious. "You believe, even though Anya was the last person to see Dad, the gun has her fingerprints all over it and she fled the scene, that it could be anyone else?"

In spite of Grady's accusations, Natasha was so concerned about Mack she couldn't help looking over at him, scanning his body with her eyes for injuries. Fortunately, he seemed less hurt than Grady did.

Aaron scowled. "It doesn't matter what we believe. We're dealing with someone we care about here. We need to remember that. Besides, Natasha's trying to help us. She's not the one who did it."

"She's not trying to help us," Grady argued. "She's protecting the person who shot him. And what are the police doing about it? Nothing! They don't give a damn about Dad. None of you do, either." He glared at Mack. "You ever come at me again and —"

"What?" Mack tried to get free, to take it up with him again, but Aaron held him tight. "You'll do what?"

"I'll kick your ass, that's what."

"Try it, and you'll get your own ass handed to you," Mack said.

Natasha couldn't believe this was happening. She'd never seen Mack like this. He was always even-tempered, congenial, fun-loving — the true baby of the family and everyone's favorite. But they were all stressed, upset, frazzled.

Grady laughed without mirth and flung a hand at them all. "I'm done with this meeting. I already know all I need to know," he said and stalked out the door.

Natasha briefly covered her mouth. "I'm sorry," she said when she dropped her hand. "That's all I can say. I have to listen to my mother, hear her side and make sure she's really to blame. She has no one else. And I don't want to be responsible for sending her to prison for the rest of her life if she's telling the truth. I just —" she drew a steadying breath "— we need some time. I know how this looks. I know you don't believe her. I admit that even I'm not convinced. But, please, ask yourself, 'What if?' She's a human being, after all. Can't we at least give the police the time they need to do their jobs?"

Mack was still breathing heavily, but she could tell it wasn't from exertion. He was furious. "Of course we can," he said, speaking for them all. "We don't have the right to do anything to her, anyway. It's up to the police to perform the investigation, collect the evidence and arrest her, if it comes to that."

Natasha nodded. "Okay. And just so you know —" she shifted her gaze from one to the next so they would all understand how sincere she was "— I get that she'll need to be punished if she did it. I'm not trying to stand in the way of that. I would never try to protect someone from the consequences of their actions — not when it's this serious — even out of love. I just hope she's not guilty and that, if we give this a little time, we'll find some proof of that."

"Dad might even come around," Rod said.

"Yes." She grabbed on to the small lifeline he'd thrown her. "I'm counting on that. I *really* hope he'll be okay, and that he'll be able to tell us his side of things soon."

Cheyenne gave her a warm smile. "I know this is hard for you," she said. "But we'll get through it."

"Hopefully without tearing the family apart," Rod added dryly, tossing a remonstrative look at Mack.

"He was the one who was out of line," Mack said.

India frowned. "He's struggling, Mack."

"We all are," Mack said. "That doesn't give him the right to treat Natasha the way he did."

Dylan shoved his hands in his pockets. "I agree. But we're all going to need to exercise some restraint over the next few days."

Natasha felt weak, drained. "I'd better go," she said. "Thanks for . . . for trying not to pass judgment on my mother too soon, in spite of . . . in spite of how it appears."

They said goodbye and Mack followed her out. "Are you okay?" he murmured, closing the door behind them as they stepped out onto the porch.

"I'm fine. Just . . . please, don't fight with Grady. Not on my account. I know how much you love him."

"And how do I feel about you?" he asked, lowering his voice.

She wanted to reach out and smooth down his hair, which was standing up after his tussle with Grady, but sighed instead. "I don't know. I know you don't want to love me, even if you do — and that can be the same as not loving me at all. You've already proved that."

TWENTY-FOUR

Grady was at the hospital when Mack arrived. Mack found him sitting with his head in his hands next to their father's bed in the small, cramped room of the ICU. When his brother realized he was no longer alone, he sat up and gave Mack a dirty look. "What are you doing here?" he asked. "You obviously care more about Natasha and Anya than you do Dad."

Or me. Was that what he wanted to say but wouldn't?

Normally, Mack didn't have any trouble getting along with Grady. A small argument might flare up now and then over who went grocery shopping last, or who mowed the lawn or did the dishes, but that was about as bad as it got. They had a good life, and they knew it. It was a big house, there was plenty of room for both of them, they had a successful business, and since they were both single, they often hung out together even after work. All without a problem. So Mack couldn't figure out why Grady was suddenly acting like an ass.

Trying to take into account what India had said earlier — that Grady was "struggling" — Mack suppressed his own temper and spoke in a low, even tone. "Can I talk to you?"

"Go ahead and talk," he grumbled.

Grady's eyes were bloodshot, and he hadn't shaved. Mack didn't think he'd even showered. "Not here." Their father didn't seem to be conscious, but Mack wanted some privacy, just in case J.T. could hear what was going on around him.

Grady hesitated as though he might refuse but finally lumbered to his feet and followed Mack down the hall.

"What's going on with you?" Mack demanded as soon as they reached the waiting room, which was, thankfully, empty.

"What do you mean?" Grady asked. "You know what's going on with me. Dad's probably going to die because we were nice enough to accept Anya and Natasha into our lives. Had we not done that, Anya probably would've followed her daughter to LA after the divorce. Instead, she stayed here because she knows we care about Natasha, that we have an ongoing relationship with her, and that makes her feel as though she can claim us as family, too. And we don't need either of them around. We've got enough dysfunctional shit going on with Dad as it is."

Mack blinked at him. Grady was blaming the shooting on the fact that they'd taken an interest in Natasha's well-being when she was in high school? That was such an outlandish stretch! "Are you listening to yourself right now? You're not making any sense. Natasha's been gone for thirteen years. She's been back to visit periodically, but . . . we've hardly done anything for her in all of that time. She was married for six of those years."

"Anya knows that if Natasha gets into trouble she could come to us and we'd be there for her. We care about Natasha. And *you* care about her a whole lot more than the rest of us."

Mack was done denying it. "So what? Why does that bother you so much?"

He seemed surprised that Mack no longer denied the accusation. "It just . . . does."

That answer — or lack thereof — made Mack believe he was beginning to understand. "Wait a second. This isn't about losing Dad. At least, it's not *only* about losing Dad. It's about change. You want your life

441

to continue on just as it was. You don't want me to get with Natasha because then you'll be the only one who isn't married."

"I've never planned on getting married."

Because of what'd happened with their mother? Because he was afraid of losing someone he loved that much? Mack could understand. That kind of loss was Mack's worst fear, too — probably the only thing he was truly afraid of. "Sometimes you have to take a risk, Grady. Give love a chance no matter how much it scares you."

"That's what you're doing?"

"It is."

"Well, that's not my problem. It's just that . . . I've always been the odd man out," he said and left the room.

Grady hadn't been entirely convincing, but another thought crossed Mack's mind, causing him to run after his brother. "Hey," he said, grabbing him by the arm to stop him before he reached the ICU. "*You* don't have a thing for Natasha, do you? You've always acted as though you like her less than all the rest of us. But maybe —"

"No," Grady broke in. "You're heading down the wrong road there for sure. She's beautiful. A guy would have to be blind not to see that. But I'm not attracted to her in that way."

442

Mack felt some of the tension leave his body. "Then why does it matter if I get with her?"

Grady didn't seem to have an answer. He stared at the floor for several seconds before lifting his gaze. "It doesn't," he said. "I hope you'll both be happy."

Natasha didn't go right back to Little Mary's. As difficult as her childhood had been, she'd had a much better life once she and her mother moved to Whiskey Creek, and she wanted to take a few minutes to see the town again.

Stopping at the park, where they put the big Christmas tree every year for Victorian Days, she got out and walked around, trying to use the time to decompress after the move, sleeping with Mack again, the shocking way her mother had arrived at her house.

She would never have known this place, or the Amos brothers, if her mother hadn't found Mack's father on a website where prisoners requested "pen pals." Natasha remembered being furious when her mother said they'd be moving yet again, but this last move had, surprisingly, turned out to be the best thing for her. She doubted she would ever have gone to college without Mack and his brothers making sure she finished high school and encouraging her to continue.

What am I going to do with you, Mom? she wondered and meandered over to a large statue of a miner with a gold pan filled with fake gold as she tried to call Ace.

He didn't pick up. That was frustrating, but it didn't surprise her. She sent him a text.

No matter how you feel about me, we have a child together. Please try to act like a decent human being and reassure me that my son is okay.

She saw the three dots that indicated Ace was responding and held her breath. He's okay.

"You really outdid yourself. Thanks for that," she muttered but was relieved to hear it. She missed Luke, wasn't used to being away from him. With all that was going on, she craved the feel of his small body in her arms.

When will you be bringing him home?

She had to know when to be back, didn't want the Grays to drive out to Silver Springs only to find her gone. She didn't want to tell them she was out of town, though. She was afraid Ace would say he was bringing Luke back right away, just to put her in a bad situation. Besides, the last thing she wanted was to have them find out that her mother had probably shot her former husband. She'd tried so hard to live her life differently than Anya, but having to test her child to see who his father was made her look all too much the same.

When I'm ready, came his response.

Natasha cursed, startling two tourists. She'd been so focused on her phone she hadn't heard them come up beside her. Giving her a scowl for the profanity, they moved farther away.

"Sorry," Natasha mumbled, but she wasn't even sure they'd heard her apology.

Give me the day and time, she wrote to Ace.

I don't know yet.

Bring him on Sunday.

Maybe.

Sunday will be a week. That's enough.

I'll be in touch later.

With a sigh, she slipped her phone back in her purse and returned to her car.

Once she reached the bed-and-breakfast, she was greeted by the day manager as soon as she walked in. "Hello, Ms. Gray. How are you today?"

Natasha was startled to be addressed by name. She'd never met this woman, either, but she supposed the night manager had made notes so they could be more personable with their guests: *Natasha Gray, young woman in #5 with long dark hair, checked in with her mother at 4:00 a.m.* "I'm fine. Thank you."

"Would you like some tea and cookies?"

Natasha looked into the sitting room to her right. It had six small tables, two chairs each, most of which were filled with other guests. "That sounds . . . good," she said, slightly surprised to find it was the truth. She hadn't had much interest in food lately. "Let me get my mother."

"Oh, I'm afraid your mother just left," she said.

"Left?" Natasha echoed. "Where'd she go?"

The woman seemed, understandably, taken aback by the question. This faux intimacy extended only so far. "Um, I don't know," the woman said. "I just saw her walk out."

Natasha left the manager standing in the hall and sprinted upstairs to her room. Where had her mother gone? And why had she left?

Her heart knocked against her ribs as her mind supplied the most likely answer. *She ran away.* How would she explain that to the Amos brothers? And did this mean that her mother would be a wanted woman? That the police would chase her down? What would the ramifications be?

Using the old-fashioned key she'd been given — there were no card keys in a place like this — she swung the door wide to find her mother's bed rumpled. Anya hadn't let the maid come in. She had, however, borrowed Natasha's makeup and rummaged through the suitcase of clothes Natasha had brought for them to share. Most everything was spilled out onto the floor, which was so typical of her mother.

Since Anya had left her phone when she "found" J.T., Natasha couldn't call or text her. She felt a moment's panic — then she saw her mother's handwriting on the pad by the land phone between the two beds. "Tell me you didn't run away, tell me you didn't run away," she chanted as she stepped over the mess, grabbed that paper and read:

I must've shot him, Tash. You're right — the Amos brothers are right. Who else could've done it? I don't remember what happened. Just the blood. I'll never forget that. But I would've remembered something if I hadn't been using, so even that's my fault. I'm going to turn myself in. I know I haven't been a perfect mom. But I love you. I hope you know that. Go back to Silver Springs and your son and forget about me. My life is essentially over while you have so many wonderful things ahead of you. That's all I care about now.

TWENTY-FIVE

Natasha rushed to the police station. She couldn't let her mother confess without first speaking to an attorney. Anya should at least have some counsel.

But by the time she parked haphazardly and ran in, it was too late. Anya had already been taken into custody.

"Can I see her?" Natasha asked Officer Howton, who'd been on the force back when she lived here. She recognized him, even though he'd lost most of his hair since she'd last seen him and his smile lines had deepened dramatically.

"I might be able to arrange that," he said, but when he came back to where she waited in a small lobby, separated from him by a thick shield of bulletproof glass, he was wearing a frown. "I'm sorry. She says you've done enough for her and you should go home."

"What does that mean?" Natasha asked.

He adjusted his gun belt as though it was cinched too tight and spoke through the small opening designed to make communication easier. "I'm afraid she doesn't want to see you."

"Seriously?"

He looked even more uncomfortable. "She said there's nothing more you can do for her, and she's done enough in her life to drag you down."

"But . . . but she doesn't even have an attorney."

"The court will appoint one for her unless —" he lifted his eyebrows expectantly "— you prefer to hire someone?"

Natasha considered her empty bank account. The only reason she'd been able to come to town in the first place was because of Mack. "I'll look into it," she mumbled and left, feeling numb.

What did she do now? Call Mack and his brothers and tell them they no longer had to worry about her mother escaping justice?

She was upset enough that she was tempted to let them continue to worry. But that was a purely emotional reaction. It was reasonable that they'd want justice. If J.T. had shot Anya, she'd feel the same. So she created a group text and sent a message to them all at once:

450

My mother just confessed and turned herself in. Thought you'd want to know. I hope your father is going to be okay.

She expected Grady to be the first to reply. He should be elated, she thought bitterly. But it was Mack. I'm so sorry. Are you okay?

What hurt the most was that her mother was finally showing some signs of maturation, enough that Natasha was tempted to believe they might've been able to have a real relationship one day. She'd never been able to respect her mother, but she respected this decision.

Still, she had to be fair.

If Mom pulled that trigger, she deserves what's coming. I understand that. I just wish she could remember doing it. That would make this easier on both of us.

Dylan: What's happened sucks all the way around. Thanks for letting us know.

Rod: More bullshit for you to go through, Tash. I'm sorry she did this.

Aaron: Hang in there, little one. You're a

451

tough chick. You've always been a tough chick.

Little one. He used to call her that when she was in high school, and because she'd found it condescending and patronizing and wanted to be considered an equal — so that Mack would treat her like a viable option — it'd made her fighting mad. Aaron used to do it on purpose, just to set her off so they could all have a good laugh, but it had become an endearment, a fond memory, and it brought tears to her eyes to see it today.

Surprisingly, she didn't receive anything from Grady. Unable to resist, she wrote: Grady? Aren't you happy? You got what you wanted.

When no one answered, she felt small-minded and petty after they'd been so supportive.

Sorry, she wrote. My bad.

Then, because she didn't feel as though she could be trusted with a phone right now, she powered it down and returned to Little Mary's, where she spoke to the day manager to see what she owed on the room and when she needed to vacate it. She was hoping she wouldn't have to drive back to Silver Springs right away — she didn't think she had the fortitude to make the long drive — and was relieved to learn the room had been prepaid until tomorrow.

What would she have done without Mack?

"Thank you," she said politely and somehow managed to climb the stairs even though her legs suddenly felt like lead weights. All she wanted to do was go back to bed. She figured she had a lot of missed sleep to catch up on. Maybe by morning her mother would change her mind about seeing her and she'd at least be able to say goodbye and promise to stay in touch.

When Mack couldn't reach Natasha, he left the hospital and went out to find her. He was afraid she'd already left for Silver Springs and didn't want her to drive unless she was feeling up to it. She'd been under so much stress for so long she looked like a strong breeze would blow her over.

Fortunately, he found her car parked at Little Mary's.

Taking the slot next to her Jetta, he went in and approached the front desk, suddenly glad he'd been the one to pay for the room. Otherwise, the manager wouldn't be able to give him any information.

"Is everything okay?" Doris asked when she saw him.

Mack recognized her from when she'd brought her Lincoln SUV into the shop to have a dent buffed out of the door before her husband could get home from deer hunting and see that she'd hit a telephone pole. "I think so. Why?"

Had she heard about Natasha's mother shooting his father? Did she know who Natasha and Anya were? An article had appeared in the local paper this morning. Maybe she'd seen it and recognized Anya.

"Ms. Gray didn't look too well when she came in a while ago," she replied. "I tried to bring her a tray with some tea and biscuits, but she never answered the door."

"I'll check on her," he said. "Can I get a key?"

"Of course. You're on the room."

A moment later, he took the stairs two at a time.

He knocked, but when he didn't get an answer, he didn't hesitate to let himself in.

The drapes had been pulled. After the brightness of the afternoon sun streaming in the windows downstairs, he couldn't see anything until his eyes adjusted to the darkness. Then he could make out a small figure in the bed on the right.

"Tash?" he murmured.

She lifted her head. "What are you doing

454

here?" She sounded both groggy and surprised, as if she'd been sleeping too soundly
to hear the door. He almost felt guilty for
waking her.

"I was worried about you."

"How's your father?"

"We still don't know."

"Go back to the hospital. I'm okay," she
said and dropped her head back on the pillow, but he wasn't going to leave her. She
meant more to him than J.T. did. She meant
more to him than anyone did.

He kicked off his shoes, climbed into bed
and pulled her into his arms. When he realized she wasn't wearing much, he wished
he'd taken off his clothes, too. He wanted
to feel her skin next to his. But he didn't do
anything to change that; he didn't want her
to think he'd come for something else.

She didn't make a sound, but he knew she
was crying when he felt teardrops soak
through his shirt.

Natasha didn't know how long she'd been
sleeping. It felt like several hours. But when
she woke up, she could tell Mack was
awake, too. Having his arms around her
made her feel completely different — better, oddly satisfied, despite everything, as
though she would survive the nadir of her

life and be just fine.

When she turned to face him and lifted a hand to touch his cheek, he hauled her closer.

"You get enough sleep?" he murmured as they entwined their legs. "I'm so worried about you."

"I'll be fine." She didn't add that having him with her made a huge difference. She wasn't going to put any pressure on him. She'd been disappointed about the paternity test, but the one good thing that came out of it was that she could rest assured that obligation would never be the basis of whatever relationship they had.

"We'll get through this."

She didn't respond. She wasn't in the mood to talk. She just wanted to *feel* him — everywhere.

Once she'd unbuttoned his shirt, he slipped out of it and tossed it on the floor. But he caught her hand when she unfastened his shorts. "I know you must feel like shit. We don't have to do this."

Except that this was how she planned to feel better. She was going to take advantage of every minute they had together before she returned to Silver Springs and left him in Whiskey Creek, to stockpile as many memories as possible to sustain her in the coming months. "I want to feel you inside me," she said simply.

Her response was all the encouragement he needed. He removed his shorts while she peeled off her panties. When their bare chests touched, she closed her eyes and wished she could capture and hold that sensation forever.

He was extra gentle in the way he touched her and kissed her, and when he rolled her beneath him, it seemed as though he was more interested in the shared experience, the togetherness, than anything else.

Neither of them spoke as they began to make love. They touched and tasted and simply enjoyed the intimacy. They were growing so familiar with each other in a physical sense, after knowing each other and caring about each other for so long in an emotional sense, that sex only built a stronger bond. Because she couldn't get over him, she knew she was probably making a mistake, but she couldn't deny herself right now.

"What is it?" she asked when he paused and smoothed the hair from her face.

"You're so beautiful. I can't believe I'm lucky enough to have another chance."

This frightened her. She didn't want to get her hopes up only to be disappointed again. "Who said you have another chance?" she asked, leery.

He pinned her hands above her head as he began to move in a more deliberate way, with powerful thrusts that also felt slightly possessive. "Are you going to turn me away?"

"I have to," she replied. "You're not wearing a condom." She was avoiding the real question by making it about this very moment and not their relationship as a whole, but he didn't call her on that. Neither did he withdraw.

"I don't care."

She tightened her grip on his hands. *"About making a baby?"*

"You don't know it yet?"

"Know what?"

He gave her a long, slow kiss. "I'm going to marry you."

"Oh, you are," she said. He'd never promised this before, but she was still afraid to trust it. What if his father died and the coming trial of her mother tore them apart? What if his brothers freaked out and made him choose them or her? What if the childhood trauma of finding his mother dead in her bed made real commitment impossible for him?

"Yep. It's true."

458

Despite her caution, his words were filling her with hope, and the pleasure he was giving her was also tempting her to believe him. "You're so sure —" she tried to draw the breath she needed to finish her sentence "— of my answer you're not even going to ask me?"

He groaned as he drew closer to climax. "You've always been the smart one," he said. "You've known all along that we were meant to be together."

At this, she stopped him. "But . . . now?" Her words fell to a reverent whisper. "My mother may have killed your father."

He framed her face with his hands. "That has nothing to do with us."

"I doubt your brothers will agree."

"Maybe they won't. But they'll accept it, because they'll have no other choice. I could never be happy without you, Tash." He pecked the tip of her nose. "I love you. I've always loved you."

Their relationship had been so confusing and hurtful at times. She could tell he felt *something,* but it never seemed to be enough. "Why now?" she asked.

"You mean why not when we made love seven years ago? I hurt you then. I was so stupid. I let you marry someone else and could've lost you for good." He rested his forehead on hers, and his breath fanned her lips as he spoke. "Can you forgive me? Please?"

She couldn't hold a grudge against him. That was impossible for her. So she wasn't even going to pretend. "Of course I forgive you. But . . ."

"Don't say 'but,' " he broke in as he licked his way down her neck.

She continued anyway. "I was just going to say that I can't think right now. We should probably talk about this after."

"I like talking about it now, when your defenses are down," he joked.

She could feel his tongue circle her nipple. "You're all I've ever wanted," she said before she even realized that she was speaking those words out loud. She hadn't meant to vocalize what she was thinking. But he was right — at the moment, he had her at a disadvantage.

"I'm happy to hear that." His teeth flashed as he smiled. "So about making a baby . . ."

Orgasm was inching closer, making it even more difficult to think objectively. "Baby?" she gasped. "You want a *baby*?"

"Why not? I turned forty-one this year. I'm getting up there."

She wasn't opposed to having another child. Not with Mack. But . . . "I don't think it would be smart," she said.

Obviously disappointed, he stopped. "Why not?"

"Because if I get pregnant, you won't be able to change your mind about me. You'll feel too obligated." There. She'd blurted that out, too — exactly what she was thinking — and held her breath as she awaited his reaction.

"I'm not going to change my mind, Tash," he said earnestly. "I'll never give you any reason to doubt my love again. I'm finally where I should've been seven years ago — ready to flip off the whole world, if necessary, and love you no matter what."

This was complete surrender. Had it been anything else, she would've argued that it was too soon to talk about something as life altering and permanent as a child together. But she'd been in love with Mack for fifteen years, so it felt more like it wasn't soon enough.

She brought his face down to hers for a long, deep kiss. "Okay," she said as she exhaled and let him take them both the rest of the way.

"I don't know if this is a good idea." Natasha smoothed her sundress as she got out of Mack's truck and looked dubiously at the hospital.

Mack hit the lock button on his key fob, took her hand and pulled her toward the entrance. "It'll be fine," he said, but he wasn't completely convinced that was true. He had no idea how Grady, in particular, might react to seeing Natasha. He only knew he was no longer going to let that or anything else get in his way. Why it took him so long to get to this point, he didn't know. He remembered how sick it had made him when he heard that Natasha was getting married, how he'd struggled for years to bury the pain and the loss, and how he couldn't help hanging on every word Dylan received from her. Mack had even secretly collected the pictures she'd sent of her and her son, had them all saved on his phone.

He supposed part of his reluctance to get together with her was that he'd dubbed her off-limits for so long and then tried so hard to remain circumspect about the fact that their parents were once married. And when she came back to town and he ran into her during Victorian Days, he felt guilty for letting it turn physical, as though he'd betrayed his brothers and what they'd set out to do where she was concerned.

Now he was finally just willing to accept reality. He was almost a decade older than she was, and they'd met in an unconventional way, but they were in love. It was that simple. He wished Lucas was his son. But Mack wanted to be part of his life regardless. What he'd said to Dylan when Dylan found out Kellan wasn't his had meant something to him, too. It was love that mattered, not genetics.

"Maybe I should take the truck back to Little Mary's," she said, her steps slowing as they drew closer. "I can pick you up later, whenever you call me."

He scowled. "Quit being a little chicken."

She scowled right back at him. "I'm not a chicken. I'm being sensitive to the situation."

He ignored the proffered euphemism. "You haven't done anything wrong. There's no reason you can't be here."

The automatic doors opened with a *whoosh,* and he felt her fingers, which were threaded through his, tighten. "I feel bad for you and your brothers," she said. "I really do. For your dad, too. But I also feel defensive of my mother. She was high when she did what she did. I know that's no excuse, not in a normal situation. But your father's an abuser, too. It could easily have been him who shot her."

Mack led her toward the elevators. "And

463

your point is . . ."

"It wasn't as if she purposely set out to kill him. She doesn't even remember it."

He let his gaze slide over to her. "She left town afterward."

She pulled away from him. "She was scared."

He understood. Anya was her mother. Of course she'd feel some sympathy for her. Natasha's split loyalties put her in an unenviable situation. But he was willing to bet what she'd said wouldn't go over very well with his brothers. "I get it. Just . . . don't say that while we're here and we might be okay."

She chuckled at his response. "I'm sorry. Sometimes I'm a little too honest."

He put his arm around her and drew her back to his side. "No worries. I love you, warts and all," he added with a grin.

She tried to elbow him, but he purposely held her too close to allow it, and they laughed as he punched the elevator button. He'd never been happier, couldn't believe that he'd finally made peace with his heart — and with her. He'd meant it when he said they'd get through this. She was the most important thing to him. He'd no longer let anything get in the way of being with her.

As they stepped into the long corridor on

the third floor, he took her hand again. "For the first little bit, maybe you'd better let me do the talking."

"Be my guest," she said. "I —"

She fell silent as soon as she looked up and saw Dylan and Rod coming toward them.

Mack braced himself for the encounter. He knew his brothers would feel a little funny about him being with Natasha in a romantic sense. They'd always pressured him to stay away from her in that way. But he was no longer going to worry about that, and they needed to get used to the change. He and Natasha could already have a baby on the way; he hoped they did. "Hey. How's Dad?"

Dylan didn't seem all that surprised, but Rod's eyes widened as he took in their clasped hands.

"Doing better," Dylan replied.

Mack knew Natasha was eager to hear their father's prognosis. The better J.T. did, the greater the chance of her mother getting out of this mess with a minimal sentence. But she didn't say anything. "In what way?"

"Vital signs are improving. No more problems with his lung. They moved him out of ICU a few minutes ago and into another room."

"I got your text on that. Thanks." Mack hoped that bit of good news, together with the knowledge that Anya had turned herself in, would be enough to get Grady to relax. "Where're you guys going?"

"To grab a bite to eat," Rod said. "Would you two like to join us?"

"No, we'll get something in an hour or so. Dad alone?"

"Aaron and Grady are there." Dylan caught Natasha's eye. "Thanks for the text about your mother. Are you okay?"

"I think so," she said.

Rod pointed to their clasped hands. "This is moving fast. Does it mean what I think it does?"

Mack lifted Natasha's hand and kissed her knuckles. "Yep."

"Took you long enough," Dylan joked.

Mack laughed. "I can be a little slow."

"Not to mention stubborn," Natasha added, which made Dylan and Rod laugh.

After his brothers said goodbye and got on the elevator, Mack kissed Natasha's hand again. "Two down, two to go."

"We don't have to do this right now," Natasha said.

"Why not?"

"Because it might be easier on Grady if I'm not here."

"I've already told him we're going to be together," he said and looked for the placard on the wall that would direct them to Room 301.

TWENTY-SIX

After having witnessed a fight break out between Mack and Grady, Natasha was nervous to walk into J.T.'s hospital room. While she was happy with Mack's sudden determination that they would be a couple regardless of what anyone else thought, she was sensitive to the fact that Grady had a problem with her right now. He'd never been her biggest advocate, but he'd mostly been supportive. It was hard to think he didn't want her around anymore.

She held her breath as Mack led her into the room, and Grady and Aaron, who were involved in some sort of discussion about the auto body shop, fell silent.

"Hey," Mack said.

Aaron rocked back in his chair. "What's up?"

Grady watched them dubiously, his lips compressed in a firm, straight line.

"Just coming to check on Dad," Mack

replied. "Dylan said he seems to be improving."

Aaron looked over at the bed, where J.T. was still hooked up to all the standard equipment. "Yeah. They're careful not to say too much, for fear it doesn't go as we hope, but I think he's going to make it."

"I doubt they'd move him out of ICU if they were as worried as they have been," Mack said.

"Exactly," Aaron agreed.

Natasha let go of Mack, approached the bed and took J.T.'s hand. "J.T., if you can hear me, it's Natasha. I'm so sorry about what happened. Just want you to know that we're all here, pulling for you."

There was no response, of course. J.T. was still unconscious, but she believed even a patient in his condition could react positively to love and encouragement.

Aaron got up to offer her his chair. There were only two in the room and Grady had the other one. "Would you like to sit down?"

"No, thanks."

"Are you sure?"

When she nodded, he returned to his seat. "I'm sorry about your mother."

"So am I." She turned her attention to Grady. "I know this has been hard for you — everything that's happened. I feel bad that my being here is somehow making it worse. You were very kind to let me live with you when I was younger and had nowhere else to go, and you've been good to me all along, just like your brothers. I'm sure you feel as though no good deed goes unpunished after what my mother has done. But I want you to know that I'll always be grateful to you, and —" she clasped her hands in front of her because the room was far too quiet and everyone except J.T. was staring at her "— and Mack and I love you."

He blinked in surprise. So did everyone else, and it got awkward for a moment. She'd been completely open and honest about her feelings, but Grady didn't know how to handle that and his brothers didn't know how to help him. The Amos brothers were good men — the best — but embarrassing displays of emotion were definitely not their style.

For some odd reason, Natasha felt like she was about to burst into tears. "You don't have to say anything," she added less stridently. "I just . . . wanted you to know."

When he saw the tears filling her eyes, Grady surprised her by standing up and pulling her in for a hug. "Mack's a lucky man," he muttered and, after a quick squeeze, left the room.

Aaron and Mack gaped at her. "You've grown soft in your old age," Aaron joked. "Your younger self would've told him to fuck off."

Mack chuckled along with him. "That's true. But I tried the 'fuck off' approach and it got Grady and me in a fight. The way Natasha handled it seems to be far more effective. 'Mack and I love you,' she said. Why didn't I think of that?"

With a sniff, Natasha grinned in spite of her tears. "It wasn't just the saying of it," she said. "It was that he knows it's true."

Pulling her up against him, Mack kissed her temple. "I *am* a lucky man," he said.

Since Mack had already paid for the room, they spent the night at Little Mary's. Natasha wanted him to sleep in with her and have breakfast, but he had to be at work at eight. He didn't want the business to fall too far behind, especially because he said it was time to hire someone to take his place, and training that person would slow things down enough as it was. As soon as he could get his replacement up to speed, he was going to move in with her and open up an Amos Auto Body in Silver Springs instead of LA.

Natasha was worried that Silver Springs

was, perhaps, too small a town for an auto body shop to be successful, but he'd pointed out that Whiskey Creek was even smaller. He said it was the quality of his work that would build his business, and she hoped that would make all the difference.

Even if it took a while for Mack to get his shop off the ground, they'd have her job, she told herself. With what he'd saved and what she could bring in, she was fairly confident they could eke by. Even if they had a baby, she had good medical insurance through New Horizons. And once they had some financial stability, she'd try again to open her own pediatric practice.

Fortunately, she could tell that was important to Mack, too. He'd always wanted what was best for her.

She was sitting at the table in the small parlor at the B and B, more hopeful for the future than she'd been since before she hired Maxine Green and her marriage went off the rails, when her phone lit up with the selfie she'd taken of herself and Mack last night.

She loved that picture. The wind was blowing his hair, he had his sunglasses on and his right arm was looped casually around her shoulders as they smiled for the camera.

472

He was so handsome . . .

To avoid disturbing the other diners — and since she was finished with her "gold rush" omelet and mixed fruit, anyway — she went outside to answer his call.

"Hello?" she said, standing on the wide front porch and looking out at the town she'd been so loath to embrace way back when she was a neglected teenager.

"You *finally* awake?" he joked.

She smiled at his emphasis on *finally*. "Barely. And I might go right back to bed."

He laughed. "I wouldn't blame you. You could probably use the sleep. But I thought you'd want to know — my father's awake."

She felt a burst of hope. "He is?"

"Yes. Grady just called. Well, he called the shop, and I answered."

"But he's treating you okay?"

"Pretty much like he used to. After what you said to him last night, I think he realizes that he has no right to try to tell me who I can love. He's just jealous that I'm moving on, and he's still single and living at home."

She could see why Grady wouldn't want to be the last unmarried brother, especially when he and Mack did so many things together. "He's a great guy. He'll find someone."

"You seem to have a way with him. Maybe you can tell him that," he joked.

She laughed. "Can your father speak?"

"Not yet. Have you heard from your mother?"

"I'm about to go to the police station to see if she'll accept a visit from me."

"You think she's changed her mind?"

"I can't imagine spending the night in jail was easy. She might be glad I came back."

"Do you want me to go with you?"

She couldn't fathom that he had any desire to see her mother. "No. You're busy at work. Just get done what you can at the shop, and we'll go over to see your dad after I get back."

"Okay."

"Mack?" she said, catching him before he could disconnect.

"Yes?"

"I'm *so* excited about our future."

"So am I. But . . . you still haven't told me you love me," he pointed out.

"Because you already know it — you've always known it."

"Still, you haven't said the words," he said, speaking softer. "I'd like to hear them some-time."

"Then it'll give you something to look forward to," she joked.

She was still smiling after she hung up, went in and packed her bags. She was planning to stay at Mack's tonight, so she no longer needed the room.

She'd just pulled to the curb in front of the police station when Dylan called her. "Hello?"

"Are you sitting down?" he asked.

She hadn't gotten out yet, but she wasn't worried about what he was going to say. She assumed he was calling to tell her what Mack had just told her — that J.T. was now awake. "Yes."

"We just asked my dad if it was your mother who shot him."

Her stomach muscles cramped. "And?"

"He can't speak yet, but he nodded."

She let her head fall forward until it rested on the steering wheel.

"Tash?"

Shit. "Okay," she said softly. "Thanks for telling me."

At least the confusion had been cleared up. At least she could rest assured that her mother deserved what was happening to her, she told herself.

But that didn't help the way she felt as she started her car and drove away instead of going inside.

Natasha felt her phone buzz. Mack was trying to call her again. He probably wanted to know if her mother had decided to relent and see her. Or he was going to tell her the same thing Dylan had — that their father had confirmed her mother's confession.

She didn't answer. She was reluctant to talk to him right now because she didn't want him to ask where she was. Since it was her mother who'd shot J.T., she'd decided to go over and clean up J.T.'s house. It wasn't as if the police needed it for anything they hadn't already done. Whiskey Creek wasn't like some of the bigger cities, where they had a forensics team to process crime scenes from shootings and homicides. This was a small town with only a few officers, and Natasha doubted they'd ever had to perform a real murder investigation. If someone was shot or killed, it was generally like this incident, where the culprit was obvious from the beginning.

Anyway, someone had to clean up soon. Otherwise, if there was enough blood on the floor, it could invite flies and, possibly, maggots. She didn't think it would be fair for Mack and his brothers and/or their wives to have to go through the trauma of dealing with that kind of mess.

Natasha had visited J.T.'s house before, so she knew where he lived. And she was pretty sure there was a key to get in on the same ring as her mother's car keys. Fortunately, Anya had left her purse behind when she went to turn herself in. The police would've taken her personal belongings when they arrested her, anyway. Now it would be much easier for Natasha to return Anya's car to the Amoses, which seemed the only fair thing to do — after she had a chance to drive it back to Whiskey Creek, of course.

She'd stopped to purchase a bucket and cleaning supplies, as well as knee pads, a mask and rubber gloves, before parking in the driveway behind J.T.'s truck.

The house — a small brown stucco two-bedroom/one bath — wasn't much to brag about and neither was the yard. Weeds choked the flower beds and large brown spots in the lawn made it apparent that it wasn't getting enough water. As she walked to the front door, she noticed spiderwebs clinging to the underside of the eaves, too, but she could tell the grass had been mowed within the last couple of weeks. She supposed that proved *some* small effort toward keeping up the place, although it was probably Mack or one of his brothers who'd come over to do it.

As a doctor, she didn't get squeamish at the sight of blood, but she'd never had to deal with a scene like this, where there was no human being to help, just the aftermath of senseless violence. Bracing herself for how it might feel to know this was where J.T. had almost lost his life, because of her own mother, she inserted the key into the lock and swung the door wide.

A wall of stale, warm air hit her, and she immediately covered her nose against the scent of rotting food and garbage. How had it come to this? she wondered. J.T. and Anya knew they couldn't get along and had no business together . . .

Pausing to put on a mask, she stepped inside, being careful to avoid the blood spatter on the tile entryway as she flipped on the light.

She was confronted with the groceries her mother must've dropped when she came in and a large reddish-brown stain on the carpet. She guessed J.T. would have to replace the carpet at some point, but she didn't want him or anyone else in the Amos family to have to cope with cleaning up the mess, so she put some music on her phone to help distract her and set to work.

Sweat rolled down her back as she carried out the garbage, but that had to be first — anything to help with the smell. Then she threw open the windows and turned on the AC so that she could breathe easier. J.T. had fallen such that the blood flowing from his gunshot wound not only soaked the carpet but also ran onto the linoleum. Her mop turned as pink as cupcake frosting as she cleaned the kitchen floor — ironic, considering the cause wasn't anything nearly so happy and appealing.

When she finished, she threw the mop away — she never wanted to see it again — and cleaned the dishes stacked in the sink. She even wiped down the counters and cupboards. She wanted to put one room absolutely right before continuing on to the next.

Stepping around the blood on the carpet, she moved into the living room, where she washed the walls to remove the fingerprint dust that seemed to cover everything. Apparently, the police department had done that much — gathered fingerprints and, presumably, taken the gun and her mother's cell phone, because they weren't there.

After three hours, she'd grown tired of her playlist and turned off the music as she started on the carpet. Getting down on her knees with a brush and a bucket of hot, soapy water, she was scrubbing hard when she heard someone at the front door. Whoever it was hadn't knocked; they were trying the knob.

Assuming Mack had found her, or one of his brothers was stopping by to get clothes or something else for J.T., she dropped her brush into the bucket and stood as the door swung open.

A tall, thin woman, who, at first glance, looked much younger than she really was — mostly because she was darkly tanned and wearing a spaghetti-strap top with a pair of very short cutoffs — walked in. Tattoos covered both arms and an ink snake climbed her throat. That also made her seem younger. But the gray streaks that ran through her long dark hair, which fell freely around her shoulders, and the wrinkles around her eyes and mouth made it apparent that she wasn't young. She had to be in her fifties.

"Oh!" She'd been so busy looking behind her, as if she was afraid someone might be watching the house, that when she nearly bumped into Natasha, she startled.

"Hello." Natasha stripped off her gloves. "What can I do for you?"

The woman glanced back at her car,

which was parked on the street at the end of the walkway, as though she regretted coming to the door and wished for a quick escape. "N-nothing," she said, her voice a raspy smoker's voice. "I — Never mind."

She turned to go but Natasha pressed the door closed before she could get back out. "Who are you?"

Long, fake red nails flashed as she pressed a hand to her chest. "Me?" She gave the impression that she didn't want to identify herself, but it would've been too awkward to refuse, so she added, "I'm . . . My name's . . . Stephanie."

Stephanie? Anya had mentioned a Stephanie. Was this the other woman? *That* Stephanie? "Vogler?" Natasha asked, recalling the last name she'd been given.

The strap on her shirt had fallen. She slid it back onto her bony shoulder as she said, "Yes. How'd you know?"

"I'm Anya's daughter. She's mentioned you to me."

Her pale blue eyes darted furtively around the apartment as if she expected Anya to appear, and Natasha suspected her of being a user, too. It made sense. Her mother had indicated that they ran in the same circles.

"Where is your mother?"

She couldn't guess? Yesterday's article

481

named Anya as a person of interest, saying police suspected this could be a domestic situation. But the local paper only came out once a week, so there'd been no follow-up to report her mother's confession. Not yet. "Why? Is that who you're looking for?"

"Hell no. She hates my guts," she stated frankly. "I just . . . I saw the car and was hoping that . . . that J.T. was back. That he was out of the hospital."

If she cared about J.T., why hadn't she been to see him? "So you know he's been shot."

"I shouldn't have come." Once again, she tried to get out, but Natasha kept her hand on the door.

"Why did you?" Natasha asked.

"I want to go. Let me out."

"Of course. Just tell me why you're here."

"Because I was worried about J.T.! I was afraid that — that Stan had killed him!" Tears suddenly filled her eyes and she covered her mouth to hold back sobs.

As hard and world-wise as this woman looked, Natasha was taken aback by the emotion. "Who's Stan?"

She blinked several times, seemingly confused. "My husband."

Natasha felt her jaw go slack. This was not the answer she'd been expecting.

482

"You're *married*?"

Stephanie forced the door open. "I'm getting out of here."

Natasha followed her out. "Can you . . . give me another second? I mean, why not? If Stan shot J.T., he has to face the consequences, right?"

"Leave me alone," she said as she scurried to her car. "I didn't mean for any of this to happen. I never dreamed he cared that much."

Once they reached her small, battered sedan, Natasha leaned on the passenger side as Stephanie power walked around it. "How do you know Stan shot J.T.?" she asked, watching J.T.'s latest love interest over the top of the vehicle.

"What do you mean?" She was too intent on escape to even look up. "He told me your mother saw him as he ran out. Surely she's told the police by now."

Natasha's heart began to pound, and her feet felt anchored to the cement. Anya must not have recognized Stan. Or because of crystal meth, she couldn't recall seeing him. "Where's your husband now?"

Stephanie yanked open the driver's door. "I don't know. He took off right after it happened."

So why had J.T. fingered Anya? "How did

Stan get hold of J.T.'s gun?"

She didn't answer. She just slammed her door, started the car and peeled off without even checking to be sure Natasha wouldn't be hurt in the process.

"She's *where*?"

Dylan looked understandably surprised when Mack confronted him, Cheyenne and Kellan in the hospital cafeteria. "At Dad's house."

"What's she doing there?"

Mack wished he knew. The message he'd received from Natasha was a cryptic one: I've found something important. Please come to your father's house. And bring your brothers. "She didn't say."

"But . . . why would she be at J.T.'s house?" Cheyenne seemed equally perplexed.

"Don't tell me she's investigating the shooting in an attempt to prove her mother innocent," Dylan said. "Anya's already confessed."

"Grandpa even said it was her," Kellan chimed in.

J.T. hadn't actually said anything. The doctor wouldn't allow the police to question him quite yet, said he wasn't strong enough. But he'd nodded when Dylan had

484

asked. What more of a confirmation was required? "I don't know." Mack scratched his neck. "I've texted her and tried to call. She's not picking up."

Dylan scowled. "Grady is just now starting to act normal. I don't want to set him off again."

"Neither do I."

"So are you going to include him in this?"

"He was sitting with me in Dad's hospital room when the text came in, so I already have. I've also texted Rod and Aaron, but I'm not sure either of them will be able to make it."

"Aaron's in Reno. He won't get here until later. But why can't Rod come?"

"Said he can't get away from the shop."

Dylan sat taller. "Really? Why? We're closed for the night. It looked like he was packing up when I left."

"He wants to finish a couple cars he's been working on, doesn't like being behind."

"Too bad Grady wasn't at the shop, too, when Natasha's text came in."

"I think he'll be okay. He's riding over with me."

Dylan's chest lifted as he drew a deep breath, and he shot a glance at Cheyenne. "Well? Should we drive over and see what's going on?"

485

TWENTY-SEVEN

Natasha had just finished cleaning the carpet when Dylan, Cheyenne, Kellan, Grady and Mack arrived. She'd been so relieved and excited by what she'd learned from Stephanie Vogler that she'd almost rushed over to the hospital to tell the Amos brothers everything she'd learned. But she was so far along in the cleaning process she'd decided to finish and simply have them come to her. It would be more private and easier to explain what'd happened if they were here instead of at the hospital, anyway.

Hearing the engines of their vehicles out front as she emptied her bucket and put it in the garbage in the scrubby, overgrown backyard, she wiped the sweat beading on her upper lip and hurried back in to greet them. Although she'd turned the air-conditioning way up, her shirt was sticking to her from scrubbing so hard to make quick work of what remained to be done.

"Wow! Is this what you wanted to show us?" Dylan ducked into the kitchen to survey the cleaning she'd done. "It looks great. Better than it ever has."

"That's so nice of you, Tash," Mack said. "Thank you, babe."

"Cheyenne was just talking about how we needed to get this place cleaned up," Dylan added, "but none of us were looking forward to it."

"I feel terrible," Cheyenne added, giving her a sheepish look. "While I was talking about it, you were over here actually doing it."

Finishing something that was so difficult gave Natasha a sense of pride and accomplishment. She loved that she'd been able to perform this service for the family who'd been so good to her. "I knew you were all busy trying to keep the shop and your families going while you supported J.T. I felt it was the least I could do, especially because we all believed my mother was the one who shot J.T."

Mack and Dylan exchanged a dubious glance. "Tash —" Mack's expression was sympathetic, but she cut him off.

"She didn't do it, Mack. I know that now."

Grady sighed as he shoved his hands into

487

his pockets. "We aren't going back to this, are we? You know she did. We all do. Who else could it be?"

Natasha's peace with Grady was tentative at best. And this wasn't going to help strengthen their truce. But she couldn't let her mother go to prison, not if Anya didn't deserve it. Pulling the letter she'd found in her mother's car out of her purse, she handed it to him.

He lowered his head and scanned it. "This letter is from my dad."

"Yes."

"He's telling your mother to move out, that he's seeing someone else."

"Yes." Natasha remembered how eager Stephanie had been to get inside the house without confronting any of the neighbors. "And that someone else is a woman named Stephanie Vogler. Do you know her?"

Dylan looked doubtful of where this was leading. "Never heard of her. But —" he took the letter and glanced over it "— this only provides motive, Tash."

His voice was overly patient, the way she talked to Lucas when she was trying to convince him of a reality he didn't want to accept. "If you didn't know the rest of the story, that would be true," she said.

"The rest of the story?" Mack echoed.

She lifted her chin. "It also provides motive for someone else."

"Who?" Kellan asked, obviously intrigued by all the drama involving his derelict grandfather.

"Stephanie Vogler's husband," she announced.

Mack tilted his head as he looked at her. "Dad was seeing a married woman?"

"He was, and her jealous husband didn't take kindly to it."

The others gaped at her as Mack moved closer. "You're saying *he* shot Dad. How do you know?"

"Stephanie Vogler told me."

Dylan spread out his hands. "When? How?"

"She showed up here while I was cleaning. She thought maybe J.T. was home, but she got me instead, and had that not happened, I might never have learned the truth, and the police might never have looked any further than my mother." She couldn't believe that the stakes were *that* high and yet the truth had come down to such a coincidence.

"Whoa. Wait a second." Mack pulled her down on the couch beside him and the others perched on chairs around the coffee table she'd just cleaned, along with the ashtray that was now empty in the center of it. "Why don't you start at the beginning and tell us exactly what happened?"

Natasha told them about Stephanie letting herself in, how surprised Stephanie had been to find Natasha instead of J.T. and how she'd blurted out things she assumed were already known but weren't. "If she hadn't believed my mother had already told the police about her husband being the one to shoot J.T., I don't think she ever would've come forward. I believe she would've taken that information to her grave, let him get away with it."

Grady didn't look entirely convinced. "But how did her husband get hold of my dad's gun?"

"Maybe she knew where it was and told him," Cheyenne volunteered.

Natasha appreciated that Dylan's wife was trying to be open-minded, but she shook her head. "I don't think so. She acted as though she hadn't known ahead of time what her husband was going to do, as though she was extremely upset by what'd happened and blamed herself for getting involved with J.T. in the first place."

"But how else could he have gotten hold of Dad's gun?" Dylan asked. "Dad keeps it in the closet upstairs in his bedroom. Some

490

stranger, or even a friend, isn't going to knock and then go upstairs to get the gun in order to shoot him."

"Maybe they were getting high together, so Grandpa didn't know what the dude was after when he was moving around the house," Kellan suggested.

"That's unlikely. The shooting happened here in the entryway." Grady pointed at the big wet spot that was the only thing left after Natasha's cleaning efforts. "Whoever it was had to have had the gun with him already. When Dad opened the door, he pulled it out and fired."

"Actually, that would place Dad closer to the door," Dylan said. "I think Dad saw it and attempted to run, which is why all the blood was about ten feet inside."

Mack jumped to his feet. "Wait! How do we know it *was* Dad's gun?"

They all stared at him.

"Most handguns look alike," he continued. "When the police arrived, they found a gun on the floor, but we were the ones to tell them that Dad owned a handgun, that Anya was living here and would know where to find it, and because she was the one to call for help, they already knew she was the last person to see him before they got here."

"Right," Dylan agreed. "And she split

right after she called, which only made her look more guilty."

"But why would the shooter drop his gun?" Grady asked, forever the skeptic. "Everyone who's ever seen a cop show knows better than to leave the weapon behind."

"Maybe he didn't mean to," Mack said. "Maybe Dad didn't run. Maybe Dad rushed him, they were wrestling when he was shot, and then Anya showed up unexpectedly and, scared, the dude ran out the door."

"Only Anya was so hopped up on meth that she didn't even remember seeing him," Natasha said softly.

Silence fell. That scenario made sense and everyone could tell.

"But wouldn't the police have searched the house and found J.T.'s gun if it wasn't the one lying on the floor?" Cheyenne asked, after they'd all had a few seconds to think it over.

Kellan nodded. "Yeah, that's what they do on TV."

"Not necessarily," Mack said. "We're not dealing with a police department that's experienced in this type of thing. They probably thought they had no need to search the house. They had the gun that was used, the blood evidence — if they even bothered

492

with that because they also had fingerprint evidence — and they thought they knew, without doubt, who the perpetrator was."

"So you think —" Dylan started, but Mack was no longer listening. After weaving through the furniture in the living room, he leaped over the wet spot Natasha had cleaned and ran up the stairs.

They all followed and found him digging around in his father's closet when they caught up to him. "No way," he said as he turned to show them a small black firearm. "*This* is Dad's gun right here."

Natasha was sitting at the kitchen table, cradling a cup of hot chocolate, when Grady walked in. It was late. She'd left Mack in bed asleep because she couldn't quiet her mind. She was too upset that the police had refused to release her mother. As soon as she left J.T.'s house, she'd contacted Chief Bennett to tell him what she'd learned, but he said he was going to keep Anya locked up until he had a chance to do some more investigating, because he considered her a flight risk. "She's run once already," he'd reminded her.

At that point, Natasha had reminded *him* that Anya had turned herself in, so she obviously wasn't trying to get away with anything, but it wasn't easy to set aside a confession. She understood that. Chief Bennett said he had to check the registration on the gun, see if there were any other fingerprints on it besides her mother's, ask the neighbors if anyone could corroborate this new story and talk to Stephanie Vogler and her husband.

The case had seemed cut-and-dried — with her mother's confession and J.T.'s agreement — so Bennett was reluctant to give up on it too soon. It was his motivation behind keeping her mother in custody that bothered Natasha. She got the impression it wasn't so much about finding the truth as making sure he and his department didn't look bad for not double-checking anything to begin with. He didn't want people talking about the fact that Natasha had figured out who the real shooter was instead of him, so if there was any chance he'd be vindicated with further investigation — any chance that her mother might be guilty after all — he was finally going to start digging into it.

"What are you doing up?" Grady asked.

She lifted her cup. "Just having a little cocoa."

"Can't sleep?"

"No. You just come from the hospital?"

"Yeah."

"How's your dad?"

"Getting better all the time."

"I'm glad."

"Why can't you sleep? I thought you'd be relieved."

She grimaced. "I am, for the most part. Just a little irritated by the way Chief Bennett treated me when I called. He doesn't want to let my mother out of jail. He's hoping she's guilty so that he won't be embarrassed for accepting what he saw without doing anything to verify it."

"I think that's a futile hope."

"What do you mean?"

"He's going to be embarrassed. There's no way to avoid that now."

She set down her cup. This was coming from her second-greatest critic? "I thought maybe you'd agree with him."

He had the good grace to look slightly abashed. "You should know that Dad was able to talk tonight, before I left the hospital."

"And?"

He pulled out a chair and sat down with her. "Once I mentioned Stephanie Vogler and her husband, it all came back to him."

"What'd he say?"

"He couldn't give me a lengthy explanation. But once I told him what we'd learned, he said it was Stephanie's husband and not Anya."

Natasha let her breath seep out. J.T. had gotten it wrong before, which didn't lend him a great deal of credibility, but the fact that he'd changed his story would help. Had he continued to insist it was Anya, Natasha wasn't sure what would've happened, even if there was proof that the gun was registered to Stan Vogler. "Did he say why he nodded when he was asked if it was my mother?"

"Said he was confused."

"Hallelujah." She took another sip of her hot chocolate. "Everything's starting to come together. Maybe we'll get out of this nightmare yet."

He watched as she put down her cup. "I'm sorry, Tash. You've had a rough life, and . . . I don't know what's gotten into me lately, but I certainly haven't made things any easier."

She shrugged. "It's okay. I can see why you might resent me. I was a pain in the ass when I lived here. You certainly got nothing out of sharing your house with me, not to mention the activities and food and other things you had to share, as well."

He waved her words away. "I've never

minded that part."

She studied him. "Then . . . what is it?"

"Nothing."

"*Nothing?* The way you've treated me — it can't all be about you thinking my mother shot your father, can it? As horrible as believing that must've been, you knew *I* had nothing to do with it."

"It wasn't just that," he admitted.

"What was it?" she asked earnestly.

He appeared uncomfortable as he shifted. "We all had crappy things happen in our childhood. I guess it's just easier for some to get past that sort of thing than others."

She guessed he was referring to his mother's suicide. "You don't think you can get beyond the past?"

"I'm not sure I ever will," he replied. "And I certainly never expected Mack to beat me to it. So maybe I'm jealous that he's found the kind of love that makes him whole. It's like they say, 'misery loves company.' As long as Mack was in the same situation, I didn't have to feel too bad about myself. I never dreamed he'd be the first to move on."

She reached out and took his hand. "You'll get beyond the past eventually, too. You're such a great catch, Grady. Someday, if you want a family, you'll find the right woman."

"There you are," Mack interrupted as he

shuffled sleepily into the kitchen. "What are you doing out of bed? Are you okay?"

"I'm fine." She gave Grady's hand a squeeze. "We're *all* going to be fine. Everyone has their demons, but we're luckier than most because we don't have to face them alone. That's the meaning of family, right? We have each other."

Grady nodded and smiled at Mack, who'd been yawning and scratching his bare chest, but Mack suddenly scowled. "Why are you holding hands with my brother?"

"I think someone else is jealous now," she said with a laugh and stood to go back to bed with Mack.

Mack felt oddly content as he settled back into bed with Natasha. He'd never dreamed he could be this happy, not after being so damn restless for most of his life. When Natasha had lived in this house with him before, he'd struggled as hard as he could to stay away from her. It was a relief to give in and enjoy what he'd always denied himself. He supposed he should've given in a long time ago. As far as he was concerned, this was fate.

"Seriously," he mumbled before they could fall asleep. "What were you doing out there with Grady?"

"Making peace," she said.

"Everything's okay?"

"It's going to be as soon as your dad gets better and my mother is released from jail."

"That's going to happen," he said. "I promise. You won't be fighting to get your mom out alone."

She snuggled closer and lifted her head to press her lips to his. "Mack?"

"What?"

"I love you," she said.

EPILOGUE

Natasha smiled as Lucas tried to help Mack unload his truck. Her son had been almost as excited as she was to have Mack move in with them, and after waiting so long, they were glad the day had finally arrived. It'd taken nearly six weeks for J.T. to get back on his feet so that he could once again help out, to a limited degree, at Amos Auto Body, and for Mack to hire and train someone to replace himself full-time.

"Look what I brought!" Mack beamed at her as he hefted an ugly recliner up the walkway toward the porch.

"Really?" she said. "You had to bring *that*?"

He looked crestfallen. "What do you mean? This was the most comfortable chair in the house. Grady and I almost got into another fight when I tried to take it — until I reminded him that I was the one who bought it years ago from a secondhand shop."

She cleared her throat. "And I suppose you want it in the living room?" she said, tentatively.

He blinked at her. "Where else would I put it?"

She'd throw it out. But she knew better than to suggest that. "Okay." She shrugged. Her own furniture wasn't much to brag about. Since she'd gotten only the dregs of what she'd owned with Ace, she supposed it didn't really matter.

He hesitated, probably guessing — accurately, in this case — that she was only trying to be nice. "Do you hate it that bad?"

She did, but she was so happy that he was finally here she'd let him bring all the ugly furniture he wanted. "If you like it, it's fine."

He flashed her a grin and, once he got close enough, gave her a kiss before he finished moving it inside.

"*I* like it," Lucas said, following closely behind his new idol, and Natasha couldn't help laughing.

"Of course you do. It belongs to Mack," she said and tried to help him lift the duffel bag he was struggling to carry in, but he wanted to do it himself.

She was about to follow them inside so

that she could check on dinner when her cell phone rang.

It was her mother. Once Chief Bennett confirmed, four days after she'd realized the truth, that the gun used to shoot J.T. was registered to Stan Vogler, he'd finally released Anya from jail. If Stan hadn't shot J.T., there'd be no reason for his gun to be in J.T.'s house, and what Stephanie Vogler had said to Natasha she'd also said to one of her best friends, so they had a better case against him than they did Anya, especially after Anya retracted her confession and J.T. insisted he'd been too drugged to understand when he nodded to indicate it had been her. No one had known where Stan was, however. They'd thought he might get away with what he'd done until Dylan and Aaron confronted some of his extended family and managed to track him down at his mother's place in the Bay Area. Bennett had arrested him just three days ago, so it felt great not to have to worry about that anymore.

"Mom," Natasha said as she answered Anya's call. "How are you?"

"Good."

After spending the last month in rehab, Anya sounded better than Natasha could ever remember. "How do you like your new place?"

Natasha had helped her rent a room in Whiskey Creek from an elderly widow who was looking to bring in some extra money. Dylan felt so bad for how they'd treated her when they suspected her of shooting J.T. that he'd offered her a job in the front office at Amos Auto Body — with the stipulation that she submit to monthly drug testing and remain sober — so she'd wanted to stay there rather than move to Silver Springs.

"About the room . . ."

Hearing the hesitation in her mother's voice, Natasha felt a trickle of her old anxiety. "Oh boy. What now?"

"It's nothing big," she hurried to say. "It's just . . . I'm not living there anymore."

Closing her eyes in despair, Natasha let her head drop into her hand. *Here it goes.* "Why not?"

"I know you won't like this, but . . . I've moved back in with J.T."

"What?" Casting a worried glance over her shoulder and through the open door of the house, where she could see Mack setting up his recliner in the perfect position to be able to see the big-screen TV he'd also brought, she forced a smile when he looked up.

"What is it?" he yelled out to her.

She waved him off. "Nothing." Turning away, she lowered her voice as she spoke into the phone again. "Please say you're joking."

"No." Her mother sounded nervous but determined. "I'm sorry. I knew this would upset you, but I'm a grown woman, and I have the right to live my own life."

"But you and J.T. aren't good together. You fight constantly. And he was cheating on you! How do you know that behavior will stop? That he won't find someone else and ask you to move out again?"

"That could happen. I don't know that it won't. We're not perfect," she admitted. "No couple is. But we love each other. That's what we've figured out through all of this."

"You won't make it if you keep using."

"That's just it. We've agreed that it's time to change our lives. We're both clean. If we stay that way, we believe everything will be different, better."

Natasha scrubbed a hand over her face. She'd heard so many of these types of promises in the past. She opened her mouth to say she was afraid her mother was only asking for more trouble — or to speculate that J.T. was merely using Anya until he could get back on his feet — when he surprised her by coming on the line.

"I'm sorry for how I've treated your mother," he said. "It took almost dying for me to realize that . . . that I've been a total ass. I asked her to move back in so that we can be together and look out for each other. It won't be easy for either of us to stay clean, but we're going to take it one day at a time and give it our best shot."

Natasha sighed. He sounded sincere, so . . . who was she to judge? It could be this time would be magic. It could be that this was exactly what her mother needed. It was what Anya had always wanted, anyway — the love and support of a good partner. To Natasha, J.T. had seemed like just another loser in a long line of losers. But it was because of him that she'd found Mack. And maybe J.T. could change. Maybe the support he and Anya offered each other would make all the difference. "I appreciate that," she said. "I hope you'll both be kinder to each other." She glanced over her shoulder again. "Do any of your . . . um . . . sons know about this?"

"Not yet," he told her. "Is Mack there? I could tell him right now, if you want me to."

She thought of the surprise she had planned for Mack after dinner. "No. It can wait." She could see that Mack was coming out of the house, so that was all she felt safe to say. "I've got to go. Tell Mom I love her," she whispered and disconnected in a hurry.

"Who was that?" he asked. "Don't tell me Ace is giving you a hard time again. What happened — did he and that woman he was seeing break up already?"

"I'm guessing they haven't, since he's only taken Luke that one time. I did hear from his mother yesterday, though. She asked if Luke could stay with them next weekend, and I agreed. I predict it's only going to get easier with the Grays. Ace is too focused on finding another wife to worry about being a good parent."

Luke had trailed Mack out of the house, and now Mack rested his hands on Luke's shoulders. "If it wasn't Ace on the phone, who was it?"

"My mom."

"What'd she want?"

She thought maybe she should give away the surprise she had planned for after dinner. He wouldn't be happy that their parents were back together, and she didn't want it to ruin her big moment. So she found the picture she'd planned to show him later and handed him her phone. "I'll tell you what my mother said in a minute. First, I want to show you this."

He scratched his head as he studied what she was showing him. "Am I supposed to know what this is?"

She laughed because he'd probably never seen one. "I took a pregnancy test — and this is a picture of the result."

He gave her a sideways look. "*And?* What is the result?"

He had to lift her phone when she slid her arms around his waist so she could rest her head on his chest. "We're going to have a baby."

He pulled back to be able to peer into her face. "Are you kidding me? I've been hoping. But when you didn't say anything . . ." An endearing grin spread over his face. "I can't believe it. That's so exciting."

"What'd you say?" Lucas asked. "Someone's having a baby? Who is it?"

She brought her son into the hug with them. "I am. In a little over seven months."

He escaped her grasp. "Is it going to be a boy or a girl?"

"I hope it's a girl," Mack said before she could respond.

"*Why?*" Lucas wrinkled his nose to show that he wasn't in favor of that at all.

Mack let go of Natasha so he could lift Luke into his arms. "Because your mother

507

and I already have a boy, right?"

He beamed. "You're talking about me?"

"I'm talking about you," he said, and Luke put one arm around Mack's neck and the other around Natasha's.

■ ■ ■ ■

HOME FOR THE HOLIDAYS

■ ■ ■ ■

HOME FOR THE
HOLIDAYS

ONE

To Natasha Sharp, nothing said Christmas like Victorian Days. She couldn't help smiling as she tasted the sweet yet salty kettle corn she and her mother had just purchased from a nearby vendor, something she hadn't had in years, and paused to admire the colored lights adorning the quaint shops and old-fashioned, Western-style boardwalk that ran the length of Main Street. The sight of the porch and yard of Little Mary's Bed & Breakfast, a historic building from the late nineteenth century, jammed with noisy revelers wearing heavy jackets and scarves while drinking hot cider or eating homemade sugar cookies, reminded her of the type of idyllic scene you'd find in a snow globe. If only she could make white flakes swirl gently onto the people as well as into the valleys of the roof and along the banisters of the building before falling thickly to the ground, the picture would be perfect.

Real snow wasn't likely, though. Whiskey Creek rarely received more than a dusting.

"What are you doing? Why'd you stop?" her mother asked, turning back in surprise.

At forty-one, Anya Sharp was only sixteen years older than Natasha, but hard living was beginning to change the fact that they used to look more like sisters — hard living and substance abuse. Although Anya didn't seem to be high tonight — *thank goodness* — she had the voice of a longtime smoker and the stench of cigarettes clung to her hair and clothes, impinging on the pleasant aromas of gingerbread and roasted chestnuts.

"Just taking it all in," Natasha said.

Trying to keep her bleached-blond hair from whipping around her face, thanks to a stiff, cold wind, Anya gave her a funny look. "Taking *what* in? The festival?"

Apparently, Anya didn't feel the same nostalgia. Although she was now divorced, she still lived in Whiskey Creek, so it was easy to take the innocence of the small, California Gold Rush town, nestled in the foothills of the Sierra Nevada Mountains, for granted. Whiskey Creek hosted Victorian Days every year, usually the week before Christmas, but Natasha hadn't been back, not during the holidays, since leaving for college six years ago. She was trying to get through med school at UCLA, and she had a job at a nearby hospital working as an orderly. The demands of both were especially high in December, so she typically visited during the summer.

"Yes, the festival," she said. "The buildings. The people." Natasha had such fond memories of this place, which was ironic. When Anya had married for the third time and told her they'd be moving yet again, Natasha hadn't been happy about it. Barely a sophomore in high school, she'd already lived in so many cities and towns, and with so many "fathers" — both those who'd married her mother and those who hadn't — that she'd almost rebelled.

She would have, if she'd had anywhere else to go. But she didn't know who her biological father was. For that matter, neither did her mother. Given the type of encounters Natasha had witnessed as a child, she had little hope he'd be anyone she'd welcome into her life and had never tried to learn more about him. Dealing with Anya was difficult enough. She didn't need another deadbeat parent. But since Anya's behavior had alienated any extended family years ago, and Natasha had no father or anyone else to step in and help her, she'd had no choice except to move with her mother.

Anya had insisted that J. T. Amos, her new husband then, would take care of them as soon as he got out of prison, that this place would be better than all the others, and for once, she'd been right. Not that Anya or J.T. could assume any of the credit. It wasn't what *they* did that had changed Natasha's life. It was J.T.'s adult sons who'd made the difference. If Rod, Grady and Mack — the three brothers who'd still been living in the house where all five boys grew up — hadn't looked after her until she could graduate, this town would've been like all the others.

"Do you think you'll ever move back here?" her mother asked.

"Maybe. One day." She spoke as though it was merely a possibility, even though she'd always planned to come back to Whiskey Creek. When she closed her eyes at night, *this* was where she dreamed of setting up her pediatric practice.

But in those dreams, she was also married to Mack, the youngest of the Amos brothers — and he didn't seem to have the same dream.

"I think the Amoses, especially Mack, expect you to move back when you finish school," her mother said as they started walking again.

Natasha said nothing. If that was the case, no one had ever told *her.*

"Are you going to see any of J.T.'s sons while you're here?"

They passed a guy Natasha vaguely recognized from high school. She nodded to say hello before responding. "I've seen them already."

Her mother's head snapped up and her gaze sharpened. "When?"

Natasha had expected this reaction. She knew her mother wouldn't like that she hadn't been included. "Night before last."

"But . . . I thought you didn't get in until yesterday."

"Actually, it was the night before."

"Where'd you stay?"

She'd stayed at Mack and Grady's — Rod was now married and had moved out — in her old room, where she'd spent the happiest years of her life. It had been wonderful to be back, to feel that sense of home. And she'd been *so* excited to see Mack. Each time she came back to Whiskey Creek, she thought something might change between them. That he'd finally act on what she believed he felt. That he'd realize they were meant to be together. But he'd been as careful as ever to avoid saying or doing anything that could be construed as romantic.

Apparently, he didn't love her the way she loved him. Or he wouldn't let himself. He was hung up on the nine-year age difference between them and the fact that his brothers considered her a kid sister.

"Where do you think I stayed?" she asked. "In my old room."

"Why didn't you call me? Why'd you lead me to believe you didn't reach town until you came to my house?"

Natasha pretended to be too busy navigating the crowd to maintain eye contact. "I didn't lead you to believe anything."

"But . . . You had to know that's what I would assume."

"Does it matter? Now that Dylan, Aaron and Rod are married, they have so much extra room at the house. And I knew I'd be seeing you soon."

Anya scowled. "Oh, I get it. Well, I'm sorry I can't provide what they can."

Hearing her mother's injured tone, Natasha took her hand. "Oh, stop. Your house might be a little cramped, but I don't mind sleeping in your bedroom." She didn't mention the many strangers who filled the living room almost every night, using the place as a flophouse. They made her uncomfortable, but her mother called them friends.

"I would've liked to go to the Amoses' with you," she said. "Why didn't you invite me?"

They'd been polite enough to include Anya in the past, but Natasha knew in her heart that they'd rather not have her around. So she'd come to town before her mother was expecting her, and she'd gone to visit the Amos brothers alone. That way, she wouldn't have to ask them — again — if she could bring Anya. And it had worked out so well. She'd really enjoyed not having to worry about what her mother might say or do. Anya embarrassed her too often. "I didn't think it would be a big deal to you. You live here. You must see them all the time."

"I run into them now and then, especially J.T. I can't seem to avoid *him*. But it's different since we divorced. I miss the boys, would like to spend more time with them." They paused to let another group cut through to reach a booth selling clam chowder. "What'd you do while you were there?"

"Just visited," she replied, but that wasn't strictly true. Mack had invited his brothers and their wives and children to come over and see her and have a big Christmas dinner. Everyone had brought a dish, and she'd exchanged gifts with them.

Some carolers, dressed in Dickens garb, were singing "God Rest Ye Merry Gentlemen." Natasha kept hold of her mother's hand as they navigated around the foursome.

"Was J.T. there?" her mother asked, raising her voice to be heard over the music.

"No." At least that was true.

"Where was he?"

"At his house, I suppose. I swung by, once I was on the way to your place, to drop off his Christmas present, but we didn't talk long. Looked like he'd just rolled out of bed."

Creases formed in her mother's forehead. "You gave J.T. a present? After how he's treated me?"

"The way you guys fought? I think you both treated each other pretty poorly. Besides, it was just a tin of candy." She'd brought some of her homemade fudge for her mother, too.

"Did he have a gift for you?"

Despite everything her mother had to say about J.T., Natasha could tell Anya still cared about him, or she wouldn't be so acutely interested in him and his sons. Natasha also suspected that Anya didn't find it entirely unpleasant to run into her ex.

Maybe they were even still hooking up now and then. Regardless, they had to see each other quite often, since they traveled in the same circles and had so many mutual friends. "Of course not. But I wasn't expecting a gift."

"Since when has he ever had the money to give anything to anyone?" her mother asked bitterly.

Anya had no room to talk. She hadn't made much of her life, either. But Natasha bit her tongue.

As they stopped to check out some jewelry and Natasha held a pair of silver hoops to her ears to see how they'd look against her brown hair, she hoped Anya would forget about the Amoses. But her mother brought them up again as soon as she put the earrings back and they continued to meander down the row of vendors.

"I bet Mack and his brothers had a gift for you."

They'd gone in together to buy her a sweater and a new smartphone, since hers was ancient and the screen was shattered. She'd made the switch this morning. But she preferred that her mother not know about the more expensive part of their gift. It would only make Anya jealous. "They got me a sweater," she volunteered before her

519

mother could ask for details.

"That's it? From five grown men? Three with wives? That surprises me. They have money. And you're their baby sister."

Natasha winced. She hated it when her mother or anyone else referred to her as part of the Amos family, because it meant that Mack would never view her in any other way. "No, I'm not. We didn't grow up together. And you and J.T. were only married for what . . . eight years? That hardly makes us related."

"You can say that after the way they took you in and looked out for you?"

Natasha gaped at her. "They took us *both* in because we had nowhere else to live. We'd just been kicked out of that crummy apartment in Los Banos when you married J.T. So you contacted Dylan and asked if we could meet him and his brothers at some steak house — that one in Sutter Creek, remember? Then, once we got there and you announced that we were their new family, you asked if we could move in until J.T. got out of prison."

"That was J.T.'s house," Anya said.

Natasha hugged the bag of kettle corn to her body so she could use her hands to pull her jacket tighter. "Not really. Not anymore. He would've lost it when he went to prison if not for Dylan." At only eighteen, the oldest Amos son had taken over his father's auto body shop and finished raising his four younger brothers. He hadn't done a perfect job as their guardian, but she didn't know a kid who could've done better at that age. He'd loved his brothers fiercely, and he'd worked hard to keep them out of foster care. Natasha had so much respect for Dylan.

"Well, they wouldn't have had it if J.T. hadn't bought it in the first place," Anya said.

"I think he owed them the house, don't you?" J.T. had gone to prison for knifing a guy in a bar, just for spouting off. Allowing his sons to take over payments on the house where they lived so they'd still have a roof over their heads was the least he could do.

"He wasn't himself when he did what he did, Natasha. His wife had just overdosed on depression meds."

Natasha was well aware of that. Mack was the one who'd found her. "I understand. But what about his responsibility to his children? Mack was only six when that happened."

"Not everyone can live their life as perfectly as you do," her mother grumbled.

Anya's defense of J.T. served as further proof that her mother was still in love with

521

him. "I've never claimed to be perfect," Natasha said. "But I've never stabbed anyone, either."

A vendor selling wooden signs with various inscriptions came up. The Tanner Residence; Here Lies the Last Trespasser. May He RIP; No Trespoopers, with a circle and a line through a dog taking a dump. Natasha chuckled at a few as her mother pulled out a cigarette. Anya was about to light up when Natasha nudged her.

"I don't think you can smoke here, Mom."

"Why not? I'm outside!"

"There're too many people."

Muttering a curse for all the "assholes" who tried to tell her what to do with her own body, she said, *"Fine!"* and put it away.

Setting her jaw so she wouldn't point out that it wasn't just her body at risk, Natasha stopped to admire some handmade ornaments.

Anya didn't pretend to have any interest. She rarely bothered with the holidays, usually didn't even put up a tree. Folding her arms, she cocked one hip while she waited, as though she was irritated or bored or both. It didn't take much to make her mother's mood deteriorate.

"So . . . How'd they treat you?" she asked once Natasha was ready to move on.

"Who?"

"The Amos brothers."

"You're talking about them again? *Why?*" They'd told Natasha they were planning to be here at the festival. She and her mother could bump into them at any moment, and she didn't want to be discussing them when it happened.

"Just answer the question. I'm curious. Was Mack excited to see you?"

Mack had been nice. But that was nothing unusual. He'd always taken a special interest in her. When she'd lived with him and Grady and Rod, he'd enrolled her in dance lessons, shown up for any events she was involved in at school, helped her with homework whenever he could, taught her how to play chess and tried to include her in whatever he did — if that was four-wheeling, seeing a movie or target shooting in the mountains — when the catty girls her age shut her out, which happened quite often. She knew he cared about her *a lot.* But he'd been careful not to let their relationship drift toward anything beyond kindness and support. "No more than Dylan and the others."

Her mother peered closely at her. "Are you upset about that?"

Shoving another handful of kettle corn in

her mouth, Natasha averted her face. "Why would that upset me?"

Anya grabbed her arm. "Oh, come on. Quit pretending. I know how you feel about Mack. We all do. So does he."

Embarrassed, she looked around but didn't see anyone she recognized. Was Anya right? Had she been that transparent?

She supposed she had. She'd been so head over heels it'd been difficult to hide her feelings. She was embarrassed about that now, especially when she remembered how she'd behaved the night before she left for college, when she'd slipped into Mack's room and offered him her virginity. She'd been nineteen at the time, old enough, but after she'd stripped off her clothes, he'd made her put them back on. His rejection had broken her heart, but the way he'd hauled her up against the wall and kissed her before shoving her out of his room suggested she hadn't been entirely wrong in assuming he'd want what she had to offer.

That certainly hadn't been a brotherly kiss.

It was, however, all she'd ever gotten.

"I'm over him," she lied. "I've been seeing this other guy named Ace."

"The *bartender* you told me about?"

"There's nothing wrong with being a

bartender." That her mother, of all people, could say that in such a derogatory tone shocked Natasha. "Ace loves his job."

"Who wouldn't? He hardly has to work."

He'd mentioned the beneficial hours. Working part-time made it possible for him to surf and do plenty of other things he enjoyed. She suspected his wealthy parents helped him out; he couldn't go boating and jet skiing and do all the other things he talked about on his income alone. But he'd never specifically mentioned that. And who was she to judge? He seemed to have ambition, talked about owning his own bar some-day.

"Do you think it'll get serious?"

She couldn't imagine it would. The only man she'd ever wanted was Mack. But she pretended otherwise. "Maybe. We've only been dating for a couple of months, so we're not exclusive, but we . . . We like each other."

Her mother eyed her shrewdly. "Mack's a fool to let anything stand in his way."

"Can we stop talking about Mack?" she asked in exasperation. "I'm sure he'll be happy enough without me. After all, he's never lacked for female attention." Although he'd rarely had a steady girlfriend, there were plenty of women who'd shown interest. She could vividly remember how heart-broken she'd felt whenever he brought one home.

"But you're the woman he wants."

She pictured the tall, muscular, rugged man she loved and remembered how badly she'd hoped he'd come to her room last night. "Even if that's true, people are complicated. And the way we met, my age at the time, your involvement with his father — I can understand why he's holding back."

"That's all bullshit," her mother insisted. "You could both be happy if only he'd quit fighting his feelings. I've watched him whenever you've been around. Last summer, when we went to the lake, you should've seen how his eyes followed you in that swimsuit when you weren't looking. I don't care what he says. He's in love with you."

Natasha wished she could believe that, but he'd never acted on those feelings, not in the way she wanted him to. "I'm fine," she said. "I still have two years of med school left and then my residency, which will take another three years."

Anya didn't respond. She'd recognized a friend and turned to greet her.

Relieved that her mother was currently distracted, and hoping that was all she'd have to hear about Mack or any of the other Amos men, Natasha was waiting for Anya when she heard someone call her name and looked up to see Dylan pointing at her from across the street. His wife, Cheyenne, his son, Kellan, who was seven, Grady and Mack were with him.

She'd known she'd run into one or more of the Amoses eventually and was glad to have found them. Even though it was more and more painful to be around Mack, at least she knew they hadn't been close enough to overhear anything her mother had said.

They smiled and waved, and she did the same. But the moment her gaze locked with Mack's, it felt as if they were the only two people on earth.

For her, it'd always been that way.

Then he said something to the others and started across the street toward her.

TWO

As soon as Mack joined them, Anya nudged Natasha. "Like a bee to a flower," she muttered.

Natasha gave her mother a dirty look. Why did Anya have to embarrass her like that?

"What'd she say?" Mack asked.

"Nothing," Natasha replied. "My mom was just trying to be funny."

"I said it's cold tonight." Anya's grin made it clear she hadn't said that at all.

Mack glanced between them, but was wise enough not to press the issue.

"Where're Dylan and the others going?" Natasha asked, eager to take the conversation in a more stable direction.

"They're hungry and the Rotary Club's selling pulled pork sandwiches."

Anya slipped her arm through his as they joined the flow of people in the street. Sometimes she tried to act like Mack's stepmother, even though he was an adult when she'd married his father. Other times she tried to act like a sister or cousin or something, since she was actually between Aaron and Rod in age, much younger than J.T. And sometimes, especially if she was drunk or high, she flirted with them shamelessly, making it obvious that she'd be willing to become a lot more, which had to make them uncomfortable. It certainly humiliated Natasha. "You didn't want one?"

He didn't pull away from Anya, but Natasha couldn't help wondering if he wished he could. "I've already eaten."

So was it merely for practical reasons that he'd joined them? Because he didn't want to wait in a long line?

Natasha could never quite decide if she meant as much to him as it occasionally seemed. That was something she'd struggled with from the beginning.

Either way, they'd spent so much time together before she left for college that it would've been far more unusual if he'd ignored her. She was just glad he was willing to suffer her mother's company in order to be with her again, especially since she had to go back to LA tomorrow. The hospital where she worked was understaffed, and she lived on a shoestring budget, so she needed to earn as much as she could.

"Want some kettle corn?" She offered him the bag and he took it and scooped out a large handful.

"Have you seen the photo booth?" he asked as he popped a few kernels into his mouth.

"Not yet. Where is it?"

"Down by the Christmas tree in the park. They're doing those old-time photos again, like the one we took your sophomore year."

She'd kept that picture on her dresser until she'd moved out. It was still one of her favorites. In it, she was dressed as a barmaid and sat on a barrel, her hair twisted up and decorated with a long feather plume, while Mack stood behind her wearing a sheriff's star on a leather vest and a fake handlebar mustache that didn't quite match his dark hair. Grady and Rod had posed on either side of them dressed like regular cowboys drinking a bottle of whiskey. She laughed whenever she looked at the tough expression on Mack's face in that photograph. She knew there were people who had seen that expression when he wasn't joking. But he'd always been gentle with her, had gone above and beyond to keep her safe and happy.

He was even the one who'd tried to have "the talk" with her. She'd never forget the night she announced that she'd been invited to homecoming and would likely be out all night. After the others had gone to bed, he'd knocked on her door and hemmed and hawed about school and the auto body shop and anything else he could think of before he managed to work up to the topic he'd come to address.

"I want you to know that . . . that this boy you're going out with might try to . . . Well, boys your age are just beginning to feel . . ." At that point, he'd shifted uncomfortably and cleared his throat before starting over. "What I'm trying to say is that this boy might attempt to do something you may or may not want him to do."

"Like what?" She'd known exactly where he was going with this. A girl couldn't grow up with a mother like Anya without learning a fair bit about physical intimacy. She'd seen things that would shock most adults — not the best example for a child to have when it came to sexuality, which was obviously what he was trying to rectify.

She'd blinked at him, keeping her eyes wide and innocent while awaiting his answer, and that was when he'd caught on that she found the conversation — and his attempt to have it — funny. "You know exactly what I'm talking about," he'd grumbled with a scowl.

"Sex."

"Yes."

"You don't want me to sleep with Jason."

"I want you to think about it, be prepared, be smart."

"What's to think about?" she'd asked.

His eyebrows had shot up at this response. "What do you mean? There's *a lot* to think about. You're only sixteen. It would be much better if you waited until you were older."

"Because *you* want to have sex with me."

His face had gone beet red. Instead of committing himself one way or the other, however, he'd said, "Because sex is much better when you're in love. And there are other things to consider — like venereal disease, pregnancy, your reputation."

"My *reputation?*"

"Yes. Gossip could make you a pariah at school."

She'd shrugged. "With a mom like mine, I'm already a pariah at school. I can't believe I even got asked to this stupid dance."

"I'm glad you did — and that you're going. I want you to enjoy it." He'd worried about her when the other kids were being unkind.

"Just don't have sex," she'd volunteered, summing it all up.

He'd sighed as he shoved a hand through his hair, which had been longer in those days than it was now. "Basically. But if you're not going to listen to me, you need to make sure he wears a condom, at least."

"Should I take one in my purse?" She'd known he'd *hate* the idea of her carrying around a condom, but she was always needling him, trying to figure out if he wanted her the same way she wanted him. He pretended he didn't, but she could feel the powerful attraction between them. Maybe she was young and naive, but she couldn't be wrong about that. Or . . . could she?

"Just . . . be careful, okay?" he'd said.

"Do you want to give me a condom?" she'd pressed.

He'd waved her off. "Forget I said anything," he'd replied in exasperation and went out and shut the door.

She still chuckled whenever she thought about that encounter. She hadn't had a mother who was paying any attention to her, and she'd never had a father, so he'd stepped in to fill whatever roles he could. He'd even taken her to the store to buy her a new dress for the dance so she wouldn't have to be so different, no less than anyone else, but finding one he considered modest enough hadn't been easy.

"Should we get another picture?" she asked as he returned the kettle corn.

"*I* think you should," Anya piped up. "Wait until Mack sees how well you fill out that waitress costume now."

"Mom!" Natasha gasped.

"What?" Her mother let go of Mack to be able to spread her hands in an innocent gesture. "Look at that curvy body of yours. You're gorgeous! I'm sure he's noticed."

A muscle moved in Mack's cheek. "I'd be happy to get another picture," he said, as if that last exchange had never taken place, and they walked past the carolers again to reach the booth that said McGee's Old-Time Photos.

THREE

Mack knew he should've stayed with his brothers, Cheyenne and his nephew. Anya was difficult to take, and each time he saw Natasha, now so grown up and in command of her life, it only got more difficult not to imagine things he had no business imagining. Last night, knowing she was under the same roof made it impossible for him to sleep. He'd almost gone down the hall to her room half a dozen times.

Instead, he'd tossed and turned in frustration and indecision. He wanted her, and he was fairly certain she still wanted him. When she was younger, she'd done everything she could to get him into bed. She was far less obvious these days, but he sensed that, even now, she wondered where they stood, whether his feelings ever crossed into that territory.

So why couldn't he act on his desire? She was certainly old enough by now to give him informed consent.

He'd asked himself that over and over again while staring up at the ceiling, but the reasons were good ones. Their relationship had never been clearly defined. They weren't brother and sister. They weren't just friends. And they'd never been lovers. But she'd always meant a great deal to him, and he knew that once he let the relationship move in that direction, there'd be no going back.

What if they didn't make it? They'd lose the love and support they gave each other now. That would hurt him, without question, but at least he'd still have his brothers and the business to fall back on. He was afraid of what it might do to her. She'd already suffered far too many losses in her life. Would it really be smart to take that chance?

Besides, Mack understood what other people would think and say. They'd accuse him of having taken advantage of her from the beginning. After what he and his brothers had endured, thanks to his mother's suicide and the stabbing that sent his father to prison, he didn't want to give the people in Whiskey Creek any more reason to disrespect him or his family. He was part owner of a successful business in this small town, and that business supported them all —

him, his brothers and their families, and J.T., too.

He sent Anya a sly glance as they wove through the crowd. If he and Natasha ever got together, it would also bring Anya back into his life and the lives of his brothers, and they were all relieved to be rid of her. Drug and alcohol issues aside, she had to be the most annoying person in the world. Mack would never be able to understand how J.T. had put up with her.

But J.T. was hard to put up with, too, so there was that.

He stopped to buy another beer before they reached the photo booth, and while they were there they happened to see Aaron, his wife, Presley, and their ten-year-old son and two younger daughters in the next line over, waiting to get some candied peanuts.

"Hey, what's going on?" Aaron asked.

"Not much." Mack offered to get him and Presley a beer, too, but they declined.

Natasha and Anya visited with Presley until Aaron was able to get the kids their peanuts. Then Natasha asked someone to take a group photo of them all, and as they were saying their goodbyes, Presley told Anya about a great wine-tasting booth she and the family were planning to visit next and invited her to join them.

Anya was obviously shocked to be invited, but she readily agreed, and they started off in the opposite direction.

"Why do you think Presley invited my mother?" Natasha asked, once they were gone.

"I guess she thought your mother would enjoy it," he said, but he knew Presley hadn't done it for that reason. The secretive smile his sister-in-law had cast him just before she walked away suggested she was doing him a favor. Although he probably would've denied it had she asked him — he'd denied a lot of things where Natasha was concerned — Presley knew he'd love to spend some time alone with Natasha before she had to go home tomorrow.

But he wasn't entirely convinced that being alone with her put him in the best position. He was already experiencing the effects of what he'd had to drink so far tonight, felt his resolve and his restraint slipping, especially as they took the old-fashioned picture and the photographer suggested Natasha — wearing a boa with her barmaid costume — sit on his lap. As he held her, wearing cowboy attire but no fake mustache this time, it felt so natural to have her close that it was almost impossible not to continue touching her afterward.

Once they received their copies of the photo, they talked and laughed about a lot of different things as they made their way through the rest of the booths. Although Mack enjoyed the food and the festivities of Victorian Days, he had no real interest in the crafts and various trinkets. Natasha seemed to enjoy looking at all the objects people were selling, however, and he was happy just to be with her.

They returned to the park because she wanted another picture, this one a selfie of them in front of the big tree. After that, they meandered away from the festival, where there were no more lights or people. He'd always been impressed by how smart she was, but as he listened to her talk, he was also impressed by how far she'd come, especially after the start she'd received in life. She was no longer the angry teen who'd gotten tattoos without her mother's permission, shaved her head one day on a whim, probably to let the kids at school know she didn't care about their rejection, and pierced her nipples — something he saw the night she came into his room and stripped off her clothes. He'd never been able to forget that sight — or how hard it had been to tell her to put her clothes back on — and it was something he couldn't quit thinking about right now. Were those piercings still there? She would always be nine years younger, but it was becoming very apparent that she was a woman now, no longer a girl. And the maturity of her mind matched the maturity of her body . . .

"What is it?" she said when he couldn't help grinning at her.

"I'm *so* proud of you," he told her. "I hope you know that."

She didn't respond. She just slipped her hand in his, and the way she smiled made it impossible for him not to grasp on. There was no one to see them, so he didn't have to worry about that. Still, he knew he'd be stupid to get anything started while she was in school. Even if they could overcome all the other obstacles, they couldn't be together for another five or six *years.* She'd already explained how long it was going to take to become a pediatrician.

Right now, however, all that seemed to matter was this moment.

She continued to talk, but his heart had begun to pound as soon as her fingers slipped through his, and he couldn't hear anything above it. He'd never stopped wanting her, despite all the years he'd been so careful not to let her know it.

He knew he should probably stay away

from her. But he also knew that was a fight he was going to lose — and he was going to lose it tonight.

The small building that housed the police station was on their right. Impulsively, he pulled her around the corner, just in case someone came looking for them, and kissed her like he'd always wanted to kiss her — with every bit of the desire he felt.

Finally.

Natasha hadn't lost her virginity until the end of her first year in college. She'd been twenty, at least three years behind most other girls she knew. Her roommates had been shocked when she told them she'd never been with a man, never even had a steady boyfriend. After watching how her mother handled relationships, Natasha had been — and still was — determined to do things differently.

She'd also been waiting for Mack. She'd fully believed they'd be together eventually. She couldn't imagine her life any other way. But when the contact they had remained as circumspect as ever, she'd begun to wonder if she'd misunderstood. Maybe he didn't feel anything. After all, he was the type who'd step up to take care of some poor girl who'd been overlooked and neglected just because it was the right thing to do — sort of like bringing home a stray puppy. He'd been good to her in so many ways. He didn't owe her his heart, too.

Once she'd realized she was taking too much for granted, she'd decided not to put her life on hold for him. She'd started dating more often and had been with three or four men over the years. Her first experience was pretty unremarkable, but her sex life had improved since. She'd slept with Ace, the guy she was dating now, for the first time two weeks ago, and she'd enjoyed it. She'd even told herself it was *amazing*.

But nothing could compare to this. Now she knew what real fulfillment and satisfaction felt like. It was Mack who was kissing her. Mack whose muscular body was pressed firmly against her own. Mack whose erection she could feel as they strained to get even closer.

When he lifted his head, she was afraid he'd pull away and it would all be over. She was tempted to cling to him, to try to crack through that warrior-like mentality to expose his true emotions. She was certain he felt *something*.

But she refused to be the grasping, desperate child she'd once been — far too eager for any kind of love, especially his. That smacked too much of her mother.

She tried to catch her breath while wait-ing to see what he'd do next. She expected an avalanche of disappointment, was already preparing herself.

But then he raised his hand, and one finger gently outlined her cheek. "Do you have any idea how beautiful you are? It makes me weak just to look at you."

"I don't care about that," she said, staring up into his dark eyes. "I don't care about anything except whether or not you want me."

His chest lifted with a deep breath, and he said, "Damn, Tash. You have no idea how much."

Those words sounded torn from him, as though he'd been reluctant to make that admission. But they meant the world to her. "Then what are you waiting for? Make love to me — at last."

"Do you really know what you're asking for?" he asked. "I'm nine years older —"

"The age difference is meaningless to me," she broke in. "It always has been."

"It's not that simple," he argued.

"Maybe not to you." Rising up on tiptoe, she caught his face in her hands and used her tongue to lightly outline his lips. "But it is to me. You're all I've ever wanted."

With a groan, he held the back of her head in his palm as he met her tongue, immediately taking the kiss to the same desperate, hungry place of moments before, and when he lifted his head again, she could tell he'd come to a decision. "Okay. Let's go."

FOUR

They were so eager to come together they almost fell inside the motel room the moment Mack managed to unlock the door, and they started kissing again immediately, before they could even get the door closed. Natasha had never felt such a rush of pleasure or such an upwelling of desire. This night had ramped up like a roller coaster, climbing slowly to the first big drop — and now she was about to come screaming down the other side.

"You taste better than I even imagined," she admitted, breathlessly.

"Let me see you," he said. "Take off your clothes, just like you did for me before."

She slanted him an injured glance. "You mean when you rejected me?"

"Believe me, that hurt me more than it did you. For weeks, even months afterward, I was tortured by the memory of what I'd missed. That night is still one of the things I think about all the time — and imagine handling differently."

"So you did want me in that way."

"How could you not know that?" he asked.

"You've done an admirable job of pretending otherwise."

"Everything I've ever done has proved how much you mean to me. But we were living together under . . . odd circumstances. I couldn't allow myself to . . . I didn't want to feel as though I was taking advantage of you in some way."

"Even though I *asked* you to make love to me?"

"You know how complicated this is."

She did. But she was no longer too young, and she felt they could overcome anything, if they wanted to be together badly enough. "It doesn't *have* to be that complicated," she said, but she was scared to cross this line, too. Her love for Mack made her completely vulnerable, stripped away the defenses she'd spent most of her life building.

She almost told him she needed more reassurance. But she didn't want to ruin this night by bringing her emotional baggage into it. She was going to do the opposite — let go completely and just . . . trust.

Drawing a deep, calming breath, she lifted

her sweater over her head and unsnapped her bra.

She heard him suck his breath in between his teeth as soon as he saw what she'd revealed.

"This would go faster if you helped me," she teased.

He grinned. "I like watching." His eyes were hungrier than she'd ever seen them. She'd barely started to unzip her jeans when he stepped forward as though he couldn't wait any longer. "They're gone," he said as his hands circled her bare waist. "I wondered."

"What're gone?"

"The piercings."

"Oh. Yeah. And some of the tattoos, too. The ones I could afford to have removed." He knew that, of course, because she'd focused on her arms first, but she was nervous and that made her talk just to talk. "I'll do more over time. I don't think the kind of tattoos I had would look very respectable on a doctor."

His hand gently cupped her right breast. "You're beautiful with or without them — the most beautiful woman I've ever seen."

As he began to kiss her breasts, she dropped her head back and closed her eyes. "This is beyond anything I could've imagined," she whispered. "Words can't even explain it."

"I agree." His hands were trembling by the time they'd stripped off the rest of their clothes. She could feel it when he cupped her face and looked down into her eyes. "Whatever this is, it's bigger than I am," he said and carried her to the bed.

Natasha woke up alone. Although Mack had spent the night with her, he'd had to get up early for work. Amos Auto Body was always slammed. But she was happier than she'd ever been — and even more in love with Mack. He'd offered to take the morning off until she had to leave, but she knew how difficult that would be to explain to his brothers. He'd be leaving them high and dry with work that needed to get done, and she had to spend some time with her mother, anyway. Anya would be hurt if she didn't.

She closed her eyes, allowing herself to remember what it'd been like to finally have Mack inside her. It certainly hadn't been a disappointment. She smiled dreamily as she relived his kisses, the care he'd taken to make sure she was satisfied, his thoughtfulness in letting her know their time together meant something to him, too. Since she had to leave today, they hadn't wanted to waste a second, so when they weren't making love, they talked or simply dozed in each other's arms. Natasha didn't think they'd slept for more than two hours all told, although she'd fallen back asleep after he left.

Her phone signaled a text. With a yawn, she gathered the energy to roll over so she could reach it on the nightstand.

It was Mack. She pushed the pillows against the headboard and pulled the sheet higher while she read.

Last night was . . . wow. I wish you didn't have to leave.

So do I. But I come back whenever I can. You know that.

This summer? That sounds like forever. Do you really have to live in LA for another five or six years?

She frowned. It sounded too long to her, too. But she couldn't give up on becoming a doctor. She was committed to it, knew that was what she wanted to be. And she'd put too much blood, sweat and tears into getting this far. The past six years didn't change anything. The next five or six won't, either.

He didn't comment on that. A few minutes went by before he sent her another message. Are you sure you don't want me to take you to lunch before you go?

No. I need to see my mom. How are you able to work? Aren't you exhausted?

Too pumped up to feel it yet. Every time I close my eyes, I see you, I feel you, I smell you. I could spend another week, at least, with you in that motel.

You'd have to buy a lot more condoms.

I'm willing to get as many as we need.

She laughed. He hadn't mentioned whether he was going to tell his brothers that they were now seeing each other. And she hadn't asked. She'd instinctively avoided topics that might pull them back to reality too soon or put a damper on their time together.

I'm glad I twisted your arm into sleeping with me.

Whatever happens, last night was worth it.

:)

Her mother called, interrupting their conversation. Mack seemed to be gone for the moment, anyway — probably had a new customer. "Hello?"

"Where are you?" Anya demanded.

Natasha hesitated. What'd happened with Mack was still so new. If they were getting together — as she hoped and believed they would — she wanted to be sure he had the chance to break it to his family first. She knew that wouldn't be easy, or the way they'd met wouldn't have been a problem in the first place. "I'm about to get some coffee at Black Gold. Would you like me to get you a cup?" she asked, dodging the question entirely.

"No, I'm fine. Why didn't you come home last night?"

"It was late. I didn't think you'd miss me."

"Did you stay at Mack and Grady's again?"

"There's an empty bedroom there for me," she said, still trying not to lie outright.

"Was it fun, being with Mack?"

"It was." That had to be the biggest

551

understatement of her life. She'd never had a night quite like last night. But she hoped her response came across as normal, even casual.

"What'd you do after I left?"

She pulled Mack's pillow to her face and breathed deeply, trying to inhale the scent of him — to hold on to *some* aspect of what they'd enjoyed together now that it was over. "After we left the old-time photo booth, we just wandered around. What about you?"

"Went to the wine booth Presley wanted to show me."

"How was it?"

"Great. Presley even paid for my ticket."

Natasha couldn't help being embarrassed about that. Anya had never been good about paying her own way. But she didn't say anything.

"I tried calling you after Aaron, Presley and the kids went home," her mother continued. "But I couldn't reach you."

Once she was with Mack, she hadn't checked her phone. "It was so loud there, I probably didn't hear it ring. Or maybe I was already in bed." She winced, wishing she'd said "asleep" instead of "in bed."

Fortunately, her mother didn't pounce on that unintended but accurate double entendre. "What time do you have to leave?"

"About two."

"You're out of school for the holidays. Can't you stay longer?"

"No. I told you I have to be at work at four in the morning."

"Call in sick."

"I can't. There'd be no one to replace me. But if we hurry, we'll be able to have lunch together before I leave. I'm on my way to your place right now." She had to check out by eleven, and it was almost ten.

"Okay. See you here."

Natasha was about to press the end button when her mother spoke again. "Tash?"

"What?"

"How will you get here? Your car's at my place. I drove last night, remember?"

"Right. I guess you'll have to pick me up."

"At Black Gold Coffee?"

"Yes."

"Now?"

She calculated the time it would take to walk there. Fortunately, it was only a couple of blocks. "In like . . . fifteen?"

"Are you sure you wouldn't rather have me come to wherever you and Mack spent the night?" her mother asked, her "level with me" tone indicating that she hadn't been fooled at all.

Natasha gripped her phone tighter. "What're you talking about?"

"I went by the house last night, Tash. Grady was there, but you two weren't."

"We must've gotten in after."

"Except that Mack left his truck downtown all night. I saw it. After everyone was gone, it was the only one parked on the street, so it was hard to miss. Does that mean something's finally happened between you two?"

Natasha hoped no one besides her mother had noticed Mack's vehicle. Fortunately, his brothers didn't keep track of him the way her mother kept track of her whenever she came home these days — something Natasha found ironic since Anya paid so little attention to her when she was a teenager. "Nothing happened, Mom."

"You expect me to believe that?" she asked. "With the way he was looking at you last night?"

"I'm telling you nothing happened!" She didn't care if that was a lie. No way did she want Anya to say anything to Mack or make a big deal about it to J.T. — or any of Mack's brothers, for that matter. It was important that Mack not feel any pressure. She'd been completely open and honest with him about her feelings. If they got together, she wanted it to be because he loved her in return, not because he felt obligated.

"You two must've gone somewhere alone last night," her mother insisted.

"So what if we did?" Natasha retorted.

This response was met with a long silence before her mother said, "I'm on your side, you know."

Natasha wanted to say, *"Since when?"* But that was resentment from the past welling up again — something she wrestled with on an ongoing basis.

Taking a deep breath, she assumed a more measured tone. "I appreciate that. I really do. But nothing's changed where Mack's concerned." Not yet, anyway. That would depend on the next few weeks. She understood that a sexual encounter was one thing and making a lifelong commitment was another. "So, can you pick me up at Black Gold Coffee?"

"Sure. Just let me get dressed."

Apparently, her mother was barely out of bed, too. But that came as no surprise. Anya didn't have a job; she lived on government assistance, stayed up late with her deadbeat friends and slept late, too.

After she disconnected, Natasha navigated to the pictures on her new phone. She

555

didn't have many, since she had yet to download most of the data from her old mobile. But she had a few from last night.

She was tempted to make the selfie she'd taken of her and Mack in front of the Christmas tree her wallpaper but decided against it and got out of bed.

As she started to dress, she noticed her reflection in the full-length mirror on the wall and paused to take a closer look. Her hair was a tangled mess, her mascara was smeared, and she had a red mark on her neck that she wouldn't be able to hide without different clothes — or at least a little concealer. She knew Mack hadn't purposely left that mark, but last night had gotten crazy.

She couldn't show up at Black Gold Coffee, not like this. It was too busy there. Someone would see her who might mention it to one of Mack's brothers.

She could have Mack come and get her. She knew he'd do it in a heartbeat. But making him leave work would be more obvious than any other option.

With a sigh, she grabbed her phone again and called Anya back. "Okay. Pick me up at Hotel Whiskey Creek."

Her mother didn't even skip a beat. "That's the old one above the Italian place?"

"Yes. Just down from the park. Call me when you get here, and I'll run out."

"I'll be right over."

Fortunately, when Natasha ducked into her mother's car, Anya didn't say anything about how bedraggled she looked or where she'd spent the night. Anya continued to let that stuff go while Natasha picked her way through those who were camped, once again, in her mother's living room. It wasn't until she'd showered and packed, and she and Anya were having lunch at Just Like Mom's — a café that served comfort food — before heading home, that she said, "If, for some reason, Mack doesn't follow up on last night . . ."

Natasha looked up from her food.

"I hope . . . I hope you won't let it hurt you too badly," her mother finished.

Natasha set her fork down. "You're the one who always insists he loves me."

"I think he *does* love you. But like you said last night, people are complicated. The Amos brothers have been through a lot, so it's natural that they'd guard their hearts. I could see his defenses going up again if you're not around to keep breaking them down."

Natasha wanted to tell her that Mack wouldn't disappoint her. Everything he'd said and done last night — even the messages she'd received today — suggested he was finally getting serious about her. "We'll figure it out," she insisted.

"You will if you move home. He won't be able to resist you then."

Natasha gaped at her. Her mother didn't like her living so far away. Although Natasha didn't believe Anya's motivations were purely mercenary, it was true that she needed things she thought Natasha could help provide. Was this a ploy to get her back? "I can't move home. Not now."

"You could if you really wanted to."

"And give up on everything I've accomplished so far? Give up on becoming a doctor?"

Her mother shrugged. "That's what I'd do. You have a good head on your shoulders. There are a lot of other things you could do. Besides, Mack has money. You won't have to worry about how you're going to live if you marry him."

Natasha refused to expect anyone else to take care of her. That was Anya, not her. "I'm not going to give up my hopes and dreams for any man," she insisted.

Anya pursed her lips. "Okay, but . . . . I hope you don't live to regret that."

FIVE

"What's wrong? You tired?"

Natasha blinked and straightened. After attending classes and studying all day, it could get difficult to remain as alert as she needed to be at the hospital, especially if it was slow. She knew she wasn't getting enough sleep. But that wasn't what was weighing her down tonight. "Not really," she lied.

Leanne Luttges, one of the nurses she liked best, touched her arm. "You look wiped out. You really need to take better care of yourself."

"You know what med school is like."

"It'll eat you alive if you let it."

Natasha managed a smile to cover the anguish she was feeling inside and headed down the hall. Fortunately, she was about to go on break. She could go outside and sit in her car, where she could eat alone and wouldn't have to worry about anyone remarking on the blank expression on her face or how quiet she'd become. She hadn't heard from Mack for several days. Right after she got home, he'd called her often, but now that it'd been six weeks, that was already changing. She could feel him slipping away from her again. The last time they'd talked, things had seemed pretty much like they'd been before their night at Hotel Whiskey Creek.

They were returning to their old lives, lives that didn't intersect very often, and she didn't know what to do about it. Although he remained as polite, supportive and kind as ever, and she could tell they'd always mean something to each other, he was retreating, which indicated he wasn't going to tell his brothers about the time they'd spent together, wasn't going to pursue the relationship.

For once in her life, Anya had been right. And it had to be about this . . .

As she sat in her rattletrap Honda, which was all she could afford, staring glumly at the people coming and going in the parking lot, she checked her phone again, hoping for a missed call from him or maybe a text. She wanted to believe she was wrong about what was happening. But she'd still received nothing, and even if she had, she knew in her heart that it was over — already. All she could do was try to throw up some kind of defense so the disappointment wouldn't crush her.

Her phone rang. She grabbed it, but it wasn't Mack. It was her mother.

Closing her eyes, she dropped the hand that held her phone in her lap while trying to swallow the lump in her throat. She couldn't talk to Anya right now. That would just make everything worse. Her mother was sure to ask about Mack, which would just bring it all up again.

Instead, she sent a text. Can't talk. At work. Everything okay?

Fine. Just missing you. Any word from Mack?

Damn it. That was the first thing Anya went to? Even in a text?

We talk every few days. She hoped her mother would leave it at that, but, of course, she didn't.

And? How's it going between you two?

Apparently, her answer wasn't obvious enough. Was she willing to openly admit it? She may as well, she decided. She had to face the truth. What good did it do to pretend?

She'd been a fool to think one night in that motel would change anything. We're just friends. Like before.

You've always been more than friends, but I know what you're saying, and I'm sorry. For what it's worth, he's making a big mistake.

I'll be fine, she insisted. But she had no idea if that was true. She didn't think she could feel any more pain than she did. It seemed as though she was moving through a red haze, one in which she could scarcely breathe. But she'd given him all she had that night, offered her heart to him on a silver platter, and, apparently, he didn't want it badly enough.

Ace, the man she'd been dating before, had been asking her out, and she'd been putting him off, claiming she was too busy with school and work. Now, feeling like a fool for almost blowing up their relationship over Mack, she sent him a text. How's it going?

She chewed her peanut butter and jelly sandwich as she awaited his response, but she couldn't taste it. There was no enjoyment to be found in any aspect of life right now, even in her studies. Especially in her studies. It was so difficult to concentrate, she had to reread everything just to gather a small portion of its meaning. Work wasn't any easier. She could barely force herself to show up at the hospital, where her shifts suddenly seemed interminable.

She shoved her sandwich back into the sack only half-eaten. She didn't have the stomach for it, couldn't eat, couldn't sleep.

This is pathetic. She had to create some handholds — fast — or she wasn't going to make it out of the hole she'd fallen into.

Her phone dinged. Ace had responded.

I miss you. When can I see you?

She stared at those words. She had to go on living, couldn't allow Mack or anything else to destroy her. If she'd learned anything from her mother's example, it was that life wasn't for sissies.

I'm off tomorrow night, she wrote back.

Awesome. Let's build a bonfire on the beach.

She sent a smiley face and hoped she'd be able to gather the interest and the energy to go out with him tomorrow night.

She ended up canceling, but they got together the following week and the week after that. At least Ace made it clear that he wanted her. And he lived in the same area she did.

She needed to forget Mack once and for all. She was determined to patch up her stubborn heart and recover. Soldier on. After all, she was no stranger to pain and difficulty.

But then she realized that might not be so simple. Although she'd been too stressed and busy to notice, something important finally occurred to her — she'd missed her period at least twice.

ABOUT THE AUTHOR

Brenda Novak, a *New York Times* and *USA TODAY* bestselling author, has penned over sixty novels. She is a five-time nominee for the RITA Award and has won the National Reader's Choice, the Bookseller's Best, the Bookbuyer's Best, and many other awards. She also runs Brenda Novak for the Cure, a charity to raise money for diabetes research (her youngest son has this disease). To date, she's raised $2.5 million. For more about Brenda, please visit www.brendanovak.com.

The employees of Thorndike Press hope you have enjoyed this Large Print book. All our Thorndike, Wheeler, and Kennebec Large Print titles are designed for easy reading, and all our books are made to last. Other Thorndike Press Large Print books are available at your library, through selected bookstores, or directly from us.

For information about titles, please call:
(800) 223-1244

or visit our website at:
gale.com/thorndike

To share your comments, please write:
Publisher
Thorndike Press
10 Water St., Suite 310
Waterville, ME 04901